Visible from the Surface of the Moon

By Scott Boyan

Visible from the Surface of the Moon

by Scott Boyan

First Print Edition. Previously published electronically as Purple Topless Carwash.

www.scottboyan.com

Purp used his fingernail to move a marble-sized wad of refried beans and cheese onto a nacho chip.

"I don't think you're right," he said.

"It's not Mexican food," Javier said.

"It's good though," Purp said.

"I didn't say nachos weren't good," Javier said, "I said they weren't Mexican food."

Purp got the chip onto his tongue, too hot. He held it there for a second with his lips open, exhaling, cooling the melted cheese.

"What you said is imprecise," Javier said. "It's a border food. It doesn't mean it isn't good."

Purp chewed the chip down. A sip from his beer cut the stinging in his mouth from the heat and the jalapenos.

"If someone asked you what kind of restaurant this was," Purp said, "what would you say?"

Javier sipped his beer. He smiled and looked into the street. An antique diesel Mercedes whined up Guadalupe, trailing black smoke onto the patio where Purp and Javier ate their lunch. Purp worked on his nachos, still a little too hot.

"You see her?" Purp said.

"Which?" Javier said.

“The Asian girl.” Purp pointed toward her with the tip of his chin while he tongued his Budweiser bottle again.

“I see her,” Javier said. “I have seen her.”

“I have, too,” Purp said.

“What about her?” Javier said.

“She’s hot,” Purp said. He figured her for twenty years old, if that, studying there with her arms folded on the table in front of her, leaning over her book. She pressed her ribs into her arms, her breasts hoisted toward the squared-off low neck of her teal T-shirt. Straight black hair hung nearly to the table on both sides of her head making drapes for her, blinders. A quarter-eaten burrito drizzled with brown sauce sat pushed to the opposite side of her table.

“She is hot,” Javier said, “and she looks smart.”

“Is that a stereotype?” Purp said.

“No,” Javier said, “she’s studying whenever I’ve seen her in here. Talk about stereotypes,” Javier flicked the neck of his bottle toward Purp and then took a swallow.

“What?” Purp said.

“Let me get my sombrero on and make some nachos,” Javier said.

“Feed them to your donkey,” Purp said. “Anyway,” he nodded toward the Asian girl. “She brings her own sauce.”

“That girl?” Javier said.

“Both times I’ve seen her. See it?” Purp said.

“Oh yeah,” Javier said. “She’s got her own hot sauce.”

“It’s not hot sauce,” Purp said. “I’ve had it before.”

“I have, too. They have it at Miss Saigon,” Javier said.

“Then you know it isn’t hot sauce,” Purp said. He broke a nacho off his pile. Cheese clumped the chips together now that it was starting to cool off. Purp dumped salsa from a black plastic cup, trying to get a little bit on each chip.

“It is a sauce,” Javier said, “that is hot.”

“I didn’t say it wasn’t a spicy sauce,” Purp said. “What I did say, was that it wasn’t hot sauce.” He finished his bottle of beer in one drag.

“If the baby sees that bottle of sauce and asks you what it is, you won’t say that it’s hot sauce?” Javier said.

“If the baby asks me that, I’ll shit my pants from having the world’s first talking baby,” Purp said.

Javier held a mouthful of beer and tipped his eyes up to the ceiling fan.

"And if it asks me what kind of food nachos are, I'll say 'Mexican' and you would, too," Purp said. He made a sandwich out of two chips hinged by cheese. He scooped salsa between them.

"You still don't know what it is, right?" Javier said.

"No," Purp said with the two chips in his mouth, a hand under his chin as if to catch what might fall out. He chewed and swallowed.

"I think it's a girl," Javier said.

"Why?" Purp said.

"Selma has three sisters, right? She has girl genes," Javier said.

"I don't think it works like that," Purp said.

"I know," Javier said, "but I think it's a girl. What do you think it'll be?"

"I think there are about seventy-two things that I can't stand talking about," Purp said. "Not only can I not stand talking about them, I can't even stand being in the same room when other people are talking them. One of those things is trying to guess what the baby will be." Purp folded a cheese-soaked chip into a taco shape and used it to scoop salsa and sour cream into his mouth. He stood to get himself another beer. Purp took his time going by the Asian girl's table, getting a good look straight down her shirt as he passed. She smelled of citrus. As he walked up to the register Purp tried not to exhale because he didn't want her scent in his nose to go away.

On his way back to the table, Purp looked at her black hair fanned out between her shoulders. The top of her white shorts left a gap under the bottom of her teal shirt and Purp could see she had a tattoo on her lower back, Celtic and symmetric.

Purp sat.

"What are the other seventy-one?" Javier said.

It took Purp a second to get re-oriented.

"People looking like other people. 'You know who you look like? Yul Brynner,'" Purp said. "Astrologic signs. 'If he's born on this day he'll be a Pisces, or the week after he'd be a Virgo.'"

Javier used a chip to scrape the last of the refried beans off his fajita combo plate.

"You said 'he,'" Javier said.

* * *

"Then we can put the crib in here with us," Selma said. She stood up from the edge of the bed, her calf muscles tight and well-defined. She'd hardly put on any weight. From the back she didn't even look pregnant. It was hard to tell anyway on her, even from the front, but for the last month there'd been a little pooch where before had always been tight abs. Selma turned and her damp blond hair whipped across Purp's face. Her breasts hadn't yet started to swell but Purp thought her nipples looked darker. He wondered if she'd get monkey nipples, like he thought some women did.

"That would kind of defeat the purpose," Purp said.

"What's wrong with that?" Selma said. She put a knee up on the bed and gathered her hair across her left shoulder to put it up in her Air Force twist, the muscles in her shoulders flexing and cutting shadows on her skin. Purp preferred her hair down but he did think it looked a little hot, the tight blond twist under her black beret.

"It's not the bassinet I have a problem with," Purp said. "I mean –

"What is the problem?" Selma said.

Purp slid up to the head of the bed and sat with his arms around his knees. His eyes followed Selma's breasts as she bent to get her thong out of the drawer. She rummaged and pulled a black one from the tangle. Purp looked at the ski-jump nipples in profile. They were darker, not bigger at all. Her ass still went straight out the back like a little shelf.

"It's either one, the bassinet or the crib –

"Well what's she supposed to sleep in? You said you don't like co-sleeping," Selma said.

"I just don't think it's a good idea to have the crib or the bassinet in here with us," Purp said. "I mean, we have a room for the baby. Let's put the crib in there and that's the baby's room."

Selma looked at Purp with her hands cupping her breasts. "That's what I'm saying," she said. "Put the crib in there and then the baby can sleep in the bassinet in here with us."

"No, but –

"But what? Where else is she going to sleep?" Selma said.

"In the nursery. Is that not what the nursery is for, for the baby to sleep in?" Purp said.

Selma slipped a nude-colored stocking over her foot and balanced her toe on the end of the bed. She unfurled the stocking, sliding the elastic garter up to the middle of her thigh.

Purp straightened his legs and pulled the covers over his lap, feeling himself swell against the weight of the comforter. He put a pillow on his belly so Selma wouldn't notice.

Selma pulled a stocking onto her other leg.

"How are we going to hear the baby crying in the night if she's down in the nursery?" Selma said.

"It's next door to us. It's right there." Purp pointed at the wall. "When we had the office in there you used to say the sound of the computer fan kept you awake –

"But that was with the door open." Selma buttoned her blue uniform skirt. It tugged a little in the front where it used to lay flat across. Selma had her uniform skirts altered every time she got a new one. Air Force skirts weren't supposed to fit as well as hers did.

"So we'll leave the door open. You'll hear," Purp said.

Selma tipped forward and reached behind her back to fasten the clasp on her thickly padded black seamless bra. Purp watched her tug the bottom of the bra left and then right into place over the bottoms of her breasts. The bra was a feat of engineering. Purp wondered who it is that designs those things. The technology of it fascinated him.

"But don't you think it would be a little cozy?" Selma said.

"I . . . don't know." Purp knew. It wouldn't be cozy at all. "I just feel like maybe it might be better to respect some boundaries, that's all."

"She won't hurt anything," Selma said.

"But wouldn't you like a little privacy?" Purp said.

"But I'm going to like to hear her breathing." Selma tilted her head when she said the last word and pushed her face forward, as if talking to a baby. She buttoned her uniform blouse up from the bottom. The light blue fabric tugged across her smooth bra, an effect created by the man at the dry cleaners who took the side seams in for her, not the designer of the uniform.

"Are you going to want to have sex with a baby sleeping right next to us?" Purp said.

Selma pinned a black plastic nametag over her right breast. "Escobar de Tejada" made the nametag longer than it ought to have been. It was one of a growing list of reasons Purp wished she'd just taken his name when they got married.

"I don't think I'm going to feel much like having sex after I have a baby," Selma said, buttoning gold Major's rank onto her shoulders. She picked up her pager and held it sideways, scrolling through a message. She clipped the pager to the waistband of her skirt and touched up her hair in the mirror. Selma leaned closer in toward her reflection, looking at the hair over her right ear. Purp looked at her ass stretching blue fabric. He looked at the back of her legs and imagined the tops of her thigh-high stockings just above the hem of her skirt. He moved his hips against the pillow on his lap.

"Hey, uh . . . I have a little situation," Purp said.

"What's going on?" Selma looked back at him through the mirror.

"Before you put your lipstick on and all," Purp said as he moved the pillow from his lap, "is there any chance you could give me a hand . . . or something . . . with this?" Purp slid the pillow off his lap.

Selma turned from the mirror and gave Purp a look with one eyebrow raised. She tugged her skirt from the hem, straightening it, and walked into the bathroom. In her reflection in the bathroom mirror Purp saw her putting on lipstick.

* * *

Purp slid the control stick back with his thumb and his fighter nosed up and to the right out of the metal canyon. He leaned forward to get a little air on his sweaty back.

"Did you get it?" Purp said.

Javier grunted.

Purp looked over at Javier's half of the television as Javier's fighter dodged obstacles and closed on the exhaust vent. Even split in two, the sixty-four inch widescreen gave them each more space than they'd have playing alone on a regular TV. Javier released his missile. It hit the canyon wall.

"Negative," Javier said "it just impacted on the surface."

The two men laughed.

Purp circled back around for another run at the exhaust vent. He met only minimal resistance as he made his way back.

"Impacted on the surface," Purp said to himself as he started the approach. "University of Pennsylvania. Ivy League," he said to Javier.

"I don't think these are doing anything," Javier said. "I'm going to go look for that plasma cannon we saw."

"You'll need a jacket up there," Purp said.

"I'll be thirty-five when I finish," Javier said.

"Eh. That's only a year older than I am now," Purp said. "Is that about how long people take, five years?" One wing of Purp's fighter caught the edge of the canyon wall.

"Yeah. The last year is pretty much just working on the thesis," Javier said. "Was that cannon over by the towers?"

"I think it was by the round thing. Aww," Purp said. He nailed an obstacle cutting across the top of the canyon and his fighter spiraled in flames into the canyon floor. His side of the screen showed a cinematic view of the burning wreck of his spacecraft. "Is anyone else in your class going back to grad school? Again?"

"That guy you met, Yuri," Javier said, "he's going to law school."

"That's cool," Purp said. "Did he do fiction or poetry?"

"Fiction," Javier said. "There it is." The plasma cannon wasn't by the towers or the round thing.

"You can teach at a university with an M.F.A. right?" Purp leaned forward and the footrest of his leather recliner slid up underneath his chair.

"It's supposed to be the terminal degree in that field," Javier said. He started in toward the entrance to the canyon. "But it's kind of like, you can't really get a teaching job until you get a book published."

Javier's fighter bobbed up and down, dodging the obstacles that Purp hit.

"But it's easier to get a job if you have a Ph.D., too," Javier said.

"Especially from U. Penn." Purp walked between Javier and the television.

"Hey," Javier said. Purp heard Javier's fighter scrape along the side of the canyon.

Purp stood beside the couch next to where Javier was sitting. Javier leaned so far forward his butt was only half on the cushion. From the side Javier looked like a bear holding a salmon with both paws. The controller looked ridiculously small in his hands. Javier approached the exhaust port.

Purp lifted his foot and leaned to one side. He bent his knee and kicked Javier hard in the shoulder. It felt solid like he'd hit a wall, but it startled Javier enough that he slid from the couch down onto one knee. His other leg crashed into the coffee table, toppling an empty beer bottle and a nearly empty one onto the carpet. Javier still gripped his controller but his fighter bashed into the floor of the canyon and burst into flames.

"Hey," Javier said, "asshole." He laughed while standing up in the space between the coffee table and the couch, one thick leg tangled under the table, both hands still locked on the controller.

"Mr. M.F.A. Ph.D. man," Purp said as he went for paper towels to clean up the spilled beer. "Maybe if you get enough letters after your name," he yelled from the kitchen, "you'll be able to finally blow up the Death Star."

"You better get something to clean this beer up, Purp," Javier said from the other room, "or Selma is going to kick your ass."

Purp walked into the living room with the paper towel roll and a cup of water as the lock on the front door clicked and Selma stepped into the entryway.

"Selma's going to kick whose ass?" Selma said, closing the door behind her. She barely stood five feet but her legs looked long, an illusion created by the extra inch she'd had trimmed from the bottom of her uniform skirt. The alteration brought the skirt out of regulation, but just barely, and if anyone said anything they'd seem like they were looking too close.

"Hola," Javier said to Selma.

"Hola! Congratulations! Purp told me about U. Penn.," Selma said. She pranced down the single step into the living room in her shiny black heels and hugged Javier. The two of them spoke in Spanish while Purp cleaned up the beer. Purp figured they were talking about school.

* * *

Purp checked his email for the fortieth time since coming in at eight. He didn't have anything he'd reply to. He wasn't expecting anything. He'd been there an hour and a half and hadn't done much other than log into his computer, check his mail, and organize his coffee.

Purp opened his drawer and took out a plastic stirrer he kept there. With his coffee cup in front of his keyboard, he poked at floaters with the stirrer. Purp poked at floaters every day. Purp loved and hated floaters, little balls of powdered creamer that didn't dissolve when he first poured his coffee in the break room. He didn't like to drink floaters. He didn't like his coffee to have lumps in it. Purp loved to fish for them with his stirrer, though, and tease them apart when he found them. He folded the stirrer in two, bending it at the middle to make little pincers. He used his pincers to crack a floater and it opened, exposing powdery innards. The broken floater bobbed, suspended on the surface tension of the coffee, a little dry island of powder. Purp pressed into the center of the island with one end of the stirrer and it submerged.

"Hoo, yeah," Max said. "Bacon. Bacon, and my sausage, and my pancakes. Pannycakes. Hoo yeah."

Purp looked at the gray cubicle partition between him and Max. He pictured Max on the other side with his bald head and his muscular shoulders digging into the breakfast he'd just brought up from the cafeteria. He pictured Max eating pancakes and looking at pictures of swimsuit models on the Internet, women a third as old as Max, a quarter as old. Purp wondered for the third time that day when Max would retire. Max was already retired once, from the Army. Now he was working on a second retirement from the University.

"There's a honey, hoo yeah," Max said. "Thank you, whoa. She's a cutie, pannycake."

"Did you say something to me, Max?" Purp said, looking at the divider between them.

"Pannycake, hoo yeah," Max said as if to himself but perfectly audible. "What's that, boss?" he said louder.

"I heard you talking, Max," Purp said. "Did you want to say something to me?" For the last couple of weeks Purp asked Max if he said something every time Purp heard Max talking to himself. Purp thought that might make Max self-conscious of all the noise he made. Purp thought it might make Max stop.

Max popped his shiny head up over the divider. "Nah, boss. Not at all," Max said. "Not at all good sir," Max said with an imitation of an English accent. "Just talking, that's all, that's all."

"Because I could hear you, I could hear what you were saying when you were talking over there," Purp said.

"Drinking coffee, boss?" Max said, his lean bronze face looking down at Purp's mug. "You put your quarter in the cup?" Max rubbed his fingers together, as if to show money. "Quarter in the cup-o?"

"Just my twenty cents, dude. I use my own mug, right?" Purp said.

"That's right. No usey no payey, right? No cupey no nickel." Max rested his chin on the divider. "You're drinking coffee already, tired boss? I don't know why you're tired, I'm the one gets up at 4:00 am, gets to the Fitness Center before they open the doors, with all them tight little asses on stair steppers they got in there. Hoo, yeah," he said. "You should get up at 4:00 am and join me there, boss. Builds character."

"I walk at lunchtime," Purp said.

"That ain't nothing." Max walked around the divider to Purp's cubicle. He flexed his biceps and held the pose. His arms looked like they would tear his shirt. He didn't have the gut of a guy who used to be fit but isn't. He just looked hard.

"Sixty-seven years old, boss. Been working out since before you were born," Max said. "But why are you so tired already? You ain't seen tired till that baby comes here. You'll be drinking coffee then, I can guarantee you that. You'll think your life is done for, if you let it get to you."

"I'm not really especially tired," Purp said.

Max leaned against Purp's desk and crossed his legs. His huge thighs squeezed into jeans.

"Hey, Purp," Arthur said, coming up behind him. "Hey, Max."

"Arthur, are you going to come work out with me and Purp here, get up at 4:00 am with us?" Max said.

"No," Arthur said. "Purp Dennis wants to talk to you about bandwidth issues."

"OK," Purp said.

"Everyone's complaining the server is slow," Arthur said.

"Slow, slow," Max said.

"I've heard that, yeah." Purp said.

"Well Dennis wants to talk to you about it," Arthur said.

"OK, well, thanks, Arthur," Purp said.

Arthur stood in Purp's cubicle as if waiting for something more from Purp.

"OK, Arthur. Thanks. I'm going to see Dennis later," Purp said.

Arthur stepped away from Purp's desk as if skeptical. Purp didn't know what more Arthur wanted.

"Nobby little squirt, huh? Nobby." Max said toward Arthur's back. Purp wasn't sure whether Max meant Arthur to hear that or not, but he figured there was no way Arthur didn't hear it. Purp wasn't even completely sure Max knew he'd said that out loud. "Slow, slow, buddyo . . . slow server no good," Max said and he walked back around the divider to his own desk.

* * *

Purp carried nachos on his tray, and two bottles of Budweiser, and six plastic cups of salsa, two each of three different kinds from the salsa bar. The Asian girl was back, reading again, and Purp took a route that brought him by her table. She wore a brown spaghetti strap halter top and a short jean skirt frayed at the hem. She'd been tanning. Purp looked at the freckles that the sun brought out on the tops of her breasts. She looked up at him and he startled, thinking she caught him looking down her shirt.

“Hello,” Purp said.
She smiled.
“You’re studying,” he said.
“Yeah,” she said.
“You study a lot. I’ve seen you,” he said.
“You eat a lot of nachos,” she said, “and drink a lot of beer.”
“You’d think I’d be fatter,” he said.
“You’re not fat,” she said.
“I know. You’d think I would be, though,” he said.
“Why would I think that?” she said.
Purp couldn’t tell if she was teasing him or if she just didn’t understand what he was saying. “What are you working on?” he said.
“Just accounting,” she said.
“What accounting are you taking?” he said.
“302. You know accounting?” she said.
“No. I don’t know why I asked that. It sounds hard though,” he said.
“Not so bad,” she said.
“You don’t finish your burritos,” Purp said.
“Nah. Too big. Why, you want it?” she said. She laughed.
“I like how you bring your own sauce,” Purp said.
“You’re a freaking stalker, huh?” she said.
Purp flushed, he felt it in his cheeks and ears. “No, I just –
“You just what, look at my book, my burrito, my fish sauce.” She counted off the three things as she said them, starting with her thumb. Purp thought she might be joking.
“You count the beers I drink and watch my weight for me, stalker,” he said.
She laughed.
“What’s your name, anyway, Stalker Girl?” he said.
“Bettywin,” it sounded like she said.
“Bettywin?” Purp said.
“Betty . . . Win,” she said.
“As in W-i-n?” Purp said.
“As in N-g-u-y-e-n. Betty Nguyen,” she said.
“Oh, Nguyen. That’s a Vietnamese name,” Purp said.
“Is that what it is? Thanks. That’s a mystery now solved,” Betty said. She took a sip from her straw, puckering her lips around it more than seemed necessary. She leaned over the table a little and looked at him while she drank. Purp looked at the black bra under her halter top.
“Now you know,” Purp said. He liked this Betty Nguyen.

"Why are you here alone today?" she said. "Big guy get tired of your shit?"

"Stalker Girl. He's coming. I actually don't know why he's late," Purp said.

Purp sensed that this was about it for Betty today. He knew when to quit, better before she got bored. "I'm going to sit down so I don't spill this," he said. "Good luck with Accounting 302 Betty Nguyen."

"I hope your friend shows up," she said.

Purp got a seat out on the patio. He burned himself a little on the black metal surface of his table and it was only April. He shifted the chairs around to get more into the shade. Purp tugged on a nacho chip and it was already stuck to the pile on his plate. The cheese had cooled while he was talking to Betty. He took a cheeseless chip and cut the stuck one free.

Chewing his chip Purp scanned the line of cars stopped at the light in front of Taco Cabana. He saw a blond head over the hood of an SUV waiting in the left turn lane. The head belonged to a girl and Purp figured she was standing on the median. The light changed and cars shifted. Purp saw the rest of the blond girl. She lifted a cardboard sign over her head and wagged her hips a few times, apparently trying to catch the attention of drivers. She wore a red T-shirt, tight, tied in a knot at the back exposing her flat, tan belly. The waistband of the girl's black shorts was so low, and the cuffs came up so high on her thighs, that it gave the effect that she'd just wrapped a scarf once around her and gone out that way. The girl swung her hips and sign in opposite directions, turning to face the cars coming the other way, the black strings of a bikini halter tied behind her neck. She stood on tip toes, feet together, to show her sign higher. Black and red letters across her ass said, "Pink."

"Que paso, vato?" Javier said as he set his tray down on Purp's table. "What's going on?"

"You shaved your head again," Purp said.

"That's why I'm late. It made a mess," Javier said. "Car wash, huh?" Javier jutted his chin toward the girl with the sign. "I hope it's not a church group."

Purp and Javier laughed. Sign Girl was moving her hips in circles, knees together. A man in a faded, dented Datsun pickup drove by in the left lane on the opposite side from Taco Cabana. His open-mouthed face turned to follow her. As he passed her she leaned forward toward his truck, shook her shoulders and said "Car wash!" so loud she could have been on the Taco Cabana patio with Purp and Javier.

"Becca is going to be pissed," Purp said. "Has she seen it yet?"

"She hasn't seen it," Javier said. "But it's not really relevant anymore. What's it for?"

"Senior trip, it says," Purp said.

Purp folded a nacho in half and put it in his mouth while he turned to look at Javier.

"We're not together anymore," Javier said.

"Oh, I'm sorry to hear that," Purp said. "When did that happen?"

"Wednesday," Javier said.

"Car wash! Woo hoo!" It was two voices this time. A dark-haired girl jogged to join the blond girl on the median.

"She actually got into Stanford, comparative literature, off the wait list and she's going to go," Javier said.

"Oh, holy shit," Purp said.

"Well, it wasn't like it was unexpected or – oh, my god!" Javier said. He laughed a special laugh he has for when something genuinely pleases or surprises him, or both.

"That's what I'm talking about," Purp said.

"Right there," Javier said.

The two girls on the median had taken off their tops, wearing bikinis underneath. The blond girl filled hers, overflowing at the top. The other girl was facing the wrong way.

* * *

"What's this?" Purp said.

"I thought you could use it," Selma said, sitting cross-legged on the bed in front of Purp. She wore sleep shorts, loose powder-blue satin, and a matching low-cut baby doll top.

Purp finished taking the wrapping off the present, a DVD. He peeled a strip of tape that was stuck to the shiny back cover. Purp turned the case over and read off the front.

"Mommy's Angel: Guide for helping new mommies get the most from their bundles of love." Purp looked at the DVD. "Thank you," he said.

"I thought you'd love it," Selma said.

"You did?" Purp said. He tossed the DVD case over toward the edge of the bed and slid his hands along the sheets toward Selma's thighs.

"Yeah, I thought you could watch it and get all kinds of good tips and tricks from it," she said.

"OK," Purp said.

"I thought we could watch it together for your birthday and maybe practice some of the techniques we saw," she said.

"Uh . . . well," Purp said. He wasn't sure how to react to this gift. Selma's enthusiasm made him feel bad for being irritated but she had to know it was kind of a bonehead move to give him that, especially wearing what she had on when she knew he'd been feeling neglected.

"Isn't the cover just the cutest?" Selma said. She stretched away from Purp to get the DVD case. She sat back up. She hugged her knees to her chest and held the DVD in front of her, showing the cover to Purp. He could see she wasn't wearing underwear under her blue shorts.

"It's cute, yeah," Purp said. "It's got a nice picture of a baby on there and everything."

"See? Little cutie, cutie," she said, turning the cover toward her and talking to the baby printed there. "Let's watch it," she said.

"Selma did you get that for me or did you get it for you?" Purp said.

"I got it for you, silly, for a birthday present," she said, giving a pouty look. "Don't you like it? Don't you just love it's so cute?" she said, drawing the last word out into a long, low note and making the baby picture dance for Purp.

"That's my birthday present?" Purp said.

"Let's watch it," Selma said. "Let's watch it right now."

"I don't want to watch it right now," Purp said.

Selma popped up from the bed and bounded over to the DVD player.

"Selma, no. I don't want to watch that right now," Purp said. He scooted off the edge of the bed and stood up behind her, pulling her arm away from the DVD player. She turned toward him.

"You won't watch it with me?" Selma said in a girlish voice, holding the DVD case behind her and leaning forward toward him, looking down the loose neck of her baby doll top and then up at Purp.

"Huh?" Purp said. Selma confused him. Was she teasing him on purpose or did she really not know it was rude to put everything out there like that for him and take it away when he went for it? He wished he were in still in bed sleeping.

Selma turned and reached for the DVD player again. Her ass in those blue satin shorts made Purp mad.

"No," Purp said. He reached over Selma's shoulder and swatted her wrist away from the DVD player. The awkward angle made him hit her harder than he intended. The DVD case flicked into the wall by the TV and fell to the floor, opening and spilling the DVD onto the carpet. The ceiling fan reflected off the shiny DVD.

"I'm not watching that now Selma," Purp said. "I mean, do you want to come back to bed, or I don't get it. What?"

Selma held her wrist where Purp had swatted her.

"You won't watch that DVD with me?" Selma said.

"I don't understand what the big deal is with the DVD," Purp said.

"I want to know, will you watch that with me or not?" Selma said.

"What did you think? Did you look at that in the store and honestly think of me when you saw it?" Purp said.

"If I said it was important to me, would you watch it?" Selma said.

"If you said it was important? What? My whole life now completely revolves around this project that is important to you," Purp said.

"This project?" Selma said.

"It's one day. It's my last birthday before the baby comes –

"You say it like you're dying," Selma said. She stepped past Purp and walked into the bathroom. In the mirror he saw her pull the baby doll up over her head. She leaned over the sink in just her shorts and looked at something on her face.

Purp turned toward the bed.

"Maybe we should go to the dealership today and trade your truck in," Selma said.

"I don't know if I feel like it, not today," Purp said.

"We have to get that done," Selma said.

Purp walked over to the spilled DVD. He bent down to pick it up. He picked up the disc by the edges and turned it over so he could put it back properly in the case, label side out. An Asian woman looked at him from the label on the DVD. She was naked, pressing her breasts together with both hands. She sat with her legs open, the hole in the middle of the DVD between her legs. "Bang Cock Nights" was the title written in flamey yellow and red letters over the Asian woman's head. Purp turned to look back into the bathroom where Selma was buttoning her jeans.

* * *

"Hoo yeah, little honey. Get me a taste of that. Mmm," Max said from the other side of the cubicle divider.

"Max, I can hear you," Purp said.

"What's that boss?" Max said.

"I can hear what you are saying," Purp said. He poked a floater. It disappeared under the surface but then bobbed back up undamaged.

"Good for you, boss. Let's see how good you hear when you're sixty-seven years old. I could hear your birth cry when you didn't even know you was making noise," Max said.

"I know, Max –

"And at the rate you're going I'll probably hear your death rattle," Max said.

"What's that supposed to mean?" Purp said.

"One thing it don't mean, is that we better get busy you showing me that server shit – stuff because according to Dennis, I'm going to be doing your job when you take your little baby vacation," Max said. "Man down, fill the gap."

"It's not a vacation," Purp said, standing to look at Max.

Max looked over the top of his monitor, pointing at Purp with a disk of glistening sausage on a fork. "You're damn straight on that point, P. J.," Max said. "Damn straight." He pulled the sausage off the fork with his amber teeth. Even the muscles in his face were cut, flexing and relaxing while Max worked the meat. If Max didn't remind Purp a few times a week how old he was, Purp would have thought he was forty. "Damn straight it ain't no vacation, and frankly speaking," Max lowered his tone. He'd been a little gun shy ever since Sensitivity Training a week before when some women in the office ambushed him during the group discussion, "that's why it has historically been the work of the female."

"No, I mean it's not a vacation, I'm not coming back," Purp said.

"I heard it was maternity leave you were getting. And that, by the way is actually something I don't understand." Max said. He stood and started to walk around to Purp's cubicle but then went back and did something with his mouse. Purp figured Max was closing his browser window so nobody would see the swimsuit model website he usually had up this time of day. That was one of the things the women complained about in Sensitivity Training.

"I thought only women got maternity leave," Max said. He rounded the partition into Purp's cubicle and squeezed into his leaning spot on Purp's desk even though Purp was already standing there.

"That's the thing though. It's paternity leave in any case, but I'm not taking leave. I'm just leaving after the baby is born in September. That's going to be it for me here," Purp said.

"Never look back, huh?" Max said.

"No, that's going to be it," Purp said.

"That means you and me got five months for you to teach me all that server . . . junk there," Max said, indicating the door to the server room.

"It's just the one server, the web server –

"I know that," Max said. "But yours got that problem, right? Ever get that straightened out? Bandwidth issue? Slowing down?"

Purp explained to Max that for a reason Purp didn't yet understand, the web server was getting heavier traffic than it should, by a factor of about a hundred, and that was causing it to bog down.

". . . and it's not like you won't have help," Purp said, "it's going to be split between you and Gilberto."

"That's worse than no help at all. That fat old Mexican pedophile fucker don't know shit from sideways –

"Max. Shhh," Purp said.

"Well it ain't because he's Mexican," Max said. "It's because he's a shit-for-brains motherfucker – anyway," Max flipped Purp's calendar to May and let it fall back down to April. "So you're taking another job or what are you doing, squirt?"

"I'm actually not. I'm going to be staying home with the baby," Purp said.

"Now that just fries my fritters right there, excuse me for saying," Max said. "Can I speak frankly with you boss?" Max clamped a hand on Purp's shoulder. It felt like Max could remove Purp's head with just his forefinger and thumb if he'd wanted. "That just ain't right."

"Well, Max, I don't really want to put the baby in daycare –

"He's got a mommy, buddy," Max said. "You're signing up to be that baby's mommy. You know that, don't you? It ain't going to be no easier that what you're doing here, I can guarantee you that. Guaran-damn-tee you that."

"I'm not doing it because I think it's going to be easier," Purp said.

"It ain't," Max said. "That little gold-leaf Air Farce blondie of yours there, Purp, she's a hell of a piece. I will give you that much, one hell of a piece. And I would tell a girl like that just about any damn thing to get up under that skirt of hers for a sniff around –

"Max, OK –

"But when it come right down to it, she's got you whipped hard, mommy," Max said. "Hard, if you're going to cut off your cock and bull and change poopy nappies all day long. You going to suckle it too?"

"I know, Max. It's just I don't like the way people do it now, just dumping them off in the morning and bringing them home for bed –

"Fire and forget," Max said.

"Exactly."

"I don't like it either."
"And she's got twelve years in," Purp said.
"Over the hump."
"Exactly. So . . . you just got to do what you got to do."
"Got to do what you got to do," Max said. "I can see it . . . but I can't see it. Know what I'm saying, boss?"
"I do," Purp said.

* * *

Purp snuck up behind her and ran the head of the putter along the inside of Selma's thigh, up her short denim maternity skirt. She was getting big enough that her larger regular clothes wouldn't fit and this skirt was new. Selma screamed and laughed and grabbed the shaft of the putter, closing her thighs on its head. She turned toward Purp, pulling the golf club out of his hands and holding it with one hand behind her like a tail. She brandished her own red-handled club toward him in a mock-threatening gesture.

Purp retreated and Selma trotted toward him keeping her thighs together on the club's head. She swung her hips to hit Purp with her golf club tail. The handle of the club hit him on the thigh. "Boom!" she said.

Purp let out a grunt that sounded like a normal grunt recorded and slowed way down for playback. In super slow motion he mimed a dramatic fall into the railing of the little bridge they were standing on at the mini-golf course by their house. He let his chest hit the railing and made another grunt, louder. Selma laughed. Purp fell in slow motion onto the artificial turf that carpeted the bridge. When he landed, he made an even louder grunt than before. People playing other holes looked over at them. Selma laughed and kneeled down beside him, beating Purp in slow motion with both golf clubs.

Purp scrambled toward the bridge's railing on his belly while Selma beat him with the clubs and he reached down into the water flowing under him. Purp wet his hand and brought it up, flicking water over his shoulder at Selma's face. She screamed and rolled back, sitting on the green fake turf and covering her head with both hands. She held onto both clubs, though. Purp dipped his hand back into the stream and flicked water at Selma, trying to be careful to only wet her bare legs and arms without getting too much water on her clothes. Every time a spray of tepid water landed on her skin Selma squealed and laughed, dodging from the spot where it hit.

Selma rolled over onto her little belly and pushed herself up while Purp splashed her. She kicked off her thong sandals and scampered off the bridge right down into the water hazard itself. She stood ankle deep and windmilled the golf clubs, one in each hand, making a noise like a big piece of machinery winding up to speed. Purp crawled down off the bridge too, to the water's edge. He didn't want to get his shoes wet. He knelt by the pool and flicked water up at Selma, wetting one hand while flicking with the other. He wasn't getting her too wet.

Selma kept up her machine noise and lowered the spinning golf clubs into the water. When they first skimmed the surface she yelled "Boom!" Water flew from the club heads. Selma's double windmill surprised Purp with its spraying efficiency. A blast from the pond nailed him in the face, and he fell back theatrically yelling "Nooo!" while the splashing machine inched toward him. He got wet, for sure, but the problem with Selma's machine was that it was getting her as wet as it was getting Purp. Wetter, maybe. He laughed a deep gut laugh while curling himself into a fetal position, still sort of trying to protect his shoes. The machine noise from Selma choked up in spurts as her own laughter broke through.

* * *

Ice break. That's what Jimmy Stewart called it. Jimmy Stewart the weather man, not the other one. The first day of the year that the high for the day broke a hundred. May 8th this year. Misters cooled the patio at Taco Cabana and Purp felt comfortable. His shoes still felt crusty from the water in the mini-golf pond the night before but he was otherwise unharmed.

Purp scooped bean onto a chip and a sign caught his eye bobbing over the roof of a Japanese pickup. "Car Wash," it said. "Senior Trip '03." Purp put the chip into his mouth. He couldn't see who held the sign. Over the last few weeks since they'd started, Purp noticed the car wash kids out there every week. He'd gotten to recognize a couple of them. The light changed and traffic moved. A feisty red-haired girl, a little chunky but not fat, held the sign wearing a bikini top and a short denim skirt that suited her even though her thighs were a little thick. She worked the sign hard, and good. She looked like she was making it her personal mission to make eye contact with the driver of every single car that passed her, wagging her tail and shaking her sunburned shoulders.

Purp sipped his beer, the outside of the bottle damp from the mist. He was on number three and Javier hadn't even showed yet. The car wash was set up on the side of a Circle K. From the Taco Cabana Purp had a good view, even though a sign posted on a dirt lot next to the Circle K, "For Sale or Lease, Build to Suit," it said, blocked some of the action.

The car wash had become Purp's favorite part of the week. Saturday beer brunch with Javier was his favorite part of the week anyway, but the car wash really made it. The washing of the cars was done mostly by what was probably a fair representation of student government types, pimply gregarious big guys, hot-looking popular guys, girls of all sorts, but for some reason a kind of loose peripheral ring always seemed to form around the sudsy kids who were actually washing cars. The ring consisted mostly of more attractive girls in little clothing who didn't seem to do much other than mill around, drifting in and out of the Circle K and the Taco Cabana, carrying sodas and burritos. These girls interacted with the actual car washers but never seemed fully engaged in the process. They'd peel off in little clusters, or ones and twos, talking on cell phones, and every once in a while they'd pick up a hose and rinse a car or scream and dodge a spray fired at them by one of the flirtatious big guys, or hot guys.

Throughout the course of the morning the girls in that peripheral loose ring would all take off their shirts at one point or another, sporting little bikini tops underneath that coordinated with their shorts or mini-skirts. The actual girls involved in washing the cars kept their shirts on for the most part, some definitely notable exceptions, but for the ring girls walking around in a bikini top near the car wash guys seemed to be a part of why they were there. They wouldn't take their shirts off right away, they'd hang around first, drifting here and there, and then it would happen in a sort of wave. Once one did it, others would do it. One girl would take her shirt off, then her friend right after, as if to keep up. Then a different little group would do it. The shirtlessness had a sort of viral propagation to it, and it didn't seem to have anything to do with temperature or time of morning either. Purp figured it to be more something social, not done out of any practical necessity.

The waves went the other way, too. The shirts would come back on. That seemed just as random. Sometimes one would put her shirt on to come into Taco Cabana or Circle K, but they'd be just as likely to come in wearing only their bikinis. But even though why and when the shirts came back on was a mystery to Purp, when one girl in a cluster put her shirt on, it wouldn't be long before the other one or two girls suited up, too, and then the wave would spill over to the other clusters, and pretty soon most of the girls in the peripheral ring would have their shirts on.

There was a subset of the peripheral ring girls, a group Purp called sign girls. The sign girls interacted more with the peripheral ring girls than the car wash girls did, and some girls migrated between being sign girls and ring girls, while crossover between ring girls and wash girls was actually something he'd never seen. The sign girls were the ones on the corners and medians who held the car wash signs, and the sign girls formed their own cluster in terms of when they wore shirts and when they did not. The number and location of sign girls varied widely. No girl stood in the same spot, median or corner, for more than ten minutes. The distribution of sign girls appeared chaotic. Sometimes there would be a sign girl one each on two diagonally opposite corners and the median, sometimes there would be two clustered on one corner, sometimes there would be three all on the median – Purp couldn't predict it but there were usually three signs and anywhere from zero to three sign girls on display at any given time. The more sign girls there were, and the more of them there were on any given spot, corners or median, the more likely they would be to all take off their shirts.

The bottoms, Purp noticed, shorts or skirts, always stayed on. No exceptions.

Purp finished the nachos and drained his beer. He was ready for another Budweiser. Javier still hadn't made an appearance, but Purp had been early and they didn't have so much of a set time anyway. When they did plan to be somewhere together at a particular time, Javier was always punctual to the minute. Purp commented on it to Javier one time, and Javier said he'd picked up the habit during his six years in the Navy.

The chesty blond-haired sign girl Purp noticed the first day of the car wash trotted across from the empty lot on the corner to the median. She didn't have a sign. She wore a purple tube-top and white shorts. The girls didn't seem to pay much attention to the "Walk" sign, they just went when they could. Because of the heavy traffic on six lanes of Guadalupe Ave., they always seemed to be trotting or running outright when they crossed, a motion made comically awkward by the thong flip-flop sandals that most of the girls had on. Purp figured the blond girl was going to hang out with the redhead on the median for a little, but she didn't even stop to chat. She kept right on going toward Taco Cabana. The redhead had her shirt back on before the blond girl even made it all the way across the street.

Purp watched the blond girl trot toward him, toward the Taco Cabana anyway. The flip-flop traffic trot and the tight purple tube top made a nice combination. When the blond girl disappeared around the corner Purp got up to stretch his legs and get himself another beer. He looked around for Javier, as if looking for Javier would make him appear. No Javier. Purp laid his empties on the red plastic tray near his greasy empty nacho plate, and he carried the whole thing to the trash.

Purp got up by the register just as the cowbell on the door tinkled. The blond girl walked in, pinching her tube top at the sides of both breasts, straightening it and hiking it up. Maybe, Purp thought, it had slipped a little when she was running. It looked like a habit to him, though, a reflex, sort of like how all the girls put their left hand over their lower back whenever they bent down so their ultra low-rise shorts or skirts wouldn't show their ass cracks.

Purp and the blond girl got to the register at about the same time. Purp pretended to read the menu so she would go in front of him. She did. Her black and purple bikini straps coordinated with her tube top. She had the straps tied in a bow behind her neck. Purp stepped a few inches to the side so that he wasn't directly behind her. This made it so he could look sideways down into her tube top, from an angle over her right shoulder. There was a space between her bikini straps and her chest, as if the straps were under tension.

The blond girl ordered a large drink to go. The cashier gave her the total and the blond girl fumbled for money.

"Shit," the blond girl said. "Shit. I left my cards."

The cashier, a girl about the same age with a shiny face waited, not annoyed but not friendly.

"Can I just pay you when I come back in for a refill later?" the blond girl said.

"Uhh . . . I can ask my manager?" the cashier said.

"Oh Christ," a heavy man behind Purp said under his breath.

"Why don't you just ring it up with mine," Purp said.

"Another Budweiser?" the cashier said to him, annoyed now. She was usually friendly to Purp, even a little flirty.

"Oh, you don't have to," the blond girl said, turning toward Purp, flushing. She looked up at him and her look of embarrassment changed to a different kind of look, the kind girls never gave Purp when he was that age, but that they seemed to more now. She tilted her chin down but kept her eyes up on his.

"No problem," Purp said. He paid with his debit card and the cashier slid him his bottle of Budweiser and a plastic cup for the soda.

Purp handed the red plastic cup back to the cashier. "I'm sorry, that was a to go drink," he said. "And can I have a cup for water?" Purp wanted an excuse to walk over to the soda fountain.

The cashier gave him a paper cup and he handed it over to the blond girl as the two of them walked over to the soda fountain.

"How's business?" Purp said. "The car wash?"

"It's OK," the girl said.

"I eat here every Saturday," Purp said. "I see you guys out there. Do you come every week?" Purp knew she did.

"Yeah, until we raise enough," the girl said.

The girl got some ice. Purp did the same. She started filling her cup with Diet Dr Pepper. Purp had to step behind her and move to her left side to get to the lemonade spout where he cold get some water. He filled his water cup while she was topping off her soda. The girl had a scar on the left side of her face. It wasn't terrible, but it was probably something that bothered a girl her age. The scar ran from the corner of her left eye to the corner of her mouth tracing C-shape. She turned her head and shoulders toward Purp while keeping her eyes on the soda dispenser. The way she moved her head made Purp think that was something she did, turn to hide her left side.

"Senior trip?" Purp said, making himself busy with a lemon. Purp didn't like lemon in his water. He didn't like the way the seeds would fall out and come up his straw.

"Cabo," she said, snapping a lid onto her cup.

"Good luck," Purp said. He turned away from the drink counter. Purp didn't want to make her find a way to end the conversation. He took a couple of steps toward an exit to the patio.

"Thank you," the girl said after him.

Purp turned back toward her, feigning a confused look. He relaxed his face into a smile and locked his eyes hard on her right eye. The side he knew she was more comfortable with. "The soda," he said. "Sure, you're very welcome." Purp's mind chased forward a second or two and he considered telling her she was wearing his favorite color, or something about his name, but the right phrase didn't come to him, so he left it at that. He turned again and stepped back out onto the patio.

* * *

The people in Javier's program knew how to party. In the two years Purp had known Javier he'd been to more parties than in the thirty-three years before that. Purp didn't know if they were good writers or bad ones, but in any case they knew what they were doing when it came to throwing a party.

"A little more," the Russian girl said. Svetlana. She had a heavy accent and Purp wondered if she could write in English more clearly than she could speak.

"Sure, I'll take a little," Purp said. He had a blue plastic Solo cup held close to his chest. It had been filled and emptied with more different drinks than he could keep track of at that point. But it wasn't like Svetlana was asking him, she was going to pour it in anyway.

Svetlana poured vodka into Purp's cup over the rum and Coke sort of looking mix that was in there already. She sloshed a little on his hand.

"Thanks," Purp said.

Purp knew about a third of the people there from coming to parties with Javier. Most of those he knew, he'd known for a couple of years now. Svetlana was one of those. She was a heavy girl, black haired and quite a bit younger than Purp, or even Javier. Javier's time in the Navy made him older than many of his classmates, but not all. A lot of them came into the program right out of college, but a handful of the twenty in his class had done other things first. Two were retired.

Svetlana drank from the bottle she'd just poured. She had Purp backed into a corner by the refrigerator. They were in the kitchen of Javier's thesis advisor Arturo Santos, a Brazilian professor who hosted parties every month but who'd done this one up special for graduation.

Svetlana leaned in closer to Purp. Soaked with sweat from the hot mass of people in the tiny adobe house, Purp felt her chest press into his arm, two cushions. Someone was trying to get a trash bag through behind her, but she didn't back off when some space opened up. Svetlana told Purp in confidential tones about Arturo's love life, while the man himself laughed by the sink with his hand on Javier's ex-girlfriend's shoulder.

Purp took a swallow of the concoction in his Solo cup, thinking the motion of his arm would back Svetlana off a little. It didn't, but the drink was kind of good. He gulped it, already so far gone it surprised him a little that he was still standing. He couldn't focus on what Svetlana was telling him but he understood generally it had to do with the professor and his tendency to run through graduate students fairly quickly.

Purp didn't remember his cup being empty but the people in the kitchen were all different and Svetlana was pouring him the rest of the vodka. He looked at the clear liquid in his cup, only just tinged with the dregs of what had been in there before.

Svetlana had turned to the subject of Turkey at some point and Purp gave up trying not to stare down the loose neck of the black tent dress she wore at the hawk tattoo on her left breast. Purp calculated that each breast must have been at least three quarters of a gallon in volume. People Purp knew kept squeezing by them in the kitchen and laughing when they saw Purp, but he didn't know why. He couldn't hear what they were saying. Javier tried to get through the kitchen, his face shiny with sweat. His bulk made it hard for him to snake thorough the crowd. Javier was headed for the screen door which led to the patio, and Purp decided he wanted to go with him.

"Svetlana," he said, waiting for when it sounded like she was switching topics or at a lull altogether. "I am roasting. I'm going to head outside with Javier."

"Well, Purp," she said, not seeming drunk at all, "if you have to leave a party," she poured his Solo cup half full from a gin bottle he hadn't seen her pick up, "always take a traveler." They laughed. It was a line from a movie they'd watched together, a little group of them over at Purp's house one time. A line they tried to work into the conversation when they could.

The way Purp felt made him think of what it's like to be an astronaut walking on the moon. He forgot the step down to the patio and stumbled onto the railing, banging his knees into a bike locked there. He half-knocked the bike over but the lock held it up. Something fell off the bike but Purp didn't know what, or where to. He made it to where Javier sat in a wooden Adirondack chair, not far from a group of students sitting and smoking. Purp sat on the wide arm of Javier's chair.

"That's one small step for a man," Purp said.

"Svetlana get you drunk?" Javier said.

"Again," Purp said. "Every time . . . I guess I got myself drunk. She poured."

"She does that, right?" Javier said.

"Oh yeah," Purp said. "She get a job?"

"No, she's going back to Moscow," Javier said.

"You did all right, huh?" Purp said. He patted Javier on the chest.

"I guess," Javier said.

"You're the only one with a book coming out," Purp said.

"That's just because of the contest," Javier said, "and it's not for three years."

"Still," Purp said. A wave of something hit him. He wasn't sure if he was going to puke or had to take a dump. Or maybe both. Neither. He laid himself down on his back on the gravel by Javier's chair. Purp tilted his head up to take a swig from the Solo cup. He rested the cup on his chest after he swallowed. "U. Penn.," Purp said. "Ivy League."

"Yeah," Javier said. He crossed his leg, putting a thick hairy ankle on his square knee. "I don't know," he said, "I don't know if it's the right thing or not."

An airplane flew across the sky, red light blinking. It passed below the moon. "One giant leap," Purp said.

Javier picked at a strip of rubber hanging off the sole of his Doc Marten.

A fire truck masked the buzz of the party. Red lights swept across the yard as the siren came and went.

"That'd be a good job, right?" Javier said.

"Astronaut?" Purp said.

"Fireman," Javier said.

Purp bent his neck and drained the Solo cup. He set the cup down on his chest. His head fell back onto the gravel and stars in his eyes mixed with the ones in the sky.

"The fireman . . . they have a room where they sleep," Purp said. "And it's like most of them have their own little room and some . . . are two to a room."

"In high school I wanted to be a fireman," Javier said. "Even in the Navy I applied for Fire School."

"From fireman to T. S. Eliot," Purp said. "That's a funny way to go."

"It was more like the other way and back," Javier said.

"Wasteland, Wasteland, Memphis, Tennessee I'm going to Wasteland," Purp said, singing. "It's a good thing," Purp said. "You're going unattached. Completely . . . unattached."

"I came here like that," Javier said.

"When you don't have that anymore," Purp said, "you'll miss me."

* * *

"Where's your truck?" Selma said.

"I don't know," Purp said.

"You don't know?"

"I don't."

"I mean, do you have any idea? Like, do you have a guess where it is? Are we talking Wal*Mart, Taco Cabana, the University?" Selma said. She didn't sound annoyed.

"Yeah," Purp said. "It could be." He curled over onto his side. He still had on his green plaid Quicksilver shirt from the night before but his jeans were off. But his socks were on. That was weird. The covers were mostly off of him and he kicked so they weren't on him at all. The air conditioner wasn't on and he was sweaty.

"It could be what?" Selma said. She wore her uniform.

"What time is it?" Purp said.

"Ten," Selma said.

Purp figured 10:00 AM since it was light out.

"You just get home?" Purp said.

"Yeah, but I didn't think you were here because I didn't see your truck," Selma said. She'd been on duty the night before.

"It's not here," Purp said. He pulled a pillow over his head, silky and cool, one of the ones in a decorative pillow sham. Selma flipped it off his head and put a regular pillow in its place. She didn't like the shams getting dirty. "Holy crap," Purp said. "I feel so sick."

"I can smell the alcohol," Selma said. "Were you actually drinking in here?"

"No," Purp said. "It's coming from me." He pressed the pillow down over his head, surprised he didn't have such a bad headache. Maybe he wasn't hungover yet. He felt sick, though. "I think I'm still drunk," he said.

"Purp, why do you do this?" Selma said, opening a window.

"It's that Svetlana," Purp said.

"With the tattoo on her tit?" Selma said.

"She makes me do it. Javier said she's going back to Russia," Purp said.

"So what are you going to do then?" Selma said.

"Maybe you could get a tattoo on your tit," Purp said.

"My tit's not as big as hers," Selma said.

"You're not as big as she is," Purp said. "Just get a smaller tattoo."

Purp poked his face out from underneath the pillow to get some air. Selma had one foot on the bed and her uniform maternity skirt hiked up around her waist. She peeled a stocking down from her thigh.

"So where is your truck?" Selma said.

"I don't need it today. You don't have to pull duty starting next month, right?" Purp said.

"Nope. I only have one more to go," Selma said. "Do you think you're going to be able to find the truck before tomorrow so we can go to the dealership to get it traded in?"

"Two problems with that," Purp said "no three. Problem one, I can't get the truck unless you drive me and you just got home so you're going to bed. Problem two, I'm still drunk from last night and I can't drive. Problem three, tomorrow is Sunday and the dealership isn't open."

"Purp," Selma said. "Christ. There's nothing I can do. It doesn't have a back seat. We have to trade it in."

"Let's just keep it. We'll keep it and get another car with a back seat, too. What if we need it?" Purp said.

"For what? For what do you need it? We can eat for a week on what it costs to fill it," Selma said. She stood by the bed naked with both hands pressing on the small of her back as if it were sore.

"I don't really have to worry about the price of gas, that's for sure," Purp said. "Yard waste. What if I want to go off-roading?"

"You don't have a place to park it," Selma said. "We have a two car garage and it barely fits."

"I'll leave it out," Purp said.

"What is with you? You know you can't do that," Selma said. "The association sent a letter the one week we left a car out, when your grandparents were here. It has no back seat, Purp. I'm sorry, we have to get rid of it."

"I'm not driving a Prius," Purp said. "Or an SUV."

"What's wrong with an SUV?" Selma said.

"They're dorky soccer mom-mobiles," Purp said.

"They're trucks, they're manly I thought," Selma said.

"An SUV is every single thing that manly is not. They're the opposite of manly," Purp said. "I'm not driving a freaking puss-mobile," Purp said.

"Aren't they for off-road too?" Selma said.

"Oh my God, they're so not for off-road. They're for hauling broods of other people's kids to and from extra-extra-curricular enrichment activities and crap you load in off a forklift from COSCO," Purp said. "And I'm not driving a Prius either."

"You don't have to drive a Prius. It was just a suggestion. They have the Civic hybrid too now," Selma said. "And you need to take a shower before I go to bed. You stink from last night, or whenever it was you took a shower last."

"I can't trade the truck in," Purp said.

"Why?" Selma said.

"I don't know where it is," Purp said. "It's in hiding."

Selma grabbed the pillow off of Purp's head and belted him in the face with it. She raised it over her head and slammed it down onto his face, over and over. When he tried to cover his face she whacked him in the balls with it, hard enough to make him cough. The exertion made Purp feel like he was going to throw up. He hollered and moaned and covered his balls and just when he did she nailed him in the face again over and over. Purp tried to cover his face and balls at the same time but he ended up covering neither very well. He was laughing and moaning and yelling for her to stop. She did, out of breath.

"It's probably at Arturo's," Purp said, rubbing his sore crotch with both hands.

"You drove Javier?" Selma said. "You picked him up at his apartment?"

"Yeah," Purp said.

"You went straight there?" Selma said.

"No, we stopped at the King's X first," Purp said.

"To get pre-drunk?" Selma said.

"Yeah." Purp said.

"You're pathetic. Who else was there?" Selma said.

"Everybody," Purp said.

"So it's either at the King's X or Arturo's?" Selma said.

"I think it's at Arturo's," Purp said.

* * *

"It is so," Purp said. He leaned his recliner back, balancing a bowl of Baked Lays on his lap and holding a bottle of Budweiser. "Can you hand me that Salsa?"

Javier passed the salsa from the coffee table over to where Purp sat. "I don't think it is," Javier said.

"It's the largest manmade structure, and the only manmade structure visible to the naked eye of an observer standing on the surface of the moon," Purp said like an infomercial pitch man.

"You can keep saying that over and over, but it doesn't make it true," Javier said. "I think you just like saying that."

"What makes it true, is that it is true," Purp said.

"It's not even wide," Javier said. "It's like the width of a road on top."

"It's bigger than that," Purp said.

"You've seen pictures of it," Javier said, "with all the Chinamen up there, riding bikes and shit. Right? It's like a road. You can't see it from the moon."

"Shh," Purp said, straight-arm pointing to the plasma screen on the wall, a television so big and so bright that Purp felt heat coming off it even back in his chair.

Javier set his beer down on a coaster and slapped the tops of his thighs.

Purp and Javier started to chant.

"D. M. G.," they said together. "D. M. G."

They chanted along with a studio audience, mostly men in their twenties, all saying, "D. M. G., D. M. G."

The men on T.V. chanted faster and faster and Purp and Javier yelled right along with them, whipping themselves into a frenzy. Purp squawked in a high raspy voice like Beavis. The chant got so fast that it lost its rhythm.

A computer-animated graphic came on-screen that looked like an old-fashioned speedometer. It had a needle on it and a red zone marked to the right of the gauge. The meter had a label under it that read: "Barkenator 5000." The men stopped yelling "D. M. G." and started barking instead. Javier and Purp barked with the men on the show. As the barking in the studio audience got louder, the needle on the meter moved to the right, getting closer and closer to the red zone. The barking got so loud Purp's left ear started to buzz and rattle. He put his finger in the buzzing ear and barked louder. The needle plunged into the red zone and the graphic changed into fireworks. Purp and Javier stopped barking and the men in the audience cheered and hooted. The screen dissolved into super slow motion footage of a busty tan Asian girl and a smaller but still huge blonde girl both in tiny thong bikinis jumping up and down on a trampoline.

"Nice," Javier said, laughing and slapping his thighs. "Two this week. There's usually one, right?"

A theme song played over the frantic cheers of the men in the audience. The women bounced in high-definition slow motion.

Words slid onto the screen against the backdrop of bouncing women: "Dude. Man. Guy."

The women dissolved away and an dark-haired man bounded onto a set that looked like a fraternity house basement, with a pool table and a bar, posters of lingerie models.

"My name is Hideo Matsuda," the man said, his arms reaching toward the ceiling, fingers splayed. About Purp's age, maybe a little older, he wore a black shirt with embroidered flames running down the front in two vertical stripes, his black hair shoulder-length. "Welcome to Dude. Man. Guy!" Matsuda pumped his fist in the air when he said the name of the show. The men in the studio chanted the name of the show with the host when he said it.

Matsuda told a couple of funny stories and ran through the order of the day. After that it was time for more chanting and then a commercial. Javier turned to look at Purp.

"If you can see it from the moon," Javier said around a mouthful of microwave burrito, "Then you should be able to see I-10 right?"

"No," Purp said, but Javier had a point.

"Are you saying that The Great Wall of China is wider than I-10?" Javier said. "I-10 is like six lanes across."

"Only in town," Purp said. "Between cities it's only four."

"It's still wider than the top of the wall," Javier said. "You've seen pictures of it. It looks cramped up there, right? It's more like a street on top than a highway."

"I-10 isn't a structure," Purp said. "I said 'manmade structure.'"

"It's a manmade object," Javier said.

"But it is not a structure," Purp said.

"So if I-10 were on top of a wall, you'd be able to see it from Space?" Javier said.

"It depends on the time of day," said Purp, improvising.

"Of course. Not at night," Javier said.

"No, I mean at noon, no. In the early morning or evening, yes," Purp said.

"What time zone is the moon in?" Javier said.

"It depends on the local time of the object being viewed. In the early morning or evening, a wall-shaped structure is visible because it casts a shadow," Purp said.

"That's kind of cheap," Javier said.

"What?" Purp said.

"It depends on the light," Javier said. "It's not like the object itself is visible, intrinsically visible based on its own properties."

"Neither are you," Purp said.

"Neither am I what?" Javier said.

"The visibility of everything depends on how it interacts with light," Purp said. "That's all our retina can detect, light."

"I wonder if I-10 is even longer than The Great Wall of China," Javier said.

Dude. Man. Guy. came back on. Javier shushed Purp before he could say any more.

* * *

"Come on," Purp said.

"Purp, please," Selma said. "Just let me go to sleep."

Purp moved his hips against Selma's ass. She laid with her back toward him. He had his arm around her waist and his hand up her satin camisole, cupping her breast. He moved his hips faster.

"Just for a minute," Purp said.

"No," Selma said. "I have to work tomorrow."

"You always have to work tomorrow. Or you're too tired from working that day. Selma, seriously. This is getting kind of ridiculous," Purp said. He kept pushing against her.

"What's that supposed to mean?" Selma said. She rolled over onto her back and looked at him.

"What's that supposed to mean? Are you serious?" Purp said rubbing against her hip.

"Purp, I'm pregnant," Selma said, pleading.

"Oh, newsflash. No kidding. It's not exactly easy for me to forget that," Purp said.

"Are you trying to forget that?" Selma said, scooting her hip away from Purp's grinding pelvis.

"This isn't about you being pregnant," Purp said. "I go to the doctor with you. He's told you both times it's perfectly OK to have sex."

"Maybe it's OK to, but I don't feel like it," Selma said. "It's not comfortable."

"Don't blame it on being pregnant," Purp said. He sat up on the edge of the bed with his back toward her. "That's just your excuse for right now."

"I don't need an excuse. I don't feel like it. I have to go to work," Selma said.

"Yeah, I have to go to work tomorrow, too," Purp said.

“Then just go to sleep,” Selma said. “Please. I don’t want to keep having this conversation every night.”

“This isn’t about the baby,” Purp said. “You know this has been an issue for a long time before the baby. For years.” Purp laid down on his back on his own side of the bed, not touching Selma. He touched himself absently. He was still hard.

“We made the baby, didn’t we? You had sex then,” Selma said, drowsy.

“Yeah, like twice,” Purp said, rubbing himself more purposefully. “I thought maybe it’d take us a few months. I was looking forward to it.”

“Mmm hmm.” Selma said, dozing off.

“I thought maybe we’d be one of those couples who said ‘We’ve been having sex every day for a year, I don’t know what else to do.’” Purp rubbed himself faster at the thought of that. “But little Miss Ovulation Strips over there, you gave me like a forty-five minute window.” Purp moved his hand fast on his boxers. “And then again the next morning just to make sure.” Purp slid down the waistband of his boxers. He’d put her on her elbows and knees that particular morning. She grunted when he slammed into her, hard. Her little fingers balled the sheets into her fists at the corner of the mattress.

Purp picked up his T-shirt off the floor by the bed. He put it over his cock and rubbed hard with his right hand. He slipped his left hand down the waistband of Selma’s panties and grabbed a handful of ass. He felt wet warmth spreading through his T-shirt under his right hand. He bucked his hips up off the mattress and then laid still for a minute. After that, Purp wiped himself off with the dry part of the shirt, wrapped the shirt into a ball around the wet spot and tossed it onto the carpet. He drifted off to sleep with his hand on Selma’s ass.

* * *

“How’d you figure it out, boss?” Max said, from the other side of the partition.

“I studied the TrafficStats reports for file activity,” Purp said.

“The whoosey whatsits? Tells you who’s going where for how long and all that good stuff? Stuff.” Max said.

It always surprised Purp a little how quick Max actually was. Max was in charge of running three Oracle database servers for the University and Max seemed to know an awful lot more about what Purp did than Purp knew about Max's Oracle servers.

"You've seen the site for the museum, right?" Purp said.

"I have, indeed. Of course, Purp squirt. My calendar module's on there that pulls from the Oracle server. Ain't nothing I ain't seen in sixty-seven years boy, nothing I ain't seen 'cept maybe that little cutie nekkid," Max said.

Purp figured that last part was probably referring to a girl Max had up on his computer monitor.

"Black beauty, hoo yeah," Max said.

Purp didn't even want to try to guess what that was in reference too.

"Well, you know there's the museum logo at the top of every page in the site, right?" Purp said.

"Indeed, I do," Max said.

"That little gif should be the single most downloaded file for the entire museum site, right?" Purp said, figuring he'd have to explain why.

"Roger that. Top of every page, P. J. Can't download diddly squat without loading that logo gif," Max said. He was spot on. That was Purp's point exactly.

"Right," Purp said.

"Except," Max said, "when they click to enlarge. That bring it up in a separate window, don't it. No logo there."

"Uh, no . . . no there isn't," Purp said. Purp hadn't thought about that. He forgot that. It was true what Max said, but as he thought about it Purp realized it didn't affect the overall point he was making. But it was true, he had to give Max that much.

"I gave that click to enlarge motherf – motherscratcher a workout when they put up them Adelson exhibit photos, remember them?" Max said. "Remember that one, Purp, them nudie photos all provocative and shit?"

"I do. So anyway, when I look at TrafficStats there are images in our archive that get downloaded literally tens of thousands of times more frequently than the logo gif," Purp said.

"Well, shee-at," Max said. "Ain't nobody click to enlarge that much, ten thousand times factor. Even nudie pictures, if everybody clicked it, and they don't, it would just be double." Max was on fire today. That is exactly the way Purp figured it when Max reminded him that click to enlarge sends no logo.

"So if you look at the page downloads, there's no traffic problem. There's plenty of bandwidth," Purp said.

"But when you look at them files it's a lot of junk coming through the pipe. That's why our server is slow, P. J." Max said.

"Exactly," Purp said. Purp liked how Max said "our" server. Max had resigned himself to the fact he was going to be doing most of Purp's job when Purp left in September since as Max often said, Gilberto was useless.

"So where's all that extra traffic coming from?" Max said.

"People are linking to our images, on our server, directly from their own websites," Purp said.

"I see. I got you," Max said.

"So every time someone loads their pages, the pages of the other sites, it makes a hit on our server to pull the image in. So they are using the image on their site, but we are storing it for them on our server," Purp said.

"They're ripping us off, bud. We're paying for that bandwidth. It's costing us more to keep our shit running because they're using it on us. They're getting the credit, and we're paying the bill," Max said "And it makes our server slow. Molasses ass slow."

"Right," Purp said. Purp liked how well Max got it.

"So what are you going to do about it, boss? What's the big fix?" Max said. "What do they pay you the big bucks for?" Max had a higher pay grade than Purp.

"OK, Max, this is where it gets good," Purp said. "You're going to like this part. Come over here on my side a minute."

Max ducked around the partition and took his leaning spot against Purp's desk. "What's going on, boss?" Max said. Purp wasn't Max' boss. "You cooking something up or what?"

"OK, I don't want you to tell anybody about this, but I've got to tell you. It's hilarious," Purp said. "You'll appreciate it."

"Classified, top secret," Max said.

"You're the only one with a clearance," Purp said. "Compartmentalized." Purp wasn't sure what that meant, but he'd heard it in the context of sensitive military information and he figured it would mean something to Max.

"Roger that, P. J.," Max said.

"What I did is change the filenames for every single image file that we use on the museum site," Purp said.

"But that broke all the links, kemosabee, no?" Max said.

"It did, so I changed every single reference on our site to match all the new file names," Max said. "To the end user it still looks exactly the same."

"Shit, that's a lot of work, boss," Max said.

"It wasn't actually," Purp said. "I wrote a little utility to do it for me and it wasn't so bad."

"You got too much time on your hands, Purp squirt," Max said. "That fixed it, though, huh? A lot of sites around the world got image not found boxes when you turned that on, eh? Red X's."

"Now that's the thing, Max. That's the thing," Purp said. "They didn't get red X's."

"No?" Max said.

"What they got is this," Purp said. He opened an image file on his computer. It was nasty porn, anal. A small woman sitting on top of a huge guy. She was facing the camera, taking it where it definitely did not fit. Purp closed the image. He'd left it up barely long enough for Max to see.

"Jesus, Mary, and Joseph, Purp squirt," Max said, covering his mouth with his hand. "You dropped the bad gas on those motherfuckers." Max stood looking at the carpet, silent for a few seconds. Purp hadn't seen him speechless before. After a while Max looked up at the fluorescent lights and smiled. "Now that right there," he said through his grin, "is a death worth dying. Hoo yeah."

"I copied that image twenty-seven hundred times," Purp said, "once for each real image in our archive."

"And you put them on our server with all the old filenames people had linked to," Max said. "You wrote a program to name all the copies, didn't you boss man."

"Exactly," Purp said.

"For how long?" Max said

"I left it like that for six hours Sunday night, from midnight to six am," Purp said.

* * *

Purp knew Javier wouldn't be there at 10:30 am for beer brunch but he'd been going earlier and earlier partly because of the car wash and mostly because he liked seeing Betty Nguyen without Javier there.

The jingling door shut itself behind Purp. Betty sat in a corner, her straight black hair brushing the table around her book. A couple of bites were gone from the burrito she'd pushed to the corner of the table. Purp didn't get why she put fish sauce on the whole thing when she was only going to eat a quarter of it. She didn't take it home, either.

Betty looked different, older. More formally dressed than usual. She wore a red button-down blouse, snug in the front, with tight sleeves slit at wide floppy cuffs which folded back on themselves baring her forearms. Her nails were done, and they usually were not. Someone had made them a half-inch past her fingertips and glossy red that matched her top. The bottom of Betty's shirt missed the top of her pants in the back by an inch. A strip of tan tattooed skin separated red from black. Purp had only ever seen her in shorts or a skirt before but today she had on black stretchy dress pants which hugged her hips and thighs then flared at the leg. She wore black strappy shoes, platform heels. The chunky heel and inch-and-a-half platform gave the impression of a Budweiser Clydesdale, in a good way. Betty's toenails matched her fingernails. Flawless and glossy.

"Hey, Betty," Purp said.

"Hi, Purp," Betty said. She looked up at Purp. He felt a thrill in his chest like someone had pulled a thing tight in there that was supposed to be loose. Purp had never seen Betty in make-up like that before. Usually she wore some, but not like this. Black eyeliner, top and bottom lid, came to a point at the corners of her eyes. She wore eye shadow in several shades of silver and bronze which coordinated with the sparkly but subtle bronzer on her usually freckly cheeks. Betty's lips looked wet with red to match her nails. Purp wondered if she'd put more lipstick on since the burrito.

"Accounting this morning?" Purp said.

"Yeah, we have a final Tuesday," Betty said.

"302?" Purp said.

"Uh huh. Good memory," Betty said. "And I don't have much time to study this weekend either."

"Aww," Purp made a sad face. "Working?" Betty had mentioned before that her family ran a nail salon and sometimes they were busy on weekends making house calls to brides.

"No, C.P.A Club is having mock interviews and I'm coordinating them with C.P.A.'s who volunteer to interview us like they would if we were applying for a job. It sucks we have to do it finals week but second semester they don't like to do it earlier because they're all busy with taxes."

"Ahh. Makes sense," Purp said. "Are you getting interviewed, too?"

"Uh huh," Betty said. She nodded her head, sending hair into her face. She shook the hair back into place.

“Your sister do all this?” He flicked his chin toward her fingernails. Betty’s red shirt stretched across the front. He saw her black bra underneath.

“You have a super-good memory,” Betty said. “Yeah, she did. She did the nails, but I did the make-up.” She tilted her face up toward Purp, stretching her neck. It caught Purp off guard when she did that. A shudder tickled down his neck and back.

“Oh yeah, I see it,” he said. He lowered his face an inch, and moved his shoulders a little side to side while she turned her head a few degrees to the left and right as if giving him the full tour. “Fancy, huh?”

“Mmm hmm,” Betty said. “Do you think it’s too much?”

“No,” Purp said. “I think you look nice, Betty.”

“Thanks,” she said.

“Good luck with the exam, in case I don’t catch you on the way out,” Purp said. “I hope the interviews get all coordinated and everything.”

“Thanks,” Betty said. “I’ll see you though. Javier’s not even here yet, huh? You’ll be back for more beer.” Betty laughed, looking embarrassed. Purp laughed with her.

“I’m not the only one with a good memory,” Purp said.

* * *

Purp ran through the list again in his head. The Motor Vehicle department made him nervous. He always felt like he was doing something wrong. He needed to get a title before he could sell the truck. Purp knew that would be an issue but he hadn’t mentioned it to Selma. He was saving it, like that was his big gun. “Oh man,” he’d said when the answers to his Craig’s List post started coming in. “How am I going to sell this without a title? All I have is the Texas Title Application. I never got a new one when we moved. The Texas one is non-negotiable because it still shows a lien. I never got a clear title from Texas when I paid it off.”

Purp had also known the dealership wasn’t going to give him enough for the truck and he’d have to sell it to someone privately, but he didn’t mention that beforehand either. He wasn’t trying to make the process go any faster.

He had the Texas Title Application, the statement from GEPCU saying he’d paid off the loan, the proof of insurance. He forgot to bring the thing he printed out that said what he needed, but he was sure he had all he'd need.

"No, no, no," a woman said behind him. Purp turned. She looked thick around the middle and had sandy-brown hair cut like a boy's. She held an infant in its detachable car seat basket and she stood beside an empty two-seat stroller. "Uh, uh – no," she said, lunging for Purp's knee, juggling the infant seat in her left arm while reaching for Purp with her right. Purp wasn't sure what he'd done wrong.

Purp felt something brush against his knee. He looked down. A walking-aged kid tugged at his pant leg.

"Pants dirty," the boy said as his mother yanked him away by the arm.

"Oh, I'm so sorry," the woman said, wiping her boy's hand on a white cloth that seemed to have materialized out of nowhere.

Purp looked down at his knee. Brown smears stained his khakis. The melted chocolate chip cookie on the floor by his foot relieved him, a little. At least it was only chocolate.

"I'm sorry," the woman said. She set the baby's basket and her paperwork on the floor and knelt. Purp saw the back of her neck and shoulders flush red with embarrassment. He thought he felt heat coming off of her she looked so red. The woman took a clean part of the white cloth to Purp's leg and it made it much worse. "I'm sorry."

"Don't worry about it," Purp said. He felt ashamed that he was actually really irritated by the stains on his pants, but he still had to go back to work. "Please, don't." It embarrassed Purp to see her on her knees like that. She looked to Purp like her days filled themselves with things like this. Her car papers slid on the floor when a door opened behind her. She kept wiping. Purp pulled his leg away from her harder than he intended while he bent to try to grab one of her papers that was getting away. His foot hit someone behind him.

The shriek of terror and pain and indignation that came from behind him silenced the packed lobby. The chubby woman on her knees in front of him looked like she'd just had a spike run through her chest. Horror and disbelief. Purp had kicked her little boy in the face. The boy must have toddled around behind while the mother was trying to clean Purp's pants. The boy sat legs open on the worn and dusty asbestos tiles, his hands twisted into fists at his chest, his mouth open in a yell that made Purp's left ear rattle. Purp reflexively blocked his ear. Blood ran in two trickles down the boy's chin while his mother scooted along the floor on her knees toward him, leaving the infant behind her.

* * *

Now Purp had waited so long he might miss it altogether. He kicked himself for not going on the way in, but he didn't want to come late. And then the parking was so bad he had to walk from the Mojave Lot. After that hike there's no way he could have found the bathroom before the ceremony started and he wanted to see Javier walk in at the beginning. Plus, he would have felt like a dork opening the door after everything had already started. And that's why he left it so long after that. He hated coming in and out of things because he felt like everybody was looking at him.

Purp handed the camera to Selma. She listened to the speaker so intently she didn't notice what he was doing until he tapped her on the lap with it. Her thighs looked shiny. She had something on them to make them look sparkly. She startled when the camera touched her leg. Purp held his head low, trying not to block the view of the people behind him. He felt like everybody was looking at him. It made his limbs feel stiff and gawky.

"Bathroom," Purp mouthed silently to Selma. He exaggerated the movements with his lips trying to make it more clear what he was saying, but maybe he overdid it because Selma gave him a puzzled look. With his head lowered almost as far as her lap, close enough he could smell the lotion on her thighs, Purp craned his neck to look up at her. "Bathroom," he mouthed again.

Selma flicked her neatly plucked eyebrows up her forehead and nodded once while bringing her eyes back to the speaker on the stage. Her look said, "Whatever," to Purp. She pursed her lips and thrust her chin forward in a look like a woman trying to regain her dignity after experiencing something beneath her.

Purp hunched himself and half-stood, staying low so he wouldn't block the people behind him. The hunch made it hard for him to step in front of the other people in his row on the way to the aisle. He felt like his butt was in everybody's face and as bad as he had to go, that was not a good thing. Standing made him feel like he had to fart and he hoped he could hold it until the aisle, at least. If he couldn't, he'd have to stand in back for the rest of the ceremony when he came back in.

Purp made it to the aisle without gassing anybody, as far as he knew. He glanced over his shoulder at the speaker on the stage. Javier sat in the second row with his head in a graduation cap, behind the Ph.D.

candidates and in front of the undergraduates. The back of Javier's head always reminded Purp of a gorilla.

A wave of it squeezed him inside and Purp doubled over, pressing his fingers into his belly against a pinch there. He could have shot himself for not just stopping on the way in. Something in the breakfast burrito at Choney's must have got him.

The door to the auditorium screeched on its hinges as Purp pushed it open. It sounded to Purp like it was yelling "Escape!"

Purp shuffled with his knees together. He saw a brown plastic sign on the wall with the outline of a woman drawn in white wearing a triangular-shaped dress. Purp figured the Men's room would be near there so he trotted toward the sign. A bubble of gas or something moved in his belly because Purp heard the noise echo in the empty corridor and he felt a stab in his gut.

Almost to the sign and not sure he'd make it, Purp had to try a fart. He knew the risk involved in that. His uncle once said to him, "Percy, when you get to be fifty, never trust a fart." Purp was only thirty-five but he'd remembered the advice anyway. He got to the sign for the Women's room, but no Men's room. Ten feet up the hall, nothing. Ten feet back past the Women's room the other way, nothing. Where was the Men's room? Purp had to let off some steam or he'd blow. He squeezed one off. It wasn't right. Something was really wrong with that fart. It was silent and hot, and Purp couldn't tell exactly when it ended. It hadn't snapped shut like a fart does.

Purp pushed into the Women's room. Single stall. He bolted the door. Pants down. On the seat. Purp figured he didn't have five seconds more before he'd have lost it out there in the hall. He chuckled to himself at the thought of that, of trying to explain to Javier he'd missed the graduation because he'd shit his pants. Selma would be looking around for him when it was over, maybe he'd be waving, trying to get her attention from the back of the auditorium. Maybe he would have just left and gone to Wal*Mart for new clothes, texted Selma where he went. But her purse was in the car. He couldn't have texted her. Maybe he would have sent a message to Javier. But would Javier even have his phone? He often did not.

Purp finished up and reached for some paper. He didn't have time to linger because he figured they'd be calling names any minute. He wanted to see Javier and he especially didn't want to walk in front of anybody while they were calling names.

No paper. A woman had balanced a six-inch strip of toilet paper on top of the plastic dispenser, probably as a warning that the paper was out. It wouldn't have done Purp any good to be warned anyway, though, it was coming whether he wanted it to or not. Purp looked around from his seat on the throne. Nothing. The room was barely big enough for a sink and a john. It looked like a broom closet converted to a bathroom back when the University first went co-ed. No cabinet under the sink. An electric hand dryer. Purp wondered if maybe all the people for the graduation caused a run on toilet paper. He lifted the six-inch strip of it off the dispenser. That's what he had to work with.

And then Purp saw the quarter-sized damp spot spreading out from the seam at the crotch of his boxers. Never trust a fart. Purp brought his chest down onto his thighs to look at the spot more closely. Nothing came to him, no ideas. A wave of panic rippled up his belly. What if it had soaked through? Purp kicked off his shoes and his shorts and his boxers. He flipped his cream-colored shorts over and spread the legs. Sure enough it soaked through, bigger on the shorts than it was on his underwear. Purp wondered why that would be. Was the fabric more absorbent? He was so screwed. He thought of the Wal*Mart plan again. It wasn't a hypothetical now, it was on the table. Selma would be so pissed, though. So pissed.

Seeing his boxers rumpled on the bathroom floor gave Purp the idea to use them as toilet paper and then maybe once he was cleaned up he could let his shorts dry a little and it might be possible to still catch some of the ceremony. If he kept his legs shut, maybe?

* * *

Javier bellowed so hard his eyes watered. His long eyelashes clumped together, wet, and a tear actually ran down his cheek. Selma shook her head and kept looking at the people around them.

"So I was like trying to hold them in the sink," Purp said, holding his hands up as if he had something stretched between the thumb and forefinger of each hand.

Purp had to wait for Javier to quiet down. Selma held her hand in front of her face while looking at the ceiling. Purp could tell by the corner of her mouth and the way her chest shook that she was laughing, too.

"And I was all, running the water real slow, trying to get it to wash through just the stain so it wouldn't smell when I came back in," Purp said.

"Oh my God, Purp. That's disgusting," Selma said, but the crinkles in the corners of her eyes told Purp she wanted to hear more.

"And then I was all holding them up over the nozzle of the electric hand dryer," Purp said.

"That was a good idea, right?" Javier said, tipping the bottom of his Dos Equis toward Purp. Javier's hand covered most of the bottle. A beer bottle looked small when Javier held it, out of scale. A forty looked more in proportion.

"Yeah, it actually was," Purp said. "It worked quick so I figured what the heck, I might as well just give them a decent wash, I mean, I had soap, I had water."

"Oh my God," Javier said, caught by another spasm of laughter.

"Not the whole thing, but I did give the crotch a decent wash," Purp said. "I tried not to get the rest of them too wet."

"Tell me you didn't put the boxers back on," Javier said.

"No, they were a loss. Cause, you know –

"We know!" Selma said, eyes wide, laughing and holding her hand up to Purp's face as if to stop him from saying more.

"I wiped with those," Purp said. "That was my toilet paper."

A girl looked over at Purp from the next table. Purp had noticed her curly brown hair before, and the tight little white tank top she filled out. It looked hot with her tan. She'd heard him, apparently, and gave him a look like, "What the crap?" One of the guys she was with turned for a second to see who she was looking at instead of him. Purp looked back at her with a wide-eyed grimace, as if to say, "Yikes!" That was the word he thought when he made the face. Her friend didn't see the look.

"Oh that's so disgusting," Selma pounded at the table with her fists, alternating left and right. Her glass of Diet Sprite jingled near her hands.

"I know, and after I," Purp said, "made use of them, you know, I guess I kind of forgot what I was doing because I dropped them into the toilet."

Javier scrunched up his face and made a sound like "oh," which turned into a blast of laughter. People from several tables looked over. Selma turned her face down and covered her eyes with one hand.

Purp finished the story over a couple of more beers and by the time they hit the highlights again, their voices were hoarse from laughing. Selma had to get up early so she excused herself and left in her own car. Purp and Javier stayed on at the King's X for super-burros, Purp drinking iced tea so he'd be able to drive Javier home later. With the burros and chips in their bellies and Purp's beer pretty much gone, Purp and Javier decided to call it a night. It was later than they thought it would be when they got back to Purp's truck. They'd been there two hours after Selma left.

"So you still have the truck?" Javier said.

"Yeah, holding on," Purp said.

"But it doesn't have a back seat," Javier said, "that's the problem, right?"

"Yeah," Purp said. He turned the key back to the accessory position and put down both windows, his and Javier's. "Hey I have something for you I didn't give you last week. I ordered it but it only came in Wednesday."

"Something for me?" Javier said.

"Yeah," Purp said. "It's under your seat. It's a graduation present."

"You want me to get it?" Javier said.

"Unless you want me reaching down between your legs for it," Purp said.

Javier fished for the package under his seat. He found it. Purp wrapped it himself in silver foil paper. It was from Christmas but he didn't think Javier would care.

"Is this bells on it?" Javier said.

"I guess, yeah," Purp said.

"That's like Christmas paper, right?" Javier said.

"I guess, yeah. You can use it for anytime," Purp said.

"It's like Christmas in May," Javier said.

"Just open it, asshole," Purp said.

"I'm just saying it's like Christmas in May," Javier said, studying the package.

"Christmas in May," Purp said.

Javier opened the package. A first American edition of Poems1909-1925 signed on the title page by T. S. Eliot.

"Holy shit, Purp," Javier said, looking at the signature. "Thank you."

Javier closed the book and held it flat on both opened palms between his knees. He looked out toward the cars gliding by the parking lot. He took a deep breath and let it out. He set the book down on his lap and looked out the passenger's window, drumming his thumb on his knee.

"Congratulations," Purp said. "Is it OK? Do you – is it something that's like, relevant . . . or?"

"Thank you, Purp. It's . . . it's perfect. I can't believe you got this for me," Javier said, putting both hands on top of the book on his lap.

"You're welcome. Congratulations."

"Hey Purp," Javier said. "I feel kind of bad." Javier looked straight out the windshield. "I'm actually not going up to U. Penn."

"Well, wherever you go, you can use it," Purp said. "He's your favorite, right?"

"Purp I like this a lot, but I'm not actually going to go anywhere," Javier said. "I think I'm done with school for a while. I'm just going to stay here for a few years, until my book comes out at least. I'm going to just get some kind of job so I have more time to write," Javier said. "If I go up there I'm afraid I'll be so busy with school it'll get too far away from me, my poetry, you know?"

"I think that's awesome. Why did you say you felt bad?" Purp said.

"Well, because I know I said I was going up there to be an Eliot scholar, but now it's going to be like I'm making lattes or something and . . . I know this cost you a lot of money –

"Oh, geez. Don't worry about that, man. I got you this because it's something you like," Purp said. "You don't have to go to U. Penn. to be an Eliot scholar. Read it on your break at Starbucks, I don't care. I'll kick your ass if you spill a latte on it, though."

* * *

"Did you think it was an appropriate way to deal with the problem?" Dennis said.

"I didn't think it was inappropriate," Purp said.

"You didn't?" Dennis said.

"Well, I mean yeah, I did think it was inappropriate but I thought it would solve the problem, too, and save us some money," Purp said.

"Percy, this isn't finally about saving money, it's about our reputation as an academic institution. What you did," Dennis said, "it undermines the reputation not only of the museum but of the entire university system."

"I don't know about that," Purp said. "It's not like it showed up on our own site or anything –

"But it was attributed to us. That's all people understand," Dennis said. "This was in the paper, Percy. This goes all the way up to the President and she is not happy. This is not the direction she wants the university to go in."

"But, I mean, who even saw it? Who really even cared?" Purp said. "Did you hear of one person personally who actually even saw one of the sites that was affected?"

“It’s not about that,” Dennis said. “This type of material on our servers, placed there by our own employees, it’s just not appropriate. There’s just no way to make this an appropriate thing what you did.”

“Well, they were ripping us off,” Purp said. “And they got what was coming to them, that’s the way I see it.”

“That’s not the way the president sees it, or me. Percy, I am a Bishop in my church. This was a real embarrassment to me, personally,” Dennis said. “Without the newspaper, without the president, this caused real hurt to me and to my family.” Dennis’ eyes watered and Purp felt the bottom drop out of his own gut. “I had to walk into my church with my five children this Sunday, Percy,” Dennis said. “No, nobody there saw the images you posted. Nobody there even knew anybody who did. But because of that newspaper article they knew the debased content of the image you used. They didn’t know how or why you did it. They didn’t know your intent. They didn’t even know your name, but they know mine and they know how long I’ve worked for this museum.”

“Dennis, I’m sorry,” Purp said. “I am sorry but it isn’t like it was you who used the images –

“I’m not sure you can understand,” Dennis said. “It doesn’t matter. What should be your shame has spilled over onto me personally.”

“I apologize for that,” Purp said. “That’s not what I meant when I did it.”

“The thing that saddens me, one of the many things that makes me sad about this is that you are a talented man. I believe that you have been given a gift to do what you can do. I’ve been working with programmers for my whole career and there’s something special about the way you solve problems. I’ve prayed on it before, when I was deciding whether or not to go with what you said on Y2K, and I’ve come to believe that what you have is a gift,” Dennis said.

“I don’t know about that –

“I believe it. And with the talent you have at your disposal, the ingenuity I’ve seen over and over again, I’m so sad to think that I know you had different ways around this problem. I know you had choices and the choice that you made is just so repulsive.” Dennis’ voice cracked and his eyes filled again. “I know it’s at the core of Christ’s teachings, of course, to forgive, and I’m not saying that I’ve –

“Dennis, I am sorry that as far as this institution goes, I’ve made trouble for the museum, but I would prefer if we kept this discussion at a secular level,” Purp said.

“Percy when your name became linked with mine in the eyes –

" Please, Dennis," Purp said. "Let's discuss the implications of this for the museum. I am sorry for your personal hurt but I can tell you that it is not going to be fruitful for us to frame this discussion in the context of your Christian faith. This is a state-run facility."

"If you will permit me to offer a suggestion to you," Dennis said, "as someone who has known you for four years now. You would not be sitting here now if in your personal life you'd developed your faith-skills as thoroughly as –

"Dennis, that is frankly offensive to me. That is not an appropriate –

"I'm not being appropriate?" Dennis said. "Bringing faith-based values into this office isn't appropriate, but using our servers to post –

"Sexually explicit material, which wasn't –

"And I am not the one who is being appropriate?" Dennis said. "Percy, I am afraid that this conversation is over."

"I guess we'll just have to agree to disagree," Purp said, standing.

"No, we won't," Dennis said. "This is the end of your time here, Percy."

"Huh? You're firing me?" Purp said.

"Yes," Dennis said.

"But you know I'm leaving in September, Dennis, when the baby comes. It doesn't make sense. I only have four months. It'll take longer to fire me than to just let me leave in September. I've got to get Max up to speed –

"You are not indispensable to the museum. You have already shown that you are capable of doing more harm than good," Dennis said.

"Oh, come on. This is ridiculous," Purp said. Selma was going to be pissed.

"The formal process will take three weeks, but I've got the approval of the president to place you on unpaid administrative leave pending your formal dismissal," Dennis said.

"Dennis, that is harsh. Is that even possible in that timeframe? I mean –

"The president thought it was a reasonable course of action –

"She did?" Purp said.

"When I spoke her to this weekend," Dennis said, "at church."

Cynthia looked up at him as Purp walked out of Dennis' cubicle. From where she sat she must have heard the whole thing. Couldn't Dennis have called him into the conference room if he was going to fire him? Purp figured Dennis wanted them to be overheard. That wasn't right either. That must have been a violation of something or other, some right of his.

"What's the good word, Purp squirt?" Max said. Purp walked past him without answering. Max stood counting the change in the coffee collection jar for about the fifty-sixth time that morning.

Purp sat down at his desk. He wrote a utility which would switch all 2700 of the images on the museum website to a picture of a chimpanzee picking its nose. Purp scheduled the program to run at 6:30 am on Sunday morning. He made it so the switch would be fixable, but not easily fixable. It wasn't even noon yet, but Purp didn't feel like working out the day. He stacked his books in a copy paper box and left everything else.

* * *

"It's OK, Purp," Selma said. "I don't want you to have to miss work."

"It's . . . not a problem," Purp said. He hadn't yet mentioned to Selma that he got fired. It had only been two weeks.

"No, I don't want you to miss work. I'll be OK," Selma said. She curled her legs up closer to her belly and wrapped an arm around her knees. She laid on her side.

"I don't think you should be alone," Purp said.

"I'll be fine," Selma said, but she didn't look fine. She wore Purp's Nike T-shirt and it felt damp to Purp as he stroked her back.

"It's not an issue. End of discussion. You're stuck with me," Purp said. A few hairs stuck to Selma's sweaty forehead. Purp brushed them back with his fingertip.

"You're sweet," Selma said.

"You seem like you're roasting. Do you want the A.C. up or something?" Purp said.

"I actually feel like I'm freezing," Selma said.

"You're covered with sweat," Purp said. He pulled on the blankets wadded up at the foot of the bed. He separated the sheet and the thin blanket from the thicker comforter. Purp straightened the sheet and thin blanket over Selma and snuggled her in. He tucked the blanket in all around her rounded belly making it look comically bigger than it actually was.

Selma opened her knees a few inches under the blanket and tugged at it, as if to wad some fabric up to keep her knees from touching each other. Purp took a cue from that and wedged one of their decorative pillows in between her legs. She left it there and made a satisfied-sounding noise, so Purp figured he did the right thing.

Purp sat on the bed next to Selma and stroked her back through the blanket. Her breathing changed and he could tell that she fell asleep.

* * *

"Well did you already tell them or could you still go?" Purp said.

"I told them. I sent back my form and I told the Eliot lady I interviewed with," Javier said.

"You told them definitely not?" Purp said.

"No, I requested a deferment," Javier said. "I deferred admission until next year."

"Well, that's good anyway," Purp said. He tipped his bottle up and drained the Budweiser. He set the empty on his greasy nacho plate. All that was left were some cheese shreds and dried beans. "You wouldn't want to go to one of the other places you got into?"

"No," Javier said. "I declined them, too, already. That would look stupid. But anyway, it's too late now."

"Is it that bad?" Purp said.

"There they go again," Javier said. He shook his head as if to say he couldn't believe he was watching this. But he leaned forward in his chair.

Purp followed Javier's look to the corner where the sign girls were taking off their shirts. The blond girl with the scar, the one Purp bought a soda, took hers off last of the three. She was by far the nicest looking of the three in her bikini top but she didn't quite fit in with the other two. One of them, a black girl with straight golden brown hair coming out in a ponytail through the back of her baseball cap, seemed to have a higher status than the other two. She kind of moved back and forth more often between being a ring girl and a sign girl than the other sign girls. She stood eight inches above the blond girl, at least, built skinny on top but with a muscular ass she showed off each week at the car wash in high-cut black volleyball shorts.

"Eh," Javier said. "It's not that it's bad, it just, I don't know, sucks."

"Is it worse than the Navy?" Purp said.

"Well, kind of," Javier said, "much worse."

"Holy shh . . . oh," Purp said. The tall black girl, the leader, pranced across the street to the median. The other two sign girls went with her.

The leader held her sign over her head and worked her hips like a stripper would. The dance she did turned her a full circle. Two college guys in a Japanese SUV, an Xterra, honked their horn frantically as they drove by her.

"At least I felt like on the aircraft carrier what I was doing was purposeful, you know what I'm saying?" Javier said. "It wasn't all these ladies coming in for their grande vanilla half-caff two-pump sugar-free 180-degree no-foam skinny lattes."

"But you have time to write, though," Purp said.

"Not even really," Javier said. "Without my teaching stipend now and with Becca not paying rent, I'm thirty-five hours at Starbucks and ten at Borders. And it's kind of hard."

"I bet it is," Purp said.

"No, I'm serious," Javier said.

"I'm serious, too. I actually think it would be hard. For one, you're always standing," Purp said.

"My feet hurt bad by the end of the day," Javier said. "Plus, just getting the bus to and from Borders takes me an hour and a half, so two five hour shifts turns into thirteen hours on the two days off I'm supposed to have off to write."

"I guess now you know, though," Purp said.

"Yeah. It was like a fantasy to do that, right? Like a millennial Thoreau living off the land," Javier said. He took a sip of his beer. "Now that right there, that would be a job."

Purp looked across to see what had caught Javier's eye. "Washing cars?" Purp said. "I don't like getting wet. And no free lattes."

One of the heavy but popular guys flicked his hose spray at a gaggle of ring girls. They screeched and bounced off in different directions, shirtless, one of them holding her cell phone up in the air. One by one they trickled back to the same spot in range of the hose guy. He hosed them again and they screamed. One of them bounded toward him and punched his arm. It did nothing. Another grabbed his wrist as if to try to get the hose. He raised his arm and her two hands came with it. Purp figured the hose guy must be getting a really good view on that one.

"They could all use a supervisor or something," Javier said.

"Now that would be awesome," Purp said. The girl holding on to hose guy's wrist hooked her leg behind his knee, as if trying to trip him.

"And fire all the guys and get the girls washing cars," Javier said.

"I bet you could actually make money doing something like that," Purp said. "You see who's going there. It's guys in their forties out doing their errands on a Saturday morning. They stop because they think it'll be the sign girls washing their cars."

"That red-shorts girl gives them a good view, though. She's usually washing," Javier said. "Did you ever notice the customers always stand on her side? They either stand by the "For Sale" sign if she's over there, or the Circle K sign if she's over there."

Purp stood up and gathered the trash, his and Javier's. "I bet you could make some serious money doing that," Purp said. He stretched his arms above his head. "You want anything from inside?"

"I'm good," Javier said.

Purp bought another two beers and a basket of chips. The battle between the ring girls and hose guy was over by the time Purp sat down again.

"You know how you could make real money doing that?" Javier said.

"Fire the guys, like you were saying?" Purp said.

"Topless," Javier said. "Like really topless."

* * *

Selma sobbed, laying curled on the bathroom floor. She gasped sharp breaths in between barking sobs, the palms of her hands pressed into her eyes. Blood smeared from her naked hip, bright red on the beige bathroom tile.

"I called," Purp said. "They're coming."

Purp couldn't breathe, as if someone had tightened a belt across his chest. He couldn't get enough air into his lungs. They wouldn't fill. Sweat ran from his hair into his eyes. He felt like he was going to faint but he knew he had to get it out before Selma saw it – saw him – there like that in the toilet. He grabbed the garbage can and tore out the bag. As soon as he did that he knew it wasn't the right thing to do. He tossed the bag and can onto the bathroom counter. The can hit Selma's perfume bottles and one of them at least clattered into the sink and broke. Purp gagged on the wave of perfume scent mixed with the bloody metallic funk already burning his throat.

Selma sounded like if she kept it up, she was going to pass out from sobbing. She choked and gagged on her sobs. Purp slid open the closet, banging the mirrored sliding door open so hard it jumped off its rollers and fell backward against Selma's clothing.

Purp tore at one of his shirts. He pulled it so hard the plastic hanger broke, flinging the hook part into the closet ceiling. The broken part ricocheted down off Purp's shoulder and landed in the toilet. On the baby's back. The yellow plastic hanger hook on mottled blood-smeared skin. Purp gagged. He looked at the shirt in his hands. A Pendleton. He brushed it against his cheek and the wool of it caught his whiskers. It flashed into his mind that this was too scratchy for a baby. He ripped down a dress shirt, blue silk, the one he'd worn when he and Selma got married. The buttons popped and its hanger flipped up and over the closet rail. Purp pitched linens out of the closet onto the floor by the toilet. Sheets, towels – the good ones, the everyday ones, the ones for messes. He threw the shirt over his shoulder and knelt on a sheet rumpled up on the floor by the toilet. The stillborn fetus was heavier than he'd imagined, and more lifelike. Fingers, toes. A nose. A penis.

* * *

Selma slept better the second night but Purp still kept waking up every forty-five minutes. He couldn't get the feeling out of his hands. The warmth, the rubbery give to the flesh. The seconds it took him to get the baby out and wrapped in the shirt and towels expanded to make Purp feel like that's all he'd ever done. He saw the wrinkly purple baby whether his eyes were open or shut. His hands felt empty. He was rubbing them in his armpits when Selma sobbed herself awake. Purp glanced at the clock, 4:00 am.

Purp felt bad that Selma woke up but he was glad for the company. He rolled over toward Selma and pulled her close to him. He buried her face in his chest and he felt his skin wet from her eyes. Purp stroked the back of Selma's head, her hair tangled and matted with sweat. Purp nuzzled his face down into the top of her head and tears ran from his eyes into her hair.

* * *

"I'll eat it like that, I really don't care," Purp said. They'd put black olives on his nachos.

"I'll get you different ones," Javier said. "It even says it on the receipt. Minus b. l. k. o. l. v." Javier slid the nacho plate back onto the plastic tray and brought it inside.

Purp couldn't have cared less about the black olives. He'd only been making conversation when he mentioned it. They forgot and put them on half the time anyway and he never said anything, but he could tell Javier was uncomfortable and just looking for something he could do to be helpful.

Purp would have rather just picked at the nachos for a while and gone home. It was the first time he'd been out when he didn't absolutely need to be and he wasn't feeling a hundred percent about it. Selma said he should go. She'd told him the week before, too, but he wasn't up for it then, not at all.

Purp thought maybe coming out for brunch this Saturday would help him get oriented a little bit but it wasn't working. With the job thing and the miscarriage one right after the other he had the rug out from under him a couple of times and couldn't quite figure his way around exactly where to go from there. He'd wake up and look at the expanse of an empty day ahead of him not knowing where to start or what to start doing. He watched a lot of TV when Selma wasn't around or when she was sleeping. He didn't want to turn the TV on in front of her. He'd been staying up until three or four once Selma started sleeping through the night again. He'd go to bed with her and once she was sleeping, he'd get back out and surf the Internet or watch TV.

"Here you go," Javier said.

"Thank you," Purp said. He slid the nacho plate toward himself. It burned his fingers. Javier must have stood right there and waited for it so he could bring it straight to Purp.

Purp didn't even feel like eating at this point. With his sleep all messed up he'd been overeating all night and then he'd feel sick during the day so he wouldn't have anything, and then he'd be starving at night again when he should be sleeping. He felt a little nauseous still from the four or five bowls of cereal he'd had before bed but he wanted Javier to think he was glad to have the nachos. He forced himself to start eating them, and to eat them as if he liked it.

"Mmm," Purp said. "If you'd just stand there and stare at them while they made my food every week, I'd get nice hot olive-free nachos all the time."

"Is it good?" Javier said.

"Yeah, it's not all stuck together like normal." Purp said.

"Hey, you don't have your salsa," Javier said, and before Purp could swallow his chip, Javier was up and in the door. Purp saw him through the window bent over the salsa bar. For a guy built like a gorilla, Javier could move. He didn't often, but he could.

"Here you go," Javier said. "You like that medium one, right? And the one with the tomatoes?"

"Mmm hmm," Purp said. He swallowed. "Yeah, exactly. Thank you."

Javier sat down. He didn't have anything to eat for himself.

"You want some of these?" Purp said, sliding the plate toward Javier.

"You don't want them?" Javier said.

"It's just you didn't have anything," Purp said. He wished Javier would eat them. The thought of eating the salsa now was making him feel like he was going to hurl.

"I'm all set," Javier said. He took a drink from a bucket of soda with no straw.

"What are you drinking there, big guy?" Purp said.

"I got a Diet Coke," Javier said.

"Huh," Purp said. "That's odd."

"Well, you're drinking water," Javier said.

"Yeah," Purp said. "I am."

Purp worked on the nacho plate. The salsa went down better than he thought it would. He thought it was funny but once he got eating a little he felt more hungry.

"Did you see," Javier said. He took a drink real fast like he was trying to swallow something down.

Purp waited for Javier to go on, but Javier just sat there. Purp ate a few more nachos, still thinking Javier would finish his thought. He didn't.

"Did I see what?" Purp said.

"Huh?" Javier said.

"You said: 'Did you see.' Did I see what?" Purp said.

"Oh," Javier said.

"Well?" Purp said.

"Nothing," Javier said.

"No, come on. Did I see what?" Purp said.

"It's just stupid," Javier said. "The car wash. Did you see it was gone?"

"Oh yeah, I did," Purp said. "I noticed that when you were in getting my food. The first time." Purp didn't feel like he had much to say about the car wash just now but he didn't want Javier to think he didn't want to talk about it.

"Yeah, it's gone," Javier said.

"I see that," Purp said. He tried to think of something else to say so it wouldn't seem like he was shutting Javier down. "Was it here last week?"

"No, it wasn't," Javier said. "It wasn't here last week. And it wasn't here the week before that, either. I guess it was like, your last week here was the last week they were here, too."

"Sounds like it," Purp said. "Maybe they got enough."

"Enough money for their trip, right?" Javier said.

"Yeah, maybe they got enough to head down to Cabo or wherever it was," Purp said, "and that was that."

* * *

"I am sorry for your loss, Percy," Dennis said, "but I am afraid at this point, no."

"I recognize the fact that it would be an odd decision, it would be for me, too, but when you think about it, it makes sense," Purp said.

"No . . . I don't see how it does make sense," Dennis said. Purp got the feeling from the way Dennis said it that he was actually trying to see how it might make sense, but couldn't.

"You don't have anybody else, right?" Purp said. "You haven't filled my position yet."

"Well, no, but you know that wasn't exactly how we were going to do –

"I know," Purp said.

"We were going to split your stuff up between Gilberto and Max, and then use the freed up position, your position, for –

"I know, but the upgrade didn't get approved yet, right?" Purp said.

"Well, no," Dennis said.

"And the re-class can't be done until the upgrade gets approved, right?" Purp said.

"So my position is still my position," Purp said.

"No. No, it's not your position," Dennis said.

"But I mean it's the same position right now," Purp said, "just not filled. It's the same pay grade and the same job classification, right?"

"Well, yeah but –

“The only thing different is just I’m not in it,” Purp said.

“That’s true, you’re not,” Dennis said. “But we’ve already submitted the upgrade for it so we can get the –

“But the upgrade isn’t even approved,” Purp said. He slapped the top of Dennis’ desk with the fingertips of both hands. “Nothing is different. Just pull the upgrade. Just unsubmit it.”

Dennis glanced down at Purp’s hands. Purp got the feeling he was making Dennis nervous. He leaned back in his chair, away from the desk, away from Dennis. Purp slid down in his chair a little so his head would be lower than Dennis’. He relaxed his arms in his lap, away from Dennis’ desk.

“Is that even possible,” Dennis said, “to unsubmit it?”

This baffled Purp. Of course it’s possible. Why would it not be possible? You just tell whoever you submit it to that you changed your mind. How could that not be possible? But Purp liked how Dennis asked a question. When Dennis asked a question, he wasn’t pushing back. If Dennis was asking questions, Purp figured, he was looking for an out.

“Sure it is,” Purp said. He tried to sound upbeat and confident, but he didn’t want to belittle Dennis either. “Sure, you can unsubmit it.”

“But we were planning to use that position to –

“But that was just because I said I was leaving,” Purp said. “If I hadn’t said I was leaving in the first place, then we just would have left things as they were.”

“Well, I might have wanted –

“No,” Purp said. “No. If I hadn’t said I was leaving in September, then nothing would have changed. Wouldn’t you agree that if I hadn’t said I was leaving, you wouldn’t have put in for an upgrade for my position?”

“I . . yes,” Dennis said. “That’s true.”

“Would you have re-classified my position if I was still in it?” Purp said.

“No,” Dennis said.

“So this is basically like I never left, as far as my position goes,” Purp said.

“You didn’t leave, you got –

“In any case my position is at the same grade and classification, exact same as it was the day I left.”

“But Max and Gilberto are already doing your job,” Dennis said.

“Well for one thing, it hasn’t been that long and the learning curve is steep, so who cares if I just jump back in?” Purp said.

"They're actually doing fine," Dennis said.

"Have they finished the new module? The interactive tour?" Purp said.

"No, but everything is running fine," Dennis said.

"And that's exactly my point," Purp said, getting a flash of inspiration. "If they have the day-to-day under control now, then that would free me up to slip back in and focus on the new module so we can get that running. You were saying yourself before I left how much you wanted that up," Purp said.

"Purp, you didn't leave," Dennis said. "I fired you."

"I know but that was just because I was leaving anyway," Purp said.

"No Purp. It wasn't," Dennis said. "I fired you because of the –

"Decision I made when I thought I was leaving anyway," Purp said. "I was making myself a martyr, trying to stop the bandwidth theft cold so you guys wouldn't have to worry about it."

"A martyr?" Dennis said, eyebrows raised.

"Well, you know what I mean," Purp said.

"Martyrdom . . ." Dennis leaned back in his chair. He put the fingertips of both hands together in front of him and looked toward the light fixture over his desk.

"I meant I thought I was leaving anyway so I figured I'd get the problem solved and have a little fun," Purp said. "Not fun, I just wanted to really put an end to it."

"No," Dennis said. "Not fun."

"No. Definitely not." Purp said. He felt like it was time to agree with Dennis on something. "I was just mad, Dennis. I wouldn't have done it if I thought I wasn't leaving. My main motivation was to just get the bandwidth theft to stop. So I could get the server back running like it should."

"That was really your main motivation, Percy?" Dennis said.

"Oh yeah, definitely," Purp said.

"It was what you would call a constructive impulse?" Dennis said. "You meant to help?"

"Yes. I just wanted to solve the problem," Purp said.

Dennis rubbed his fingertips together, looking down at his hands. Purp felt like Dennis could use some quiet time to think. Dennis seemed as if he were considering his options and Purp took this to be a good thing. At least Dennis hadn't made up his mind completely. There was still a chance.

"Then why," Dennis said, looking over his hands at Purp, "the stunt with the chimpanzee picture? What was constructive about that?"

It didn't go well for Purp after that. He could sidestep the porn image swap but the chimpanzee thing, that was something he couldn't get around. He'd meant that as an act of sabotage and he couldn't see any other way to read it. He and Dennis wrapped it up and Purp left Dennis' cubicle as amicably as he could manage. The two stood and shook hands and Purp told Dennis he'd still be willing to come back if Dennis changed his mind at some point.

"I'm sure I won't," Dennis said, "but I appreciate you coming to talk to me today anyway. And Purp, I'm sorry again for your loss. We can't know what the Lord has in mind for us but when he is ready, you and Selma will be blessed, I am sure. It's a sad thing and it happens too often. I know this from experience."

"Thank you, Dennis," Purp said. It surprised Purp that he actually felt comforted to hear that Dennis had been through something similar.

Purp left Dennis' cubicle. Cynthia looked up from her desk as Purp walked by. Purp nodded at her and smiled.

Purp made it down the hallway without seeing anybody he knew. Nobody at the coffee pot. There was no money in the contribution jar. Max would be pissed about that. Purp stepped into his old cubicle. He smelled Max' breakfast. Purp leaned his head over the partition between him and Max.

"Hey soldier," Purp said.

Max looked up, a sausage on his fork.

"Purp squirt," he said. "The monkey man. Them was a lot of monkeys, monkey man. A lot of monkeys for old Max. I made my monkey money that day. Fucking Sunday morning."

"Yeah, I'm sorry about that," Purp said.

"Sixty-seven years, ain't never seen nothing like that, boss," Max said. "Couldn't have did it on a Tuesday, huh? Sunday's the fucking day of rest, Purp."

"I noticed you got it cleaned up pretty fast. Like really fast," Purp said.

"Nope," Max said. "I didn't hardly do shit."

"Gilberto did it?" Purp said.

"Nope," Max said. "I didn't want to fuck with it, or, mess with it or whatever, and I sure didn't want Gilberto to mess with it. I didn't even call the Mexican motherfucker. So I just restored the whole damn server from a backup and wiped the thing clean. Didn't take me twenty minutes."

"Oh," Purp said. It had never even occurred to him that somebody would have been able to undo his chimpanzee image swap like that.

"Yep," Max said.

"That was a really good idea," Purp said.

"Been having good ideas since before you was born, P. J.," Max said. "I heard what happened, too, and I was sorry to hear it. I know you were looking forward to that baby, Purp. Say what you will, there ain't nothing like it, having a baby. Can't even imagine life before it once it comes."

* * *

"I don't even . . . what?" Selma said. "When were you planning to tell me, Purp?"

"Well, it just never –

"Never what? Never occurred to you to mention that you don't go to work at your job anymore?" Selma said.

"If you would just let me say something without –

"Say it. Say it. You've got a lot to say, apparently. Tell me. What?" Selma said.

"Well, I mean, it was like that same week you weren't feeling well," Purp said, "and I didn't want to mess with it then."

"But six weeks? Or whatever it's been?" Selma said.

"Right after that though . . ." Purp said. "And I just, you know."

Selma stood in the kitchen in her uniform, her purse on the counter. She looked older to Purp, and tired. She'd put on years in the last month.

"I just couldn't then," Purp said.

"So you just lied to me? You decided to just get up every morning and lie to me?" Selma said.

"I never actually did lie. I said it wasn't going to matter at work if I stayed home with you while you got better," Purp said.

"That is a lie. That is," Selma said. She slapped her hand on the counter. "A lie is not telling the truth. It isn't just saying what isn't true."

"What was I supposed to do? You were so sad and sick. And I was, too. I didn't," Purp said, "it just didn't seem important enough compared to what was going on."

"It wasn't important? That you quit your job?" Selma said.

"I was leaving anyway, in September. It just happened earlier, that's all," Purp said. "It's not like it mattered in terms of money or anything. That's not an issue."

"That's another thing," Selma said. "You think you're so rich but that money isn't going to last, Purp. You can't count on having that the rest of your life. Not with the TVs and stereos and videogames and satellite radio and all the stuff you seem to need. It's a lot but it's not enough to get you through the rest of your life."

"Selma, that's insulting. You know –

"I know you're burning that money and it isn't going to last. That was a lot of money, Purp, and it should be more now but it's less," Selma said.

"You talk to me like I don't understand. Selma, I went to work every day," Purp said. "I could have quit that job a long time ago but I know it's not enough for the rest of my life. I kept up my job –

"So you want a medal for that?" Selma said. "You want me to put you in for an award because you went to work every day? Jesus Christ, Purp. I just got out of work. What did you do today? What did you do yesterday? What did you do all day the first day I put my uniform on and went back to work in my maternity skirt with no baby in my uterus? What did you do that day? Did you watch TV? Did you go drink beer at Taco Cabana –

"That's not fair," Purp said. "That is so not fair. You told me to go out. You're the one who told me you thought it would be good for me to get out of the house –

"You were probably glad I went back to work so you could sit here and –

"That is too much. Just stop there. Selma I have not been glad about anything since . . . I haven't, Selma." Purp said.

Selma opened the refrigerator. She looked into it like she was looking at an exhibit in a museum. She shut the door without taking anything out. She opened the pantry door and looked in there, too. She shut the pantry.

"What are you going to do? What are you going to do for money?" Selma said. "Have you been going on interviews without telling me, too?"

"I'm just getting back on my feet a little now, after everything," Purp said.

Selma turned to him and gave Purp a full blast of her look. She tugged at her uniform blouse, straightening a wrinkle.

"You're getting on your feet?" Selma said. "Why don't you just go back and tell Dennis what happened. I'm sure he didn't fill your position. It must take them forever, like us."

"I can't do that." Purp said.

"Why? Just go back and tell him. Say what happened and you want your job back," Selma said.

"I'm not going to do that," Purp said.

"Why?" Selma said.

"I'm just not," Purp said. "Anyway, I'm ready for something different."

"Well have you sent out resumes?" Selma said. "Are you on Monster? I know SAIC gets a lot of IT people from Monster at our shop. I could talk to LeDon."

"No, don't talk to LeDon," Purp said. "It's not that, I could get another IT job but I think I want to do something different. I think I want to use some of the money to start my own business."

"Like what? Consulting?" Selma said. "You did do freelance work. That's a good idea. You could do that from home and then if we tried again . . ." Selma poured herself a glass of water from the dispenser in the freezer door.

"I don't know if freelance work," Purp said, "I don't know. But something. I think I want to use the money to start something, because like you said I'm spending it."

"You are," Selma said.

"And you're right, I shouldn't be," Purp said.

"You've got to be careful what you do with it, though," Selma said. "It's still an awful lot of money."

"I know Selma. I know," Purp said. "You don't have to talk to me about it like I'm a kid. I did make the money in the first place."

"You did make it, Purp, but it isn't like it was hard," Selma said.

"That's rude," Purp said. "What?"

"It's not like you're the only one who got rich in the nineties, Purp. People who had money got rich," Selma said.

"Yeah, but they lost it, too. That was the hard part, not losing it," Purp said.

* * *

"It's hot," Javier said.

"I know. I can't even touch this table," Purp said. He poured water onto the black metal table and smeared it around with a napkin. He stood up and wiped the napkin on his chair, on the front part of the seat where the backs of his legs touched, and on the arms. "What are you wearing jeans for?"

"I have to work after this," Javier said.

"After beer brunch?" Purp said.

"Yeah," Javier said. "I'm lucky to get hours. They had to shift us all around." Javier scooped salsa onto his chicken and wrapped it in a tortilla. "I'm way up on Mission and Fred Jackson today."

"Whoa. Up in the 'burbs, huh?" Purp said. "That's a long way for a city boy like you to go to make a latte."

"You mean like what's a Mexican doing in the suburbs?" Javier said.

"No, not like that," Purp said. He couldn't tell if Javier was joking or not. "I didn't think artists had much use for the suburbs. It's so ordinary."

"They do if they need hours," Javier said. "You know how long it takes me to get up there on the bus?" Javier worked on building his next fajita. "An hour and twenty minutes. That's two hours and forty minutes for a five hour shift."

"That sucks," Purp said. "Did they give you any idea when your store is going to be fixed?"

"They don't know yet," Javier said.

"It was the fireworks, huh? That started it I read?" Purp said.

"That's what they said. Subway and Guillermo's was bad, real bad, but our place is in decent shape," Javier said. "I was in there to get my stuff out of the back and you'd barely even know anything burnt."

"Too bad you weren't working on the fourth," Purp said. "With your fire school training and all."

Javier laughed. He'd been kind of grumpy all morning but this he laughed at. The laugh seemed to release the tension in him a little.

"I know," Javier said. "Except I ended up working in the galley. I could have swung into action, though, anyway."

"That would be awesome," Purp said. "To see you swing into action."

"But you'd hardly know our place burnt. It's just a little heat damage in the corner of the back room," Javier said. "Thermal fractures in the block."

"I'm not too sure what that means," Purp said, "but they've got you bussing out to the suburbs for it, huh?"

"Yep," Javier said.

"Why don't I ride you up after here?" Purp said.

"It's not that close to you, either," Javier said.

"I could go to that Target out there. The nice one. And they have the GameStop," Purp said. "They have everything out there. The movie theater." Purp dropped a nacho onto the patio. He picked it up and laid it on the edge of his plate. He didn't like having a straggler there like that so he ate it. "I'll go to Target and GameStop and Lowe's and a movie and by that time I could just head over to Starbucks and get one of your lattes. Probably be time to ride you back in, after all that."

"Selma on duty today?" Javier said.

"Yes. She is, in fact," Purp said.

"If you don't mind going up there," Javier said.

Purp worked on his nacho plate. Javier finished his fajitas. Purp was on his third beer but Javier only sipped another soda, Purp figured it was a Diet Coke.

"Plus, maybe we can get some beers in you on the way back," Purp said.

"Better than this," Javier said. He raised his plastic soda bucket to Purp as if in a toast.

Purp looked out at the corner, the median, the side of the Circle K by the empty lot.

"This place isn't the same without the car wash, huh?" Purp said.

"No," Javier said. "I got used to it being here, right?"

"Me too," Purp said. He scanned the dirt lot across from Taco Cabana. The one behind the "For Sale or Lease" sign. "I've been thinking of what we were saying that one day," he said.

"About what?" Javier said.

"About how a guy could make some serious money running a car wash," Purp said. "Especially if he had girls doing the washing."

Javier stretched his arms straight and over the back of his chair, behind his head.

"Yeah, I bet he could," Javier said.

"And if the girls were topless," Purp said.

"He'd make a lot more," Javier said.

Purp got up and cleared the table leaving only the two drinks. He went inside to throw his trash away. He came back out and sat down behind his half-empty Budweiser.

"I think I'm going to do it," Purp said.

"Do what?" Javier said.

"The car wash. 'Purple's Topless Carwash.' I think it could work," Purp said.

Javier laughed, but this time not like he thought it was especially funny.

"I'm serious," Purp said. "I think I'm going to look into it."

"No," Javier said. "I don't think you can do that, can you?"

"Why not?" Purp said.

"I don't know," Javier said. "They have rules and things, the city. They're not going to let you do that."

"I don't see why not," Purp said. "People have strip clubs."

"Maybe," Javier said. "I don't think so."

"I think they will," Purp said. "It's like a strip club, and you get your car cleaned. What's the harm in it?"

* * *

Purp had it all in a program he bought, software meant for people trying to get bank financing, but Purp wasn't planning to apply for a loan. He thought it would be nice to have it organized, though, and he thought it would look more official when he showed it to Selma. He figured she'd be harder to convince than a lender, anyway. He had it printed at FedEx Kinko's. He knew Selma always did that when she had a presentation at work.

The girl behind the counter slid an envelope across toward Purp as if it held something fragile.

"Thank you," Purp said. The Kinko's girl had acne scars on her cheeks. Purp wondered why nobody had helped her get treatment before her scars got so bad. She was a sweetie, though, and she looked great in her snug little golf shirt and khakis, the uniform at the copy place. Her nametag said "Asusuena." She wore highlights in her hair that Purp knew were expensive. Shadows on her arms showed muscle definition. She must work out. Purp liked how she took care of herself, even with the scars. He figured she probably did well with the guys, in any case.

"Here you go," the counter girl said.

"How do you say your name, anyway?" Purp said, nodding toward her nametag.

"Susie," she said.

"Thanks, Susie." Purp said.

"Five copies, spiral bound," Susie said. "Clear cover and purple back cover."

"Perfect," Purp said. He paid for the copies with his debit card. "Thank you." He slid the bag off the counter and turned to leave.

"What is it?" Susie said. "The topless car wash?"

Purp turned back toward Susie. He felt his face and ears get hot. He knew he'd turned red. He felt embarrassed to tell her, but also excited.

* * *

"I don't know, Purp," Selma said. "Is this the only thing you can think of to do?" She shut the refrigerator door and took a drink out of her water bottle, draining half of it. With her head tipped back sweat dripped down her throat and collected in the hollow between her neck muscles before running down between her breasts.

"It's not the only thing but it's a thing," Purp said.

"It's got nothing to do with your training or your background or anything," Selma said. She sipped her bottle. She'd lost every ounce that she gained when she was pregnant. Purp thought she looked more toned now in her black sports bra than she had before. She'd been running daily, to and from the gym three miles away.

"I don't think it matters, if I'm passionate about it," Purp said. He'd read a book about talking to banks to get a business loan. It said that it helped to be passionate about your business.

"Passionate? About naked women washing cars?" Selma said.

"Well, not passionate. Enthusiastic?" Purp said.

"What's the point of it?" Selma said. She reached up into the cabinet where she kept her vitamins. The abdominal muscles on her side rippled. Her ass tightened in black Lycra short-shorts as she stretched on tip-toes to reach.

"The point of it?" Purp said. "I don't understand the question."

"Why would someone go to this?" Selma said.

"Why? Why do they go to a strip club?" Purp said. "Why do they go to a car wash?"

"Why wouldn't they just go to a car wash, and then a strip club?" Selma said. She leaned over the sink to get water in a cup for her vitamins. She always did that, took her vitamins with water from a cup instead of her water bottle. Individually defined cables stood out running up and down the back of her tan thigh. The shorts she had on weren't even covering everything she had back there. Purp thought the guys in the gym must have gotten an eyeful today.

"Two reasons," Purp said. He'd expected resistance, which is part of why he wanted to make his presentation as official-looking as possible, with the spiral-bound packet he had made and a Power Point slide show showing sketches he had of the facility superimposed on satellite photos of the empty lot. "The girls are wet, your car gets clean, and you can do this in the day and it's not weird. And you don't even have to get out of your car so it's not as embarrassing as going into a strip club."

"That's four reasons," Selma said.

"Exactly," Purp said.

* * *

"They moved the closing up a day," Purp said.

"That's when you sign the papers?" Javier said.

"It is," Purp said. "That lot is going to be mine by the end of the day. I think. I don't actually know how long it'll take to record."

"That's awesome," Javier said.

"Yeah. It's at one, so do you mind if we stop on the way back down to your place?" Purp said. The light changed and Purp made a right onto Mission.

"Of course not," Javier said. "Thanks for picking me up."

"No problem. I had to go to Best Buy anyway. I needed a new laptop for the business stuff," Purp said.

"Didn't you have one?" Javier said.

"I wanted one just for PTC. The other one Selma uses a lot," Purp said.

"That's what you're calling it?" Javier said.

"For short," Purp said.

"Did you get it?" Javier said.

"Get what?" Purp said.

"The laptop," Javier said.

"No," Purp said. "Do you want to stop at McDonald's? The place is actually on Mission so we have time."

"I could use a chicken sandwich," Javier said.

"Well, do you want to go somewhere else?" Purp said.

"I'll get one there," Javier said.

Purp fiddled with the satellite radio. He got something on he thought Javier would like better. "I can't believe they're still not done with your store," Purp said.

"That wall had more structural damage than it looked at first," Javier said.

"The one between you and Guillermo's?" Purp said.

"Yeah. So Guillermo's is moving and they're expanding our store onto that space," Javier said.

"That's going to be a huge Starbucks," Purp said.

"The biggest in the state, they say," Javier said. "They had a meeting to show all the displaced partners the plans for it, kind of like so we know we have somewhere to go back to when it's done."

"That's cool," Purp said. He pulled his truck into the drive-through. There were two lanes, left and right. Two cars could order at the same time, side-by-side.

"What is this?" Javier said, looking at the drive-through setup.

"I know, huh? This is how they roll in the suburbs. High tech," Purp said.

"How do they do it at the window, though?" Javier said. "Are there two windows, too?"

"No, these two lanes funnel into one on the other side. It seems weird but it's McDonald's. I'm sure someone studied it," Purp said.

"It seems like there would be a bottleneck on the other side," Javier said.

"It does. But I don't think there is," Purp said. "Maybe they timed it and found out it takes people twice as long to order as it takes for the guy at the window to give you your food."

"That's weird," Javier said.

"It is, but they must know," Purp said.

"How do they know which car goes with which order?" Javier said.

"I don't know," Purp said. "Maybe by sight. Maybe they just remember which car goes with which order. I'm sure they have a camera on you when you order."

"You think?" Javier said.

"Yeah," Purp said.

"But they set these things up so retarded people can run them," Javier said. "They're not going to set something up that requires somebody to keep straight which car goes with which order."

"Well they could be like, 'Order seven, gray pickup. Order eight, yellow Mazda.'"

"I don't think so," Javier said. "Plus there's probably a money window and a food window, right?"

"There is," Purp said.

"So how would the order taker and money window person tell the food giver which car goes with which order?" Javier said.

"He could type it in," Purp said. "Maybe it doesn't matter. Maybe it's just if you order first, you get to the merger first. If the left car orders a little before the right car, then the left car will get to the window first."

"That could be," Javier said. "It would get there first, right?"

Purp noticed he'd been sitting there waiting to get up to the order speaker for a while. Cars jammed both drive-through lanes.

"What the fuck?" Javier said. He jutted his chin toward the car in front of them.

"I know. This is taking forever," Purp said. He looked in his rearview mirror. Two cars behind him, too. "And I have to be there by one." He thought about trying to get out of line but the side of the building blocked him in on his left side, the second lane blocked him in on the right.

* * *

"This is it. It's done," Purp said. He'd parked in the center of the dirt lot and walked around the front of his truck toward Javier who was slower getting out of the passenger's side.

"Official?" Javier said.

"Official," Purp said.

"Did you buy it or are you renting it?" Javier said.

"No, man, I bought it," Purp said, "that was what the closing was for last week."

"The one you missed," Javier said. "I didn't know if that was just like signing the lease papers or something, like when you get the keys to your apartment."

"No, I bought it," Purp said. "This is my own piece of dirt." He squatted down and clutched a handful of gravelly earth. He let it run through his fingers.

"How far down?" Javier said.

"Huh?" Purp said.

"How far down does it go?" Javier said.

"This gravel?" Purp said.

"No, how far down is yours?" Javier said.

"I . . . don't know. It never occurred to me before to ask." Purp said. He stood and stretched his arms behind his back. A breeze whipped dust up against him. Purp heard pebbles hit his truck. It was September already but the little wind still felt like a hair dryer. "When I'm hungry

I can head over to our patio." Purp pointed across Guadalupe to Taco Cabana. "Short walk."

"It couldn't be all the way down," Javier said. "Some Chinaman would have something to say about that on the other side, I'm sure. It must end somewhere. There must be a rule about that."

"I'll take my break and walk across the street to meet you for beer brunch on Saturdays," Purp said. "I'll eat nachos and monitor my domain."

"It won't be beer brunch if it's a break," Javier said. "You'll be going back to work after."

"Who cares? I'm the boss of this operation. If I come back drunk, who's going to say anything about it?" Purp said.

"I guess so," Javier said. "But you'll probably want to keep on your toes."

"Maybe," Purp said. "But how hard can it be?"

"I'll sit over there on the patio and drink beers and watch your car wash," Javier said. "That'll kick ass over the crappy little high school one, any day."

"Negative, Captain," Purp said. "There's going to be a wall around the whole thing. You won't be able to see it from anywhere but inside."

"Or from the air," Javier said.

"Well, yeah, if you're in a helicopter you'll be able to see down into it," Purp said. "But as a practical matter, notwithstanding Ana Ng boring peepholes up from below, you won't be able to see it from the outside."

"And from those dorms," Javier said.

Purp hadn't thought of that. "Yeah," he said. "Yeah. And from those dorms." He studied the angle from the upper floor of the dorm building across Powell Avenue down into his lot and figured Javier was right.

"Where people drive in and out, too," Javier said. "You'll be able to see it from there. I bet there's a rule against that. A regulation."

"I got you covered there," Purp said. "The entrance is going to be off of Guadalupe there by Circle K." Purp pointed over toward the curb cut that was already there, next to where the high school girls used to have their car wash. "The exit is going to be back there onto Powell." Purp pointed to the back corner of the lot adjacent to Zia Records.

"They're going to have to drive over the sidewalk and down the curb?" Javier said.

"No," Purp said. "That's going to be part of the construction, cutting the curb and making a driveway through there."

"How do you do that?" Javier asked.

"A concrete sawing and coring company," Purp said. "Anyway, stay with me. You won't be able to see into the entrance or exit because it's going to be curved."

"Huh," Javier said. "How does that make it so you can't see?"

"It'll be a curved entrance, and exit, one lane and it'll have a high wall on either side of it," Purp said.

"Huh," Javier said. "If it's curved enough, you won't be able to see in, right?"

"Exactly," Purp said.

"Is there room for the curve?" Javier said.

"There is," Purp said. "Good question. I actually got out one night and measured it over there at that high-tech McDonald's drive-through."

"You measured it out there?" Javier said. "They didn't say anything?"

"I went late. I measured it pretty carefully," Purp said. "They have a tight curve from the left order speaker over to the pay window on the other side of the building, but it's nothing getting my truck through there. I took the dimensions of that curve and superimposed them on a satellite image I got of this lot on the Internet –

"Holy shit," Javier said.

"I did, and it fits easy. There's actually room for a bigger radius than that on both the entrance and exit," Purp said. "And with walls along both sides of where you drive, there's no way somebody will see in from outside."

"Except for the dorm," Javier said.

"And helicopter pilots, and Chinese miners," Purp said.

Javier walked a few steps toward the street. He put his hands on his hips and looked left and right, up and down Guadalupe. Thick rush hour traffic flowed across six lanes.

"When you drive in, where do you get out and watch from?" Javier said.

"You don't. You drive in and park in one of three slots," Purp said. "You stay in your car while the girls wash it. You get a great view of the girls while they're washing your car, and a decent view of the girls on the other two cars, too."

Javier tipped his face up to the dipping afternoon sun over Guadalupe. The sun made reddish highlights in a halo around Javier's wooly mass of tangled curly hair. He turned. "That was a good idea, Purp," Javier said.

"Which?" Purp said.

"That curved driveway thing," Javier said.

"I got it from this autistic lady I saw on the Discovery channel," Purp said.

"She designs topless carwashes?" Javier said.

"No, she actually designs abattoirs. Do you know what they are?" Purp said.

"Abattoirs? No," Javier said.

"Master's Degree in writing?" Purp said.

"Not all of us can be as educated as you. What is it?" Javier said. He hooked his thumbs in his belt loops and all of a sudden Purp thought Javier looked scary.

"A slaughterhouse. She designs the passageways that the cows walk along before they kill them. She makes it so the cow can't see what's coming up ahead," Purp said. "So they don't freak."

"It's like the Purple Topless Slaughterhouse," Javier said.

"Purple's Topless Slaughterhouse," Purp said.

"So I guess I won't be able to see it form across the street," Javier said.

"No. Definitely not," Purp said. "Not any of the action, anyway."

"That sucks," Javier said.

"If you're out there at Taco Cabana looking in, I'm not making any money off you," Purp said. "You've got to come in and get your car washed if you want a piece of the action."

"I don't even have a car," Javier said.

"No car, no wash," Purp said.

"But what if I wanted to check it out?" Javier said.

"You, personally?" Purp said. "Are you joking? I'm going to have a huge-ass picture window in my office on all of this. You're going to be sitting in there with me, drinking beer."

"No, not me personally," Javier said. "I mean what if a guy has no car, a student, say, but he's got money and he wants to check it out. It seems like there would be a lot of people like that, in this neighborhood especially."

"Huh," Purp said. "Huh."

"It seems like there should be some way to watch what's going on from inside," Javier said.

"I could sell tickets," Purp said. "You know when you go to an automatic car wash how there's that little hallway all along with windows in it? Kids look through? Everybody looks through."

"Yeah," Javier said. "It's cool to see the car getting all clean and shit."

"I could have something like that," Purp said. "A gallery. I could charge people a couple of bucks or something to go in there and hang out and watch."

"To just stand there?" Javier said.

"I don't know," Purp said. "I don't know, I could put seats in there or whatever. Stadium seats."

"No," Javier said. He laughed. "No." He looked directly at Purp. "You know what you need in there?"

"What?" Purp said.

"You need a Starbucks in there, Purp," Javier said. "You need a Starbucks in there with a huge ass glass wall so kids can sit in there after class and hang out and watch the car wash."

"That's awesome," Purp said. "A car wash café."

"A car wash café," Javier said. He bent over and slapped his thighs. "Holy shit," Javier said. He laughed a belly laugh. "And a bar."

"Oh yeah, dude," Purp said. He laughed. "That's what I'm talking about right there. Right there." Purp slugged Javier on the shoulder. Hard enough it made Purp's knuckles hurt. Javier barely seemed to notice.

"It'd be like beer brunch every day," Javier said. "You could have nachos up in there and people would sit and eat and hang out and you'd be making money both ways, on the car wash and the café."

"You could teach me how to pull shots," Purp said. "And how to run my galley."

"I could," Javier said. "That I could do."

* * *

Purp sat behind his laptop at a patio table, his papers weighed down with a stone on one side of the computer. On the other side, he had most of a breakfast burrito left and half a bottle of Budweiser. The morning sun warmed him up a little, now that it was getting higher. September had taken a chilly turn but not too chilly for Purp to still work outside. Purp worked facing his dirt lot, keeping an eye on his domain. Taco Cabana had become his office lately, once he licked the problem of how to power his laptop. He'd spent a thousand dollars on four batteries and a car charger, so he always had fresh power. He picked up wireless at Taco Cabana from somewhere, too, so he even had Internet.

Purp scrolled through a city website explaining the difference between a beer and wine permit and a liquor license. He'd read the same paragraph three times and still hadn't focused on it enough to be able to explain what it said to anybody.

Daydreaming off of the liquor license website, a blond girl caught Purp's eye. She pulled into the Taco Cabana parking lot off of Guadalupe. Purp could only just barely see her in her faded burgundy Taurus but he knew she was hot. In any case, she was more interesting than the website he was reading so he kept an eye on her while she got out of the Taurus.

Purp was not disappointed. She stood her tan legs on platform sandals and the denim skirt she wore was shorter than mini. The frayed little hem of it barely covered a couple of inches of her smooth-looking thighs. The skirt was almost useless as she walked across the parking lot. On top she wore a wide-necked off-the-shoulder billowy white lacy pullover shirt that looked soft and thin as it fell around her pushed-up breasts, bulging up out of her scoop-necked top. She clopped along past the patio, a faded green denim purse slung over her shoulder. A scar caught Purp's eye, a C-shaped arc from the corner of her eye to the corner of her mouth. Purp knew this girl. This was the sign girl he'd seen at the beginning of the summer, the one he'd bought a Diet Dr Pepper.

Purp closed his laptop and got up, leaving the computer and his papers on the patio table. He walked inside and got in line behind the blond girl. Nine inches taller than her and standing at an angle to her, not directly behind, it was easy for Purp to get a look down the front of her shirt. Purp remembered her looking good, but not this good. She had a better tan than the last time he'd seen her, but she wasn't over-tan like so many of the girls around the university area seemed to be. She looked like she lost a little fat, too. Not that she had weight to lose, she just looked more toned than she had before when she still had a little bit of a young-girl roundness to her. The wide elastic neck of her white shirt fell off both shoulders, and she'd put something glittery on them and across her chest. Clear plastic bra straps snaked out of the front of her shirt and down into the back. Purp saw through her white shirt and down its neck that the bra itself was black. She looked up at the menu with her hand on her hip, tipping an ankle so that the side of her meaty sandal laid against the tile.

"Excuse me," Purp said. "I think I remember you."

The blond girl turned to look up over her shoulder at Purp.

"Hey," she said. She made it a two syllable word, drawing it out. "I thought I saw you outside."

"I was outside," Purp said. "That was me."

"You bought me my soda that one time," she said. "I remember."

The cashier finished with the customer in front of them. The girl stepped over to the register but kept talking. "I have my purse this time, so I could pay you back," she said.

"You could by me a soda?" Purp said.

"Sure," the girl said. She gave a chuckle-laugh. Her breasts shook with it. "That'll make it even." She ordered a breakfast burrito and a soda for herself. Purp ordered his soda over her shoulder and she paid with a debit card out of her denim purse.

"I never carry cash," Purp said to her.

"Me neither," the girl said. "If they don't take a card, I'm screwed."

"Thanks," Purp said, taking his cup from the cashier. "Thank you for my soda," Purp said to the girl.

"You're welcome," she said. She stuffed the receipt with her order number on it in to the back pocket of her skirt. Purp caught a glimpse of the top of her black thong when she pushed the paper down into her pocket.

They walked over to the drink dispenser together.

"Diet Dr Pepper, right?" Purp said.

"Holy crap good memory," she said. "Stalker." She pursed her lips and tilted her chin down, glancing at him as if over glasses, except she didn't have glasses on. She wore earrings that looked like tiny handcuffs. A silver stud rested in the side of her nose. "Just kidding," she said. She kicked Purp in the shin with the toe of her sandal.

Purp felt that touch ripple up the inside of his leg.

"Seriously, how do you remember that?" she said. She poured Diet Dr Pepper into her cup.

Purp stood on her right side as she worked the dispenser. He remembered she didn't seem comfortable with him looking at her from the left last time.

"I don't drink much soda," Purp said," but when I do, I like Diet Dr Pepper, too. And it's hard to find a place that has it in a soda fountain."

"I know," she said. She topped off her drink. "It is. I hate that. That's why I used to walk over here to get it instead of going into the Circle K," she said.

"When you guys were doing the car wash?" Purp said.

"Yeah," she said. "They have it in bottles at Circle K."

"Oh, no," Purp said. "It's not the same in bottles. I like it much better with ice in it."

"I know, me too," she said.

"It tastes more like regular Dr Pepper that way," Purp said. He wanted to know the girl's name and he thought about just introducing himself but he figured that the longer he went without doing that the less it would seem like he was hitting on her.

"I know. That's so true. Sometimes I think they gave me regular by accident when it has ice in it," she said.

Purp finished pouring his soda. He and the girl moved away from the soda dispenser so the next person could use it. A heavy college guy stepped up after them, obviously checking out the girl.

"Of all the diet sodas, I think Diet Dr Pepper tastes the most like regular," Purp said.

"Me too," she said. "I hate other diet sodas."

Purp didn't want to push his luck. He thought ahead to a whole line of questions about the senior trip and the car wash fundraiser but it didn't seem like the right time for it. He wondered if he left her a way to do it on her own, if she might come and sit with him.

"Hey, I left my laptop outside on the patio," he said. "So I don't want to leave it out there unattended too long." Purp had the urge to thank her for the soda as he turned away, or to say it was nice bumping into her, or even to introduce himself at this point, but he didn't. He felt like the less he closed the conversation at this point, the better. If he could give her the feeling that they were still talking, like their conversation was still incomplete, the more likely she'd be to find a way to continue it. He didn't want to make it easy for her to think of their interaction as over.

"Yeah, that won't last long out there," she said. "My burrito is still not out."

Purp thought the mention of the burrito was a good sign. He walked out onto the patio without another word. Certainly not a good-bye. His laptop was still there, and his papers hadn't blown away.

There were three empty tables on the patio. Two next to where Purp was working, and one on the other side of the doorway. People were sitting and eating at the rest. One of the two tables next to Purp had trash on it. Purp gathered the trash and bussed it over to the third empty table, the one not by him. He liked his odds better that way, with the only two clean empty tables next to his.

Purp sat down behind his laptop. He opened it and stroked the touch pad so it would come out of suspend. Somebody inside called a number over the speaker and Purp looked in. The blond girl reached up under the heat lamp for her burrito. Purp looked at his laptop screen, pretending to be interested.

The blond girl came out onto the patio with her tray. She set it down on one of the empty tables next to Purp, not the one that had the trash on it in the first place.

"Hi," she said.

"Hi there," Purp said. He tried to sound friendly.

"I'm going to go in and get some salsa," she said.

"I'll watch your burrito," Purp said. "And your Diet Dr Pepper."

While she got her salsa, Purp shifted his chair and the laptop a few inches so that he'd be facing where it looked like she was going to sit without the laptop blocking his view of her legs in that little skirt. That, Purp thought, was going to be spectacular.

The blond girl came back with four cups of salsa. She sat down at her table, her right side toward Purp, scar hidden.

"This pico de gallo is my favorite," she said. "I like to mix it with the chipotle."

"Mmm," Purp said. "That sounds good."

"I'm all talking, bothering you," she said.

"Definitely not," Purp said. "I'm kind of bored. I've been working a while today." He slid the laptop more out of the way so she wouldn't think he was so busy with it. "My name's Purp, by the way."

"Purr like a cat?" she said.

"Purp as in short for Purple," Purp said.

"That's a pretty name," she said.

Purp got a lot of different reactions to his name but that was one he'd never had before.

"Mine's Gina," she said. She looked like she thought Purp was going to get up to shake her hand or something.

Purp stayed where he was. He felt like shaking her hand, but he thought it might come off as dorky.

"You said you're working, what are you working on," Gina said.

"I'm starting a business," Purp said, "and I'm working on getting the licenses for it and stuff like that."

"What kind of business?" Gina said.

"It's a car wash," Purp said. "And it's going to be right there on that dirt lot." Purp pointed.

"The sign's gone," Gina said. "Did you buy it?"

"I did," Purp said. "You know about running car washes on this corner, huh?"

"Oh yeah," Gina said. She sipped her drink but still hadn't taken the foil off her burrito. "Let me tell you. Every fucking Saturday for like six weeks. Every Saturday morning."

"Yeah, I used to see you guys out there. I come here with my friend every Saturday," Purp said.

"I know," Gina said. "I saw you. A lot of the girls noticed you out here all kicked back, hanging out with your buddy."

"You did?" Purp said.

"Oh yeah," Gina said. "We thought you guys looked cool, like real adult guys."

"Huh," Purp said. He didn't expect that.

"Not old or anything," Gina said, "just like, not like high school guys."

"Well, thanks," Purp said. "About the not old part."

"No way," Gina said. "What are you like twenty-five? Do you go to school here?"

"I'm thirty-five," Purp said.

"Holy shit," Gina said, "are you serious?"

"I am," Purp said.

"Really?" Gina said.

"Yes."

"Wow," Gina said. "You don't look it."

"Well thank you," Purp said. "So do you have any pointers for me? About running a car wash?"

"I know the secret to it," Gina said.

"You do?" Purp said.

"I do."

"Can you tell me?"

"I could," Gina said. "But you're technically the competition, right on our corner."

"But you graduated," Purp said. "It said 'Senior Trip' on your sign. So you're out of the car wash business now."

"True," Gina said. "True." She bit her knuckle. "OK, I'll tell you then."

"What is it?" Purp said.

"If you want customers at your car wash," Gina said, "you have to get girls in bikinis to hold signs for you on the corner. It works every time."

Purp laughed. Gina laughed with him. Purp thought about bringing up the fact that Gina was a sign girl herself. He didn't want to embarrass her but he thought since she was the one who brought it up it might be worth the risk.

"I noticed," Purp said, "that you were usually one of the girls out there with a sign. Was that your job?"

Gina looked at him for a second with her lips pursed, as if in a little scowl. Purp wasn't sure whether or not he offended her. Maybe he came off creepy saying that. Then Gina twisted her mouth to one side and tilted her eyes up and to the side as if trying to see something over her left shoulder. Purp took this look to be one of mock-deliberation.

Gina leaned forward in her chair and looked straight at Purp with her chin tilted down. She cupped her breasts with both hands, pushing them up further out the neck of her loose top.

"Hell yeah," Gina said, holding her breasts. "I shook these all the way to Cabo. She looked down at them, one then the other. Then as quick as she'd done it she was back leaning in her chair, her hands folded on her shred of a little skirt, looking around the patio theatrically as if to say, "Who, me?"

Purp felt his neck and ears get hot. Then his cheeks. She'd caught him off guard. He knew he was bright red and he hoped that Gina couldn't see that in the sunlight on the patio. He tried to laugh, but it didn't work out.

"I," Purp said. Nothing came to him. "OK, wow. I guess . . . that's a good marketing tip."

"You guess? I gave you the secret to running a good car wash and you guess it's a good tip?" Gina said.

"No, you're absolutely right," Purp said. His face felt sweaty now but he felt that the flush had passed. "Since you told me a secret and all, I feel like I should tell you one, too."

"Oh?" Gina said. She still hadn't opened her burrito but her Diet Dr Pepper was almost gone. "Juicy."

"Well, you're not far off with the sign girl thing," Purp said. Purp waited for a second. He wanted to make sure he was going to say this. Purp felt like since she'd already brought the subject of boobs up, she might be comfortable with the car wash. "I actually sort of got the idea from . . . you," Purp said. "And your friends, actually?"

"You did?" Gina said.

"I saw the guys driving slow when you were out there, blowing their horns," Purp said. "The car wash is actually going to be a topless car wash." As soon as he said it Purp was sure Gina would grab her burrito and run. He knew he'd gone too far.

"Topless?" Gina said.

"Yes. Yep," Purp said. He cringed, waiting for the shoe to drop. He couldn't think of a way to salvage this.

"Topless like," Gina sat straight up in her chair, throwing her shoulders back. She cupped her breasts.

Purp snuck a glance at a couple of the other tables, to see if Gina had caught anybody's attention. It didn't seem like anybody saw.

"Exactly," Purp said. "Just like that."

"What the crap?" Gina said. She sounded more amazed than offended. "Can you even do that?"

"Sure," Purp said.

"You are going to be freaking rich," Gina said.

"You think?" Purp said.

"Hell yeah," Gina said. "How much are you going to pay the girls?"

* * *

"I don't think so," Javier said.

Purp couldn't hear Javier well. Javier worked with his back to Purp and the noise from Javier's shovel scraping rocky soil made it difficult to hear him. Sweat soaked through the back of Javier's sweatshirt wetting the waistband of his jeans, darkening them in a crescent across the ass.

"But why mess with the other stuff?" Purp said. "All anybody is going to care about is the bar." Purp panted from the digging. He and Javier had made it half way around the perimeter of what would be the main building, digging the footings so they could put up block walls. The main building was going to be the office and the viewing gallery for spectators. A smaller building toward Zia Records would be the locker room and lounge for the girls.

"I don't think so, Purp," Javier said. "That's a mistake."

"What is?" Purp said.

"Saying they're only going to care about a bar," Javier said, grunting out his words in between shovel strikes. Javier dug like he was looking for something he lost and wanted back, bad. Purp only had to shovel out what Javier already loosened. "This isn't a strip club."

"OK," Purp said.

"It's not," Javier said. "A guy who wants to go to a strip club will go. He's a guy who has already been indoctrinated into that world. He knows how to go to a strip club."

"What do you mean, 'knows how to go'?" Purp said.

"A guy who knows that system, who knows that world," Javier said. "Do you know how to go?"

"You park, you go in, you pay –

"Do you go to strip clubs?" Javier said. "Do you know what money to bring, how much? Do you know why you want to go to the V.I.P. room? Do you know how to ask a girl there?"

"I . . . am not a big fan of strip clubs so much, no," Purp said.

"It's a whole language. To go, you have to know how to go, right?" Javier said.

"You seem to be the expert," Purp said.

"I know that language," Javier said. "But what you have here," Javier straightened himself in the trench, stopping for the first time in a while. He held his shovel out in one arm to indicate Purp's dirt lot. "Is a place for people who don't know how to go to a strip club."

"But it's too much hassle, the food and the coffee –

"Espresso," Javier said. He jabbed the point of his shovel into the rocky earth. "Purp, if you try to make this into a strip club it isn't going to work. I'm telling you that right now."

"But why wouldn't guys want to sit in a bar here and watch what's going on?" Purp said.

"If you make people feel like this is a strip club, then they guys who like strip clubs won't come. The guys who go there want a lap dance," Javier said. "They don't want to see girls through glass. This won't interest them so much."

"Too soft?" Purp said.

"Yes," Javier said. "This is a place for the man who is not comfortable going into a strip club. The man who doesn't know how to go to a strip club."

"But it's the same physical facility on the same lot," Purp said. "You're getting kind of grad-school on me. I'm not sure this is so theoretical as you're making it."

"Of course it is. If something new works, it works because the theoretical basis of it is sound," Javier said. "This is not sound, a strip club where people come in the day to drink and look at girls through glass at a distance of twenty-five feet."

"Well, closer if they're in their cars –

"I'm not talking about car wash guests, I'm talking about café guests," Javier said. "Car wash operations is a completely different thing. I'm not talking about that."

"So why have the bar if it isn't going to work?" Purp said. "I don't get what you're saying. I thought you liked the idea of a bar at first."

"I'm saying it's not a bar," Javier said. "For one, there's no show unless there are cars to wash. People get their cars washed in the day, bars are busy at night." Javier dug so ferociously Purp could hardly shovel himself or he'd miss what Javier said. "Two, this is too tame for the strip club crew. They're not interested. This is for the younger guys, all the college dorm guys in this neighborhood, guys goofing around, and guys like us out having a laugh when our wives think we're at Circuit City looking for a new computer on Saturday morning."

"OK, so guys like that don't like to go to a bar?" Purp said.

"Yes and no," Javier said. "Not at noon on a Saturday after they went out the night before and didn't get any." The dark sweat stain on Javier's back now covered shoulder to shoulder. "Purp this has to be a combination of Starbucks and Johnny Rockets, but with a full bar."

"OK," Purp said, "I thought you just said it wasn't a bar?"

"It's not a bar, but I didn't say guys weren't going to want a drink." Javier said. "They want to feel all bad-ass about it, like they're doing something edgy, but our guys are going to be a little intimidated to come in unless it's an environment they know how to read." Javier panted, stopping for a second. "A place where they're already comfortable, except there happens to be topless beautiful women washing cars outside."

"Almost like they came into Starbucks to study or to Taco Bell to get a burrito and, 'wow, there is some seriously awesome shit going on next door, check it out.'" Purp said.

"Yes," Javier said. "Yes. These are college guys who aren't as hardcore as they want people to think they are." Javier threw his shoulders back and twisted from side to side. He turned in the trench to face Purp. "This is for guys like us sitting at the Taco Cabana watching the high school car wash across the street. We could have gone to a strip club any Saturday for beer brunch, but did we?"

"No," Purp said.

Javier turned away from Purp, back toward the end of the trench.

"No. We came to Taco Cabana. This has to be an OK place to go on a Saturday morning or you're up against strip clubs and you'll lose," Javier said.

"I guess it's like going around the competition, and –

"What the fuck?" Javier said. He jumped backward knocking Purp down into the dirt.

“What?” Purp said. Javier stood over Purp, straddling him in the trench. Purp’s elbows burned from scraping on rock.

“Snake,” Javier said.

“What?” Purp said. He scrambled from between Javier’s ankles and out of the trench. “Where?”

Javier pointed with the handle of his shovel. A snake, the thickness of a Sharpie marker, rattled its tail and hissed at them from the corner of the trench.

“How did he get in there?” Javier said. “He must have fallen. A little guy.”

Purp dug in his pocket for his cell phone. He dialed 911 for the fire department, putting his finger in his left ear. He turned away from the trench toward Taco Cabana and out of the corner of his eye he saw Javier climbing from the trench, still holding his shovel.

Javier tapped Purp on the shoulder, shaking his head “no.” He dragged a finger across his throat.

“Mistuh Kurtz – he dead,” Javier said. He pointed into the hole with the blade of his shovel, the dust on it clotted with something damp. The snake writhed in the dirt, in three pieces.

* * *

Purp shifted his chair so he got a better view of Betty’s thighs in black fishnet tights under a floppy black pleated skirt. She wore stompy gray Ugg boots.

“I really appreciate all your help with this,” Purp said. “All this help for free I feel like I should be paying you.”

“Nah,” Betty said. She shook her head side to side so that her black hair, gathered in a high ponytail almost at the top of her head, shimmered like a fountain. “I’m not certified. It’s good practice.”

“But it’s like every week I’ve been asking you all this stuff,” Purp said. Purp wasn’t sure who he would have asked if he hadn’t known Betty. He would have had to pay somebody, definitely, but he didn’t even think he’d have gotten as much useful information from a working C.P.A.

“No problem,” Betty said. “It’s a funny business, but I actually think it could be pretty solid.”

“I’ll think about what you told me,” Purp said.

"It might be better than what you're doing. You'd be able to leverage that cash you've got and protect yourself at the same time," Betty said.

Betty had given Purp a lot to think about over the past few weeks. He had a question for her here and there whenever he bumped into her in Taco Cabana since the semester began and she started coming back. The basic idea Purp took away from their conversations more and more, though, was that he didn't know as much as he thought he did about starting a business like the car wash.

"There's Javier," Betty said. Purp had been meeting with Betty so often on Saturday mornings before beer brunch that Javier and Betty got to know each other. Javier stood up at the register. Purp hadn't noticed him come in.

"Are you super busy today or do you want to hang with us for a little?" Purp said to Betty.

"I can hang out for a while, but at noon I have to go to the salon because my mom has a bridal party coming there to do all at once," Betty said.

"Hey, gang," Javier said. He carried four bottles of beer and a receipt for his food that wasn't out yet. "Are we going to eat in here?"

Since Betty was going to sit with them for a while they decided to stay where they were, at Betty's table. Javier's food came and Purp went up and bought his nacho plate. After chatting for a while the subject came back around to the car wash.

"It's a stupid move," Betty said. "It exposes you to all kinds of liability."

"But I don't want to mess with all the paperwork and meetings and all that kind of stuff," Purp said. "Don't you have to have officers, like a treasurer or something?"

"You got to at least form an L.L.C.," Betty said. "If one of those girls slips out there washing cars, or if somebody gets food poisoning in the café, if you don't protect yourself you're going to expose your assets when someone tries to recover damages from you."

"I don't want to expose my ass," Purp said. Neither Betty nor Javier laughed. Purp felt dumb for saying that.

"Your assets personally will be exposed to liability if you don't incorporate this thing in some way," Betty said. "Any investments you have, your house, Selma's assets, Selma's wages, someone can take that if there is a judgment against you, any of that unless you incorporate."

Betty went on, finishing her rant about setting the car wash up as a corporation. It made Purp nervous. The more he got into it the more he realized there was too much for him manage with this project. Purp hadn't been sleeping so well, thinking of all the things that could go wrong and all the deadlines for the permits and licenses.

Purp was glad when it was almost time for Betty to go. She'd done a lot of thinking about his business for him, and he appreciated it, but she was on a roll this morning and the more she talked the more anxious Purp got.

"Thanks again, Betty," Purp said as Betty started gathering her things.

"No problem," Betty said. "It's fun for me. Your business illustrates a lot of the problems we've been talking about in my Entrepreneurship class. I'm actually going to use it as my case study."

"Well . . . OK," Purp said. He wasn't crazy about the idea of Betty telling a bunch of people what he was up to.

"I mean, if that's OK," Betty said.

"Sure," Purp said. He couldn't exactly say "no" with all the help she'd given him.

"OK then," Betty said. She wiped her fish sauce bottle off with a napkin. She put it into her backpack and when she did, she pulled out a magazine, a poetry journal Purp recognized as one Javier had published a poem in the year before. "Thank you." Betty slid the journal across the table to Javier. "It was beautiful. I read the whole thing but I liked yours the best."

Purp never saw Javier giving her the journal. He wondered when Javier had given it to her.

"Thanks," Javier said. "But it's not the best. I was lucky to be in there."

"I thought it was the best," Betty said. "I can see why you won that contest. I can't wait until your book comes out."

"It's not for a while," Javier said. "I can bring you the manuscript though if you want."

"Sure," Betty said. "I was never into poetry but something about yours makes it seem . . . real or something. You're a really good poet."

"I wonder how many good poets there are," Purp said, "pulling shots at Starbucks." Purp instantly felt like an idiot for saying this.

Betty, who was already standing up to go, slipped her arms through her backpack straps. The pack pulled her shoulders back and stretched the fabric of her button-down gray plaid top tight across her chest. The hem of her little black pleated skirt brushed so close to Purp's face as she wriggled into her backpack it made Purp feel flushed. She gave Purp a look like maybe she didn't understand what he just said.

Javier looked down into his plate of fajitas, working on organizing some shreds of chicken and onion that he'd left there for the last twenty minutes, untouched. They all of a sudden seemed to be intensely interesting to Javier, the way he bent his face down over them.

"No," Purp said, "I mean, Javier is a good poet, definitely. I mean, how many other good poets are there, like when you go in there, to Starbucks."

Betty stood with her hands on her hips looking down on Purp. She gave him a look like "Are you trying to be an ass, or what?" Her brow scrunched up, her head tilted to one side, her mouth open a little. She stood with her legs apart, the fishnet thighs a foot from Purp's face. She was almost Purp's height in those boots she had on and he couldn't help but look at those legs.

"No, I mean, like," Purp said, "you don't think about it when you're getting a latte but the guy behind the counter, you never know, he might have a Master's degree, you know?"

"Thanks again for the journal," Betty said to Javier. "Definitely bring me the manuscript. I don't want to have to wait for the book to come out."

"OK," Javier said. "But it's not that great."

Betty left.

"You know what I mean, right?" Purp said. "I just mean it's weird how like if you're a really good basketball player, you end up playing in the NBA but in poetry, it's like there's no equivalent. You know?"

Javier went back to organizing his leftover chicken.

"No, I mean, if you're a good poet," Purp said, "a really good poet, which you are, in our society there's no like poetry NBA. You can either teach other people who want to become really good poets, or like work at Starbucks or wherever."

Javier leaned against the back of the booth. He tipped his beer up, draining the almost empty bottle he slid away a half hour ago.

"There should be something like that, you know?" Purp said. "Like an NBA, for poets where they all get together and compete. They should make as much as NBA players, good poets. Like you are. You could call it the NPA. It would be awesome. They could get endorsements for stuff like . . . dietary supplements like ginseng or like cool berets like the ones Samuel L. Jackson wears, what are those?"

"Kangol," Javier said.

"Yeah," Purp said. "Like Kangol, the official cool beret of the NPA."

* * *

Hideo Matsuda pumped his fist on television in time with the frothed up members of the studio audience for Dude. Man. Guy. On Purp's plasma screen Hideo looked the same size he might have been if her were standing right there in the room with them. The show cut to a commercial for antiperspirant using a NASCAR driver as spokesman.

"Oh, yeah, that's good, right?" Javier said. He held his hand under his chin, as if to catch anything that might fall. Three plates of nachos sat on the coffee table in front of him.

"That one's my favorite, too." Purp said. "That's the recipe from maybe three weeks ago? Four?"

"The one with the chicken wings?" Javier said.

"Yeah," Purp said. "That was the one when I had the chicken wings left over from Miss America and I cut them up and put them on the nachos the week after for D.M.G. ."

"That's right. That was good then, too," Javier said. He sampled a different plate.

"Buffalo wing nachos. But these aren't the same chicken wings from then, right?" Javier said.

"Oh no," Purp said, "that chicken isn't even chicken wings at all. It's breasts I cubed and baked in the same sauce I used for the Buffalo wings. I was trying to make it like we would, you know, in bulk."

"The breasts are going to cost you more," Javier said. "Did you try it with thighs? You can get those a lot cheaper."

"Eh," Purp said, scrunching up his nose and shrugging his shoulders. "I'm not too crazy about thighs."

"Could you tell on nachos, though?" Javier said.

"Yeah, I could tell," Purp said.

"I bet if you added it up over a year's worth," Javier said, "it would be a lot cheaper to use thighs. And I doubt anybody would care."

Hideo Matsuda came back on so Purp and Javier turned to the show. Purp loaded up a plate for himself with all three different kinds of nachos on it. He settled into his recliner to watch the first segment on D.M.G. , a story about raucous homecoming celebrations on college campuses across the country. Beniko Kumi reported the story for D.M.G. and as she usually did, she became the story whenever she was on camera. With her signature school-girl skirts and knee-high loose socks on, it didn't seem like the guys she interviewed even remembered what they were celebrating in the first place. At LSU a chant of "Be-ni-ko" rose up so loud she stopped trying to say what she'd written and just turned her back to the camera, standing on her tiptoes to hold her microphone over the frenzied throng.

Purp and Javier ate and watched, then when the commercials came on ate and talked about the differences between the three different nacho recipes Purp made.

With the nacho plates empty, the D.M.G. theme song playing, and eight empty beer bottles on the coffee table, Purp turned down the volume on the television. The next show was a reality program about a family in Florida that builds motorcycles and he wasn't too interested in it. Javier didn't like it either. But they often left it on anyway, with the volume down, while they hung out after D.M.G. .

"Thanks for taste-testing the nachos, Javier," Purp said. He felt like he stumbled a little on the t's in "taste testing." Maybe the four beers in a half-hour had caught up to him, he thought. Those on top of the two he drank while getting the nachos ready in the kitchen, talking to Javier.

"Your welcome, Purple," Javier said. "For taste-testing the nachos."

It sounded weird to Purp to hear Javier use his full name, or even to use his name at all. Purp had just used Javier's name, though, so he figured Javier was making fun of him. Purp felt like an idiot for using Javier's name, now, but all evening he had been trying to say something and he didn't exactly know where to fit it in or how to bring it up.

"Javier," Purp said.

"Purple," Javier said.

Now it was making Purp nervous. He was having a hard enough time as it was.

"Stop that," Purp said.

"Stop what?" Javier said.

"Using my name," Purp said.

"You used my name," Javier said.

"I know," Purp said. "I know I did. But I'm trying to say something."

"You are saying something. You keep saying my name," Javier said. "It kind of creeps me out."

"I know," Purp said. "It creeps me out, too. I mean, not me saying your name creeps me out, you saying my name."

"OK," Javier said.

"Javier," Purp said. "Will you be my partner?"

Javier leaned forward on the middle of the couch. He sat right on the edge, usually, and it always made Purp uneasy. Now Javier was on the edge but rolled forward, too, with his forearms resting on his knees. He stared straight ahead at the coffee table in front of him.

Purp thought maybe Javier hadn't heard him, but Javier sat so still and quiet Purp figured no, Javier must have heard.

"Homey don't play that game," Javier said.

"What?" Purp said?

"I don't roll like that," Javier said.

"Like what?" Purp said.

"I'm flattered, but . . . no," Javier said.

"But you seem so interested in it, and you help me so much. I just feel like it's getting too big to take care of all on my own –

"What?" Javier said. He seemed a little insulted now. "But you have Selma –

"Yeah, but she's so busy with work, and she's not that into it anyway," Purp said. "And I'm not talking about as an employee, you know, me paying you –

"What the fuck are you talking about?" Javier said. He twisted all the way so he was sitting sideways on the couch, looking at Purp.

"What are you talking about?" Purp said.

"I don't know. Seriously," Javier said, "what?"

"The car wash. I want to know if you'll work with me at the car wash," Purp said.

Javier stared at Purp. The look on his face softened and he smiled. He shook his head and turned back to sitting on the edge of the couch.

"Jesus Christ," Javier said. "I'm a little drunk."

"Me too," Purp said. "Me too." Purp felt like he'd missed something but he was embarrassed to ask what. He always tried to seem less drunk than he was around Javier, because he didn't want Javier to think he was a wuss.

Javier sat and looked at the trash on the coffee table again.

"I can't," Javier said. "I'm getting my insurance through Starbucks now and it's kind of . . . I need the hours."

"But I'm not talking about as an employee," Purp said. "I mean as a partner."

"But I am a partner, at Starbucks," Javier said.

"No, I mean as a partner partner," Purp said. "A real partner. A part owner. You and me owning it together."

Javier shook his head. "I don't have the money for that," he said.

"I'm not asking for money, I'm saying for the work you're putting in, all the ideas you have, everything, I want you to be my partner," Purp said.

* * *

"It's not going to take that down," Purp said. He had to yell over the engine noise coming from the Bobcat mini-loader. The engine whined and vibrated right behind his driver's seat making Purp's ass go numb.

"Just hit into it," Javier said. He motioned to a rise in the earth on the dirt lot, only about ten inches over ten feet back, but sloping diagonally across the lot in the corner by the Circle K.

The rise needed to go in order to get the lot down to the grade stakes Purp and Javier pounded in every eight feet in a grid across the entire property. The rest of the lot was fine, toward the intersection where they'd dug footings, but it sloped up too much in the back corner.

"It won't cut that much dirt," Purp said.

"It's a tractor," Javier said. He leaned his face right up to the cage. "That's what it's for."

"It's a skid-loader. It's not an excavator," Purp said. "You've got to hit that with your pick to break it up so I can clear it out of there."

Javier laughed.

"I'm not joking," Purp said. "This blade won't push into that. That's hard earth."

"I know," Javier said. He still looked like he thought Purp was joking.

"OK, just start breaking that up with the pick," Purp said.

"Back through the whole corner?" Javier said. "You're telling me to take it down all through there?"

"Yeah, we have to get all of that out of there to get it down to grade," Purp said.

"What good is this thing for if it won't dig that out of there?" Javier said.

"Well, would you want to carry all that dirt out of there by wheelbarrow and pile it up with shovels?" Purp said. "This all has to go down to the dirt pile so on the day we rent the dump truck we'll be able to load and go all in the same day. If we didn't have the Bobcat we'd be wheeling it down there by hand."

"That's going to be a lot of picking," Javier said.

"I know," Purp said. "This is a lot of work."

"Why do I have to be the guy doing the picking?" Javier said.

"Well, we have one pick," Purp said. "And we have one Bobcat."

"I think we should go get another pick," Javier said.

"In the time it takes us to get out to Home Depot and get another pick, we could have had this cleared out," Purp said. "Plus then it'll be time to eat, and we'll get sidetracked over there having a burrito at Leo's and the whole time we're paying for this thing by the hour. Come on." Purp made a flapping gesture with his hand toward the rise that needed to be cleared.

"Come on?" Javier said. "Come on? Look at my hands." Javier held his palms up, reaching around to the Bobcat's open front where there was no cage.

"Jesus," Purp said. "You need to get yourself some gloves."

"I can't pick all that out of there," Javier said. "We're going to need another pick or you're going to have to take a turn on it."

"If I'm picking, and I'm driving the Bobcat, what are you going to do?" Purp said.

"I'll work the Bobcat," Javier said.

"But you don't have a license," Purp said. "You can't drive a car, how are you going to drive this thing?"

"I don't have a car," Javier said. "That doesn't mean I don't have a license."

"You have a driver's license?" Purp said.

"I do," Javier said.

"Huh," Purp said. "I did not know that."

"Plus it's not a car anyway," Javier said. "And you don't even need a license for it. I can't pick that out of there with these hands like this."

Purp climbed out through the open front of the Bobcat. Javier squeezed himself in. His bulk made it hard to reach the controls, one black plastic grip on each side of the driver's chair.

"Like the Devastator," Javier said, a tank they'd used a few nights before in a video game Purp rented. The Devastator controlled with two sticks. Javier kept bumping his elbows because there wasn't enough space for him to move the levers at his sides.

"Exactly," Purp said. He showed Javier how to work the bucket, how to tip his wrists in and out to make the bucket raise and lower, tilt forward and back.

"I think I got it," Javier said.

"Can you buckle the belt?" Purp said.

"No," Javier said. "It's down there in between. And I can walk faster than this thing."

Javier backed up over a grade stake, splintering it into the dirt. He didn't seem to notice. After that he took a full lap around the dirt lot, looking like a gorilla in a go-cart. He had a knack for the controls. He zig-zagged over to the dirt pile and scooped earth into his bucket. He raised it six feet up and tipped the bucket so the dirt would fall back on the pile. The cool wind blew falling dry dust back into the Bobcat, into Javier's face. Dust swirled around the Bobcat's intake and exhaust. Javier stood up and leaned out the front of the cockpit, dust clouds puffing from him as he patted his jacket and jeans.

Javier rolled back over to where Purp stood. He made the Bobcat spin in place, turning a full circle before pointing it at Purp.

"I got it," Javier said. "It is like the Devastator. But without the chain gun."

"Good thing," Purp said. "Or we might not have anywhere to get lunch." He nodded over toward Taco Cabana.

"I'm going to take a crack at it," Javier said. He didn't give Purp time to say anything.

Javier backed up the Bobcat. This time between rows of grade stakes, not hitting any. He rolled forward toward the dirt rise at full speed, about the speed of a slow jog, the speed where it's too fast to walk, too slow to run. He had the bucket down a few inches off the ground, skimming the gravel as the Bobcat rocked forward and back.

The blade on the front of the bucket slammed into the dirt rise. It didn't even bite the earth. It was like it hit a solid wall. The Bobcat stopped dead but Javier kept going out the front. His arms flailed in front of him, swimming in air, but his feet must have caught a little on the dashboard because he went horizontal. He landed face and hands first onto the rocky soil.

Javier laid still with his face on the dirt and his arms out to his sides. His knees rested on the floor of the bucket and his shins leaned against the bucket's top. Javier's feet poked up into the air.

Purp ran. It looked like Javier might be dead.

"Are you OK?" Purp said, falling to his knees beside Javier. "Are you all right?" He grabbed Javier's shoulder and tried to roll him, but he didn't budge. Purp pulled on Javier's shoulder with both hands. Then he thought maybe he shouldn't be moving him because maybe his neck was broken. But he wasn't moving anyway. "Hey, are you OK?"

Purp rocked back on his knees, noticing he had blood seeping though his own jeans. He must have cut himself when he kneeled down, but he didn't feel it. Purp fished in his pants pocket for his cell phone. He flipped it open and dialed 911. He told the operator what happened but he couldn't even remember the address on the lot. He had to give the cross streets.

"Hey," Javier said. He lifted his head off the dirt to look over at Purp. He moved like he was sort of testing whether or not he even could. Bits of gravel poked out from his cheek, each pebble ringed with blood. Blood and dust browned his lips.

Javier rolled himself over to one side. His legs got tangled up on the bucket. Blood stained both shins. His jeans were torn off pretty much from the knees down. He pushed himself into a sitting position, half in the bucket half out.

"Holy fuck," Javier said. "It just impacted on the surface." He looked up at Purp and let out a belly laugh. The laugh echoed off the side of the Circle K.

Purp laughed too. Not as hard as Javier, but he laughed with him so long they were still laughing when they heard sirens coming down Powell Avenue.

* * *

"Are you sure it shouldn't be back further from the sidewalk?" Selma said. She wore a silvery quilted jacket over her jeans. She stepped up onto the concrete pad from the dirt. She managed fine in the four-inch heels of her fuzzy gray boots. A little white headband she had on made her look like a snow bunny, like she was ready for the slopes. A chill in the air reddened the tip of her nose.

"What would go in between?" Purp said.

"More café parking?" Selma said. "Or something. It seems awfully close to the sidewalk."

"There will be café parking on the side there, by the entrance," Purp said. "And then on that side, too. But I like how it's close. It's no closer than Zia or Taco Cabana. It's inviting. I think it's better for University walk-ins like that. More like a city street, like it's meant for walking to."

"Won't people see in?" Selma said.

"I want them too. You see in when you walk by Starbucks," Purp said. "Or Johnny Rockets."

"But won't they see through to where the girls are?" Selma said.

"Well," Purp said. "Huh. I guess I'll have to put something up or something, because they would, wouldn't they. They'd be able to see right through to the glass wall."

"Could you just make this solid?" Selma said. "Not a window?"

"Nah," Purp said. "I want it to be light and comfortable in there. I'll figure something out."

"If this was back further from the sidewalk people wouldn't be able to see in so well," Selma said. She stood on the edge of the concrete pad near the sidewalk and motioned with her arms, as if to scoot the pad back toward the middle of the lot.

"Well, it's kind of not really relevant at this point," Purp said. "The slab is poured."

"Can't you bust it out and move it back?" Selma said.

"No," Purp said.

"Why? It should be back further," Selma said.

"Gosh, Selma," Purp said, shaking his head. "It's not even a remote possibility. The plumbing is in, the electrical is in, the slab is poured." Purp stomped his foot on the concrete pad to show how solid it was. "You don't just bust it up and pour it again."

"Better now than when you get the walls higher," Selma pointed to where Javier and Purp had experimented with laying the first block wall at the back corner of the office.

"It would cost a fortune to do that, Selma." Purp said. "Breaking it out and hauling it off, no." Purp shook his head. "It's not even a possibility. This part of the slab cost forty-thousand dollars. Just this part, not all that," Purp motioned over to where the driveway and car wash area had been poured, too."

"I'm just saying," Selma said. "It seems like it could be further back."

"But anyway," Purp said. "Do you like it? I was excited to show it to you."

"It doesn't look like much yet," Selma said. "I thought the walls you were telling me about would be higher. That's the next thing, huh? To make the walls higher?"

"Yeah," Purp said, "it is, but why do you do that? Why is it always the next thing?"

"What, I'm just saying, that's the next thing, right?" Selma said.

"It is the next thing," Purp said, "but you're always doing that to me, every time I do something."

"Doing what?" Selma said.

"You're always with the next thing and the next thing," Purp said. "It's like I do something, and I get all excited to show it to you, and your reaction to it is always, 'Now all we have to do is this,' or, 'Now we just need to do that.'"

"I'm just looking at it," Selma said.

"You're not looking at it," Purp said. "Every time I do something, or a project around the house, or anything, I show it to you and you don't look at it. You're just always right in with the next thing."

"Like what? I do not," Selma said.

"You do. You so do," Purp said. "It took me two hours to put your bathroom mirrors up like you wanted and I show them to you and in two seconds you're all, 'This will look nice when we get the new light fixture up.'"

"I was just thinking it would," Selma said.

"But that's the thing," Purp said. "When someone does something nice for you, it's nice to just look at what they did and say, 'Wow, thank you, that looks nice. I can't believe how nice it looks. You did a good job.'"

"I said it looked nice," Selma said.

"Yeah, but it's like you never enjoy what's already been done," Purp said. "You never spend any time on enjoying the part that's already finished, it's just like once it's done, it's done. It's as if the part that got done was always like that."

"That's not true," Selma said. "What do you want me to put you in for an award because you put the bathroom mirrors up?"

"I just want you to look at the mirrors and say they look nice," Purp said, "and just make it seem like you appreciate something I did before assigning me the next task with your, 'Now all we need to do . . .' thing you say."

"Well I'll write it up then," Selma said, "and you can get your award for putting up two medicine cabinets."

"Why do you have to trivialize it, Selma? I'm telling you it's something that bothers me," Purp said. "I don't even like doing projects around the house anymore because I get myself all anxious because it's like a countdown to when you're going to come in and say, 'Now all we need to do . . .'"

Purp walked toward where his office was going to be. He stood as if he were looking out his window at the car wash girls. He imagined the tile he was going to pick for his floor.

"Sometimes when I do something around the house," Purp said, "and I call you in to show you, when you walk through the doorway I literally just start counting in my head, ten, nine, eight, and I swear to you before I hit 'one' you will say something that begins with the phrase, 'Now all we have to do is . . .' I swear to you. And it's never something that 'we' are going to do, it's always something you are assigning to me to do."

"Well, I don't really think about it," Selma said, "it's just my way."

"Maybe you should start thinking about it," Purp said. "It makes me feel bad. I don't like your way, OK? It really upsets me." Purp bent down to pick up an orange plastic cap sitting on the concrete. He pressed the cap down onto the end of the rebar rod it had fallen off.

"When I finished painting the baby's room, three colors – three different colors, walls and ceiling. Six edges where two colors meet and I knew every damn inch of those edges had to be millimeter perfect or you'd put your finger on it. When I finished painting the baby's room," Purp said, "you know what you said? Do you? You came in and looked at it and said, 'That's going to look really nice when we get those curtains up.'"

"I said it looked nice," Selma said.

"You said it was 'going' to look nice, it was 'going to look nice' when 'we' got the curtains up. And you knew it wasn't 'we' that was going to be putting up the curtains, it was me," Purp said.

"Fine I'll put my own curtains up from now on," Selma said. "Next time I make a nursery."

"That is so not even close to the point," Purp said.

* * *

"No, not quite," Betty said. She shook her head. Black hair whipped bare brown shoulders. Purp thought she must be chilly in that shirt, a gray ribbed-neck sweater with a neck hole so wide it opened over both of her shoulders, slipping down the sides of her arms. Betty seemed like she thought it was funny how Purp didn't get what she was saying. Purp wasn't ashamed that he felt confused. For one thing, it was hard for him to concentrate with Betty wearing that sweater. It was kind of hard for Purp to concentrate with Betty around at all. But what he didn't get was how Javier already seemed to know all about what Betty was saying.

"It's to separate them," Javier said, picking at a scab on his cheek. "To keep them apart."

"Thanks," Purp said. "I know what 'separate' means."

"The verb and the adjective?" Javier said.

Purp laughed. So did Javier and Betty.

"That isn't going to heal if you keep picking at it," Betty said.

Javier stopped picking at his face. He reached under the table with both hands. Purp knew it was to pick the scabs on his shins.

"But what's the 'them'? What are we keeping separate by doing this?" Purp said.

"The two separate businesses," Betty said.

"Car wash and café?" Purp said.

"No," Javier said. "The property and the car wash."

"What about the café?" Purp said. "Where does that go?"

"That's all part of the car wash, part of PTC," Betty said. She crossed her legs under the table. Sitting on her side of the booth, Purp watched her thighs move under a black wool skirt with a slit up the side almost to her hip.

"OK," Purp said.

"But the way I think you should set this up," Betty said, "is to incorporate two different L.L.C.'s. One for the car wash, the whole thing, car wash, café, whatever. That's the partnership between you and Javier."

"Got it," Purp said.

"The other L.L.C. is for the property and building as a separate business," Betty said.

"So since you bought that," Javier said, "that's not a partnership. You and Selma just own that whole thing outright."

"But you lease the property and the building to the car wash business," Betty said. "And that way if somebody gets hurt on the premises, like they already did," she jerked her thumb toward to Javier, "the assets you and Selma have, like your house and her income or whatever are insulated from the liability."

"So Javier owns half the business since he's my partner," Purp said, "but I own the building and I rent it to the car wash."

"Right," Betty said with a nod that flicked her hair forward across both sides of her face. "Unless Mr. Busy Fingers bleeds to death from picking his scabs under the table. Then you're just on your own."

Purp chuckled. Javier put his hands on the table. He flicked something off his finger toward the floor.

"That's cool," Purp said. "That's cool." He tore a nacho off the pile on his plate. He'd let his nachos get cold because he didn't want to eat in Betty's ear while she was talking. Purp folded the chip into a taco shape and scooped some beans and sour cream into it.

Javier finished his second Dos Equis of the morning. Betty gathered her things and slid her quarter-eaten burrito back toward her. She tightened the top on her fish sauce and wiped it clean with a napkin. It looked like she was getting ready to slide out of the booth and leave.

"Are you taking off?" Purp said.

"Yeah, I have Entrepreneurship small group at one thirty," she said.

"But you have time," Purp said.

"It's way over in Wilson though. And I have to carry my computer," Betty said.

"Well," Purp said, "I had something else I wanted to talk to you about today, but we got going so long on the corporation stuff I didn't get a chance to mention it."

Betty finished putting away the pens she was using to draw things out for Purp, and the highlighters, and the paper, and everything. She sat with her purse in her backpack and her backpack on her lap.

"What is it?" Betty said.

"I wanted to ask you," Purp said, "we wanted to ask you, both of us," Purp nodded to Javier and Javier nodded once back at him, "if you wouldn't mind joining us with this thing. If you would like to work for us at the car wash."

"Washing cars with my shirt off?" Betty said. But she said it funny, like she knew that wasn't what Purp meant.

"Huh," Purp said. It kind of caught him off guard what she said, even though he could tell she knew that wasn't what he meant. The idea certainly did appeal to him. "Well, sure if you wanted, but that's not what I meant. I meant would you like to come to work for us as our administrator and bookkeeper? You've helped us so much with everything, and you know much more about this stuff –

"Sure," Betty said. "I have to get to Wilson, though." She slid out of the booth holding her backpack. The back of her skirt clung a little to the vinyl bench and as she stood Purp caught a flash almost all the way up the back of her thigh. "I'll see you guys."

"Bye," Purp said.

"Bye, Betty," Javier said.

Betty slung the backpack over one of her bare shoulders as she walked away. She tugged at her sweater, pulling it up a little where the backpack made it slip too low.

"She seemed to take that in stride," Purp said.

"Yep," Javier said.

"I thought she'd need more convincing," Purp said. "Or be more surprised, or something. Huh."

"Nope," Javier said.

"I was all like nervous to ask her," Purp said, "like I was asking her out or something."

"You get nervous when you ask a girl out?" Javier said.

"Yeah, I guess," Purp said. "Don't you?"

"Not so much," Javier said. "What are they going to do, say 'no'?"
"Well, yeah," Purp said.
"No, I mean, what's the worst they can do, say 'no'?" Javier said.
"Yeah, I guess that's the worst," Purp said. "I guess I don't really know now if I'd get nervous or not. I'm not a single stud like you."
"No," Javier said.
"I still think it was kind of weird," Purp said. "She didn't even think about it."

* * *

"Try not to almost kill yourself again," Purp said.
Javier climbed onto the upper level of the scaffolding. He didn't seem to have any trouble at all getting up there.
"Ha, ha," Javier said. "you're freaking hilarious."
"OK," Purp said. "Try to almost kill yourself again."
Javier did laugh at that.
"I'll toss them up to you?" Purp said. He held a concrete block in both hands and mimed a motion like he was going to toss it up to Javier.
"I don't know about 'toss,'" Javier said.
"What's a better word?" Purp said.
"I mean, maybe you're going to hand them up to me, right?" Javier said. He leaned over with his hands on his knees to look down at Purp. Standing on the scaffold, Javier's feet were only at about the level of Purp's chin, but Javier called down to Purp as if from a great height.
"No," Purp said, "I mean, I'll toss a bunch up to you –
"A bunch?" Javier said.
"Well, one at a time, of course," Purp said. "How could I toss more than one at a time? I'll toss a bunch up to you, you stack them up, there on your platform, and then when we have a bunch up there, I'll climb up and we'll lay them."
"Oh, I thought you'd hand me one, I'd lay it, then you'd hand me another one, like that," Javier said.
"No, I'm going to toss you a bunch, then we'll both lay them together," Purp said.
"Why?" Javier said.
"It's more efficient," Purp said.
"How is that more efficient?" Javier said. He kneeled down onto the platform and gripped the edge of a scaffold plank. His face was only

two feet above Purp's head but he still talked loud like he was up on top of a three-story building.

"I don't know, man," Purp said. "Let's just get these blocks up there before the mortar sets in the mixer."

"Here." Purp handed a concrete block up to Javier. Javier took the block, still kneeling, and set it toward the back of the scaffold platform.

Purp handed up another block. Javier set it beside the first.

"That wasn't a 'toss,'" Javier said. "I'd say you're handing them up." The blocks moved faster now as they got a little rhythm.

"Well, I didn't figure on you kneeling down like that," Purp said.

Hand, stack, hand, stack.

"What's wrong with kneeling?" Javier said.

"I'd have to say the kneeling is," a block slipped in the handoff, but Purp grabbed it so it didn't fall, "the kneeling is a little wussy, I'd have to say."

"It's wussy," Javier said. "How's that?"

"I don't exactly know," Purp said. "But the kneeling is definitely a little wussy."

"What's wussy about me kneeling?" Javier said.

"It's just not manly," Purp said.

"That's a logical fallacy," Javier said.

"It's just if you think about it," Purp said. He handed up another block. The stack on the scaffold platform was high enough now that Javier had to stand to stack the blocks. "Think of all the times you see professional masons laying block, or professional tradesman of any kind, really, they're never really kneeling, are they?" Purp tossed a block up to Javier.

"I guess that was a toss," Javier said. He stacked the block.

"What's the difference between a toss and a hand?" Purp said. He tossed another block.

"For a toss to be a toss," Javier said, "the block, in its transit from you to me, must exist for a period during which," he caught another block, "it is neither touching my hand, nor yours." He stacked the block on the back of the pile he'd built, starting a new row.

The back tier of blocks on Javier's stack peeled loose. It bent back off the scaffolding as if Purp were watching it on TV in slow motion. Ten or fifteen concrete blocks tumbled off the stack, crashing into the scaffold poles, slamming onto the planks, shaking other blocks loose from the stack. One of them bounced off the scaffold plank near Javier's foot and missed Purp's face by four inches. It grazed Purp's shoulder before slamming into the concrete pad and shattering. The crashing and banging stopped, blocks strewn, dust rising.

"Holy fuck," Javier said.

"Wow," Purp said. He looked at his hands and feet, checking to make sure everything was still there.

"You told me to try not to almost kill myself," Javier said.

"I did," Purp said. "Yeah."

"You didn't say to try not to almost kill you," Javier said.

* * *

"I'm sorry," Betty said, "I'm sorry." A puff of a scent like citrus rolled in with her.

Purp closed the door behind her and looked at Betty's red button-down sweater, stretched tight and opened lower than he would have expected, even from her. Purp hadn't ever seen Betty show as much cleavage, and she wasn't exactly shy on other days, either. In that sweater, Purp thought, Betty would have to do an awful lot more than show up late to make him mad. He'd miss D.M.G. now because she was late, but with Betty in his house instead, he didn't care so much about whether or not he saw D.M.G. . She set her backpack down on the tile and shimmied out of her black leather jacket.

"I'm sorry," Betty said, "I just couldn't get out of there. I couldn't leave during the gift exchange, did you get my text?"

"Yeah, don't worry about it," Purp said. "We're just testing nachos and watching TV."

"And drinking beer, I see," Betty said, looking at the five empties on the coffee table. She stepped down into the living room.

"And Jack Daniels and Coke," Purp said.

"Hey, Betty," Javier said. He leaned forward on the couch and rearranged the empty bottles and glasses on the coffee table, as if trying to make it look like there weren't so many.

"Got one for me?" Betty said.

"Oh, yeah," Purp said. "Of course." He walked into the kitchen. "Budweiser, Dos Equis, or Jack and Coke?"

"Diet Coke?" Betty said.

"I don't," Purp said.

"Dos Equis then. Nice house, Purp," Betty said. "It's beautiful."

"Thanks," Purp said. "Did you find it OK?" He brought a bottle of beer out for Betty, a fresh one for Javier, and a Jack and Coke for himself.

"Oh yeah," Betty said. "Good directions."

Purp handed two beers to Betty and she passed one along to Javier sitting next to her on the couch. Purp muted the TV and scooted his recliner a couple of feet so he could see Javier and Betty better.

The three of them got their meeting started. Betty had downloaded a bunch of forms for Purp and Javier to sign to get the business set up the way she said it ought to be. Betty had everything ready to go, all organized in file folders in her backpack. She even had the forms filled out for them already. She had little Post-It flags that said "Sign Here" with an arrow wherever Purp and Javier had to sign. Purp liked those flags. He thought Betty was worth twice what they paid her. A few times he'd wished they made her a partner, too.

"The blue flags are for Selma," Betty said. "Is she here?"

"No," Purp said. "She's in San Antonio."

"Oh," Betty said. "I thought she'd be here. I'd like to meet her."

"You will. What does she have to sign?" Purp said.

"She has to sign this form from the county to re-record the deed on the lot in the name of the property-holding LLC, because her name's on the original deed, too," Betty said.

Purp caught the gist of what Betty said but he thought it would be funny to pretend he didn't.

"Oh . . . kay," Purp said. "I will get her to sign that." He looked over at Javier, trying to appear comically puzzled. Javier nodded in a way he probably meant to look dignified and looked back at Purp as if to say, about Betty, "Not bad. Not bad."

Betty shuffled the papers back into the folders she had for them. Purp could watch her lean over that coffee table all night. He even turned his chair more so he could see better. He wished they had more paperwork to sign but Betty was so efficient it didn't take long for them to finish.

"Now the other thing," Betty said, opening a spiral-bound packet of color charts and spreadsheets, "is the cash on hand issue." She pulled out three more packets, handing one to Purp and one to Javier. Purp figured maybe the extra packet was supposed to be for Selma.

Purp flipped through his packet. It had a clear plastic cover and a purple vinyl back cover. Nice touch, he thought.

"I was going through the numbers you gave me and I think your labor and food cost estimates you made are much too low. I also added in rent because the property-holding LLC should be getting rent from the car wash, for the lot and building," Betty said.

"I'm renting the building to myself?" Purp said. Now he really was confused.

"Sort of. It's better for taxes on the car wash side and it's more professional. It protects you later if you wanted to sell the car wash because if you don't have rent on your books it'll be weird for a buyer to try to figure out what kind of profit to expect. Anyway," Betty said.

"Anyway," Purp said.

"So after I fixed up what you had, look on page three there," Betty said, "you don't have enough cash on hand. Not nearly. You have enough for four months of operating costs."

"Well, that's pretty good," Purp said. He looked over at Javier. Javier nodded and shrugged his shoulders as if it sounded good to him.

"You need six months, minimum," Betty said. "And that's why new businesses fail, Purp, because they don't have cash on hand."

"Yeah but by four months' time we should –

"You should nothing," Betty said. "Nothing. Don't count on a dime for a year."

"A year?" Purp said.

"What do we do for a year?" Javier said, leaning forward on the couch.

"Cash on hand," Betty said. "Six months is textbook, to have cash on hand for all projected expenses for six months, but those businesses fail. I'm telling you that right now. We're going to have a year on hand. That'll give us a cushion –

"A year's worth of expenses?" Purp said.

"A year. In the bank. On the day doors open," Betty said.

"Where are we going to get that?" Purp said.

"From you," Betty said, "if you have it. From other investors, I know some. And if we have to, we'll have to finance some of it, maybe cash some equity out of the lot. Who is that?" Betty looked up at Purp's muted sixty-four inch plasma. "Nice TV, by the way."

Beniko Kumi held a microphone on television. D.M.G. had started during the meeting. Beniko wore a plaid skirt and striped stockings that went up over her knees, leaving four inches of skin between the tops of her stockings and the hem of her school-girl skirt. She tilted her head back, laughing, apparently at something the man she was interviewing just said. The light-brown ponytails sticking out the sides of her head shimmered with her laughter.

"She's so pretty," Betty said.

"Oh, I'm sorry," Purp said. He fished the remote out from his chair cushion. "We don't need that on now."

"No," Betty said. "Can you turn that up a second?"

Purp took the TV off mute. Beniko and the man she was interviewing were talking about his business. The man rented adult DVDs from his website and sent them to customers in the mail. Beniko asked him all about how his business worked as the two of them walked through his facility.

"What is this show?" Betty said.

"It's just a dumb show, it's kind of obnoxious," Purp said.

"Dude. Man. Guy.," Javier said. "We watch it every week. D.M.G. ."

"Oh, I've heard of that," Betty said. "Is this the one with the Japanese guy?"

"Hideo Matsuda," Javier said. "Is he Japanese?"

"What the hell else would he be," Betty said. "But I didn't know they had more serious segments on it like this, interviews."

"If you call a website that rents porn serious," Javier said.

"Look at the machine sending them out," Betty said. "That's labeling what, two per second? It's been running the whole time they've been standing by it. That's a lot of DVDs. That's serious."

Betty watched Beniko Kumi finish her interview with the porn guy.

"Anyway," Betty said. "The last thing I had on my agenda, I don't know if you guys had stuff too, but the last thing I had was about the name." Betty looked at Purp. "I have it with the apostrophe on the forms right now," she said, "but before I turn those in, when I drop those off that's going to be the name. Are you sure you want the apostrophe?"

"Yeah, I'm sure," Purp said. "That's how I want it."

"Purple's Topless Carwash?" Betty said.

"That's the deal. Javier already said he doesn't care," Purp said.

"I don't care," Javier said. "It's just always what he called it before he made me a partner."

"I don't care about that," Betty said, "but it's hard to say."

"It is not," Purp said. "It's just as easy as the other way."

"Purple Topless Carwash is a lot easier to say," said Betty. "And to write, and it looks cleaner, and it's easier if you sell it –

"What's with all the selling it tonight?" Purp said.

"I'm just saying," Betty said. "Plus what if it gets big, and it's franchised. They won't all be yours, but they could all be purple. It just looks silly with the apostrophe. It doesn't seem scalable to multiple locations."

"McDonald's," Purp said. "Eighty-bagillion served."

* * *

The building inspector, Arturo Munoz, stood on the concrete pad with his back toward Taco Cabana. He had his hands jammed down into the patch pockets of a thigh-length suede barn jacket, holding a clipboard in his armpit. He shivered his head down into the upturned faux-sheepskin collar of his jacket.

"I'm doing you a favor," Arturo said.

"A favor?" Purp said. "What the heck kind of favor is that?"

"I'm not saying you have to tear down what you've got up," Arturo said.

"Of course I'm not tearing down what I have up," Purp said. "Of course not."

"It isn't really 'of course not' actually," Arturo said. He kicked a stone off the pad and it bounced farther than he probably thought it would, landing in the right lane of Guadalupe. If a car had been going by, the stone would have hit it.

"Why would I tear it down?" Purp said.

"Well, that's really what should be done here," Arturo said.

"But it's totally up to code," Purp said. "Every single thing. Look at the rebar." Purp grabbed onto a rod of rebar sticking up out of the waist-high wall of what he planned to become the kitchen. "There's a third more than the code says we need."

"It isn't that," Arturo said. "I can see that. You're doing a nice job, you are."

"Why didn't you say anything at the pre-pour inspection," Purp said, "before the pad went in."

"Because you had licensed subs do the plumbing, the electrical, and a licensed sub was going to do the pour—

"But there was no general contractor at that time, either," Purp said.

"I know," Arturo said. "I know, now. That wasn't right. And that's why I'm telling you that you don't have to tear this down to the pad, because you did have your permit and that first inspection."

"Stop with the tearing it down," Purp said. "That's ridiculous."

"I'm not saying you need to tear it down –

"I know you're not," Purp said, "because that's completely out of the question. Do you know how much time we spent laying this block? My partner and I laid every single one of these blocks ourselves and it's to the permitted plan to the quarter of an inch. Everything is up to code."

"Not everything," Arturo said.

"What?" Purp said. "What isn't to code?"

"The code is that commercial construction has to be performed by a licensed general contractor," Arturo said.

"No, no," Purp said. "It does not."

"Look, I deal with this stuff every day, mi'jo and I know what I'm talking about," Arturo said. "You're walking a fine line here between continuing on and having to rip all of this block out."

"But I built my own house," Purp said. "I didn't have a contractor's license for that. I just had to live in it for what, a year or something?"

"Primary residence for twelve months," Arturo said. "That's because it was residential. A commercial property is a different ballgame."

"Oh, no, that's such bullshit," Purp said.

"I don't know what to tell you," Arturo said, "but if we keep the visibility of this down, and you get a general in who will sign off on this block you've put in already, then you can move on from there."

"I can't do that," Purp said.

"This block, technically, all needs to come out of here," Arturo said. "You know, you were talking about you want to talk to my supervisor, you want to talk to this person, you want to talk to that person. You can do all that, but you know what? You know what's going to happen if you start going up the chain like that? You're going to have a general contractor in here with a front loader and a roll off dumpster clearing all this block away down to the pad, because that's all that's to code."

"No," Purp said. "It is to code."

"It's not to code," Arturo said. "Code is that a licensed contractor needs to do or sub out the work. It doesn't matter the rebar is on twenty-four or forty-eight, it matters who set the block on it and you don't have a license."

"I don't have the budget for a general contractor," Purp said. "Can't I just have more inspections, something?"

"I – no. It doesn't work like that," Arturo said.

"You know what this place is, right?" Purp said.

"I do," Arturo said.

"You know we can work something out," Purp said, "between us. For after, when we open."

"I don't follow you," Arturo said.

"I'm saying if you can cut me a break on this end of it," Purp said, "there are going to be a lot of girls here who owe their jobs to me when we open."

"I am afraid not," Arturo said.

"No, I'm serious," Purp said. "As a friend of mine, I'm telling you, when you came back to this place you'd get the V.I.P. treatment, you know what I mean?"

"Absolutely not," Arturo said. "In fact, no. No, just leave it at that, I don't even want to acknowledge having had this part of the conversation. Now I'm actually offended, and I'm going to leave it at this: you can leave the block up, but you're going to need a general in here to finish construction and sign off on everything between the pad and now."

"All I'm saying is –

"I know what you're saying, and it is offensive to me," Arturo said. "You need to stop all activity on the jobsite so that the next time I come here, I'm dealing with someone with a general license, not you. If there's anything else that happens other than that, this block is coming down."

* * *

The waiter set down a plate of Pad Thai between Purp and Selma.

"Is there anything else I can get you?" the waiter said.

"Another glass of water, please?" said Javier.

"Do you have any nuoc m'am?" Betty said.

"Certainly," the waiter said. "Water, nam pla, anything else?"

Javier shook his head, the others murmured, "no, thank you."

Just as the waiter was out of earshot, Purp said, "One thing you could do for me," as if to the waiter who was by that time in the kitchen, "is get those Christmas decorations down before it's Groundhog's Day already." Purp nodded to a Christmas wreath and two cardboard cutout angels on the wall over the cash register.

Javier and Selma laughed, and Purp did, too. Betty just looked at the decorations.

"I'm so sick of Christmas," Purp said as the laughter died down. He said it mostly toward Betty, who still looked at the angels. "When January comes I just want it gone, all of it."

Javier, Betty, Purp, and Selma passed dishes and scooped food, sharing the three entrées they'd ordered between the four of them. They ate a little and talked before Betty got them back to business.

"So with the two investors I have who are interested," Betty said, "it isn't that much left to finance back against the lot to offset the additional expense of the general contractor."

"It seems like you're going to have plenty of money, though," Selma said. She slipped a shrimp between her lips with chopsticks.

"It seems like it, I know," Betty said, "but it's not a lot of cash compared to the operating expenses we forecast."

"But Purp says you're planning to have enough money on-hand to pay the bills for a year?" Selma said.

"Yeah," Betty said. "That's what it's going to take to keep it running."

"How do you know that?" Selma said.

"That's what everybody says," Betty said. "I've heard in a few different classes that's the main reason new businesses fail. Not enough cash on hand."

"It seems excessive," Selma said. "Isn't the business going to make enough profit to pay its own bills?"

"Eventually," Betty said. "But you can't count on it. Not for the first six months, anyway."

"So why don't you just have six months' worth of money available," Selma said. "That'll give you enough to pay a big chunk of this new huge expense of having to get a contractor to do the work now." Selma looked over at Purp. He could tell from the look she gave him she blamed him for now having to get a contractor. She was nervous when they'd built the house something like this would happen. Purp remembered telling her back then she seemed almost disappointed it had worked out for them to do that, because she'd seemed so sure something would go wrong.

"Because we want to be sure everything goes all right," Purp said. "We want to play it safe."

"If we become profitable before that, that's great," Betty said. "But the cash is going to give us the staying power we need to get things running well enough to turn a profit."

Purp slid a spring roll, a leftover from the appetizers, onto his plate. He squeezed the rubbery rice-noodle skin of it between the ends of his chopsticks. The spring roll felt like something that was born the way it was, not something put together by a person. He ate it in two bites. Purp forgot to dip it into the peanut sauce that came with it, even though for him that was the whole point of eating a spring roll, to get the sauce. He used his chopsticks to stab at a clump of white rice on his plate, breaking it up into smaller clumps, then breaking those, then breaking those until he was separating individual grains of rice which he nudged into a grid pattern, ranks and files.

"Who are these investors you have lined up," Selma said to Betty. "Do you even know them?" she said to Purp.

"I don't, no," Purp said.

"Are they reliable?" Selma said to Betty. "How do you know they even have the money?"

"Well, one is my uncle," Betty said. "And the other is my cousin."

"If we need the money," Purp said, "why can't we just finance more out of the lot?"

"You could," Betty said, "but I thought you wanted to avoid that as much as you could."

"Which is cheaper?" Selma said to Betty.

"It depends on how you look at it," Betty said.

"Which one costs less money than the other one?" Selma said.

"I know what cheaper means," Betty said. "But it depends on when you mean. And how you look at it. A bank loan is cheaper overall, if the business does well. But you have to start paying it back right away, as soon as you get it." Betty wound a rice noodle around her chopstick with a single flick of her wrist. She held onto it. "Which is the whole point, to have cash that first year to help with bills."

"We wouldn't have to pay the investors that first year?" Selma said.

"No. We wouldn't have to pay them back the first year," Betty said, "and after that their interest rate is lower since they'd get an ownership stake."

"An ownership stake?" Purp said. "We'd be giving them part of the business?"

"That's the deal they agreed to, yes," Betty said.

"So for the whole rest of the life of the business, they'd be coming around looking for money?" Purp said.

"Well, they'd be owners," Betty said.

"That sounds like a bad deal," Purp said. "I don't want the Vietnamese mafia sniffing around for money every week for the rest of time. I say bank loan."

"How much money are we talking about," Selma said.

Betty didn't answer. She seemed pre-occupied with the remnants of her Pad Thai, her face down toward her plate. The top of her forehead and the tips of her ears glowed red.

Purp was used to Betty fielding the financial questions, but she wasn't talking so he stepped in and told Selma how much they needed.

"Purp and I will kick in the rest," Selma said to the top of Betty's head.

Betty didn't look up.

Purp looked at Selma. He didn't have enough of his own money left to make up the difference Betty said they needed, not with paying the contractor. Selma could only mean that she was pitching in with her money, money she had since before she and Purp even met. She had money from her mother's insurance policy that she never let them touch, not for anything. Not even in the nineties when Purp could have tripled it, quadrupled it.

Betty still kept her eyes on her plate. Javier sat leaning back in his chair with his arms crossed high over his chest. He looked at Betty.

With all eyes on Betty, she looked up from her plate, her crisp black eyeliner blurred just a smudge under her left eye.

"Excuse me," Betty said. She slid her chair back and stood, taking her purse with her.

* * *

Guadalupe seemed like a ghost town the week of Spring Break. It felt to Purp like it was early on a Sunday morning, but he knew it was Wednesday, noon. He and Javier, and Betty, sat outside at a patio table. It was the first time they'd sat outside all season. Purp faced the street, and the car wash. He couldn't take his eyes off the place. It sat there exactly like he'd pictured it. He still had a hard time believing that the place he'd sketched out on his computer stood right across the street from him now, looking back across Guadalupe at Taco Cabana.

The café sat on the corner, with windows on Guadalupe and Powell, inviting walk-ins from either direction. The double front doors angled kitty-corner, pointing toward the center of the intersection, made it seem like cars stopped for the light at any of the four sides of the intersection were all looking at the front of the place.

The curvy wall around the car wash, the mason called it "serpentine," was a change over the original design and Purp thought it looked much more interesting. The mason said it was stronger like that, too, and at each point where the wall curved away from the sidewalk, Purp planned to plant a mesquite tree, or palo verde.

Purp liked how the serpentine wall echoed the sweep of the curved driveways in and out of the car wash. Purp had driven his truck through the curved entrance and exit twenty times before convincing himself the driveways weren't too tight to get through. Then he woke up one night in a panic that they were too narrow and tight again, so the next day he rented an Expedition from Enterprise and drove that through, too. It fit fine. That made him nervous the openings were too big, though, so then he walked to every point on the block from which he could see the car wash and he took a picture of the entrance and exit, to make sure he couldn't see anything inside from that angle.

Since it only just started to get warm and Purp hadn't yet had a chance to admire his work from the Taco Cabana patio, he had a hard time following the meeting. He tried to focus back in on what Betty told him.

"And after we pay for that," Betty said, "we're done with the general contractor. Yay!" she said. She clapped her hands noiselessly in front of her, twice.

"That worked out, right?" Javier said.

"It did," Purp said. "I wasn't crazy about paying the bills, but I actually doubt we'd hit June fifth if we'd have done it all ourselves."

"Do you think we still will, even with?" Javier said.

"I don't see why not," Purp said. "Do you?"

Javier shrugged. Betty shook her head.

"I mean, we still have two and a half months," Purp said. "I think we'll get it done."

"What happens if we don't?" Javier said.

"Then we don't," Purp said. "We're going to be somewhere near there, though." Purp looked away from the table again across at the car wash. "Look at it," he said. "It looks like it could open today if we had to."

"It does look awesome from here now," Javier said. "There's a lot to do though, right?"

"Speaking of that," Betty said, pressing what looked like the page down key on the laptop Purp had bought for her, "Marshall Electric is asking if we could give them their other half."

"I don't know," Purp said. "I don't really think so, no. They still haven't hung the track lights yet, and the bathroom fixtures. No, tell them we'll wait until it's done."

"But they say they can't hang the fixtures until the painters come, so it's not their delay," Betty said.

"They shouldn't have done any of the finish electrical before the painters come," Purp said. "No, we'll pay them when they finish the job."

"I don't think he's going to be that happy about that," Betty said. "Since it's not his fault we won't let him finish."

"No, they're fine with that," Purp said. "That's not unusual. How are the licenses coming, have you heard anything?"

"Food's all set," Betty said.

"That class was a bitch," Javier said.

"I know, huh?" Purp said. "I thought it was going to be like this blow-off thing, like traffic school or something."

"That exam was actually hard," Javier said.

"That was a lot of school for making nachos," Purp said.

"I'm actually afraid of chicken now, after that," Javier said.

"So food's all set, liquor is pending," Betty said.

"You haven't heard from them?" Purp said.

"Just that it's pending," Betty said. "I'm going to give them a call later today and see."

"I feel like chicken is this toxic substance, now," Javier said.

"It's like you need a Haz-Mat suit," Purp said.

"It's like that one Seinfeld when his dad has all these flashbacks –

"Speaking of TV shows," Betty said, talking over Javier. "You guys remember that one show on Spike TV? The one we saw at your house like around Thanksgiving? Dude. Man. Guy?"

"Of course we remember it," Javier said. "We watch it every week."

"I don't know if I mentioned this," Betty said, "but I emailed them a few weeks ago and told them what we're doing. I didn't think anything would happen, but a producer called me this morning and they're going to send that girl we saw out here to do a story on us this summer after we open, maybe in July."

Purp and Javier just sat and looked at Betty. Purp wasn't sure he'd heard right. He looked over at Javier who didn't seem to have gotten it, either.

"Beniko Kumi?" Javier said. "From D.M.G. ?"

"The Japanese girl, the reporter," Betty said.

"She's coming to do a story on us?" Purp said.

"On the car wash, yeah," Betty said.

Purp didn't say anything. Neither did Javier. Betty looked at them like maybe she did something wrong. Javier looked at Purp and opened his mouth. He leaned forward in his chair and put both hands on his knees, letting out a barking belly laugh so loud Purp was sure they must have been able to hear it inside Taco Cabana.

* * *

"I don't know why," Purp said. "I guess because it says 'Business' on it and she knows I'm starting a business?" Purp got into the left turn lane. He knew he'd be there a while until the light changed up ahead at the next intersection. He wondered why Best Buy didn't have a light by it so it was easier to get in and out.

"And why Titanic?" Javier said. "That just doesn't seem right. There's just no guy who would want that for a birthday present."

"Well –

"That's just kind of cold, right?" Javier said. "To give a guy Titanic?"

"That I actually do understand," Purp said.

"Is it her favorite movie or something?" Javier said.

"Well, it's actually one of my favorite movies," Purp said. "I'm returning it because I already have it."

"Oh," Javier said. "Oh."

The light up ahead turned red and the traffic thinned down enough for Purp to make his left. Purp felt his phone vibrate in his pocket.

"Yeah," Purp said, "so if I didn't already have it on DVD for like the last five years already, it would have been a pretty decent gift. He found a spot near the back of the lot. His phone vibrated again to tell him someone had left a voicemail. "Let me see who this is." He slipped the phone from his Jeans. It was Betty.

"It is a pretty good movie though, right?" Javier said. "It's a good story."

"Yeah. I'm going to see what she wanted," Purp said. He called Betty back. He got out of the truck while he was talking to her. Purp grabbed a plastic bag from the space behind his seat, the bag with the birthday gifts from Selma he was returning, the Titanic DVD and some business software.

Purp and Javier walked toward Best Buy while Purp talked to Betty. They got up to the front of the store but Purp stopped, staying out front to finish talking to Betty. Javier stayed with him.

"All right . . . OK . . . OK, thanks," Purp said. "No, it's not your fault. OK, thanks. By."

“You got your receipt?” Javier said.

“I do,” Purp said. “I even have the presents this time.” It was the second time Purp and Javier had been to a Best Buy that day. The first time he’d forgotten his gifts.

“What did Betty want?” Javier said. “Is she still coming tonight?”

“Yeah,” Purp said. “She had some kind of bad news. We didn’t get the liquor license.”

“Oh, fuck,” Javier said. “That’s not good, right? What are we going to do?”

“Well, it’s not that bad,” Purp said. “We weren’t actually denied it, but Betty called the guy who sent her the letter and he said that from the documentation she sent him, he can’t quite picture what the business is going to be.”

“What do you mean he can’t picture it?” Javier said.

“He was telling her he was kind of confused whether or not it was a strip club,” Purp said.

“Oh, that is bad,” Javier said.

“So he’s going to have to do a physical inspection after we open,” Purp said. “She said he gave us a provisional license –

“So we can serve then, until he does the physical inspection?” Javier said.

“No, actually,” Purp said. “The provisional is that everything is done and in the computer, ready to go as if we had the liquor license. But before he actually issues the certificate, he has to come over.”

“So what the fuck good is that?” Javier said.

“It’s faster. Betty said he told her he’d be there within two weeks of when we open, and if we pass then we’ll have the certificate within five days,” Purp said.

“So no six months again,” Javier said.

“No,” Purp said. Purp and Javier walked in through the electric doors. A man at the front of the store put a pink tag on the two items in Purp’s bag. There wasn’t any wait at the customer service counter.

“Hello guys,” the girl at the counter said. “Can I help you?” The half-inch gap between the girl’s tight blue golf shirt and super-tight khakis caught Purp’s eye. He guessed that wasn’t part of the uniform. Her name tag said “Clarissa.” Purp liked the way her khakis stretched over her ass and thighs but then flared out below her knee. He couldn’t see her shoes but he thought she’d be wearing Vans.

“Hello, Clarissa,” Purp said. He tried not to sound at all like Anthony Hopkins. He figured she was sick of that. He also thought there was a decent chance it wasn’t her name at all, and that she just grabbed the nametag out of a basket they have out back. Her over-dyed straight black hair and maroon lipstick made Purp feel like she might have an edge to her, somebody who might choose a "Clarissa" nametag just for the effect of it, or the irony. He wondered what kind of clothes she normally wore. He was worried he sounded like he was trying to sound like Anthony Hopkins when he said, "Hello, Clarissa."

"You have a return?" Clarissa said. "Or an exchange?" She sounded more perky than Purp expected given her mildly Goth look.

"I'd like to exchange this stuff," Purp said, "and then just pay the difference to get a GPS receiver."

"OK," Clarissa said. "The software is fine because it isn't opened at all, but I can't do an exchange for the DVD unless it's for the exact same item. Was it defective?"

"No, I didn't even play it," Purp said. "I do want to exchange it, though, just for something different."

"I'm sorry I can't do that on the DVD because it's been opened," Clarissa said.

"But it's not even played," Purp said.

"But it's opened," Clarissa said. "See?" She showed Purp where he'd cut the security tape along the edge with his Leatherman when he opened it on the bed the morning of his birthday.

"Well, I opened it, yeah," Purp said. "But I have the receipt for everything."

"If the DVD is opened it's not returnable," Clarissa said. "Unless you exchange it for the exact same DVD, like if it was scratched or something."

"I did open it," Purp said. "But Clarissa, you strike me as the kind of girl who has bent a rule or two in your time, am I right?"

Clarissa smiled. She pivoted behind the counter, standing on one foot.

"Am I right about that?" Purp said.

"Yes," Clarissa said. She tilted her chin down by an angle Purp could just barely notice. Three or four degrees, if that, keeping her eyes on him.

"And I know this place has screwed you over. They give you shifts all weekend on short notice when you have concert tickets, stuff like that?" Purp said.

"That is all very true," Clarissa said. "But –

"It's just a matter of pushing a couple of keys for me," Purp said. "You're a smart girl, I can tell –

"Oh, please," Clarissa said. She laughed. She kept her eyes on Purp.

"OK, maybe your grades aren't the best, but I know you know some code, some way around, to get that computer to let me exchange this DVD," Purp said.

"I actually don't," Clarissa said. She made a sad face. "And it is opened. Which means you could have bought it, watched it, and are now just returning it. That would be stealing."

"I did open it. But not to watch it," Purp said. "My wife gave it to me for my birthday and I thought she was playing a trick on me."

"She wasn't?" Clarissa said. "She was actually giving you Titanic for your birthday?"

"See what I'm working with here?" Purp said. "I mean, giving a guy Titanic for his birthday?"

"That is kind of sad," Clarissa said. She wrinkled her nose and slid her mouth to one side.

"I thought she'd done like this elaborate joke," Purp said. "I thought she bought a different DVD and just really carefully took the security stickers off. I thought she switched them."

"But it was really Titanic, huh?" Clarissa said.

"It was," Purp said. "It was."

"How sad for you," Clarissa said.

"You know what I thought she put in it?" Purp said.

"What?" Clarissa said. "About a Boy?"

"No," Purp said. "No. I thought she did a switch on me," Purp lowered his voice and leaned over the counter a little even though the store was pretty much empty. "I thought she put a porn DVD in there to surprise me."

Clarissa laughed. "Well," she said, "there's always that drawing scene. That's pretty hot."

"That is, actually," Purp said. "But it's not what I thought was in there."

"That's a sucky birthday," Clarissa said. "But I can't return an opened DVD."

"You could," Purp said.

"I can't," Clarissa said. "But I can exchange it for exactly the same thing."

"But," Purp said. "If I wanted the same thing, I'd just keep this one."

"Or the one you already have," Javier said.

"But listen," Clarissa said. "If you exchange it for the exact same thing, then your new one will be unopened."

"How will I know if it has porn in it if I don't open it?" Purp said.

Clarissa laughed. "The receipt I give back to you will have it marked on it that you exchanged it. And it'll show in the computer if they look it up by your credit card number. But if you lose your receipt, say, and take the new DVD back to a different Best Buy, and you don't give them the same credit card to look it up, then they'll give you store credit for it. Which is what you want, right?"

"Exactly," Purp said.

* * *

Purp and Javier straightened folding chairs around a card table. They had four chairs and a table in the office and four more chairs set up in a row in the café area. They figured they'd do the interviews in the office, and the girls could wait out in the café. The place wasn't painted and the electrical work wasn't completely done, but they thought it would be more professional to have the interviews right there at the carwash than at Taco Cabana or Purp's house.

Purp moved the table closer to the window. Then he and Javier straightened all the chairs around it again. They'd gone through this four times, moving the table, straightening the chairs. Moving three chairs in a row on one side of the table, then putting them back one on each side of the table.

"Do you think it's light enough in here?" Purp said.

"Oh, definitely. That window is bright. You have those work lights anyway, right?" Javier said.

"I do," Purp said. "Do you think I need them? I have plenty of time to get them."

"I think it's fine with just the window," Javier said. "Should you put your laptop on the table?"

"Oh, yeah," Purp said. "That's a good idea. That'll make it look more professional."

"Plus then you can put the names in the computer," Javier said.

Purp stepped outside to get his laptop from the truck. When he came back in, Javier had moved the table back from the window two feet and straightened the chairs.

"You know what we should have done?" Purp said. "We should have taken pictures."

"That would be awesome," Javier said. "That would be so awesome." Javier sat down in one of the folding chairs. "When are the first ones getting here?"

"Betty is giving two of them rides," Purp said. "They are supposed to be here at noon."

"Those are the two she knows?" Javier said.

"Yes," Purp said.

"Those are the two Asian ones, right?" Javier said.

"I didn't know they were Asian," Purp said.

"I think Betty said they were," Javier said.

"I don't remember her saying that," Purp said.

"Maybe it was when you weren't there?" Javier said.

"Maybe," Purp said.

"Let's put the table over here instead," Purp said. He slid the table to a different corner, closer to the window. Almost the whole north wall of the office he and Javier were going to share was a window looking out on the car wash bays. Purp loved the view from the office. Even without a car wash going on it looked nice with the curved walls and the trees making what looked more like a courtyard than a topless car wash. The view of the mountains to the north looked better than Purp thought it would, too. He thought the wall was going to block more of the mountain view than it did.

Purp and Javier arranged the chairs so that the girl being interviewed would sit with her back to the window on one side of the table and the three of them would sit on the other side of the table in a row.

Purp looked at the setup. He stood in the middle of the office on the newly laid saltillo tile with his arms crossed. The tile and the block walls made the room echo.

"If she sits there," Purp said, "it's so bright out we won't be able to see her face good."

"That's true," Javier said. He walked over to the window. "Can you see my face from there?"

"Not so good," Purp said. "And that's kind of the whole point."

"Not the whole point," Javier said. "There are at least a couple of other points I'm going to be checking out."

Purp and Javier laughed.

"Speaking of that," Purp said. "I just kind of assumed we were not, but . . . are we actually auditioning them today?"

"You mean like having them wash a car?" Javier said.

"No, but, I mean," Purp said. "Are we like going to be . . . actually getting a look at them today?"

“Topless?” Javier said.

“Yeah,” Purp said.

Purp and Javier shuffled the table and chairs and laptop back away from the window, setting everything up with one chair on each side of the table.

“Are we?” Javier said.

“I don’t know,” Purp said. “I guess it makes sense?”

“I guess,” Javier said. “I hadn’t thought of that.” He sat down again, knocking his leg into one of the other chairs so it wasn’t straight.

Purp straightened the crooked chair.

“But with Betty here, though?” Javier said.

“What? She’s going to be here every day,” Purp said. “And they’re going to be right there.” Purp nodded toward the three car wash bays, staggered and at forty-five degree angles to the window.

“What are we going to be like, ‘OK, your work history looks good, could you please take off your shirt for us?’” Javier said. “Holy fuck.”

“I don’t know,” Purp said. “Did you ever watch those casting call videos they have on the Playboy website? Like when they go to Boston or Dallas or wherever looking for CyberGirls?”

“Yeah, I guess, right?” Javier said.

“Yeah. That’s how they say it, isn’t it?” Purp said. “They take a couple of pictures, then they say like, ‘OK, now we’d like to get a couple of shots with your top off, are you comfortable with that?’”

“We need a camera,” Javier said. “How can you say that without a camera?”

“I know,” Purp said. “It won’t work without a camera. The first few pictures are just to get them comfortable.”

“You need to go get your camera,” Javier said.

“And my work lights,” Purp said. “It’s not bright enough in here.”

* * *

Selma held a fabric swatch next to a paint sample card in front of the Home Depot, looking at the colors in the sunlight. Betty stood beside her and moved Selma’s wrist, looking from the fabric to the paint card and back to the fabric. Purp stood in the shade by a hot dog cart with Javier. It was pushing a hundred degrees out and Purp didn’t have little shorts on like the girls. Javier ate a hot-dog. He didn’t seem like he could care any less about what was going on.

"It's too similar," Betty said. "If that's the color for the side wall, then it's going to be too much like the fabric for the couch."

"No it's not," Selma said. "It's not too similar at all."

"Is that the couch sample?" Betty said.

"No, that's the one for the benches by the door," Selma said. "This is the couch one." She dug in her purse for a different fabric sample. She pulled it out, with a third piece of cloth, and held all three like a fan in one hand while she moved the paint card against each one.

"OK," Betty said. "That makes more sense."

"I think it's great," Selma said.

"It looks better in the sunlight than it did in there," Betty said.

"It'll coordinate well with the way the purple on the outside came out," Selma said.

"I don't know," Betty said, "I was kind of hoping not to have so much purple inside. I was hoping it would be more earth tones like the Starbucks where Javier works."

"Me too," Purp said. "I didn't quite picture such a purple theme inside, too."

"It's going to be great like this," Selma said. "It's going to look very regal. You'll see."

"I do like how the outside came out," Javier said. "I didn't know how that was going to look, but it actually looks pretty good, right?"

"I like it," Purp said.

"OK then," Selma said, "so we'll go with these."

The four of them went back into Home depot to order the paint. They didn't have to wait for it to be mixed since the painters were going to pick it up from there in the morning. When they were done they didn't waste time getting back to Selma's car. They packed into the Focus, girls in front and guys in back. The heat from the inside of the car choked Purp when he sat down. They'd forgotten to put the sunshield up when they went in.

"They should be just about done," Betty said once Selma had made her right onto Mission.

"Done?" Purp said. "I thought they were coming at two?"

"No," Betty said, "they said they should be done around two."

"They've been there this whole time?" Purp said.

"I guess," Betty said. "They should be just about done, anyway."

"That's too bad," Purp said. "It would have been good to be there to make sure everything goes OK."

"Well," Betty said, "we'll see it now."

"I guess we will," Purp said.

Selma got them across Harrison and onto Guadalupe without any trouble. The traffic on Guadalupe slowed them down though. As they worked down toward Powell Purp caught a glimpse of his purple building.

"I think you can see it better now that it's painted," Purp said.

"I think so, too," Selma said.

"It's bright," Betty said.

"No airplane is going to run into it by accident," Javier said.

"I don't think one would, anyway," Purp said. "Even if it was still gray."

"Well it definitely won't now," Javier said.

"I don't see a crane up," Purp said. "They must have the sign up already."

"I can see it on the side," Betty said. "It's up."

Purp squinted to see the new sign. He caught a glimpse of it but a truck rolled beside them in the left lane and blocked his view.

"I wish I knew they were going to be there so early," Purp said. "I would have been there."

The truck fell back behind them. Purp could see the sign.

"It looks nice," Selma said. "Very nice. Just like the picture you made on the computer, Purp."

"That's awesome," Javier said. "It's huge."

"The color came out nice," Betty said.

The sign did look nice, but something about it didn't strike Purp as right. Selma made a left into the café lot and Purp re-read the sign as she turned.

"It's not right," Purp said. "They messed it up."

They got out of the car and all walked back to where they could see the sign best.

"What's not right?" Betty said.

"Look what it says," said Javier.

"Purple Topless Carwash," Betty said.

"Exactly," Purp said. "That's not the name of the business, remember?"

"Fuck," said Javier.

"Purple's Topless Carwash, Betty," Purp said. "Purple's."

"That's not what I told them," Betty said. "I swear I told them Purple's."

"This is why I wanted to be here," Purp said. "You can't just plan to have someone come do something like this and then go away."

"You have contractors here all the time," Betty said. "You aren't here every single time they come."

"But not something like this," Purp said. "I thought you told me they were going to be here at two, not be finished at two."

"Well, I think it actually looks better like this anyway," Betty said. "It's easier to say."

"But it's not the name of the business," Purp said. "This isn't the right sign. Call them up, Betty, this isn't acceptable. Do you have the number?"

"It's inside on the paperwork," Betty said.

"Go in and get it," Purp said. "This isn't what I paid for."

Betty trotted across the lot toward the front door in her thick-soled sandals, her black hair fanning and flopping back and forth behind her. She straightened her tube top with both thumbs before she got her keys out of her purse. She opened the door and popped back out after only a few seconds.

Betty walked back across the lot toward them holding papers, her head down.

"I'm sorry," Betty said. "I wrote it wrong or something." She held the paperwork from the sign company out for Purp to see. There was a grid for her to write in on the form, one block for each letter of the sign. She'd printed "Purple Topless Carwash" neatly in the grid.

"Oh, man," Purp said.

"They're going to say it's our fault," Selma said.

"It is easier to say, though," Betty said.

"Will you stop with that?" Purp said.

"But it is," Betty said. "I'm sorry, though. It's just so much easier to say that way I guess it stuck in my head like that." She took the paperwork back from Purp. "Plus, it's nicer if you wanted to sell it. Or franchise."

* * *

"There should be some place for them to sit," Purp said. "Like an awning or something." Purp stood in the office, leaning against his desk. Javier sat at the chair behind his own desk.

Betty poked her head in the door.

"Front door's open," Betty said. "Are you sure the gate's open?"

"It's open," Purp said. "Back gate, too."

"Why aren't you in the kitchen," Betty said to Javier.

"There's nobody in the café," Javier said.

"Don't you have prep to do?" Betty said.

"It's done," Javier said. "I'm ready."

Purp looked out at the girls. Twelve girls. They looked uncomfortable with nothing to do. They stood in their sandals and purple shorts, wearing white T-shirts and tank tops with the PTC logo on them in Purple. Most of them tied their shirts in a knot behind them, exposing their bellies and pulling the fabric tight across their breasts. One girl, Tara, seemed to be their leader. The alpha girl. She showed up with the neck of her T-shirt cut down so low it was hardly doing her any good at all as a shirt. The girls liked the shirts, and they liked how Purp had four different ones so they could pick. They grumbled a little at the last minute about the shorts, though, they weren't crazy about the way they were cut. Purp worried earlier that half of them were going to flake out altogether, but he insisted on the shorts. Now they milled around the wash bays in clusters, reminding Purp of the ring girls he used to see at the high school car wash next door. They shuffled around with their arms crossed in front of their chests. Purp thought they looked fantastic even with their tops on. But he wished they had somewhere to sit, something to do while they waited.

It happened. 9:04 am. A black Ford Escape rolled in through the curved entryway.

"We got one!" Purp yelled. "We got one! Betty, come here."

"That's our first one, right?" Javier said. He stood and leaned on his desk, too, like Purp.

The Escape crept in slowly, as if the driver were trying to figure out how things worked. Tara, the alpha girl, reacted to the Escape first. She put her hands over her head and waved the driver toward the first wash bay, shaking her ass while she waved both hands over her. As the driver inched toward her bay, Tara walked toward the SUV. In the instant since the truck arrived Tara changed from an antsy-looking college-girl walking around with no place to put her arms into a walking fire hose of sexual energy. She fluffed her curly black hair with both hands and she walked with a liquid ripple that ran from her hips to her shoulders with every step she took. She leaned into the open driver's window, her knees straight, legs together, her hands more than shoulder-width apart on the door. Purp couldn't see but he could imagine the way she leaned that the driver was getting a serious eyeful of her C-cup breasts pulled together tight by the knot in her shirt so that they bubbled up through the deep V-slit she'd made in her PTC shirt.

"She looks good out there," Betty said from behind Purp. "She has the approach down good."

Money changed hands. 9:06 am. That was their first dollar in Tara's hands. Their first twenty dollars. Maybe more, the way Tara leaned in through that window. She carried the money over her head toward the slot in the wall and turned once, a full slow turn around as if dancing to music Purp couldn't hear. She slipped the bills into the slot.

"Woo hoo," Tara said, loud enough Purp heard it through the window like she was standing in the office. She pulled a chain next to the money slot and rang the bell, loud.

"Woo hoo," the girls chanted back to her all at once. It was an organized call and response, like they'd planned it out beforehand.

"Girls, come on," they all chanted, Tara included. They clapped three times.

Purp loved it. He hadn't coached them to do that, but he loved it. He figured Tara must have organized the chant and it couldn't have been more perfect. They sounded like cheerleaders chanting that, and Purp couldn't even imagine how he hadn't thought of telling them to do that.

Melanie and Elizabeth squeezed their hoses onto the sides of the Escape while Tara took her time walking toward the front of the SUV, stopping wide-legged just far enough from the truck's front so that the driver could probably see her perfectly from hair to sandals. She slipped her fingertips under the tightly pulled hem of her T-shirt and peeled it up over her head, tossing it behind her toward Purp's window.

"Woo hoo," the girls chanted together.

The horn on the Escape blew, frantic. Purp saw the driver pushing the passenger's hand away from the wheel. They looked like college guys, with a University sticker above their rearview mirror.

Then it was one by one, domino-style, the shirts fell. Purp wasn't even prepared for how good it would look. He thought it up, the whole set-up, but it wasn't any preparation at all for what it would actually look like with the truck there, and the hoses and the curvy-walled courtyard with the trees, and the tits. Everywhere, the tits. Purp couldn't believe how good the girls did. It unleashed something in them, it seemed like, when Tara rang that bell and called them to action. They didn't look like girls at work, they had a look on them like the girls did on the Spring Break videos advertised late at night. They seemed to be competing for the chance to work the driver's and passenger's windows, leaning their wet chests into the glass. Watching them soaking that Ford Escape Purp had a problem growing in his Jeans. He had to sit down behind his desk.

Javier sat, too.

"They look good," Betty said. "Real good." Betty stood with her face six inches from the window, her hands on her hips, the purple on her nails the exact same shade as her purple leather pants and her four-inch plastic hoop earrings. She wore a PTC tank top, too, like the washers. She looked out at her girls like a mother hen even though she was their same age. "That's twelve girls on one car, though. We need more cars in here."

"You know what I forgot?" Purp said. "I can't believe I forgot."

"What's that?" Betty said.

Even against the backdrop of twelve wet topless girls Purp liked looking at Betty better.

Javier looked at Purp.

"I forgot sign girls," Purp said.

"Oh my God," Javier said. "The sign girls." Javier scrambled to his feet.

Purp hadn't expected Javier to jump up like that, but they'd all been a little touchy the past week leading up to opening. Purp heard Javier digging around in the storage closet on the other side of the office wall.

"Here we go," Javier said. He had a stack of fluorescent purple poster board they bought at Walgreen's on Wednesday, thinking they'd use it to make signs with. Betty had said a few weeks ago that they should have nice signs made up, professional-looking signs, but Purp and Javier liked the idea of doing it old-school, with signs like the high-school girls used to make. They thought the image of those hand-written signs would appeal to the men driving by, evoking the fantasies they might have had before driving by other car washes.

Purp, Javier, and Betty made three signs. They thought they'd take three girls off the courtyard and put them on signs out front, leaving three girls per wash bay. The Escape drove off clean while they made signs. The shirts came back on and the energy changed again. Everything slowed down outside. As they finished the three signs, though, a gray Nissan Xterra rolled in and the process started all over. The bell, the chant, the clapping, and the shirts came off again. The first time was no fluke. If anything, the girls got it down smoother and sexier the second time around. Purp realized they had no music, either. He'd have a good system installed to give them something to move to.

Betty gathered up the signs and clopped out to the courtyard in her clunky sandals. She pulled Rachel, J.J., and Nicole off washing. The girls toweled themselves off while Betty talked to them. They took their time getting their shirts back on, too. They didn't seem self-conscious at all in front of Betty. Betty and the sign girls walked together out the exit driveway.

A guy's voice, a youngish sounding guy, called through the office doorway.

"Are you guys open yet, or no?" The guy said. He stuck his head into the office but he didn't look at Purp or Javier. He had on a backwards University ball cap and he kept his eyes on the window, glued to the action.

"Oh, fuck," Javier said. "The kitchen."

"Yeah, we're open," Purp said. He stood up. He had completely forgotten about the café. "Sure we're open, sorry. This is our first day open. Come on, we'll get you squared away."

"I've been waiting," the guy said. "I walk by here every day and I could see what you were doing."

"Well come on, let's get you something to eat," Purp said.

"OK, hang on," the guy said. He walked over to the front doors, opening one of them. He leaned his head out and called to somebody Purp couldn't see. "Yeah, they're open," the guy said. "Let's roll."

Two more guys came around the corner. They walked in through the door the first one held for them. Three café customers already. But they kept coming around the corner now, the guys did, a group of them all together. They streamed in and set their backpacks down like they knew where they were going. It actually seemed like a little bit of a scramble for the seats closest to the glass wall. The three became five, seven, ten, twelve. Twelve guys all at once. No, fifteen. The door closed behind the fifteenth customer. Fifteen guys at once for the first party. They staked out their seats with backpacks and sweatshirts. One of them, a skinny tan guy in red basketball shorts who couldn't have been twenty-one, just set his ball cap on a chair right by the window so nobody would get his spot. The guys clumped up at the register, some of them seemed torn between reading the menu on the wall and watching the action through the glass. The guys gasped and then laughed when Elizabeth, soaking wet now, leaned her breasts against the driver's window of a red Acura RSX. "Oh yeah," one of them said. "That's what I'm talking about, right there," a different one said. A third one just stood in the middle of the café and barked like a dog. Nobody seemed to be in a hurry to order their food.

Purp got behind the register and Javier settled himself in behind the food prep station. All three wash lanes had cars in them, three girls to a car. The view of the action was stunning, even from behind the register on the opposite side of the dining area from the glass wall. There was not a bad seat in the house. Purp thought it looked much better with the three lanes all washing. He didn't know where to look first.

Purp realized he hadn't seen Betty in a while and then he spotted her. She was out in the courtyard by the entrance driveway chatting it up with a customer in a Navigator waiting for a wash bay to open up. It looked like she was standing there taking money and directing the flow. Man, she looked good out there with her hair up in a top-sided ponytail and her purple leather pants. She looked like she was running the show. Purp wondered if there was a chance she'd wash, in a pinch.

"Can I have a, uh, Buffalo nachos and medium Dr Pepper?"

"Sure can," Purp said. "That's our specialty." Purp called over to Javier, "Buffalo."

"Got it," Javier said.

Purp got the Dr Pepper. He gave the kid a large for being the first customer. "Four-fifty," Purp said. "Even." Purp had insisted that the prices be even, including tax. He tore off a receipt and handed it to the customer. "Your number is at the top. Yours is one hundred, our first customer. You might want to save that."

"I'll have that, too," the next guy said. "with a Pepsi though."

"Another Buffalo," Purp said.

"Got it," Javier said.

Purp took more orders. Another group of five or eight shuffled in while Purp was working on the original fifteen. He couldn't count them anymore as they came in, but he knew he was pushing his thirty chairs. The fire marshal said his max was sixty-five, but Purp knew only thirty could sit.

Javier grunted and huffed with all the food, slopping beans on the prep counter and knocking over a steam pan full of black olives. Purp looked at the flat-panel touch-screen monitor over the food station. It was showing twenty open orders. The computer ran software Purp wrote. He tapped at the screen and got it to sort by the items ordered, not by order number. He saw a group on the list of five people who had all ordered bean burritos and nothing else. He slid over to help Javier and knocked out all five bean burritos at once.

"Five, eight, eleven, twelve . . . and fourteen," Purp called. Bean burritos. Next he made a batch of five Buffalos assembly line style, too. He cranked out ten orders in like three minutes that way. That knocked it down so it was reasonable for Javier. He poked at the screen to re-sort by order number and went back to working the register.

Purp glanced up and saw all three wash bays wet. The girls worked it hard. Lacy danced in front of a little Ford Ranger, swaying her hips to a slow beat with her hands over her head, wet blonde hair stuck to her back. She wore a straw cowboy hat with the brim heavily rolled, dipping down in front of her eyes. Purp figured it belonged to one of the two guys in the truck. The two of them in the Ranger clapped their hands and laughed, dancing, too. Purp wondered if maybe Lacy danced to music coming from the Ranger. He needed a sound system, absolutely needed it. That was dumb not to have it. He'd get Bose outdoor speakers put in all around the courtyard, eight or ten of them, with a head unit and CD changer in a weatherproof box outside so the girls could put in CDs or hook up their iPods and play whatever they wanted. Whatever would get them moving like that, Purp thought, was what it would sound like out there. They obviously wanted to dance.

Purp saw Betty with her head back, laughing probably, leaning at the open window of a Toyota Supra. The Supra looked good for twenty years old. So did Betty. It occurred to Purp he didn't actually know how old Betty was, but he guessed maybe she was about that, now that he thought about it. She seemed older. He always thought of people younger than him as being his same age, but it struck him that Betty was barely older than the car she leaned on. Behind the Supra Purp saw two cars waiting. Because of the curved driveway and wall he couldn't see any further back than that, but the way the bays had been continuously full, he wondered if the cars were backed up onto Guadalupe.

Purp took orders, Javier made food. The tray for twenties had a good fat stack in it and Purp wondered if Betty put enough change in the safe to get them through the day. The mob in the café just got thicker throughout the morning. Some of the original fifteen were still inside but Purp didn't care people were lingering. The café concept was that people would want to hang out a while, maybe order something twice.

A police man inched his way in through the crowd of mostly college-aged guys. He looked like he was trying not to bump anybody with his equipment as he threaded through up to Purp. The wide officer did a good job of not stepping on anybody. Purp knew the policeman wasn't in the café for the food. Or the girls.

"Hello," the officer said to Purp. His nameplate said Serna on it.

"Hi," Purp said.

"Whoa," Serna said. "Wow, nice view." He looked out the glass wall. "That's not something you see every day."

Purp and Serna laughed.

"Well," Serna said. "I guess you do." He gave Purp a look that Purp thought said, "lucky bastard."

"Starting today," Purp said.

"Listen, do you think I could speak with the manager here," Serna said. "Is he or she available?"

"I'm the owner," Purp said. "How can I help you?"

"I know you're just getting started here today," Serna said. "But there's a little bit of a problem out on Guadalupe."

"What's going on? Are the girls OK out there?" Purp said. He got a sinking feeling like maybe one of them got hit by a car or something. He all of a sudden wished he'd never sent them out.

"They're fine where they are," Serna said. "You can get a permit for them to be there on the median, actually, but that's no big deal. You'll want it at some point."

"Oh, OK," Purp said. He liked Serna. "Sure, I'd like to get that because they really helped once they went out there."

"I bet they did," Serna said. "Have you been out there to see them? They're working those signs for you, my friend."

"I haven't had a chance," Purp said.

"But anyway, your traffic is backing up onto Guadalupe," Serna said. "Which actually isn't something you can be cited for, but it's backing up into the intersection. I'm going to have to call a traffic officer to wave people off your line so it doesn't block the intersection. Is there something internally you can do to accommodate more cars?"

* * *

Purp sipped a beer and watched the traffic flow from a patio table at Taco Cabana. It looked much smoother now. Much better than last Saturday. It hadn't been a problem so much during the week but they had done a steady business every day. The overflow concept kept Guadalupe clear. Purp liked how the cars in the overflow area had a good view of the girls, too, while they were waiting. It gave the customers a better value. The café lot was full. Purp couldn't do anything about that. Twelve guys baked in the sun outside the front doors, waiting to get into the waiting area. They needed an awning or something to keep them in the shade.

Purp set his beer down and turned to look back toward the counter. He'd seen Gina walk into Taco Cabana and he wasn't sure whether or not she saw him. She was hard to miss in her cutoff denim shorts with the pockets longer than the raggedy hems, but she hadn't waved or smiled on her way in like she usually did if she saw him. Gina was just paying at the register, getting her card back from the cashier. She wore a backless white apron top held in place only by a halter strap tied around her neck and another ribbon-thin strap tied around her ribs. It looked like she'd gotten a tattoo on her back since Purp noticed last. Purp thought he saw it poking up out of the top of her low-rise shorts, on her lower back. It was hard to tell from the patio.

The sound of a car horn, long and angry, distracted Purp. His eyes darted toward the PTC entrance. He was worried traffic had backed up again onto Guadalupe. It was a false alarm, though. Purp couldn't tell who had blown the horn, but it didn't seem to have anything to do with the carwash. Probably somebody didn't notice the green left turn arrow.

"Hey there," Gina said. She'd come out onto the patio holding a basket of chips and a soda, Purp figured it was Diet Dr Pepper. She smelled like cocoa butter or vanilla. Her shorts were crazy. The frayed hems on them squeezed her tight-looking thighs so high up it looked more like she had on a bikini bottom than cut-offs. The golden brown skin on her thighs shimmered with what looked like a faintly glittery lotion or oil she must have just put on in the car, it looked so freshly applied. The pockets sticking out longer than the shorts were at the same time ridiculously trashy looking and overwhelmingly alluring. Purp had just come from his office a half-hour ago, his office with an almost floor to ceiling window looking out onto twelve sudsy mostly-naked girls but seeing Gina standing with those shorts right near his face it was like he hadn't seen a woman in months.

"Hi, Gina," Purp said.

"Are you busy?" Gina said.

"No, I'm just checking out the traffic," Purp said. "You want to sit down?"

"Sure," Gina said. She arranged her chips and drink and purse at the seat next to Purp. She scraped the metal chair across the brick patio and sat down.

Gina crossed those brown glimmery thighs. The shorts were cut so high it was more like a thong underneath than shorts.

"Did you buy those," Purp said, "or make them?"

"What?" Gina said.

"Your shorts," Purp said.

"You don't like my shorts?" Gina said, making a motion like she was trying to pull them down, but there was just so little of them it wasn't any use.

"Oh," Purp said. "I like your shorts. I like them . . . a little too much. Did you cut them like that or is that how they came?"

“This is how they came,” Gina said. “They’re just from Target.”

“I think I might get those for the girls then,” Purp said. “That could be our new uniform bottom. We have these purple hot-pants now, like Hooters girl shorts, but they’re kind of cheesy. Some of the girls have been wearing their own bottoms.”

“I noticed you guys were open now,” Gina said. “I haven’t been in yet, but I went over one day with some friends. It was so crowded we couldn’t get in.”

“You came by?” Purp said. “Are you serious?”

“Of course,” Gina said. “It’s like the place right now. Everybody’s been trying to get in. I went with three girls and they told us it would be like an hour for a table for us.”

“It was just the four of you?” Purp said.

“Hell yeah,” Gina said. “No boys allowed.” She laughed. “One of my girlfriends knows Alyssa, do you know her?”

“Of course I know her,” Purp said. “I know all the girls. I hired them.”

“We wanted to watch her work,” Gina said. “She is a popular girl these days, let me tell you.”

“Yeah?” Purp said.

“Her coolness rating,” Gina said, “through the roof.” She pointed up with her thumbs. “T. T. R.”

“Have you talked to her?” Purp said. “Does she like it?”

“I don’t know her, only through Emily,” Gina said. “But Emily says Alyssa loves it. Loves. It. She doesn’t have to go tanning anymore, every single guy knows who she is now, and she’s taking home like a hundred and fifty a shift in tips, average.”

“I’m glad she likes it,” Purp said.

“Loves. It.” Gina said. “I hear there’s a waitlist now, huh?”

“Well, it’s just like first come first serve,” Purp said.

“No, for girls,” Gina said. “For washers.”

“There is?” Purp said. “Betty didn’t mention that. She’s the one who handles the administrative stuff. We haven’t had to hire any new yet.”

“That hot Asian chick I see you in here with sometimes?” Gina said.

“That’s the one,” Purp said. “She didn’t mention there’s a waitlist.”

“Hell yeah,” Gina said. “I’m on it.”

“Really?” Purp said.

“Really. I went over there on Saturday, after the first week but –

“Gina, you don’t need to be on the waitlist,” Purp said.

“The Asian chick, Betty, she told me –

"I don't care what she said, Gina," Purp said. "That's my name on the sign there, sort of. If you want to join the crew, you can walk across the street with me right now and you're on the crew."

* * *

"Do you really like that guy?" Purp said. It was a Wednesday morning and two bays were wet. Not bad at all. Six girls washing, just right. One car waiting with Guadalupe clear. Purp was learning how to staff better now that he had more numbers to work with.

"Brad?" Javier said.

"She is so freaking hot it's not even funny," Purp said. He watched Gina dance in front of a hardtop BMW Z3. The girls took turns being front dancer. Front dancer was their favorite. The bass beat rocked in through the glass from the Bose system that went up last week.

Purp stood with his arms crossed in front of the office window. Javier sat on his desk looking out, too.

"I still can't believe you got her to wash," Javier said. "Every day she works I can't believe that is the same girl we used to watch out there."

Gina leaned over the hood of the BMW, using a move Tara invented. She turned her ass to the hood. Purp thought Gina had the best looking breasts of any of the twenty-five girls on the payroll.

"We used to go nuts just seeing her in a bikini top," Purp said. "Did you interview him?"

"Brad?" Javier said. "No."

"It doesn't seem like he knows what he's doing," Purp said. "At all."

"Betty liked him because he's part of the regulars," Javier said. "She recruited him. She thought it would be decent for the hang-out concept, kind of like how the girls have their friends come in to watch them."

"Now that is something I did not expect," Purp said. "Not at all. Hot girls on both sides of the glass. Hot girls other than Betty inside."

Purp and Javier laughed.

"But I don't understand how you didn't interview him," Purp said. "It's café ops. It's your lane."

"I know," Javier said.

"And if you don't like him," Purp said, "it's your lane he's in. You have to step up, man."

"I know," Javier said. "I better see what's going on." Javier stood up and walked out into the café. Purp followed him.

A couple of guys waited to order while Betty showed Brad how to prep chicken breasts for the Buffalo nachos. Purp wondered why she showed him prep when there were customers at the register.

Purp glanced out the glass wall. Gina danced with J.J. by the passenger's window of the Z3. Gina and J.J. held hands and pressed their chests together. It was a new move this week and it seemed to drive the customers nuts. A couple of them came back through for another wash since the girls started doing it. Purp insisted that every car get washed in exactly the same way whether the car had just come through or not.

"Oh, man, check it out," a customer said, a football-player looking guy sitting by the glass wall, talking to his friend using a laptop at the next table over. Laptop-guy looked up to catch Gina and J.J. pulling apart, water running down their chests from Elizabeth's hose arching over the low roof of the BWM. It was a hundred and ten degrees out and the girls did not mind being wet, not at all. It had actually gotten too sunny for them and Purp called for quotes to get an awning put up, metal roof, over the wash bays.

Purp slid in behind the register, keeping his eyes out the glass wall on Gina and J.J. now dancing ass to ass with their hands on their knees. Javier stepped behind Purp and walked over to the food line by Betty and Brad.

"Hi there, can I help you?" Purp said to the back of the customer standing first in line at the register. Purp got the feeling that the customer could have stood there all day watching Gina and J.J.

"Oh, sorry," the customer said. He turned around to face Purp. He ordered a fajita burrito, chips and salsa, and a Diet Dr Pepper. Purp had the soda rep replace the Diet Sprite with Diet Dr Pepper when Gina came on board. Purp poured the drink when he heard the cowbell on the door jingle. Three sorority-type girls in knit shorts and halter tops, one in a tube top, came in laughing.

"Oh my God there she is Nicole," one of them squealed. She clapped her hands and baby step shuffled over to the glass wall in her flip-flops.

"Nicole, yay," said the one in a tube top. She ran over to the glass wall. Purp saw the Greek letters alpha, chi, omega screen-printed on the butt of her short-shorts.

The girls that came in treated the washers like rock stars. Purp wondered if maybe he should get shorts like that printed up that said

"PTC" on the ass. Maybe the girls would like that since it seemed to be such a status symbol for them to wash and all.

The cowbell on the door jingled again. Betty put up the bell to keep with the bell-ringing theme outside and it rang so often that Purp hardly noticed it. A man walked in, a tree of a guy in his forties. He wore a golf shirt tucked in and khakis with a braided leather belt. That was unusual. All of it. Purp knew that this guy was not a customer. It was very rare for Purp to see anybody come in anywhere near his own age, and when they did, they weren't guys dressed like this one. Guys hardly ever came in alone, either.

"Welcome to PTC," Purp said. "Can I help you?"

"I'm Horatio Pendragon. Hello." He shook Purp's hand. Mr. Pendragon smelled delicious, something between vanilla and nutmeg. "I'm here for an appointment with Ms. Betty . . . Nuh-goo-yen?" He spoke with the wisp of an accent, Purp could barely hear it whispering up. Maybe he was Swiss a long time ago, or Austrian.

"I'm Betty Nguyen," she said, running it together into one word like Bettywin. She stepped out from behind the food line and shook Horatio Pendragon's hand. "I am the administrator and bookkeeper."

Horatio Pendragon looked a little afraid of Betty. He looked like she surprised or shocked him in some way, but Purp couldn't tell how. Betty was dressed pretty tame, compared to lately, so it wasn't that. She just had on jeans and a PTC tank top. Maybe Purp was just getting used to her, though. Betty in a tank top could definitely set a guy back for a second, especially one so much taller than she was.

Javier and Brad worked on the fajita burrito. The first one came back because Brad put guacamole in it and Javier hadn't noticed. Purp wasn't sure how well Javier would train Brad if Betty weren't right there with them.

"Mr. Pendragon this is Javier Abdul," Betty said. "He's the owner here."

Javier reached over the sneeze guard and shook Mr. Pendragon's hand. He went back to making the burrito with the same un-gloved hand.

"Mr. Pendragon this is Percival Johnson," Betty said. "He's the other owner here. Mr. Pendragon is from Liquor License and Control, he's here to do our physical inspection so we can get our liquor license."

"My name is Horatio," Mr. Pendragon said to Purp, "so I know what it's like to have a name like 'Percival.' I feel for you." He shook Purp's hand again. The guy was a hand-shaker. And it took him longer to let go than most people. But Purp didn't mind it.

Purp laughed. The name joke caught him off guard, and the hand-holding. He didn't expect Mr. Pendragon was the kind of guy to crack a joke like that. Purp thought it was a funny joke, too.

"I go by Purp. Long story. How about you?"

"Harry," Mr. Pendragon said.

"Like Harry Potter," Purp said. He had absolutely no idea why he just said that.

"Exactly," Mr. Pendragon said. "Except with an e-n-d-r-a-g-o-n instead of an o-t-t-e-r."

This cracked Purp up. He thought it was hilarious. They weren't going to have any trouble at all getting a liquor license. This guy was awesome. He and Mr. Pendragon laughed while Betty, Javier, and even Brad just stood there and watched, as if they'd missed something.

* * *

Purp drained the dregs out of the bottom of a bottle of Budweiser and tossed the empty into the trashcan beside his desk. It clinked against the others in there and he made a mental note to empty the can before Betty came in and said something about it again. He bent into the mini-fridge he'd put in behind his desk and pulled another bottle out by its neck. He popped the top off the new bottle and walked to the office window. Girls washed in three bays, the way it had been every Saturday all month since they opened.

Purp staffed what he called his lucky thirteen on Saturday. He had thirty-five girls on staff total, and a waitlist to join. Everybody wanted to work the lucky thirteen. Three girls each on the bays and the street signs, he had permits for them now, and the greeter made thirteen. Purp moved the bell and the money box with the slot in it over near the entrance driveway, and it was the greeter's job to fluff the customer up a little, get his money, make him happy he stopped by, ring the bell, and if traffic was heavy, direct the driver to the area of the courtyard they called overflow. Five cars could wait in overflow. With a decent view of the wash bays while they waited, overflow was just part of the experience for the customer. The ones Purp talked to actually liked when overflow was on.

Purp gulped at his Budweiser while he watched what was going on in overflow. He had Marissa on greeter. Girls didn't particularly like being on greeter too much. It wasn't hard but it wasn't as sexy because they weren't in the bays and they had to wear their PTC shirts. It wasn't as social, either, because there was only one greeter. The plus side was they got to interact with every single customer, and since the girls knew a lot of the customers from outside anyway, that was the fun part of greeter for them.

Purp wasn't too happy with Marissa on greeter, but he had a rotation and it was her turn. The guys liked her, a stunning girl, six-feet tall and African-American, with light brown curly hair that she wore loose down to the middle of her back. She wore a PTC T-Shirt knotted at the back and slit down the front almost to her belly. When she bent over to lean into a yellow Mazda 3 Purp saw the bottoms of her ass cheeks poking out of the new uniform cutoff shorts from Target. She definitely looked great and danced well in the bays but her traffic management on greeter wasn't the best. She didn't do a great job reminding the guys whose turn it was to drive into the next empty bay. Purp finished his beer and smelled smoke. Maybe somebody tried to light up in the café.

Purp turned toward the office door and a foggy haze drifted in. It hit his nostrils full force and there was no way it was cigarette smoke. It smelled like microwave popcorn someone left in too long, but more intense even than that and mixed with a greasy smell, too.

Purp's left ear rattled and buzzed against the shrieks of multiple fire alarms. He set his three-quarter empty bottle down on something uneven and it spilled onto his desk, running onto his chair. He heard the murmur of people in the middle of something real. His eyes stung with it when he stepped out of his office into the café, the smoke much thicker there. Kids filed out the front doors in a pretty orderly way. One girl in fluffy pink slippers with sunglasses on her head stood and held the door for people as they walked out, waving their hands in front of their faces. Another girl in a super-short skirt bent to unplug her laptop, keeping her knees together under white smoke that filled the café to waist-height.

Flames whipped behind the window in the door of the convection oven, white smoke billowing out the back of it like a fog machine. Brad stood in front of the oven looking at it with his hands on his ears.

"Rescue. Rescue," a voice said from behind Purp. It took Purp half a second but he recognized it as Javier through the sounds of the fire alarms and the shuffle of evacuating guests. Javier plowed Purp into the wall. Metal brushed against Purp's arm. Flames squirted out from the convection oven, from the back and also all around the crack where the door sealed. Javier thudded by Purp carrying a fire extinguisher. Purp didn't even remember that they had a fire extinguisher. Javier walked the long way to the food line, coming in from behind the register.

“Rescue,” Javier said. “Rescue.” He used the fire extinguisher to push Brad, who seemed paralyzed, all the way to the end of the food line and around the counter. Then, like it was something he did every morning, with one hand Javier snapped open the circuit breaker panel on the wall by the food line and popped each breaker shut down the line of ten of them or so that were there. The amount of smoke rolling out the back of the convection oven dropped by half as soon as Javier did that. Purp heard sirens outside. He glanced at the glass wall. The car wash seemed to be running normally. He saw Betty out there talking to Marissa, pointing back toward the café.

Purp heard the sink turn on, full blast. Javier soaked a bar mop towel that he then used to protect his hand while he opened the metal handle on the convection oven. A blast of smoke poured out of the oven and the flames flared up. It looked like Javier might have gotten a face full of it but he pounded the inside of the oven with a continuous jet from the fire extinguisher, walking backward as he sprayed, keeping the extinguisher's nozzle exactly on target, sweeping it a few inches from side to side as he killed the flames.

* * *

Purp lifted his head off some papers he had on his desk. There was a wet spot on a file folder. Purp wondered if the moisture came from the cup of Jack and Pepsi by his keyboard or if maybe he'd drooled a little while he was sleeping. He didn't remember falling asleep. He wiggled his mouse to see what time it was. Crap it was only noon. He felt like he needed to go to bed. He couldn't tell if he was still drunk from the fourth of July party the night before, or maybe just from what he'd had to get himself going this morning.

“They're here,” Betty said.

Purp turned to see where she was talking from. Betty stood in the office doorway.

“Come on,” Betty said. “They're here.”

Betty had seriously turned it on today. Even Purp was surprised at how good she looked, and he was often the first to point out that she was the hottest girl in the place. It looked like her mom and sister had done her nails and makeup. She had her Purple leather pants on and the inch-long acrylic claws on the tips of her fingers looked like they'd been painted with the same dye as the leather. Purp had never seen the shirt she had on. It looked like a PTC tank top but the logo on it was done in shimmering gems instead of being screen printed. Betty's D-cup breasts bulged out the top of her custom-made tank top and Purp figured she must have some kind of new bra on because her tits were squeezed up and together exactly as if Betty herself was cupping them with her hands from below, lifting.

"They're ready to go," Javier said. He stood behind Betty in the office doorway. Even Javier looked done up. He had his hair trimmed and styled with gel in a chunky messed-up effect on top. He wore a simple black one-pocket T-shirt that Purp had never seen before. It suited him. The fabric made Purp think that it was no T-shirt from Wal*Mart, that was something that came from Dillard's or Macy's. Javier was so wide he was the kind of guy it was hard to tell whether he was fat or not, but he definitely didn't look it in that shirt. He looked good. Javier's jeans were new, and not pants he picked out. They were dyed a deep shade of indigo blue with the thighs faded pale, yellow stitching around the turned-up cuffs. The fancy pants gave the beat-up Doc Martens Javier wore a look like they'd been beat like that on purpose.

"That's right," Purp said. "It was supposed to be noon, huh?" He stood up, unsteady. He needed to use the bathroom, he couldn't quite tell which kind. Maybe both. His chin felt wet. He wiped it with the back of his hand. It had been drool on the file folder.

"Uh huh," Betty said. "Is that what you're wearing?"

He looked down at himself. He wore his green plaid Quicksilver shirt, black Guess baggy jean shorts, and Clark's sandals. It was what he wore for the party the night before, so he didn't think it was so bad. It was dressed up for him. It was a little wrinkly, though. And there was something on the bottom of the shirt, but it didn't show so bad.

Purp walked out into the café. Betty reached over him to fix his hair a little. It gave him goosebumps to have her touching his head. The café gleamed under the television lights. The chairs were all full, but nobody was standing like usual. It wasn't noisy like it should be. The kids seemed like they'd been arranged and they were afraid to move in case they messed something up. A crowd on the sidewalk, all along the windows, pushed for a peek inside. The guys out there started to holler and pound the glass. Purp turned to see Beniko Kumi walking out of Betty's office. The guys outside started to chant "D. M. G." and Purp was worried they might break the window. Two big dudes, Samoan-looking, stood inside the front doors wearing black shirts with the letters

"D.M.G. " in yellow on the back. These guys dwarfed Javier's size. They kept an eye on the crowd through the glass.

Beniko Kumi put her arm around Betty and looked at Purp. Beniko stood six inches shorter than Betty and wore a little gray pleated schoolgirl skirt with white fluffy loose socks that came up past her knees. She smelled like strawberries, or at least like a chemical that was supposed to smell like strawberries. Standing side by side, Beniko made Betty look like just an average girl off the street. Beniko glowed with something that actually just made Purp hurt inside when he looked directly at her.

"I'm Beniko," she said, holding out a hand to Purp, keeping her other arm around Betty's waist. "Nice to meet you."

Purp took her hand. It felt tiny in his, like in a dream when something feels smaller than it ought to, out of proportion. Purp got this flash of a thought, like he wished bad that he could just die right then, at that instant, so that the last thing he would see would be Beniko Kumi with her arm around Betty Nguyen. He couldn't even hear the guys outside chanting anymore. It was like his whole world compressed itself so that nothing else had ever happened other than shaking Beniko Kumi's little hand.

* * *

Purp and Javier sat on café chairs in Betty's office. On a shelf a stone vase of scented oil, bamboo reeds splayed out of its narrow neck, gave the room a gingery smell.

Betty leaned across her desk showing Purp and Javier a graph she made.

"It's café ops that seems to be the place where there's room for growth," Betty said.

"That makes sense," Purp said. "We don't even have the liquor license yet. But I don't always have three bays wet, either, so I have work to do, too." Purp popped the top of a Budweiser he was keeping on the floor so Betty wouldn't see it until as late as possible. She gave him an annoyed look. "What," he said. "This is a working meeting, no?" He took a long drag on the bottle. "Plus," he said, "it's four o'clock somewhere, right?"

"I don't –

"After I take food cost out, I'm almost all beverage sales right now," Javier said, talking over Betty. Javier had been getting between Purp and Betty more and more since Betty got so annoyed with Purp for being drunk when Beniko Kumi came. "And that's just with soda. Imagine what that would be like if just a quarter of those guys bought a Jack and Pepsi instead."

"That is a lot of money," Purp said. He ran his finger down a spreadsheet of the beverage numbers, estimating what Javier said it would be like if a quarter of those bought alcohol.

"The other thing," Javier said. He slid a pie chart out of Betty's folder. "Is that of course all my guys who buy a soda buy only one. And that's still where my money is coming from. Imagine if half the guys who bought a beer bought two."

"Or if they're like Purp, four or five," Betty said.

"Betty, order up," Brad said from the café.

"I've got to get my burrito." Betty stood up. "Excuse me."

"You're all primed up there for some serious cash once old Mr. Pendragon comes through for us," Purp said.

"I know," Javier said. "It's a lot of covers, right? When you add it up over the six weeks?"

"Especially since this is supposed to be the hardest time," Purp said. "This is supposed to be when we're making our mistakes."

Betty came back in with a burrito on a plate in one hand and a bottle of fish sauce in the other. She lifted her knee and used it to spin her office chair around so she could sit in it. The move gave Purp a nice view of the inside of her thigh under the short hem of a gray pleated skirt Purp hadn't seen her wear before.

"I know," Betty said. "We don't seem to have made many mistakes. Not so far anyway." She sat down and opened the top of her fish sauce bottle. Purp smelled vinegar mix with the scented oil.

"Did they tell you when they're going to show us on D.M.G. ?" Purp said to Betty.

"Not 'till next season," Betty said. "They actually can those Beniko segments. It looks like he's talking to her, but he's not. So they start showing the new ones in January."

"So maybe January?" Purp said.

"January, February, who knows," Betty said. "Could be any time all season. Spike TV ordered twenty-six episodes for next year, which Beniko told me is a lot, so who knows."

Betty started in on her burrito while Purp and Javier looked through the graphs and spreadsheets on her desk. Purp looked at the daily counts for car wash. He had dailys from cash receipts and from his plate camera, but he didn't yet have hourlies. He thought about how to tweak his license plate software to give him hourly counts.

"I want to try to up-sell sodas," Javier said. "See these covers?" Javier pointed to a cell on the spreadsheet. "These are food, non-drink. That's just not right, right? They could have all had a soda. With the way the margin is on the food line, it's a complete waste to give somebody a Buffalo with no soda."

"If they sit they drink, I think. That should be your mantra," Betty said. "Also," she finished swallowing a mouthful of burrito, "I know you guys are pretty firm on the refill thing."

"Definitely," Purp said. "That's cheesy not to have refills. I wish we'd put the fountain on the other side of the counter."

"So what good does the 24-ounce do you?" Betty said. "You're selling the same amount of soda for less money, and it costs me more to buy two different sized cups instead of one."

"Good point," Purp said. He finished his beer while Betty put her head down to saw a corner off her burrito. Purp looked at the crisp part in her black hair. He loved when Betty parted her hair down the middle and wore it to both sides.

"Just one size though?" Javier said.

"It'll be especially cheaper when we go to the logo cups," Purp said.

"Mmm, hmm," Betty said, chewing. She swallowed. "That's right, too."

"If we keep on top of this stuff, there's a lot of little things that are going to add up big onto the huge base we already have right now," Purp said.

"We have the fundamentals," Betty said.

"We have customers lining up, car wash and café," Purp said. "And they're going out both doors happy."

"And coming back," Betty said. "Those were interesting numbers you had on the license plate analysis, Purp." She slid her quarter-eaten burrito to the corner of her desk toward Javier.

Javier picked up Betty's burrito and took a bite of it off of the same part where Betty just ate. Fish sauce dribbled down his chin.

"I can't believe you wrote that program to snap the plate numbers on the greeter line like that. That's like James Bond shit," Betty said. "You should work in IT."

The three of them laughed.

"That's what they pay me the big bucks for," Purp said.

"Anyway," Betty said. "Speaking of that, we're taking enough in that we can start paying you guys now."

"Oh, thank God," Javier said, his mouth completely full of burrito.

"I don't know," Purp said. "I don't want to deplete more cash on hand."

"It's killing me, Purp," Javier said. "I've got to get out of Starbucks. It's too much with both."

"There's enough, actually, that we can pay you guys and reduce our weekly draw on cash," Betty said.

"Seriously?" Purp said.

"Even right now, yes," Betty said. "And when we get the liquor license, I don't even project we'll need the cash anymore. We can just use it for outside debt, and then we're done."

"That's awesome," Purp said.

"Let's start giving you guys a check with the rest of us on Thursdays," Betty said.

"That sounds good to me," Javier said.

"I concur," Purp said.

"How much are we talking?" Javier said.

* * *

Selma laughed so hard she choked. She stuffed bills down into her bra while Purp reached in after them, from the top and bottom, grabbing more boob than money. Selma squirmed on the kitchen floor, fighting Purp off. She kicked her feet and money slid in all directions. Purp slipped on it. Bills slid under the table, the refrigerator.

Purp had gone to the bank and gotten his whole paycheck in ones. He planned to spend it all the next afternoon on dinner, drinks, mini-golf, and a movie. It really wasn't that much as far as paychecks go, but it looked like a big fat stack on the kitchen table when Selma came home and the two of them went nuts with it.

Purp flipped Selma over on her belly and lifted her up by the web belt of her camouflaged uniform pants. He grabbed a handful of bills and stuffed them down between her ass and the back of her thong. She screamed and wriggled, slapping at Purp's ankles. Purp jammed handfuls of bills into her pants. The pants fit snug over Selma's round ass anyway, but with the money in them the seat bulged, lumpy and ridiculous.

Selma swept her arms on the floor as wide as she could, making a sort of snow angel in the money, except on her belly instead of her back. She wadded the swept pile together between both hands and leaned to one side, crushing the bills down into the ruined stretched neck of her brown T-shirt.

Purp pressed Selma onto her back. She held her hands over her breasts, as if protecting all the money she had stuffed in her shirt. Purp kneeled on Selma's shoulders and gathered up a bundle of cash from under the kitchen table. He stuffed it down the front of her pants while she screamed and kicked and writhed against him.

* * *

"It's ridiculous," Purp said. "It's fucking ridiculous." He kicked his trash can and beer bottles flew. One of them broke. He stood with his hands on his hips, looking at the mess on the tile. He snatched the soda cup from his desk and gripped it so hard the lid popped off from one side. He pressed the plastic lid back down onto the wax cup. "I can't even believe it." Purp walked over to the window. Two bays wet on a Tuesday morning. The gray sky outside made it look like it was going to open up and pour any minute even though it wasn't even noon yet. It hadn't slowed down for the monsoon like he thought it might. He had a line one day the week before when it was actually raining. Pouring. The girls put on a good show then, too.

Purp sipped his Jack and Pepsi. He pumped it into him through the straw until it made the rattle noise that told him it was time to mix another drink. Outside Gina and Alyssa did the chest-together dance by the driver's side of a Boxster. The two of them, Gina and Alyssa, that was their specialty. Gina slid her knees down the outsides of Alyssa's wet thighs, running her hands down the sides of Alyssa's dripping breasts and over her belly, down her hips, gripping Alyssa's tan thighs with her fingertips just inside the hem of Alyssa's jean short-shorts.

"That guy seemed pretty into the place, right?" Javier said.

"Harry Pendragon," Purp said. "What an ass."

Purp opened his bottom desk drawer and took out a bottle of Jack Daniels. He poured four fingers' worth into his thirty-two ounce wax soda cup. He snapped the lid back onto the cup and walked out into the café. The café looked good, especially for so early, about half the tables covered. He had to work with Javier to get some kind of breakfast burrito for these guys, though, especially with the semester starting in a couple of weeks. Fucking Brad could barely handle re-heating the fajita chicken, how was he going to manage short-order eggs? He'd have to with no liquor license. This was going to have to be about the food.

Purp opened his soda cup and filled it the rest of the way with Pepsi. He took a couple of slugs of it before putting the lid back on. He walked into Betty's office while she was still on her cell phone. He stood by her desk and looked down at her while she finished her conversation. Betty was speaking Vietnamese. She snapped her phone shut.

"What the fuck, Betty?" Purp said. "What did you say to the guy?"

"What do you mean what did I say to the guy?" Betty said. "You were here, you didn't seem that interested in him."

"I didn't seem interested in him?" Purp said. "I was nice to him. I chatted him up."

"You told him your name," Betty said. "It wasn't exactly like you got into the technical details of things with him."

"You lined it up. I didn't even know he was coming," Purp said. "I had customers to take care of."

"I told you he was coming," Betty said.

"You did not," Purp said. "The first I heard of it was when he walked through the door."

"That is not true," Betty said. "I told you he was coming. I have it in my notes when I told you, even."

"You didn't remind me then," Purp said, "if you even told me at all."

"I did tell you, and once he was here you knew he was here," Betty said, "and you backed off of it like I'm supposed to know how to take care of all this and I don't."

"You sure seem like it," Purp said. "You seem like you think you know what you're doing. You're always bossing me around like I'm the one who works here and you own it."

"If you had so much to say to him you should have said it when he was here," Betty said. "You wouldn't have even known how to apply for the liquor license."

"I was working on licenses and permits before you even came on," Purp said. "I hired you to do it and now we have no liquor license. Do you even realize how serious this is?"

"Do I realize it?" Betty said. "Are you completely drunk or do you just not even know what you're saying? Do I realize? You wouldn't know how much money came into the box outside if I didn't tell you. You wouldn't know –

"I would know, but I hired you to do it," Purp said. "I own this place and I hired you to do this job. It doesn't mean I couldn't do it. I bought the clock on the café wall so I could see what time it is when I walk by. I bought you so I could focus what I'm doing without –

"You bought me?" Betty said.

"I bought your services, yeah," Purp said.

"You didn't buy me," Betty said. She stood up and walked out into the café.

Purp walked after her.

"I bought your services to make my life easier," Purp said. "If you're not making my life easier, I'm not sure what I'm paying for."

"I'll tell you what you're paying for," Betty said. "You're paying to run this business, and not paying me very well, either. You hired me because you knew you could get me cheap and –

"I hired you because you have nice tits," Purp said. "And I liked looking down your shirt. And I have a thing for Asian chicks, too. You're a fucking decoration, as if we needed more of that."

A couple of the guys at the café tables looked at Betty standing in her PTC tank top, one hand on her chest and her other on her hip. Betty breathed shallow and fast, her face tilted toward the floor.

* * *

Purp stood under the new awning outside the front door. Not even noon yet and jewel-sized drops fell hard enough to make rivers by the curbs on Guadalupe. Tail lights glowed in the entrance driveway. That would be weird, to be on overflow when it was raining, even.

Purp wanted to walk across to Taco Cabana but he'd get soaked. It was blowing, too, and he only liked sitting on the patio. He had to get out, though. He'd just drive home. He wasn't that drunk. He was upset about the license, that was all. He'd just go home and cool off. But his car keys. He had to go back in for his car keys, crap.

The cowbell jingled him into the café. Brad looked up from the food line and then back down right away, as if he didn't want to make eye contact with Purp. A few of the café guys looked at Purp, though. They glared at him, mutinous. He felt his face flush. The tops of his ears burned. He walked over to his office doorway and he heard Betty inside his office, crying.

"He's not pissed at you," Javier said.

"I don't want to leave, but," Betty said. She sniffed twice. "I shouldn't have to tolerate that."

"He's bummed about the license," Javier said. "I'm sure he knows it's not your fault."

"I work so hard for this place," Betty said. "I didn't take summer school so I could," she sniffed, "help you guys get all set up so that when the semester," she sniffed, "started you'd be OK."

"He's Purp, right?" Javier said. "He didn't mean –

"I only registered for five units this semester," Betty said. She sucked in a deep, jagged breath. "I changed my whole schedule, plan."

Purp walked into the office, trying not to look at anything other than the keys on his desk. He couldn't help taking a glance, though, at Javier standing by the office window with both arms wrapped around Betty. She looked like a little girl next to him, like his thigh was as thick as her waist. Betty sniffed, her head on Javier's chest, her face toward the wash bays. She didn't seem to notice Purp walking in. Purp made eye contact with Javier, though. He couldn't read Javier's look. Purp walked super-quiet over to his desk, snatched his keys, and popped back out as quick as he could.

* * *

"As economically different from a strip club as possible," Betty said. She sat behind her desk wearing her button-down red blouse with the flared cuffs, all but the top button fastened. She'd been looking mostly at Javier during the meeting, but she hadn't been ignoring Purp, either.

"And that's to differentiate ourselves from the way that they operate?" Purp said. He'd been trying to say back what Betty was saying, but in the form of a question, so she'd know he was listening.

"That's right," Betty said. "If you use Hooters as a case study, you see they're not set up anything at all like a strip club and they have a full bar."

Purp fought back the urge to point out that Hooters girls wear shirts. For the last few days he'd been trying to just completely lay off the subject of boobs whenever he was around Betty. He'd been trying to lay low altogether after he came back to apologize. This was the first day he'd been in for more than just staffing.

"Don't all strip clubs have a full bar?" Javier said. "They have dollar tequila shots at Foxy? I don't get what the big deal is."

"Foxy is in the county," Betty said. "This is city limits here."

"What about Empress?" Javier said.

"That place is a dive," Purp said. "Have you ever been there?" he said to Javier.

"No," Javier said.

"Me neither," Purp said. "I drive by on Jefferson, thought. It's a pit."

"They don't have any license at all," Betty said. "They had beer and wine, but they lost it in ninety-eight because of the neighborhood complaints."

"That place was there long before the rich people decided those houses behind there were cool," Purp said. "Those things are expensive back there. You could get one of those for under a hundred when I was in college."

"It's B.Y.O.B. now," Betty said.

"Huh," Purp said. "I did not know that."

"And if you look at us on paper," Betty said, "it kind of looks like that's the way we operate. We treat the girls like independent contractors."

"We don't officially employ them." Purp said.

"We don't," Betty said. "They stuff the box, we get a cut of it. We're basically renting them the lot out there."

"Isn't that a good thing? I thought I was saving us a lot of hassle setting it up like that." Purp said. "I mean, doesn't that make it look more separate?"

"It makes it look separate," Betty said, "but it's exactly like a strip club that way."

"How does Hooters do it?" Javier said.

"Just like a regular restaurant," Betty said.

"Which is what they are," Purp said.

"They pay an hourly wage with tips onto that," Betty said.

"The girls don't mind how it is now, right?" Javier said.

"No," Purp said. "I still have a waitlist. But Betty is saying that when we go that hearing we want it to look –

"As much like Hooters as possible," Betty said.

* * *

Gina sat at the bus stop on Guadalupe. Crossing back from Taco Cabana Purp saw her up there by Circle K. He saw her legs, first, and then noticed who they were connected to. He wasn't in a hurry to get back to work so he walked up to where she waited. She'd changed out of her uniform into a denim skirt and a black zip-up hoodie with Tinkerbell on it. Her blond hair fell freshly styled and loose around her shoulders. Purp figured Gina had taken a shower and used the blow dryers he put up in the locker room for the girls since he noticed they were bringing their own. Collecting hair care and beauty products to stock the locker room had become a kind of duty for Purp, and a little bit of a hobby, too. He liked knowing Gina used Paul Mitchell detangler and Rachel used Neutrogena conditioner.

"The Taurus give out on you?" Purp said as he got up to the bus stop.

"No," Gina said. She kicked her feet back and forth, dangling them off the bench. "I actually got rid of it."

"Are you getting a new car?" Purp said. "Or a different car?"

"No, I don't want to pay for it anymore," Gina said.

"Am I not paying you enough?" Purp said.

"Kind of the opposite," Gina said. "I'm making enough now that I can afford a place with no roommate. If I get rid of my car."

"Well, that's good . . . right?" Purp said.

"Definitely," Gina said. "It's a pain not having a car, but it's so much better not having a roommate." She drew out the "so" and made her voice low when she said it. "I was sick of the hassle, because the other place was in my name. Everything."

"That's a pain," Purp said.

"Yeah," Gina said. She adjusted her hands on the bus bench under her thighs while she kicked her feet. She either didn't know or didn't care that from where Purp stood he could see a flash of her green thong every couple of kicks.

"I could use a break," Purp said.

Gina laughed. She looked up, playful, leaning toward him. She didn't seem to turn her scar away from him as much lately. "You just came from Taco Cabana," she said. "You need a break from your break?" When she leaned forward Purp caught a peek of the green bra she wore under her Tinkerbell sweatshirt. That's all she had on underneath. Purp saw Gina's tits for hours at a time three or four times a week when she worked, but seeing her with her clothes on all of a sudden was driving him nuts.

"I know," Purp said. "But I don't feel like going back right now."

"Tough day?" Gina said.

“Kind of,” Purp said. “Betty’s been kind of working me pretty hard.”

Gina laughed.

“What?” Purp said.

“Who’s the owner?” Gina said.

“It doesn’t exactly work that way as much as you’d think,” Purp said. “I’d be so screwed if she quit. And I’ve been trying to give her some room the last couple of weeks because she and I had a fight.”

“I heard about that,” Gina said.

“You did?” Purp said.

“Oh yeah,” Gina said. “News travels.”

“Did Betty tell you?” Purp said.

“I don’t really know Betty so well,” Gina said. “I think Brad told Rachel. That’s usually how things come from inside.”

“Huh,” Purp said. “Does Brad talk to Rachel a lot?”

“They’re kind of going out on and off,” Gina said. “Rachel introduced Brad to Betty when she heard you were looking for a kitchen guy.”

“Huh,” Purp said. “I kind of suspected maybe Betty and Brad were a thing, sort of. He just appeared one day and she was training him.”

“Betty and Brad?” Gina said. “Hell no. Nobody knows who Betty’s going out with.”

“I doubt she has a boyfriend,” Purp said.

“Oh, she does,” Gina said.

“Really,” Purp said. He kicked the gravel by the bus bench. The sun was heating up his back. It was almost October but is still had some bite to it, and Purp didn’t want to get sweaty in his rayon shirt. “Where are you headed, anyway. I’ll give you a lift. I seriously have to get out of here for a while and I feel like going for a ride.”

“I’m going home,” Gina said. “It’s not far,” she kicked her feet and looked up at Purp, taking one hand out from underneath a thigh to shade her eyes, “but it kind of takes a while on the bus.”

“I’ll take you,” Purp said.

“OK,” Gina said.

Purp got an eyeful when Gina hopped off the bus bench. He wondered why she would leave her sweatshirt zipped down so low if she was about to ride the bus. She tugged the hem of her skirt down after she stood up, wiggling her hips to get it straight. The stone-washed denim had a butterfly appliquéd over one thigh and a flower over the other. Purp took her backpack off the bench for her and Gina slung a little purse over her shoulder, barely big enough for a wallet. They walked to the café lot where Purp had his truck. Purp went around to the passenger's side to let Gina in. She got in with a flash of her green thong that Purp had a hard time believing was an accident. Purp shut the passenger's door and he saw Gina through the window already reaching across the cab to open his door for him, her Tinkerbell sweatshirt sliding up, showing the tattoo on her back.

Purp got into the truck. Gina gave him directions and they headed up Guadalupe.

"Is that like an Army uniform?" Gina said.

Purp glanced in his rearview mirror at Selma's uniforms hanging in plastic bags from a hook in the space behind the truck seats.

"Air Force," Purp said. "Those are my wife's. I got them from the cleaner's at lunchtime."

"Aww," Gina said. "How sweet."

"Yeah," Purp said. "She gives me tasks. She gives me these lists on yellow sheets."

They talked a little about Selma. Mostly Gina asked and Purp answered, not offering more than he had to.

"So what makes you so sure Betty has a boyfriend," Purp said when the conversation turned back around to people at PTC.

"Lacy saw her at Walgreen's," Gina said. She leaned over the console closer to Purp, lowering her voice as if she didn't want anybody to hear. "At the Pharmacy, picking up a Nuvo ring."

"Huh," Purp said. "How did she know what she was getting?"

"She heard," Gina said. "She heard the guy explaining it to her how it worked."

"Huh," Purp said. "That's embarrassing."

"I know," Gina said. "I'd die."

"Maybe she's just being prepared," Purp said.

"Maybe," Gina said. "But no way. Girls don't go for their appointment unless they absolutely have to. Or unless they have really bad zits. Which she does not."

* * *

Purp used his soapy hand to play with himself in the shower. He was just about done. He woke up twice during the night thinking about Gina sitting on the bus bench, and Gina getting into his truck. He thought about like seven different ways he could have tried to go up with her when he dropped her off instead of saying, "Well, OK, see you Friday, huh?" He thought of turning her around with her back toward him, leaning her over onto the seat of the truck with her feet still on the pavement. He thought of sliding the hem of her skirt up over her thighs and what she'd look like standing there looking over her shoulder at him with her elbows on the passenger's seat. He thought about hooking his thumb under her green thong.

"Did you get a chance to get my uniforms yesterday?" Selma said. Purp hadn't noticed her come into the bathroom.

Purp stopped playing with himself real fast and turned to face the tiles. Selma looked through the glass shower door at him. It didn't seem like she noticed what he was up to.

"Huh?" Purp said. He'd heard her, but he was just trying to buy a second to collect himself.

"Were you able to get my uniforms for me yesterday?" Selma said, speaking louder and more slowly into the glass.

"Uh, yeah," Purp said, trying to make it seem like he was busy washing his armpit and couldn't turn around. "They're still in my truck. The key's in the hall table drawer."

Selma left the bathroom. Purp hoped she hadn't caught him. He went back to Gina, still bent into his truck looking back at him, except now her thong pulled tight against her spread ankles. He finished himself off and cleaned up.

"Who's Regina?" Selma said.

"What's that?" Purp said. He stood in the shower with the water off, drying his legs.

"Who's Regina?" Selma said.

Purp wrapped the towel around his waist and stepped out of the shower.

"I don't know who Regina is," Purp said.

"Well, she left her purse in your truck," Selma said, holding up Gina's little wallet-purse.

"Oh, that's Gina," Purp said.

"Gina?" Selma said.

"The blond girl with the scar," Purp said. "I gave her a ride because her car was broken. Or, she sold it."

"She washes?" Selma said.

"Yeah," Purp said, pulling on a pair of boxers. "The little one with the scar. You've seen her."

"OK," Selma said. She set the purse down on the bathroom counter. "That's real nice, Purp."

"I just gave her a ride," Purp said. "Betty was annoying me."

"Not that," Selma said.
"What?" Purp said.
"If you don't know," Selma said, "You don't know."

* * *

"No, not at all," Betty said. "It isn't anything like that." She sat at the edge of her chair in a gray satin long-sleeved button down top and black slacks that flared at the ankle.

"Well, I would say it is something like that," Vic Caputo said. He sat across the conference room table from Betty, Horatio Pendragon on his left, Barry Epstein on his right. "I mean, there are men who come there paying to see naked women."

"The women aren't naked," Betty said. Javier sat on the other side of her from Purp, but Purp saw Javier shaking his head in support of what Betty was telling the board. "They don't wear shirts, which it is their right not to do outdoors on private property. And the men we're concerned with are not the ones in the cars, remember. They literally never set foot inside the premises during the course of their transaction."

"They're not paying to get their cars washed," Vic Caputo said.

"That may or may not be, but it is irrelevant," Betty said. "You're getting hung up on the car wash customers. That's not relevant to our liquor license application because those are separate customers who do not set foot in the café portion of our operation."

"It is very difficult," Horatio Pendragon said to Vic Caputo, "like she says, to even physically get from the car wash into the café, the way the traffic flow is."

"We've studied it," Purp said, "and we only get a three percent conversion from car wash customers to café. It's not something we promote."

Betty slipped a spreadsheet from her sleek inch-thick black briefcase on the table in front of her and handed it across to Vic Caputo.

"To give you something to compare that to," Purp said, "Mr. Abdul actually sat over on Father Kino and Adams for sixteen hours one day." Purp looked at Javier and Javier nodded to the men across the table in a way he seemed to want to look dignified.

"That's over by where there's that Chevron on the corner with the Java Dave's next to it?" Javier said.

"I know where you mean," Barry Epstein said.

"Me too," Horatio Pendragon said.

Vic Caputo nodded his head.

"If you count the customers who stop at that Chevron," Purp said, "two percent drive into the Java Dave's parking lot and either go through their drive-through or go inside."

"So for the purposes of analysis," Betty said, "you can ignore what's going on with the car wash."

"Except for the naked women," Vic Caputo said.

"The topless women," Betty said.

Purp looked over at the stenographer transcribing the meeting on a weird little computer at the head of the table. That guy was getting an earful.

"And I would appreciate it if you would be more precise about that," Betty said, "since you know that the fact they wear bottoms is significant with respect to the law."

"It is," Horatio Pendragon said. "Absolutely. It is an important distinction with respect to strip clubs."

"Which this is not, in any case," Betty said. "Ignoring the car wash customers, we're speaking only of those people who enter the café as being relevant to our application. These customers engage in no financial transaction which in any way links them to the women washing cars. They don't pay a door fee, they don't buy a ticket, there exists no mechanism by which they can provide the car wash women with tips, and the employees washing cars are neither compensated nor incentivised in any way by the fiscal performance of the café itself. One thing has literally nothing to do with the other."

"Except for the fact that your café would be empty if there weren't bare-breasted women spraying themselves down with hoses outside the large glass wall that looks out onto your car wash," Vic Caputo said.

"Not empty," Horatio Pendragon said. "The Buffalo nachos there are quite good. Competitive with the quality of the food in the Taco Cabana across the street."

"Which has a beer and wine license," Betty said. "Mr. Caputo, you seem to be linking your decision about our liquor license with the fact that our café has a view of what's going on in the adjacent car wash."

"I do link it, because that's the primary motivation for your customers to enter your premises," Vic Caputo said.

"You would agree," Betty said, "that we'd get in trouble at the café if we all of a sudden put a booth up near the trailhead at Benjamin Mountains State Park and started charging admission to supplement our income, right?"

"Of course," Vic Caputo said.

"And Larocca's, which has an excellent view of the state park, has a liquor license," Betty said.

"Larocca's is in the county, not the city," Vic Caputo said.

"But for the purposes of argument, Larocca's couldn't put up a booth at the trailhead of the Benjamin Mountains any more legally than we could, could they?"

"No," Caputo said.

"So the fact that they have a better view of the mountains than we do doesn't necessarily imply that they have a more closely defined legal connection to the place that is being viewed, right?"

"No," Caputo said, "But –

"Do you think their patio would be full of people on dates all weekend long if it didn't have such a great view?" Betty said.

"It wouldn't. Not at all it wouldn't. It's the view that makes that place," Horace Pendragon said. "You don't have to drive all the way to the end of Gooseneck for Italian food of that quality."

"Now their view is important to their business, but I'm sure nobody took their view into account when giving them a liquor license," Betty said. "The Sausage Pot sits right in the middle of Sorority Row with girls walking back and forth all day long to campus and to the fitness center right behind there. From their patio you see more than you see at Hooters, much more, but I'm sure you didn't consider that to be an important factor when you gave them a beer and wine license. And they are in the city. They're packed with laborers and tradesmen every weekday at lunch."

"It is true," Horatio Pendragon said to Caputo, "that it's physically as much two different places as adjacent neighbors would be. The customers in the restaurant do not in any way pay, interact with, or influence the girls in the car wash."

"We're not charging admission," Betty said. "We're making money solely off our table covers in the café portion of the operation. And a view of a place does not inherently imply a business relationship with that place."

* * *

Purp carried a silver tray with two beers on it, a Corona and a Budweiser. A card stood folded to make a tent beside the Corona, a purple number one on it next to a PTC logo. He had a number two done up the same way next to the Budweiser. He walked the tray from behind the register out to the café dining area where a guy in a university tank top sat with a girl in a brown strapless fly-away baby doll dress over jeans, her sunglasses on her head. Other customers stood around the seated couple. Brad, Javier, and Betty leaned on the divider wall between the entry area and the café, Betty holding a Nikon digital SLR camera Purp had bought when he was first setting up the PTC website.

Betty snapped pictures while Purp lowered the silver tray onto the table between the lucky couple. The Nikon whirred like a printing press to keep up with all the pictures Betty took.

Purp lifted the Corona so the crowd, and Betty, could see it better. He popped the top of it with his Leatherman, for dramatic effect. A wisp of vapor rose out of the neck, the soul of something trapped in the bottle coming home to PTC where it belonged.

"The first beer ever sold in PTC goes to," Purp said, "Jeremy Wheeten." He handed the beer down to Jeremy. The crowd cheered and chanted "PTC" while Jeremy drank. Jeremy won the right to buy the first beer at PTC in an essay contest. Javier selected Jeremy's out of a stack of one hundred seventy-five one-page essays they'd received from people explaining why they should be the first to buy a beer. Jeremy had only written half a page, but on the bottom half he printed a copy of a receipt he'd scanned into the computer, a receipt for a Buffalo and a soda dated 5 June, 2004, at 9:52 am, order number 100. He'd been the first café customer the day they opened.

"The second beer ever sold in PTC goes to Jeremy's invited guest," Purp said, brandishing the bottle of Budweiser, "the lovely, and graceful, and elegant, and stylish, and beautiful, and smart, and in good shape, and nice tan-having, and sunglasses-on-head-wearing Ms. Brandi . . . Mazon!" The crown cheered and chanted again. Purp had almost lost her last name for a second while he stalled with the epithets, but he thought it probably just came off as funny. He kneeled on one knee and handed Brandi her Budweiser. She laughed, embarrassed, covering her mouth with one hand and taking the beer with the other while leaning away from Purp.

They handed out beers by name to nine other runners-up that Javier chose from the stack of essays. Purp figured they'd just randomly flip through the papers and pick a few, but Javier spent half a day going through each one and sorting them all into smaller and smaller piles until he had it narrowed down to the final ten.

The party in the café worked out great. They all had a fantastic time and at five-thirty Javier carried a spreadsheet out to where Purp was giving some pointers to Jerra, a new Thai girl who didn't quite seem to be a natural at wash dancing. Javier showed the spreadsheet to Purp, the gross figures for the top ten full café days Javier had ever had.

"Guess where we are right now," Javier said.

Purp gave him a number.

Javier shook his head.

"Add five hundred," Javier said, "to that." He pointed with a thick finger to the highest grossing day they'd ever had. "And that's where we are right now. And that's only at five-o'clock."

Purp walked into the café with Javier and half the tables had at least one beer on them. Everybody seemed like they were having a great time. Brad squirted sour cream on five Buffalos he had lined up assembly-line style. Purp glanced at the touch-screen, it was sorted by order item. He flicked his eyes to the glass wall. Jeera danced in front of a Navigator beside Elizabeth. Elizabeth had a much better rack but Jeera writhed, maybe she would work out, black hair stuck to her narrow wet back, a black band tattooed around her thigh like a garter, three inches from the hem of her shorts.

Purp walked around behind the divider wall between the kitchen and the prep line area. Clear plastic garbage bags filled with beer bottles clogged the little hallway where they kept their prep cooler and their back stock of dry goods. Purp poked his head back into the kitchen. Javier stood beside Brad, helping him assemble a row of burritos.

"We're going to need a few of those blue recycling barrels," Purp said to Javier's back.

"They don't take glass," Brad said over his shoulder to Purp.

Purp ducked back into the storage hallway and dug behind cans of jalapenos on the top shelf of the dunnage rack where they kept most of their back stock. He stood on a flipped-over mop bucket to reach. He pulled down a case of forty-eight bottles of nuoc m'am that he'd bought the day before and hidden from Betty. All day since the ceremonial first beers Purp had been meaning to give his present to Betty but one thing kept coming up after another. He hoped she was still even in her office.

Purp carried the box of fish sauce through the café. It was hard to even move in there. The party atmosphere had held on all day. Purp tapped at the bottom of Betty's door with his shoe. She opened the door.

"Hi," Betty said.

"Hi, Betty," Purp said. "Can I come in for a second?"

"Sure," Betty said, stepping to the side of her doorway to let Purp pass in front of her.

Purp got a little shivery chill in his back, brushing so close to Betty's black cotton sweater, gray buttons pulling the fabric tight across her chest. Her room smelled of something like mulled spice. Purp thought maybe she'd changed the oil in her bamboo diffuser.

"What do you have there," Betty said. Purp's arms covered the sides of the box he set down on Betty's desk.

"I have something for you," Purp said. "I got this for you at New Saigon."

"From Mrs. Ho?" Betty said.

"I don't know who from," Purp said. "But it wasn't a Mrs."

Betty laughed.

"That's a lot of fish sauce," Betty said.

"You seem to use a lot, I noticed," Purp said.

"You think?" Betty said. She leaned against her open doorway with he arms crossed over her breasts and her legs crossed at the ankles.

"Is it all right if I sit down?" Purp said. Betty nodded and Purp sat down on the edge of one of her guest chairs, not leaning back into it or making himself comfortable. "Yeah, I, uh . . . noticed that you were putting it on your burrito the other day," he said.

"The other day?" Betty said. She smiled at Purp, still leaning on her doorframe. Her smile seemed to Purp like the look she'd give a sick distant relative her parents had forced her to visit.

"I think it was the other day," Purp said. "Or the day before that. Or the day after that."

Betty chuckled, but only just barely, a laugh-like rush of air through her nose. Three staccato puffs of it.

"Or maybe the other week," Purp said, "or a couple of times a month anyway for the last twenty months."

"Twenty months?" Betty said.

"Yep," Purp said.

"What's that?" Betty said.

"That's about when I ever saw you for the first time," Purp said. "Twenty months ago."

"You remember that?" Betty said.

"I don't remember the exact date," Purp said. "But I could probably narrow it down to three or four if I had a calendar. I'm pretty sure it was a Saturday in February, maybe early March."

"At Taco Cabana." Betty said.

"That's right," Purp said. "You were studying."

"I still am," Betty said. She pointed to the open book on her desk, keeping her arms crossed.

"Oh," Purp said, "I'm sorry to bother you." He started to stand up.

"It's all right," Betty said. "I needed a soda, anyway." She pivoted out her office door. "You want a Pepsi?" she said through the open doorway.

"Sure," Purp said. "I would."

Betty came back in with a thirty-two ounce cup in each hand. She gave one to Purp. The cups were the plain ones, the ones with no logos. She'd taken the extra time to get those from back stock instead of grabbing the printed ones which cost more. Betty sat down behind her desk.

"So do you like your fish sauce?" Purp said. "Is it the right kind?"

"I do," Betty said. "Thank you."

"Well, thank you," Purp said, "for . . . everything."

"OK," Betty said.

"I mean, at the hearing," Purp said, "you were unbelievable. It was just like, I couldn't even believe how good you were at that hearing."

"Huh. Thank you," Betty said.

"There's no way we would have a beer and wine license if it weren't for you," Purp said.

"I thought you were bummed we didn't get the full bar," Betty said.

"Betty, it's not just the license," Purp said. "I just want you to know that I know, and Javier knows, and everybody knows, that this place runs because of you." Purp picked at the fabric on the arm of Betty's guest chair.

* * *

Purp looked down at an orange square spray-painted on the concrete. Mist blew onto his glasses from the wash bays. The mason, distracted by being so close to the car wash, didn't seem to be listening to Purp at all.

"They can't go like this," Purp said. "They have to go down the other sides. That was my whole point."

"Yeah," the mason said. Greg Hughes.

Purp hired Greg to build an awning over the wash bays. It was going to be more like a roof over half the courtyard than an awning. They'd made it through the monsoon and the sunny season fine all right with no cover, but Purp wanted to put propane heaters out for the girls when it got colder and he never did like how they got so much sun anyway.

"No, listen to me," Purp said. "Look." He pointed to the row of orange squares on the concrete, each one showing where a support post would be for the awning.

"They just can't be there," Purp said. "That'll ruin the whole look of the courtyard. See these?" Purp waved his arm at three of the squares.

"Yes," Greg said. He seemed like he was trying to pay more attention. He turned his back to the wash bays.

"There just can't be any pillars between the windows and my wash bays," Purp said. "That's why I was saying they need to go in rows along there and there."

"But the span is twice as long that way," Greg said.

"I don't care how long the span is," Purp said. "We'll get iron big enough to support the span. Saving a nickel on the girders is not important. Blocking the view of the wash bays, that's my business."

"The posts will have to be bigger to support the heavier iron," Greg said.

"That's fine," Purp said. "If you could just calculate it and re-lay it out for me, but in a different color, then I'll see what you've got."

Purp and Greg finished up talking about a few details with the awning and Purp came back inside. Greg walked over toward the lowered tailgate of his truck parked in the corner of overflow.

"Hey, Purp," Javier said. He stood behind the counter between Brad and Janissa. Javier had been training Janissa all week. Janissa was on register and Brad on food line.

Purp poured himself a Pepsi. Halfway thorough he realized he forgot to use a plain cup. He thought about dumping his soda into one but then decided that would more than defeat the purpose.

"How's it going?" Purp said.

"Great," Javier said. Something about him seemed weird. "This is going to be so much better. Now I can jump on the line in a rush, or shift Janissa over and take register myself. Under three minutes is my goal."

"That's awesome," Purp said. "That roof is going to be nice, too."

"We're moving up," Javier said. He seemed like there was something he wanted to say but was saving it, or waiting for the right time, or something.

"We are," Purp said. "Is, uh, something going on?"

"Do you have a minute?" Javier said. That was a bad sign. Purp wasn't sure Javier had ever said that to him before.

"Sure," Purp said. "What's up?"

"Betty was asking earlier when you were out with the contractor if when you came in, we could go see her in her office," Javier said. He looked directly at Purp while he talked and he stood unusually straight, not leaning on the back counter or anything. But he had a smile, sort of. Like he was fighting one back or something.

"OK," Purp said. He had no idea what to make of any of this at all.

Purp and Javier walked into Betty's office, Javier in front, through the open door. Javier just walked right in without knocking on the frame or anything. Javier sat and Purp sat, too. Betty seemed to be expecting them, with a closed file folder on her desk. Two Christmas wreaths hung on the wall on either side of Betty's bookcase, red velvety bows and golden ornaments.

"Purp," Betty said. Something was seriously freaky. That was the second time in only a few minutes that either Betty or Javier had used his name. They usually only did that when he was in trouble. "I have something I would like to discuss with you, and with Javier." She sat straight in her chair, with a similar fought-back smile look to what Javier had on in the café.

Purp got this flash like he felt as if he were getting fired or something.

"What have you got for us?" Purp said. He leaned his forearms onto the edge of Betty's desk.

"This is a special month," Betty said. She touched her fingertips to the file folder between them.

"Can't beat Christmas," Purp said.

"This is the first month we've been in operation that we don't have to use any cash on hand to pay our expenses," Betty said. She looked like she was announcing the birth of her sister's first son or something. She opened the file folder like a magician's assistant.

"None at all?" Purp said. He knew what she'd said, he was just trying to stall for just the right thing to say. Betty seemed so excited Purp felt pressure to show the right response. "That is fantastic news."

"We're completely self-sustaining as of this point," Betty said. "I project that we'll be able to cover all of our expenses, with salaries for the two of you, from here on out."

"That was fast, right?" Javier said. "To get there in six months?"

"Unbelievably fast," Betty said. "Especially with a new-concept start-up."

"What about Janissa?" Purp said.

"She's in the projection. There's actually one hundred hours in the projection for café help," Betty said.

“That’s way more than I’m using now,” Javier said.

“Now the awning will come out of cash, though, right?” Purp said.

“Yeah,” Betty said, “we’ll have to use cash for that but the projection does even have facilities improvement in it, it’s just the awning is too big.”

“That is awesome news. The way you were talking at the beginning, I was thinking we’d be a year before we got to this point, if then. Congratulations,” Purp said. “To both of you.”

* * *

“So I said, ‘You can’t get out of your car,’” Purp said. His throat burned from talking so loud over the Friday roar in King’s X, his eyes and nose watering from an evening’s worth of secondhand smoke. “And he said, ‘What kind of car wash do you have to stay in your car?’” Purp tipped up the last of his Jack and Coke, ice glacier-sliding into his nose. He better order another before last call, maybe two. “And I said to him, ‘It’s the kind you have to stay in your car.’”

Betty giggled a snorting laugh, holding one hand in front of her nose and her Cosmopolitan in the other. Javier did his silent head-shaking laugh, looked up at the ceiling, and then polished off the Dos Equis he’d been working on.

Purp felt like he had to go to the bathroom but he wasn’t sure how well he would be able to stand.

“That’s like the kid we had that one time who came in with his lunch and his water bottle and sat down near the glass wall with his laptop,” Javier said.

“Yeah, he was all camped out there doing his work and eating Cheez-Its,” Purp said.

“And it wasn’t that busy so I was kind of like, waiting to see if maybe he’d order something later,” Javier said. “And then he leaves.”

Purp and Betty laughed.

“But then the next day he comes back again,” Javier said. “And he pulls out a fucking frozen pizza.”

Purp laughed around a piece of ice he was chewing. Betty laughed so hard she sloshed a few drops out of her Cosmo. She looked at Purp with a comical “What the crap?” look.

“And he asks me if I have an oven I can cook it for him in,” Javier said.

The three of them laughed. Betty put her face down almost nose to the lacquered wood tabletop while her back shook with laughter. She held her martini glass out to one side as if not to get any on her.

Purp ordered himself another Jack and Coke and a beer for Javier when the waitress came by for last call. Betty was the one-drink wonder, they called her. She could get herself red-face trashed on half a Cosmo and that was it for the evening. They talked about PTC and the customers, and the girls, and Brad, and Janissa. Before long Purp was chewing on ice again, sucking out the last of the flavor from his drink.

" . . . and boom," Purp said, miming being slammed to one side. "I was just like, flattened into the wall, dazed. I was all, 'huh? What?'" He looked around the King's X as if her were confused or stupid, imitating himself. "And he barrels by me with this huge-ass fire extinguisher I didn't even know we have, going 'Danger. Danger.'"

"No, 'Rescue,'" Javier said.

"Oh yeah," Purp said. "Rescue. And he just plows into the smoke and blasts the crap out of the convection oven, like it was just something he did every day, you know, saving us all from a fiery death and everything." Purp shrugged his shoulders and jutted his chin out, trying to imitate Javier.

Betty was just finding everything so hilarious. Purp hadn't ever seen her have such a good time. Javier laughed and then made a robotic-looking pantomime of a guy putting out fires with a fire extinguisher.

"This is awesome," Purp said. He was even starting to sound drunk to himself. He held his empty cooler over the table, as if making a toast. "We should celebrate our financial self-sufficiency . . . every day." He slurred and butchered his toast, partly because he really was drunk and partly because of the comic effect he thought it would have. "Every day, at least, that we sustain our self-sufficiency."

Javier clinked his beer to Purp's glass. Betty stood a little and leaned over the table, reaching to bump her drink into the other two. Purp liked the look of her leaning forward and reaching up, even though her black button-down shirt didn't show a whole lot, not buttoned up as high as she had it.

After a couple more stories Javier got up to go to the bathroom. Purp lost count of how many beers Javier had, but Javier walked through the King's X just like he'd walk through the café at ten in the morning. Javier stopped to talk to a guy and a girl at a table near the bathroom. The guy had on yellow-tinted glasses and the girl wore a thrift-store looking shapeless dress with black combat boots. Purp recognized them from parties.

"Who are they?" Betty said, nodding toward the couple. "They're not regulars."

"They're people Javier went to school with," Purp said. "They're in his program, behind him."

Javier slid a chair over to their table and sat on it backwards, folding his arms on the chair's back. The girl in combat boots gestured to Javier with sweeping hand movements.

Betty leaned her folded arms onto the table, her drink in front of her. Purp looked at her thigh, squeezed tight into jeans and crossed over her other leg. Betty kicked her high-heeled foot forward and back and Purp watched the rhythmic contractions of her thigh muscles under the taut denim. Purp looked at the side of Betty's breast. The way she leaned forward onto the table her breasts bulged against her snug-fitting shirt. Purp imagined Betty straddling him, leaning over him at that same angle and unbuttoning her shirt, her breasts spilling out.

"Thank you, Betty," Purp said.

"For what?" Betty said.

"For today," Purp said. "For getting us to this point. It's a big accomplishment."

"You don't have to thank me," Betty said, "it's your business."

"We wouldn't be at this point today without you," Purp said.

Purp leaned toward Betty and put his hand on her thigh. Her head jerked, turning toward him, black hair whipping his face, the berry scent of shampoo mixed with cigarette smoke. Purp put his face to hers and kissed her lips.

Betty pulled her head away after half a second. She scooted back in her seat and looked at Purp, wiping her mouth with the back of her hand. She looked down at her shoe.

Purp leaned back into his chair. With his forearms on the table he jingled the ice in his cooler glass. At the other end of the room, Javier swung his leg over the backwards chair like he was getting off a horse and walked into the bathroom.

* * *

"Not much," Purp said. "I just hung out with Selma. We went out for a nice dinner at Kabob and Curry and then came home and hung out." He sat at his desk and looked out into the courtyard. It looked a little strange with some of the support columns built, but no awning.

"Hung out?" Javier said.

"Yep," Purp said. He watched J. J. dancing with Monica, a brand new Latina girl. She was the chubbiest girl he'd ever hired but she could shake her ass hot enough that guys would probably drive through just to see her dancing with her shirt on. And she had enormous tits, too with nipples pointing practically straight up. That didn't hurt.

"Is that what you call it?" Javier said. He had his feet up on his desk, reading "Hugh Selwyn Mauberley."

"Call what?" Purp said. He saw Tara, on greeter, leaning into a beat-up Escort. He only scheduled enough girls for one wash bay, a greeter, and a sign girl. He figured it would be a dead day. They thought about not even opening, but now cars backed up into the entrance driveway. It looked like Tara might have to send them to overflow but Purp couldn't see how far back the line went.

"You call it hanging out?" Javier said.

"Oh," Purp said. "No, that's just what it was. We had a big dinner, we came home, we watched the ball drop, and that was that, Mattress Man."

"Come on," Javier said.

"I'm serious," Purp said.

"No way," Javier said.

"I'm telling you, it's not good," Purp said. "After Dick Clark – well, Regis, I went to sleep. I didn't even hardly drink last night."

"OK," Javier said.

"How about you? What did you do?" Purp said.

"I went to Arturo's party," Javier said.

"That is an awesome party," Purp said. "I mean, just on a regular day it's an awesome party, let alone."

"I know," Javier said. "I wasn't there too late, though."

"Nice," Purp said. "Nice. What, did you meet one of the little first-year chiquitas there or something? They must be all over you with your book coming out."

"No," Javier said.

"But you left early," Purp said.

"Yeah," Javier said.

"So you left to go play DS?" Purp said. "Did you get any stars? Or your Wing Cap?"

Javier laughed.

"So you left a party early," Purp said. "But you didn't meet someone there."

"No," Javier said.

"So you went with someone?" Purp said.

"I actually did," Javier said.

"The mystery DS-giver?" Purp said.

"In point of fact, the same," Javier said.

"Who?" Purp said. He spun in his chair and swiveled around so he was facing Javier. Purp leaned forward, his hands on his knees. "Someone from here?"

"Maybe," Javier said. "It was a long night. It's hard to remember."

"The new girl, Monica," Purp said.

"No," Javier said. "But she is hot."

"Janissa," Purp said. "I noticed you talk to her a lot."

"That's because she's my girl," Javier said. "I talk to Brad a lot, too. I only have two employees. But she is hot, too, though. Anyway, that would be inappropriate since I'm in her chain of command."

"J. J.," Purp said.

"No," Javier said. "But she is hot."

"Jeera," Purp said.

"Does she even work here anymore?" Javier said.

"No," Purp said. "She actually left for Foxy."

"Traitor," Javier said.

"No way," Purp said. "She couldn't quite make it here, so she had to go there. It's a step down, definitely."

"Well," Javier said. "She may not have been a traitor, but she was hot. You're on a 'J' theme, right?"

"Lacy," Purp said.

"No," Javier said. "But she is hot."

"Tara," Purp said.

"No," Javier said. "But she is hot."

"Rachel," Purp said.

"No," Javier said. "But she is hot."

"Brad," Purp said.

"Homey don't play that game," Javier said. "But he is hot. Also, chain of command issue again. But you do have the right first letter."

"The right first letter?" Purp said. He ran through the list in his mind. He didn't have any girls on it with a 'B.' He tried to think of ones who had left. "From here?"

"Yes," Javier said.

Purp worked it over. Outside Alyssa leaned onto a yellow Mercedes CLK, her hands spread wide over the hood. She kept time to Black Eyed Peas gyrating her ass with as much dexterity as a conductor holding a baton in his fingertips, cranking her hips to the left for two pulsing beats, then two beats to the right and back again. It caught him. Not just one thing, a few of them at once sliding up from below and grabbing at his guts, pulling them down. The hug in the office after the fight. The smirk like he knew what she was going to say already on self-sufficiency day. Accepting Brad without questioning it. All kinds of things. Things from way back.

"Betty," Purp said.

Neither one of them said anything for a while. Purp watched Alyssa dance. He wasn't sure what Javier was doing. Alyssa stood on tip-toes with her hands on her knees, legs spread, her back to the CLK. She kept the beat with her ass to the driver, looking over her shoulder at him. Her front faced the office window, though, and Purp wasn't sure who was getting the better show, himself or Mercedes guy. "Huh," he said. "I did not know that."

Javier tossed "Mauberley" onto his desk. He didn't say anything for thirty seconds. He looked out at Alyssa now, too.

"I know you didn't," Javier said. "So . . . don't sweat it, in December, right?"

"Fuck," Purp said. He exhaled a long, slow breath. All the air bled out of him. "She told you about that."

"Yeah," Javier said. "But I know you didn't know."

Purp sat forward with his forearms on the desk. He looked out at the undone masonry work for the awning. Two of the twelve pillars were almost done. He hoped the rest would go faster now that the holidays were over. He hoped the roof would keep the heat from the propane heaters in better. Not that it mattered today, he wasn't even sure they were on. The digital thermometer on the wall by his desk told him most sensors in the courtyard read over seventy degrees.

"How long?" Purp said. "A long time, huh?"

"Yeah," Javier said. "A while."

"That wasn't news?" Purp said.

"It was just kind of like, never a good time to bring it up, right?" Javier said. "And she's kind of weird about it."

Purp wiggled his mouse and went to a website he'd made showing a map of the courtyard and the average temperature in each part of it for the last hour. He had it shaded green for seventy to a hundred, red for above and blue for below. Most of the courtyard showed green, except the south side which faded into aqua and then blue right by the building. He thought about hanging more sensors on the new columns to get a more accurate grid.

"We should start watching D.M.G. again," Purp said.

"New season, right?" Javier said.

"Yeah," Purp said. "But either way. We should hang out more, outside here."

* * *

"Jesus Christ," Purp said. "Are we married or what?"

Selma yanked the blankets over to her side, tucking them in behind her. She faced away from Purp.

"I'm serious," Purp said. "This is starting to get ridiculous. It's already ridiculous." Purp pulled the covers back over to his side. He felt stupid being naked – and hard. He covered himself up. "I don't even know what to do anymore. Just tell me what I'm supposed to do and I'll do it."

"It's not what you do," Selma said, "it's what you don't do."

"What is that supposed to mean?" Purp said. "Is that something you heard on Oprah or something?" He got out of bed and went over to his armoire, fishing a pair of boxers out of his drawer in the dark. He held them up close to his eyes, looking for the side that had the tag on it. "That doesn't even mean anything. I wish you would just tell me something instead of talking in these annoying Dr. Phil clichés."

"Not everybody hangs out in such a literary crowd as you," Selma said. She sniffed. "It's not that easy for me."

"Easy?" Purp said. "What's easy? Nothing you do is easy. Is that what you tell the Colonel? Do you say, 'Oh, I didn't get it done because it isn't easy?'" Purp stepped into the boxers. They didn't feel right. He put his finger in the fly, the fly buttons inside. Inside out.

"I'm under a lot of stress," Selma said.

"You know what?" Purp said. "So am I. So is everybody. You keep telling me it's going to get easier when you get promoted –

"It is," Selma said.

"It isn't," Purp said. "You've been telling me that our whole lives. Since like six months into our relationship. It's going to get easier when midterms are over, you'll feel more like having sex then. You'll feel like it when the semester is over. When you graduate. After Basic Course after you get promoted, after you get permanent party Air Guard –

"Those are all true things," Selma said.

"And in none of those cases did anything get better," Purp said. "None. You just keep telling me how much better everything is going to get when you get to the next phase of your job, and I'm telling you, I'm sick of waiting."

"That isn't fair," Selma said.

"It is fair," Purp said. "What is 'fair' anyway? That's another Oprah word."

"Why do you keep saying that?" Selma said. "I haven't even seen Oprah in years. Is she even on still?"

"What? Are you serious?" Purp pulled on a pair of sweatpants. Damn it. Backwards. "Of course she's still on. Of course. How could you not know that Oprah was on TV? Where the fuck else would she go? Her magazine cover?"

"I'm not that up on my TV like you, I'm actually busy at work," Selma said.

"I'm not busy?" Purp said.

"You have an enormous TV in your office," Selma said.

"Which I hardly turn on," Purp said.

"Because you're staring at college girls' wet tits all day," Selma said.

"Maybe I'd be less interested in that if I got a little action once in a while," Purp said.

"That's not fair," Selma said, whining. "You know it's been hard since the baby."

"You know what?" Purp said. "I am sick of hearing about the baby."

"You're what?" Selma said.

"I am," Purp said. "It was a year and a half ago. It happens to like half of the people who get pregnant. So what, I'm just not supposed to have sex anymore now because you had a miscarriage a year and a half ago?"

"Well it didn't seem to affect you much then, either," Selma said.

"It didn't seem to affect me? Are you joking?" Purp said. "I was freaked out. Seriously freaked out."

"You got over it awful quick," Selma said.

"I did get over it," Purp said. "In a normal amount of time. I'm not going to hold onto it for the rest of my life and stop having – and you know what? I am sick of hearing about that. That's just another one of your crutches. 'It'll get better when I get over losing the baby.' It's just another phase of your life you can blame for your lazy attitude toward –

"Lazy?" Selma said. "You think I'm lazy now? I go to work at –

"I don't care when you go to work," Purp said. "You're always telling me about this big mystical work ethic you have, how hard you work. I'm telling you you're lazy when it comes to doing the work of being in a relationship. You're awfully lazy about that. You might have a work ethic, but your home ethic sucks." Ribs sore from laying on his side so long, Purp sat up on the edge of the bed in his boxers. Sitting didn't agree with him. He wasn't sure which was worse, the headache he got from sitting up or his sore ribs and stiff shoulder from laying down. If he laid back down and fell asleep, though, Selma might come home and find him in bed, and he didn't want that. Purp shuffled into the kitchen and poured himself a Jack and Coke. He thought that might do the trick for the hangover, if that's what it was. He couldn't quite tell if he was hung over or still drunk but he had to get some in him anyway, before he could face trying to shave and wash up. While he poured, Purp's cell phone vibrated in the bedroom, one short pulse. A missed call.

After he made himself look like he might have gone to work, dressed and shaved and hair pulled back, Purp poured another Jack and Coke and a bowl of Goldfish crackers. He made his drink with ice in a thirty-two ounce plastic tumbler that Selma bought for her fruit smoothies.

Purp settled himself onto the recliner with his food and drink and turned on the TV. Oprah. She had Dr. Phil on. They talked about these four people on there who looked terribly overweight. Special kind of chair overweight. Everybody was crying on there and pouring out the things that seemed like they'd been in there all their lives. Dr. Phil did a great job helping them get right to the core of what was going on, and it was kind of similar for all four of them. Purp had heard people making fun of Dr. Phil for being a little heavy himself and trying to lose weight, but Purp got it. Purp understood what it was like to be a coach at something maybe you weren't the best at yourself. He couldn't dance, and he didn't think people would pay to see him with his shirt off, but Purp knew how to coach the girls, to get them psyched up about what they needed to do to get the job done. It wasn't too different from what Dr. Phil was doing.

Purp sipped and watched and munched on his goldfish. He liked to take a little drink in his mouth while he had Goldfish in there, half-mashed. It got fizzy all of a sudden when the Coke hit the crackers. Effervescent, Purp thought.

Purp's phone vibrated in the bedroom. He didn't feel like getting up. He figured whoever it was, they'd deal with not being able to talk to him for the afternoon. He had Marissa on greeter, and she'd been at it long enough she could handle whatever came up. He wouldn't have minded, either, if Betty noticed he was gone and needed him for something. She'd been making him feel more and more useless.

The house phone rang. Telemarketers, probably.

Dr. Phil hugged one of the overweight men. Thick tears drained out of both the heavy man's eyes. The poor guy couldn't even stand up off the platform they had him on to give Dr. Phil a hug. Dr. Phil had to lean way in to reach, and his arms barely opened wide enough to get around the guy's shoulders. Dr. Phil didn't seem to care how awkward he looked bending over like that with his ass to the camera, his suit coat bunched up around his wireless mike transmitter. Dr. Phil was making a lot of money, and there were a ton of people watching, but if you took it all away, Purp thought, all the lights and money and advertisers and everything – if you stripped it all away, it was just Dr. Phil giving this big fellow a hug, trying to come up with something to say to him to help him feel a little better about the world. Purp figured Dr. Phil would do that anyway, lights and money and crowd or not.

The locked turned in the front door and it was way too early for Selma to come home.

"What are you doing here?" Selma said before she was half in the door. "Are you OK?"

"I am . . . OK," Purp said. It felt like his brain moved a little faster than his mouth was giving him credit for.

"What are you doing?" Selma said. She closed the door behind her, not a slam but loud. She stood on the tiles in her tight little Air Force skirt, hands on her hips with her legs apart. Purp knew those stockings didn't go all the way up. He thought about her maybe straddling him there on the chair.

"Hanging with Phil," Purp said.

"What?" Selma said. She tossed her purse and keys onto the hall table.

"This . . . man is really something," Purp said, "else. Something else."

"Where have you been?" Selma said. "Everybody was worried about you. They called here all morning and nobody answered. Didn't you hear the phone?"

"Technically, I heard it," Purp said. "But I did not hear it in the morning." Purp started to rub his crotch through his jeans. He felt himself getting hard.

"You just decided not to go to work and not call anybody?" Selma said.

"I'm the boss," Purp said. "I don't have to tell Betty where I'm going, when. She works for me," Purp pointed, arm straight but wavering, at Selma, "not the other way." He let his arm down onto his lap. He thought it still felt wrong from sleeping on it funny, but that would be a long time for it to still not feel right.

"What about Javier?" Selma said. "He didn't know where you were. He called me and asked if you were OK."

"And that I am," Purp said. "Everybody can relax now."

"I left work early," Selma said. "I thought you got into a car accident or something."

"I'm fine," Purp said. "Fine. Did you miss me?"

"Did I miss you?" Selma said.

"When you," Purp said, "thought I was dead." Purp rubbed his crotch faster.

"Purp this isn't funny," Selma said. "You can't just not tell people where you are."

"Come here," Purp said. "Come climb up here right now." He unzipped his pants.

"What?" Selma said.

"Kneel on this chair over me," Purp said. "Hike that little skirt up. Let me slide your thong to one side and –

"You are seriously not right," Selma said. "Seriously. I just left work early because I thought you got injured or lost or something."

"I'm not lost," Purp said. "I'm right here." He gripped his dick as if to wave it at Selma.

"Do you hear yourself?" Selma said. "You need help or something, Purp."

"I need help?" Purp said. "Because I want to fuck my wife a couple of times a year?"

"Purp, no. There's not even a chance I'm going to have sex with you right now," Selma said. "That is just completely out of the question. You're just not right in the head if you'd think I would have sex with you right now. You're disgusting."

"Disgusting?" Purp said, still stroking himself.

"If you think making me worry all day something happened to you so I have to rush home early and find you drunk and masturbating in the living room is going to get me in the mood, then you just know nothing. Nothing at all," Selma said.

"I'm not disgusting," Purp said. "I don't have to wait around for you to fuck me, I'll tell you that much."

"What's that supposed to mean?" Selma said.

"I have other options," Purp said. "I work with a lot of naked hot girls every day. I wouldn't have any trouble at all getting one of them to fuck me. No trouble."

"You think those girls would have sex with you?" Selma said. "Purp, they're like twenty years old."

"If there's grass on the playing field," Purp said. "Play ball."

"Those girls wouldn't touch you," Selma said. "You're their clown."

"Play ball," Purp said. He started rubbing himself fast, like he was going to finish.

* * *

Purp left work early. He'd fought so bad with Betty over the short box that Betty cried. The video wall ran way over what Purp thought it would, and he needed the extra cash to get it done. Javier had to get between them and herd Purp back into the office. Purp fell asleep at his desk and Javier woke him up to tell him to go home. Javier said Betty didn't want to stay there with Purp the way he was, and she didn't have much time to get everything done for tax day. Javier said it might just be best if Purp went home and slept it off a little so everybody could get back to work. Javier walked Purp out to the car.

Purp didn't have room to pull in. Selma left the Focus in the middle of the driveway at an angle, the hatch and both back doors open. Purp left his truck at the curb, blocking the neighbors. Walking in he saw Selma had the Focus packed up. Selma walked out of the front door carrying a pair of black combat boots in each hand. The boots had a mirror shine on them and Purp was surprised to see Selma letting them rub together.

"What's going on?" Purp said. He knew what was going on.

Selma didn't stop but she answered him in a neutral tone. "I'm going to my father's for a while."

"That's not necessary," Purp said, following her to the car.

"It is for me," Selma said. "It's kind of getting to where it is for me."

"What's it going to solve?" Purp said.

"It's just too much," Selma said. "Why are you home so early?"

"I just stopped by to get my flash drive," Purp said.

* * *

"It's for the video wall," Purp said, "why do you care? Why is it such a big deal to you?"

"It's stealing," Betty said. She stood beside her desk, in loose cutoff sweats and a baggy University T-shirt.

"Stealing from who?" Purp said. "Not from you. You get paid. How many raises have you gotten?"

"You're stealing from the business," Betty said. "You're not paying taxes on that money you're skimming out of the box. It's not legal."

"I'm stealing from the business?" Purp said. "I am the business."

"You're not the only owner," Betty said.

"Is that was this is about?" Purp said. "Ask him, he doesn't care."

"He kind of does care," Betty said. "But he won't say anything to you. You're stealing from him, too. And the government."

"I don't care about the government," Purp said. "And it's an investment. It's going to make the café look so much better. It'll be the whole wall."

"If it's an investment, just do it right," Betty said. "Just tell me how much you need and what it's for and if there's money I'll budget for it. I'll cut you a check. Why is that so hard? We can sit down with Javier and discuss it, plan it out."

"That's a pain in the ass," Purp said.

"It's not so hard. You don't need to be just running to Best Buy with a wad of cash in your pocket every other day," Betty said. "This isn't your ATM."

"Twelve screens, the whole wall," Purp said. "Every one a different camera angle on the bays."

"It's a lot of equipment. I know what you're spending, Purp. I'm not stupid. And I know how you do things, you're not getting cheap stuff, I know," Betty said.

"There won't be anything like it," Purp said. "Not anywhere. And I can use the feeds on the website. If I get twelve streams of this place on that site I can monetize that. I'm talking about real money. Huge money. Potentially more money than we take in here, bricks and mortar."

"I don't doubt it. That's not what I'm saying," Betty said. "It's just the way you're going about it is completely the wrong way to do it. This equipment is all depreciable. Every penny of it over years, and years. I don't need it for the fifteenth because that's last year, but for FY zero five if you can't recreate what you've taken out of the box and give me some documentation for all of this, we're losing out on massive capital expenditures. You're ripping us off so bad by not letting me do that right. You're ripping us off for years, and years."

"It's not your money to tell me what to do with it," Purp said. "I own this place, not you."

"I know," Betty said. "You remind me of –

"I remind you because you seem like you keep forgetting," Purp said. "You order me around like you're my boss, but you forget. You're not. You're just a little college girl who puts numbers in a spreadsheet."

"Do you have absolutely no idea what I do here?" Betty said. "Do you know how to do anything I do? You make a schedule of which girls come in when. Do you think that is running a million dollar plus business? Is that what you think it takes to run this place?"

Javier walked into Betty's office behind Purp.

"Come on you guys," Javier said, "cool it. It's annoying for the customers out there."

"Cool it," Betty said. "Cool it? He's ripping you off, tens of thousands of dollars, more than that, and you just want him to be quiet?"

"I want you to be quiet," Javier said. "You're the one yelling."

"Do you care?" Purp said to Javier. "Do you care that I'm using box money to build the video wall?"

"That's not the point," Javier said.

"You're the one who's going to benefit from it," Purp said. You're the one who'll have twelve fifty-sixes of wet tits and ass in your café all day. It's got to be better than looking at her in those ratty sweats and listening to her bitch at you all day. I feel sorry for you. She'll have you so whipped down you'll wish –

"Come on," Javier said. He walked into Purp, not pushing him so much as moving him along, out of Betty's office. Javier rolled Purp like Purp didn't weigh anything at all. In only a couple of steps Javier belly-bumped Purp right out of Betty's office.

"And it's not all for the video wall, either," Betty said over Javier's shoulder. "You guys need two Xboxes in your office? You need two plasma screens in there? For what? That's for the customers? And the digital video thing we're paying a hundred and fifty bucks a month for from Time Warner? That's for what? Why don't you guys just take the money at the end –

"OK," Javier said. He turned around and walked into Betty's office, taking Betty with him. Javier shut the door behind them.

Purp stood in the café. He heard Javier talking over Betty's rant on the other side of the wooden door. Purp caught the eye of a guy who was looking at him. The customer flicked his eyes toward the glass wall and sipped his beer, as if pretending he hadn't just been staring at Purp.

* * *

"Thanks for dinner," Gina said. She sat in the passenger's seat of Purp's truck.

"You're welcome," Purp said. "I had fun."

"I'm sorry about the wine thing," Gina said. She uncrossed her legs. The slit in the side of her dress opened up and Purp saw the wheat-tan skin of her thigh framed by the floral print of her knee-length sundress.

"Oh, geeze, don't worry about that," Purp said. "I wouldn't have ordered it if I thought you weren't twenty-one. I'm the one who's sorry."

"I felt like an ass," Gina said. "But you could have still had yours."

"It was totally my fault," Purp said. "Don't even worry about it. I just assumed you were twenty-one. It seems like such a long time ago you graduated."

"I know," Gina said. "It seems like forever."

"Well, thanks for having dinner with me," Purp said.

"Happy birthday, again," Gina said. "I wish I knew before. I would have gotten you something. Do you have any big plans for tonight? Are you and Javier going to party or something?" Gina shook her shoulders when she said that, as if to mean dancing. Purp glanced down the scoop-neck of her dress.

"No," Purp said. " We don't hang so much anymore like we used to."

"The shit you were telling me about with Betty?" Gina said.

"Yeah," Purp said.

"So no plans?" Gina said. "On your birthday?"

"Having dinner with you," Purp said. "That was a fun birthday."

"Aww," Gina said. She made a sad face. "That's so sad."

"That I had fun with you? That's sad?" Purp said.

"No," Gina said, "that you have nothing to do on your birthday."

"I did have something to do," Purp said. "I went out with you."

"I mean like after that, though," Gina said. She ran her fingers through her blond hair. "What are you just going to go home and watch TV on your birthday?"

"Pretty much," Purp said. He had three saved episodes of Curb Your Enthusiasm on his DVR he hadn't seen.

"Well," Gina said. She sounded timid. "I have a T.V." She bit her bottom lip and tilted her chin down, looking up at Purp. "And I also have a bottle of wine, too, in case you still felt like having a glass." Gina leaned onto the center console, her knees together but her ankles apart. "I mean, it's probably not like the kind you like or anything but –

"I would love to come up," Purp said. "And have a glass of your wine." Purp tapped the back of Gina's hand with his fingertip. He saw her almost naked several days a week but tapping the back of her hand with his fingertip felt to him like the most intimate gesture. "But . . ."

"But you have to get going?" Gina said. She pursed her lips and twisted her mouth to her scar side. She actually looked disappointed.

"But," Purp said, "I really," he let his fingertip linger on the back of her hand. The he dragged it, stroking her skin. "I really, really, really . . . have to go to the bathroom. Can I use yours?"

Gina laughed. She wrinkled her brow and touched her chin, like she was deliberating.

"Definitely," she said. She opened her door and hopped out of the truck. She left her purse on the floor mat. Purp leaned over picked it up for her before he got out, too.

Liquid wax trickled off the candles into pools on the mirror, lava flows, the translucent rivulets turning opaque as they hit fresh glass and cooled. The wood floor under the mirror grew stalagmites, the accumulation of multi-colored dripped-off wax, left there, it looked to Purp, for months. Gina had a mirror set up like a shelf under her window, a full length mirror laying flat on three concrete blocks, one supporting the middle and one under each end. The only light in her room came from the streetlight outside and the fifteen or twenty candles she had lit on the mirror.

"Happy birthday, again," Gina said. She clinked her glass on Purp's. They each had half a glass of Chardonnay left, the last of the bottle they opened when they came in. Gina sat cross-legged on her full-sized futon in her floral sundress and Purp leaned on his side, his knees bent so that his body curled in a little C-shape around Gina, his knee touching her foot and leaning against her hip. Gina's dress fell loosely over her legs and between her thighs, six inches above her knee.

Purp sipped his wine and set the glass down on top of the stack of plastic crates Gina had for a night table. Gina leaned her arm on the side of Purp's thigh, using his leg like an end table, or an armrest. Purp touched Gina's knee with his fingertip, slowly tracing a circle on her skin the size of a quarter. He let the circle get larger and larger with each turn. Gina had on Dave Matthews. She swayed with the music, her eyes on Purp, brushing her side against the fronts of his thighs as she moved back and forth.

Purp's fingertip circles got larger and larger until he was just barely stroking the entire circumference of Gina's knee with each turn. He came around to the top of his circle, the inside of her knee the way she sat cross-legged, and let his finger stop there for a second. He looked at his own skin against her tan knee. Half as slow as he was moving it before, Purp let his fingertip wander against the inside of Gina's thigh, not in a straight path but curved, toward the front of her leg, then toward the back, but always creeping up higher on her thigh. He barely touched her, just grazing the tiny invisible hairs on her skin. Back and forth until his finger brushed the hem of Gina's hiked-up dress. He slid his finger along her thigh under the fabric only far enough to hide his fingernail. He felt Gina open her legs wider, just a half inch, and then he let his finger retreat back along its zig-zagged path to her knee. Gina sighed.

Gina leaned and set her wine glass on the candle mirror and then sat back the way she was before, her hand open on Purp's thigh. She slid her hand up to his hip, slowly, as slow as he moved his fingertip on the inside of her thigh. He dragged his finger up toward the hem of her skirt and then down to her knee. They stayed like that for a while, listening to the music, Purp tracing patterns on the inside of Gina's tight golden thigh, she rubbing the back of his leg, her fingertips slipping into the space where his own thighs met. After moving up and down her thigh so many times he lost count, Purp stopped his finger just at the hem. He set another finger beside the first, then another, then another. Four fingers brushing the inside of her thigh. Gina slid her hand further around the back of Purp's leg, wedging her fingers between his legs from behind. She opened her legs wider and rocked her hips toward Purp, her other knee pressing between his thighs. Purp opened his legs a couple of inches, grinding against her knee. He knew she could feel him hard through his jeans on her leg.

Purp slid his four fingers up under Gina's dress. He nestled them in the spot where the inside of her thigh met her body. He felt it warm there, and wet. She made a soft humming sound and sucked in a deep breath. Gina laid back on the futon, her hands on her flat belly. She stretched one leg out and hooked it around the small of Purp's back.

* * *

Purp tried to make it to the soda dispenser before Betty noticed him coming in so late, or Javier. Javier wasn't behind the food line or the cafe, probably in the office. Purp didn't care so much if Javier noticed when he came in to work, he mostly just didn't want Betty to see. Purp slipped in behind Janissa to get himself some Pepsi. Brad had five breakfast burritos on at once. The guy was getting to be a little bit of a legend himself the way he cranked out burritos. Janissa was supposed to take turns with him but it always seemed like Brad on the line and Janissa on register.

"Hey Purp," Betty said from behind him.

"Good morning," Purp said over his shoulder to her. He waited for some foam to die down before he squirted another jet of Pepsi into his cup. He left a few fingers empty in the cup so he could top it off with Jack from his desk. He needed a drink to get going.

"Late start today, huh?" Betty said.

"Not so much," Purp said. "I was working on a few things at home. Trying to get the video feeds working on the website."

"Telecommuting," Betty said.

"Exactly," Purp said. He walked around Betty toward his office door, trying to end the conversation.

"I hate to bother you," Betty said, following him toward his door, "but I'm trying to get everything straight for the month end and I was wondering if you had something for me from the box?"

"Oh yeah," Purp said, "I was going to get that together for you this morning." He walked into his office. Betty followed him in.

"Because I don't have anything down for the last three days of April," Betty said, "and it's already the second." Betty leaned against Javier's desk with her arms crossed.

"Yeah," Purp said. "I said I'd get it."

"Morning, Purp," Javier said. Javier sat behind his desk looking at his monitor. He didn't look at Purp, or Betty. He looked like he was copying numbers off a paper form into a spreadsheet.

"Hey, dude," Purp said to Javier. Purp rolled his desk chair back and sat down. He set the thirty-two ounce cup on his desk. He didn't drink any. He was waiting until he could mix it and he didn't want to mix it with Betty standing there. "OK, I'll bring that over to your office in a little bit," he said to Betty. Outside two bays washed. Susie, a new redhead girl slowly turned a complete circle with her arms over her head, swaying her hips to the courtyard music. Purp could only hear the beat of it. Susie moved well, a University basketball cheerleader, but her skin was so fair Purp wasn't sure how she'd hold up in the courtyard even with the awning. He definitely couldn't use her on sign girl. She'd get an awful burn.

"Have you been smoking?" Betty said to Purp.

"No," Purp said.

"You smell like weed," Betty said.

"Well, not this morning," Purp said. "Last night I did, a little, but not today. I had these same jeans on, maybe that's why." Purp logged into his computer, trying to look busy. He started up Visual Studio. He learned a long time ago at the museum, you put that up and nobody messes with you. "OK then, I'll get that money to you later on."

"I'm trying to get this done," Betty said. "I've got to get out of here early today so I can study for my Econ final on Thursday." She walked around to the front of Purp's desk, leaning against it with both thighs. The sweat shorts she had on were so short, bare skin touched the desk. Can you please just give it to me? I don't care if you do the paperwork, I'll do it for you."

"I haven't really sorted it out," Purp said, "which was from April and May. I'll get it done."

"I'll do it," Betty said. "Please." She leaned over, her knuckles on Purp's desk. He flicked a look at her out the corner of his eye but he couldn't see much down the neck of her loose T-shirt.

"Betty will take care of it, Purp," Javier said. He kept his eyes on his monitor. "She'll get you caught up and you can start fresh on it from today." Javier rolled the scroll wheel of his mouse. It ticked up and down, moving the spreadsheet into a screenful of empty cells and back to what Javier was working on. "You just got a little behind, it's been busy ever since Spring Break finished."

Purp opened his bottom drawer. He wanted the Jack but he grabbed the green vinyl bags instead. If she wanted the cash so bad, let her mess with it. The bags felt light. He unzipped one, empty. Maybe he'd consolidated it onto just one. Second one, empty. He felt his ears go red and his pits start to sweat. His back prickled. He could feel the third one was empty, too, because it weighed only as much as the other two. He unzipped it. Empty. Betty watched him, still leaning on his desk. He felt his scalp burn, like she was shining a heat lamp on it.

"Oh yeah," he said. "I had it under these file folders." He had no idea what he did with the cash. He took the bottle out of his desk drawer and set it under his desk so he could get the file folders out. He knew the money wouldn't be there. He took the file folders out and set them on his desk. There was nothing underneath. "Oh no," Purp said. "I gave it to you, didn't I? That's right. I dropped off April the day before yesterday after you left. It's in the safe. All I have is yesterday, here." Purp leaned to one side and pulled out his wallet.

"You didn't put it in the safe," Betty said. "I went through the whole safe before you came in today. It's not in there."

"Did you put it somewhere else?" Javier said. "When was the last time you remember seeing it?" Javier said, still scrolling his spreadsheet up and down.

"I put it in the safe," Purp said. "I swear I put it in there the day before yesterday. Are you sure you don't have it?" he said to Betty.

"Come on," Betty said. "You spent four days of the box?"

"I didn't spend it," Purp said. "You lost it. Go look for it again. Maybe it got stuck in the turnstile."

"It did not get stuck in the turnstile," Betty said.

"Well, here's for yesterday, anyway," Purp said. He took a stack of bills out of his wallet. He counted out seven-hundred twenty dollars. He put twenty back in. "Here's seven-hundred bucks." He handed the money to Betty. "Get yourself some PTC shirts with it. We have an image to uphold."

* * *

Purp sat at a back café table, one of the ones along the six-foot high glass block wall between the entryway and the seating area. He wanted to check out how the video wall looked from this particular table, the one with the worst view of the courtyard. He sat with Jeremy, a devoted regular, a kid in a basketball jersey and flip-flops.

"What do you think?" Purp said.

"Freaking awesome, Purp," Jeremy said. "It's so freaking awesome. That was the only stressful thing about coming here, trying to get close to the glass wall."

"I don't know why I didn't set it up like this to begin with," Purp said. He looked at each of the twelve plasma screen TVs on the video wall, each one showing a different live feed from the wash bays, four cameras per bay. Purp sprayed purple ovals onto the concrete floor of each bay so the girls would know where to be, to show as much on camera as possible. "Except it was expensive."

"It's so much better," Jeremy said. "It's like a totally different place now."

"I can control the cameras from inside, too," Purp said. "From home, even."

"That is so freaking awesome," Jeremy said.

Javier walked over to where Purp sat with Jeremy.

"It looks great, doesn't it?" Purp said to Javier.

"It does," Javier said. "Sure makes my day better, right?"

"I hope so," Purp said.

"Hey, you almost ready?" Javier said. "For Betty? She's waiting on us."

"OK," Purp said. He stood. He mimed a whipping motion at Jeremy and made a sound like the crack of a whip. "Peace," he said to Jeremy.

"Later," Jeremy said.

Purp followed Javier into Betty's office. She had a file folder on her desk. She looked like she'd been tanning recently, or outside. Betty started the meeting for them as they sat down, going over the numbers she had for May. It had been a decent month. Not a record or anything, but average, good.

"And that," Betty said, "is with a lot I know we lost from the box."

Purp felt his cheeks flush and his forehead wrinkle. He looked Betty in the eye.

"Well I mean," Betty said, "I know all spring there was a lot coming out of the box. For the video wall," she said, nodding at Purp, "which definitely looks great."

"It does, Purp, it looks great," Javier said.

"And that was a big expense, and I wish we had more receipts from it," Betty said, "but I'll do what I can and I'm glad it's all up and working and everybody's happy with it. And it's done."

"The customers love it," Purp said.

"Absolutely," Betty said. "I've heard them. They love it."

"Yes," Javier said. "It worked out great."

"And now that it is completely done," Betty said. Purp thought her attempt to sound upbeat was getting a little thick. "I think it's a good time to change the way we do our cash handling a little, to streamline it."

"That's a good idea," Javier said.

"To make it better for both sides of the house, café and car wash," Betty said.

"Because we don't need that cash going out for the video wall any more," Javier said.

Ambushed. Betty sounded almost convincing, but Javier just sounded like he was reading off his lines.

"So I was thinking," Betty said, "and I mentioned it to Javier the other day, too, that we could increase our cash handling efficiency if we follow what I've outlined here." She opened her file folder and started going through her presentation.

Betty flipped her charts and spreadsheets in front of Purp and Javier. Purp felt bad that Javier was sitting there pretending he'd never seen them before. Betty explained to them how their receipts from the car wash weren't what she expected based on the plate camera database, and that she could account for a lot of that with the equipment costs but even so, money was getting lost between the box and the safe. It deflated Purp, seeing Javier there nodding his head. He couldn't tell which one was the dog and which one was the pony.

The end result of all of it was that Purp was out of the cash handling loop. Betty would get the box in every day, and she'd stock a new petty cash safe in her office with a hundred dollars a day for Purp and Javier to use to buy small-ticket items. It was a digital safe, "real easy to get in and out of securely," she said. She had a log book in there, a three ring binder with the PTC logo on front, for Purp and Javier to write down how much they took, and for what.

* * *

Sipping a new Jack and Pepsi Purp watched the girls finish up the last car for the day. Thirteen girls on one powder-blue Mustang. That guy was getting his money's worth, the last customer through the last bay on the fourth of July. He had a DoD parking sticker on his windshield, too, and an Air Force haircut. Good for him. The girls even walked along on either side of the Mustang all the way to the exit driveway. Nicole shut the gate behind the Mustang and Marissa locked it.

It had been an unbelievable day. Purp planned for three bays, but he even pulled the sign girls and squeezed in a fourth wash lane. He thought people might not figure they'd be open for the holiday, but there was more traffic than he could handle. The café was hopping all day, too, but not so much more than a regular day. Groups of guys wandered in together on their way to and from barbecues and parties.

The girls stood out by the exit gate, soaked, hot. The sun was almost down but Purp's temperature plot said the whole courtyard was still over a hundred. The girls didn't seem to mind. It looked like they were laughing and talking, just hanging out together in the courtyard before breaking up to shower and head off to their Fourth of July parties or wherever it was they went. Gina and J. J. danced a little to a song that just came on. Purp would have thought they'd have been all danced out by now. But they danced, silly, and shook their wet hair at each other. Gina looked up at Purp and waved at him. J. J. and Elizabeth looked over toward the office to see who Gina was waving at, then they hip-checked her and laughed. Purp figured Gina had told the girls about them and he didn't mind. He asked Gina to keep it a little low-key at work so nobody got irritated, and she'd been doing a pretty good job.

Seeing the girls out there hanging around, not rushing off like they were sick of the place, made Purp feel like going out there and splitting the box between them and wishing them a happy Fourth. He hadn't seen Betty go out yet to get the money. He wanted to see the looks on their pretty faces when he handed them a big pile of cash. He wanted the smell of damp hair and sunscreen and money in his nostrils. He wanted Gina talking to him after about how nice of him that was while they cuddled up together to watch the fireworks in the back of Purp's truck. Purp wanted the girls to think Gina's boyfriend was cool.

Purp sipped down the rest of his Jack and Pepsi, sidestepped out of his office, and made a dash for the courtyard door. He stopped short, his shoes skidding on the concrete damp with overspray. He didn't have his keys. He popped back in. Betty's door was shut. Javier, bent behind the register, counted his till while Brad and Janissa cleaned. Purp snatched his keys off his desk. Monica and Susie walked toward the changing room and the rest still milled around by the gate. Purp slipped out of the courtyard door again and headed straight for the box, looking for the key on his ring while he walked. He found it.

"Marissa," Purp said over his shoulder while he walked, "could you please ask the girls to hang on a minute?"

"Sure, Purp," Marissa said.

Purp all of a sudden got this crappy feeling like what if Betty changed the lock on the box. He hadn't tried to open it since she started the new cash handling system two weeks before and he wouldn't put it past her at this point to put a different lock on there and tell him it was to make it more efficient. His hands shook a little as he reached for the box and he felt he would be getting red if he didn't have a tan. What would he do now after telling the girls to wait if he couldn't get the box open? He fumbled with his key. He looked back and Marissa was leading the girls over to where Purp stood. They probably guessed what he was up to. It was one of his favorite things, splitting the box. The key wouldn't go. But it looked like the same lock. It looked exactly the same. He steadied his hand on the top of the box and turned the key around the other way. It went. It went. He got the box open and reached in to feel it thick with bills. He jammed his arm down into it and felt money all the way to the bottom. He pulled it out in handfuls and sorted it on the concrete, holding it down with his shoe.

The girls went nuts. They crowded around in a half-circle, some of them singing, most of them dancing with their arms in the air. They didn't seem to care at all that they were topless. A hundred degrees in the courtyard, Purp wished he was topless, too.

Purp got the bills sorted out in four piles. He took three twenties off the top for tonight and left it up to Marissa to divide the rest. Gina hugged him from behind while he was still squatted down by the money with Marissa. Purp almost tipped over, Gina's wet tits pressed onto his back. Purp fell forward onto his hands, a cage of thighs in short-shorts all around him. He'd die happy if that was the last thing he saw.

Purp hung out with the girls for a minute in the courtyard until he could tell Monica and Susie had somewhere to be but were staying to be polite. So he made it seem like he had to get back in to help Javier clean up, which he did have to do. He walked back into the café, telling Gina he'd meet her over at Taco Cabana after he was done and she was showered.

"Did you just give away the box?" Betty said. She stood with her arms crossed in the middle of the café dining area. She looked better than she had in a while, in a jean skirt with an appliqué flower on it and a pink sleeveless knit shirt with a high-cut neck. She had a flower in her hair, by her ear, to match the one over her thigh. It looked like she had something glittery on her tan legs, too. Maybe she and Javier were going out somewhere. Purp hadn't asked Javier what he was doing for the holiday.

"What?" Purp said.

"What?" Betty said. "It's right there." Betty pointed through the glass wall to the box. "Hello?" She waved her arm up at the video wall where a couple of cameras showed an angle on the box, too.

"No, I mean 'So what?'" Purp said.

Javier walked around from behind the register. He leaned on a café table, his knee brushing Betty's thigh. He looked at Purp. A sad look.

"Purp," Javier said, "we have a system now."

"So I gave them a cut," Purp said.

"It's not your cut to give," Betty said.

"I gave them some money for working hard on the holiday," Purp said.

"We all worked hard on the holiday," Javier said. "So did Brad. So did Janissa. So did Betty."

"So did Javier," Betty said. "You don't see him stuffing money in his pocket from the till."

"Is that what this is about?" Purp pulled out his wallet. "Is that what you're talking about?" He took three twenties out of his wallet.

"That's part of it," Javier said. "But you had a big day out there. That's what we're all here for."

"Well here then," Purp flicked the twenties into Javier's face. Javier tipped his head away, like a moth had brushed his eyelid. "Go buy your girlfriend some dinner."

Javier let the bills flutter to the tile floor.

"We don't need to go back over this," Javier said.

"We're not going back to you ripping off the box every other day," Betty said, "Or every other whole week."

"It was one time, OK?" Purp said. "One time."

"One time plus a lot of other times," Betty said. "What do you get off, like some kind of pimp, throwing money around at them?"

"A pimp?" Purp said.

"You want the naked girls pawing all over you for cash," Betty said, "is that it? Are you compensating because Selma won't have sex with you?"

"Betty, I think he just –

"You need to grow up, do you know that?" Betty said, talking over Javier.

"What do you know?" Purp said. "What are you like twenty-two years old or something, little Miss Business School?"

"You just stole how much money?" Betty said. "That's embezzlement. It's not right. You're going to kill this business if you keep doing that. You just embezzled a whole day's worth of cash. Do you know that? On multiple video feeds streaming on the Internet?"

"Who's going to care?" Purp said.

"It is irresponsible," Javier said. "It's not good for our records."

"Now you're some kind of accountant all of a sudden?" Purp said. "Because you're fucking a little bean counter? Does it rub off on your dick or something?"

"At least he doesn't need to give girls money so they'll like him," Betty said. "Lure girls half his age into bed with him by throwing cash around."

"Half my age?" Purp said. "I'm not that old. I thought you were the math whiz. And who are you to talk about that?"

"Couldn't get laid in high school so you're back for Round 2?" Betty said.

"What are you, Dr. Phil now all of a sudden?" Purp said. "You're really talented. According to Beniko Kumi you're the brains behind this operation, you're the superstar CPA student, and now you're a top-notch pop psychologist on top of everything else. You're really helpful. But you know what? Making spreadsheets isn't that special. I could hire some dude to come in here once a week and do what you do. If you really want to be helpful to this business, stop telling me what to do and get out there in the courtyard with your shirt off. I'd have to get a bigger box if you got those tits wet out there. Now those are something special."

* * *

The woman detective talked to the girls out in the courtyard. Rachel stood with her hands over her nipples, fingers interlocked. So did Nicole, standing next to her. Tara and Susie crossed their arms over their chests, with their hands on their shoulders. Another woman, a uniformed officer, talked to Gina by one of the pillars that held the awning up. Gina had a towel over her shoulders like a shawl. She leaned against the masonry. It looked like she was crying. A man in uniform stood by the entrance gate that he'd just shut, staring out into the curved driveway where there was nothing to see. Lacy stood off to the side of the detective, shoulders back and her hands on her hips, looking fierce.

"Can I just grab them some shirts or something," Purp said to the man detective, Darius Butcher, standing between Purp and Javier in the office.

"No," Butcher said, but not in an unkind way. "Officer Dice or Detective Sergeant Margolis will help the women get what they need to be comfortable. I would prefer if you didn't have any contact with them at this point"

Purp turned away from the window in his office. Javier sat in his rolling desk chair with his hands on his knees, looking down at his feet.

Purp looked at the junk on his own desk. A digital voice recorder he bought to keep track of ideas and things he needed to do. His new watch he hadn't even worn yet, its instruction manual next to it he'd been reading when the police came in. His radio with the digital tuner he bought so he could listen to NPR while he worked. A police radio hissed and squawked out in the café where another uniformed officer stood behind the locked front doors. Purp heard Betty talking to a third detective in her office. Purp couldn't make out what they said. They had the door shut.

Detective Butcher sighed and put his hands on his hips, fingers on his back and thumbs toward the floor. He turned away from the window and looked at Purp.

"I mean," Butcher said to Purp, "it's on her driver's license."

"I don't know what to tell you," Purp said. He kept looking down at the top of his desk. At the things on it.

"You said you don't think you want to talk without your council," Butcher said. "I understand that. But before you invoke that right, I just have to know. Just one human being to another. Before this blows up into a big thing for you."

Purp looked at Butcher's face. Smooth and shiny. He had crinkles in the corners of his blue eyes. A pierced ear with no earring in it.

"Did you really not know? I mean, really deep down," Butcher said.

"I swear to you," Purp said. "I didn't know."

"Did she not seem a little young to you?" Butcher said.

"Detective, they're all young," Purp said. "That's what we're doing here. That's what we're selling." Purp wondered if maybe he shouldn't have said that. "I know she graduated from high school. I just honestly didn't give it any thought. It's not like it even occurred to me. Especially not now. I mean, she's worked here for what, Javier, a year already?"

"Just after we opened," Javier said. He put his elbows on his knees and clasped his hands behind his neck, still staring down at his shoes.

"Do you think she lied on her paperwork?" Detective Butcher said.

"I honestly don't know," Purp said.

"You do keep records," Detective Butcher asked.

"We do," Purp said. "Good ones. I'm sure Betty is showing them to the other detective right now."

"She must have lied when she filled out the application," Detective Butcher said.

"That's the thing," Purp said. "It was crazy after we opened, and I don't think she went through the same process as everybody else. I hired her. I personally gave her the job."

* * *

Detective Butcher dropped them off after they got done at the police station. Purp wasn't sure if they'd be allowed back in but Detective Butcher said it would be fine. He said they could go in and out as they pleased but that the car wash was closed. Purp wasn't sure what to expect, like maybe yellow police tape around the whole building or something, but when they drove up in Butcher's white Focus, the car wash looked just like it always had. Except closed.

Purp shook Butcher's hand and the three of them, Purp, Javier, and Betty, walked into the café. The video wall was still on, showing the empty courtyard lit by streetlights and the moon. The officers serving the search warrant had locked the doors and turned out the lights, but Purp figured they didn't want to mess with figuring out how to get the video wall off. Purp turned it off while Javier turned on the café lights and got himself a soda.

Javier and Betty sat down at a table in the café and looked at Purp. He thought they would just go in so Purp and Betty could grab their keys and get out of there, but it looked like they expected him to sit, too, or say something. Purp walked over to their table and stood with his hands on the back of an empty chair.

"How could you not know?" Javier said. He held his arms wide and his hands open over the table, fingers splayed.

"I swear to you," Purp said. "I didn't know. I mean, did you know?" he said to Javier.

"He's not fucking her," Betty said.

"Betty, please," Purp said. "I know. I know."

"You screwed us over so bad," Betty said.

"The subject just never came up?" Javier said. "Like, 'hey, how old are you, anyway? Am I going to go to jail if I have sex with you or anything?'"

"I don't think he cared about that part," Purp said. "Did he even ask you about it?"

"Not really," Javier said. "He asked how you knew her, I said how. From Taco Cabana."

"Me too," Purp said.

"Me too," Betty said.

"We are so screwed," Javier said. "I can't believe you didn't know she was seventeen. I just can't believe it." Javier put his forehead down on the table and let his arms fall straight toward his ankles. He just stayed like that without moving. Betty scratched his back with her fingernails in slow circles.

"I hope Mr. Needleman can get us out of this," Betty said. "This is not going to be cheap." Betty didn't sound as upset as Purp figured she'd be. The whole way home in Butcher's car the thing Purp dreaded most was the tongue-lashing he was going to take from Betty. He would have walked away from the whole business altogether if it meant he never had to hear about it from Betty, but now she didn't sound so bad.

"He didn't tell me at all how they knew," Purp said. "Or why now."

Betty started dragging her nails in diagonal lines on Javier's shirt.

"Me neither," Betty said. "I asked the lady detective and she said she couldn't say."

"Could it have been one of the other girls do you think?" Purp said.

"Maybe one of them was jealous of you and Gina," Javier said.

"I don't think so," Betty said. "So many people come through here, they just knew she was underage and said something."

"But why would someone go to the trouble of reporting that?" Purp said. "I mean, one of our customers? If they're our customers, they like it here."

"Maybe a girl on the waiting list, just trying to get a spot to open up?" Betty said.

"Could be," Purp said. "But girls do come and go, it's not like there's never an opening."

"Maybe someone saw her on D.M.G. ," Javier said. "Recognized her, right?"

"Maybe," Purp said. "But why would someone who watches D.M.G. go to the trouble of reporting that?"

"Just goofing," Javier said. "It could have been a guy she knew who is too young to come in himself."

"Ex-boyfriend?" Betty said.

"Who knows," Purp said. He dragged the café chair back and sat down with Betty and Javier.

* * *

Gina stood on the steps up to her apartment in a black sports bra and volleyball shorts. She had her hair in a ponytail close to the top of her head. She swung a plastic grocery bag by her side, letting it hit her thigh and spin so that it twisted shut. She held it away from her body and it spun back the other way. She had her things in the bag, her things from the car wash that Purp just dropped off. He cleared out her cubby for her in the changing room.

"Because I didn't think you'd hire me if you knew," Gina said.

"I wouldn't have, of course," Purp said. "Of course not."

"Would you have fucked me?" Gina said.

Purp looked at her face. She looked straight at him, not turning her scar away at all. It took Purp longer to answer that question than he would have thought. It was one thing to think he wouldn't, it was another to see her standing there in her tight little shorts with beads of sweat on her golden thigh.

"I guess," Purp said, "I wouldn't?" He knew it wasn't true as he said it. "I probably would have. I guess it's more like, would you have fucked me if I hadn't hired you?"

Gina twirled the bag, letting it twist and untwist, banging it every once in a while on her thigh. The sun burned the back of Purp's neck.

"It's kind of like, we wouldn't have known each other so well if you hadn't ever hired me," Gina said. "It's all mixed up in that."

Purp put a foot on the step, the side of his sandal touching the side of Gina's shoe.

"It still doesn't make a whole lot of sense to me," Purp said. "You only graduated a year early. So if you did it regular, you would have graduated three months ago. So aren't people eighteen when they graduate?"

"November birthday," Gina said.

"Huh," Purp said. "That's weird."

"It sucks," Gina said, turning her knee in and bonking Purp's sandal with her heel.

"So you'll be eighteen in four months?" Purp said.

"Uh huh," she nodded, her top-pony flipping over her forehead.

"Well," Purp said, "there's that, anyway."

"Uh huh," Gina said.

"Maybe we should put one of those countdown clocks on the website," Purp said, "like they had for Mary-Kate and Ashley."

Gina laughed.

"I doubt we'll be open by then, though," Purp said. "If they let us open back up at all."

"I'm sorry," Gina said.

Purp laid flat on his back with his head in the cabinet and looked up. He pointed to the bottom of the steam pans that held the hot items on the food line.

"Holy crap it's dirty under there," Purp said.

"How does it get dirty under there?" Javier said. He squatted down by Purp.

Purp didn't think Javier could see it just by squatting.

"I don't know, but it's dirty," Purp said. "Filthy. Don't you clean under there?"

"I didn't know it was dirty," Javier said.

"Didn't you look?" Purp said.

"I'm not out looking for things to clean," Javier said. "If things look clean, I'm happy."

"You've got to be more thorough than that," Purp said. "Roaches could live off this stuff caked on under here."

"You help us close all the time," Javier said. "I never saw you under there with a flashlight when we're trying to get out of here at night."

"Man, if the health inspector saw this crud," Purp said.

"He'd what?" Javier said. "Shut us down?"

"Well, yeah," Purp said.

"You already took care of that," Javier said.

"Ha, ha," Purp said. "You're a regular comedian."

"You did," Javier said. "And I'm not joking."

"When we re-open, man, you've got to get into a better cleaning routine," Purp said. He flicked a cake of brownish substance off the bottom of the stainless steel pan.

"I think we have bigger things to worry about than some dirt underneath the counter," Javier said.

"Not really," Purp said. "This is our chance to step back and get some of this stuff right."

"I don't know," Javier said. "Sometimes I think maybe this might be a sign."

"Of what?" Purp said.

"My deferment expires next summer. If I don't enroll by then, that's it," Javier said.

"You heard Needleman," Purp said. "This is going to be all right."

"He said it could take months," Javier said, "even if they let us re-open."

"This is our opportunity to re-engineer," Purp said. "Betty said we'll be all right for a good long while if I don't charge us rent until we open." Purp scraped the side of the steam pan and some crud fell onto his shirt. "Which obviously I won't."

"That doesn't help me much pay my rent," Javier said. "Or Betty. Or any of them. At least I have money saved up now. The others were all just making hourly wages like normal people. They're not getting paychecks until we open."

"We'll be all right," Purp said.

"You'll be all right," Javier said. "This isn't so much a real thing for you, right? I mean, you had money to begin with, you put it into this place, and you got your money back. So you're back where you were except you own this property now. The rest of us, not so much me for a while but still, the rest of us need a paycheck."

"I know," Purp said. He sat up out of the cabinet and flicked brownish flakes off his shirt onto the tile.

"You put a lot of people out of work," Javier said.

* * *

Betty slid the brochure across her desk toward Purp. Javier didn't look at it. He'd stopped pretending he didn't know everything Betty was going to say before she said it.

"What do we need it for?" Purp said.

"It'll take care of the whole problem," Betty said.

"There's nothing to take care of," Purp said, "the system we have works fine."

"It's completely automated," Betty said.

"It'll be broken half the time," Purp said. "It'll be more of a pain in the ass than it's worth. I don't like it."

"Nobody will have to go out and get the box," Javier said. "Or count it, or deposit it."

"It's much more secure," Betty said. "And it'll take debit cards, too."

"The cash in the bill feeder," Purp said, "Loomis just comes and gets it?"

"They sure do," Betty said. "And they stock the fives and tens. Every day. The record keeping is totally streamlined, too. All I have to do is download the reports from the machine and import them into

QuickBooks. The guys just swipe their card or put in their money and the light turns green."

"It's like a robo-greeter," Purp said.

"Uh huh," Betty said. "And that way nobody gets tempted to take money out of the box, either."

"Nobody meaning me?" Purp said.

"Nobody nobody," Betty said.

"You either?" Purp said. "Nobody as in you won't be tempted to take money out of the box?"

"Well, I don't actually ever take money out of the box," Betty said, "but I guess."

"So when you say 'nobody will be tempted,' you mean I won't be tempted," Purp said.

"Not you specifically," Betty said, "I just mean the potential for theft will be reduced."

"So you won't be tempted to steal from the box anymore?" Purp said.

"I don't steal from the box," Betty said.

"The only people who handle the box are you and me," Purp said. "So if this isn't to prevent you from stealing out of it, then it's to prevent me from being tempted, right?"

"I guess," Betty said. "I just think it'll be better."

"You're saying you want me to spend forty-five thousand dollars," Purp said, "on a robo-greeter with no T and A, and no personality, who doesn't know any of the customers by name, and who can't decide when to use overflow and when not to? And that'll be broken half the time anyway?"

"It's more secure," Javier said.

"No. It's not going to happen," Purp said. "I'm not going to pay Loomis forty-five thousand dollars just to keep me from every once in a while taking some money that's mine anyway. And then how much a month for the pick-up service? No."

"It's not just your money," Javier said. "And we're not going to go through this again."

"Whose is it?" Purp said. "Yours? It's your money now?"

"It is his money," Betty said. "You guys are partners."

"Will you stop telling me who owns this place?" Purp said. "It's not you," he said to Betty, "so you better keep your mouth shut. That robo-greeter would be a step closer to automating you out of a job here, so maybe it isn't all bad."

"What the fuck?" Javier said. "We're just showing you something we think will help."

"You're so concerned about me taking money from the box now?" Purp said to Javier.

"He's always been concerned about it," Betty said.

"So he sent his yappy little attack dog after me instead of telling me himself?" Purp said.

"Purp, that's enough," Javier said.

"That's what she is," Purp said. "She's your little attack bitch, huh?"

"That's not appropriate," Javier said. "And it's beside the point. Betty and I don't want you stealing from the box anymore. Period."

"What?" Purp said. "Are you serious? You're the boss now?"

"I'm your partner," Javier said. "I own half of this business."

"You own half of this business?" Purp said. "That's a joke."

"What's that supposed to mean?"

"I gave you something to do instead of working at Starbucks when your little poetry thing didn't work out and now you're all calling the shots?" Purp said. "Look at you, the big business man with his hot little trophy girlfriend."

"You didn't give me anything," Javier said. "I worked for this place. I bled for this place to make it happen."

"You kept me company while I started it," Purp said. "Without me you'd be pulling shots and sliding lattes across the bar until you just gave up and got a job teaching high school English."

"Well what the fuck have you done for us lately?" Javier said. "I don't see my bank account getting any bigger lately since you got us shut down."

"I got us shut down?" Purp said.

"Of course you got us shut down," Javier said. "Of course. You're a God damned pervert having sex with little high school girls. You're lucky you didn't end up in jail." Javier stood up and looked down at Purp.

"This isn't getting us anywhere," Betty said. "Guys, let's just call it a day."

"I'm the pervert?" Purp said. "What? You're Mr. Straight-and-Narrow with your little mommy in the room, huh? I don't remember you looking away when Gina was out there on the corner in her bikini swinging a car wash sign over her head. I don't remember you looking away." Purp stood up and put his face near Javier's.

"I didn't hunt her down like some kind of pedophile stalker," Javier said.

"You're telling me you wouldn't have fucked her?" Purp said.

"Purp, please," Betty said.

"No, tell me," Purp said. "If the situation was reversed, would you? If you didn't have the good fortune of somehow getting laid by Miss Saigon here? Which congratulations, by the way, that is an unbelievable score for you."

"Stop, now." Betty said. She stood up and walked around her desk, ending up behind Javier.

"I don't need your gimpy little stripper girl," Javier said. "And if you were worth a crap, you wouldn't need her either. If you weren't turning more into a crazy-ass drunk every day you wouldn't have to bother with scar faced little runaways because Selma wouldn't have left you in the first place."

Purp balled his hand into a fist and swung it at Javier's face. His hand ended up hitting Javier's collar bone and sort of glancing off the bottom of Javier's jaw.

"Ouch," Javier said. He rubbed his chest. Javier swung his fist at Purp and hit him in the side of the forehead.

Purp's head snapped to one side, but it surprised him that it didn't hurt more where Javier hit him. He barely noticed it. He didn't lose his footing or anything. He'd bumped his head worse than that, plenty of times.

"Aww, fuck," Javier said. "Fuck me." He held his punching fist with his other hand, cradling it like he'd done some serious damage to it. "Ouch."

"Are you OK?" Betty said. "Oh my God, stop." She pulled at Javier's hurt arm.

Purp stood facing Javier. Javier shook out his sore hand, looking down at it. Purp wasn't sure if the fight was still going on, or if he should take his turn to punch, or what. Javier seemed more interested in his hurt hand than in continuing the fight. Purp shoved Javier as hard as he could, both of his hands flat on Javier's chest. Purp felt his wrists bend back. It sent an electric tingle into both of his forearms. That couldn't be good. He pushed himself backwards a couple of feet until his back hit into the office wall. That made a boom sound but it didn't feel like much either. The shove sent Javier a half a step back, too. He stepped on Betty's foot and she went down. Purp saw her smack her head into the edge of her open door. The door barely even swung an inch when she hit it. The top of her head slammed into it right on the edge, pushing it straight back into the hinges. Thud.

Betty yelped and rolled over onto her side, grabbing her head with both hands, legs splayed, one flip-flop still under Javier's Doc Marten. Her jean skirt hiked itself up indecently showing her red thong. Javier turned but he looked too high, where her head had been when she was standing, not on the floor. Purp half fell, half dove around Javier, as if to catch Betty. A reflex completely after the fact. Betty was already down. Purp kneeled beside her and tried to pull her hands away from her head so he could see if there was any visible damage. Betty swung her elbows, crying, trying to fight him off. Javier stepped over her and straddled her hips, trying to lift her from her armpits as if standing her up would somehow fix the problem. All Javier managed to do was lift her torso a few inches, then she wriggled so much Javier dropped her onto the tiles while Purp kept trying to pry her fingers out of her hair. Purp heard her head knock into the Saltillo. She kicked and caught Javier between the legs, but it didn't seem to get the goods because Javier just reached under her armpits to get a grip again.

* * *

"No, we just put ice on it," Javier said. He put a peanut butter cracker in his mouth, the last one from a pack of six. "It left a lump though. For like three days," he said, chewing the cracker.

"Is it any better now?" Purp said.

"It's going down," Javier said. "She said it's not sore anymore, but I can still feel the lump."

"You should have gone to the Emergency Room, or somewhere," Purp said. "You can get a bleed from something like that even a few days later."

"That's what I told her," Javier said. "I've seen that on E.R., right?"

Purp sat down on the futon in Javier's apartment. Javier was in his desk chair so there really wasn't anywhere else for Purp to sit unless he cleared off one of the breakfast bar stools which Javier had piled so high with books it seemed like it would be kind of risky to move them.

"You should definitely keep an eye on her," Purp said.

"I know," Javier said. He took a sip from a two-liter bottle of Diet Pepsi. "Her ankle is bothering her more than her head, though."

"She twisted it when you stepped on her?" Purp said.

"Yeah," Javier said. "I guess. I didn't even realize I stepped on her foot."

Purp looked at Javier's pillow, stained like Javier had drooled on it and not changed the case. Purp knew for a fact Javier had enough money in the bank to put a down payment on a little place of his own, at least.

He definitely did not need to still be living in his basement studio apartment he'd had all through grad school.

"Is she coming back?" Purp said. "To PTC?"

"I haven't asked her," Javier said. "I think she will."

"Do you want her to?" Purp said.

"I guess," Javier said. "I don't know. If she wants. Do you?"

"Shit yeah," Purp said. "What would we do if she didn't come back?"

"I know a lot of it," Javier said. "What she does."

"The QuickBooks stuff?" Purp said.

"No," Javier said. "Not really that."

"That's not what I mean, though," Purp said. "We could hire someone for that." Purp flipped the pillow over so he didn't have to look at the stain. The other side of the pillow looked worse. It actually had something red on it, like taco sauce. "It's just," he saw legs walk by the slit of a window over Javier's desk, a girl's legs, "it wouldn't exactly be PTC without her around, you know what I mean?"

"I guess," Javier said.

"It wouldn't," Purp said. "She's part of the," he couldn't find the right word for a second, "magic." Purp tugged Javier's Afghan blanket over the pillow so he wouldn't have to look at it. "Is your hand OK?"

"Oh yeah," Javier said. "It hurt like a motherfucker for a second but it went right away."

"That was weird," Purp said. "I didn't even feel you hit me hardly."

Javier polished off the Diet Pepsi. He fiddled with the wrapper of another six-pack of Austin peanut butter crackers.

"We suck at fighting, right?" Javier said.

"We'll have to remember that," Purp said, "in case we ever get in the shit."

"We need to develop better fighting skills," Javier said.

* * *

"I know but I never did really like the way it looked so much," Purp said.

"What do you mean?" Javier said. "You loved it."

"But it's like half the space almost is taken up by entryway," Purp said.

"I don't know," Javier said. "Taking down the whole wall?"

"It's nothing," Purp said. He stood from his chair in the café and walked over to the divider between the café and the entrance area. He rapped on the glass blocks that kept people on the sidewalk from seeing through the café all the way out into the car wash. The blocks were Purp's idea to begin with, blocking the view from the street while still letting light through. "This will come down like nothing," he said. "This wall was laid after the tile went it. It won't even mess up the floor."

"Could we get it done in time?" Javier said. He sat at the table in the middle of the empty café where he and Purp had been brainstorming.

"Done in time?" Purp said. "Are you serious? Needleman says February at the earliest. If it gets dismissed at the first hearing."

"Well yeah, so, could that all get done by then?" Javier said. "I want to open as soon as we can if they say we can open back up."

"Javier, of course," Purp said. "I could have this whole divider down in like two hours. It's not going to take me five months. It was four loads of glass blocks in my truck, remember?"

"As long as it can get done in time," Javier said.

"It'll give us room for like seven or eight more tables," Purp said. It's going to be awesome.

"They won't be able to see," Javier said.

"They'll be able to see the video wall," Purp said. "And check this out." He held his hand open at the level of his mid-calf. "I'm going to put a riser in along here, two steps up like this. That'll give them a bird's eye view right through to the glass wall and it'll look freaking awesome, too."

"What are you going to block off the windows?" Javier said.

"Nope," Purp said. "Not at all. We take the glass bricks from the divider and put up screens, like here." Purp drew his toe across the tiles in front of one of the windows. "One in front of each window, floor to ceiling. All glass bricks. But only in front of the windows."

"Huh," Javier said. "That would look cool."

"It'll look better than it does from outside now," Purp said.

"But would you put the glass brick walls that far behind the windows?" Javier said.

"Yeah," Purp said, "like three feet behind each window. That'll even give us a little space there for apparel displays or to suspend banners or whatever we want. Like at the Apple store at El Mercado."

"Oh yeah," Javier said. "Yeah like how they hang the displays there right by the window."

"Exactly," Purp said. "Except they use roll-down fabric screens, we'll have permanent glass block. I'll put two rows of halogen tracks in on top, suspended, and one down here under the sill. We'll be able to light anything we wanted. Holy crap."

"What?" Javier said.

"Human mannequins. That would be so freaking awesome."

"Real girls?" Javier said.

"Standing totally still," Purp said. "People love that. They always love that."

"That's awesome," Javier said.

"That'll sell apparel merchandise, I guarantee you," Purp said. "And if it doesn't, it sure will give the guys something to look at while they're waiting to get in since we won't have an indoor entryway anymore."

"We'll need a bigger awning out front," Javier said, "across all the windows, not just the door."

"Exactly," Purp said. "That's what I'm talking about right there. And speakers. The music from the courtyard. The window girls could be dancing, even."

"Holy shit," Javier said. "In their shirts of course, right?"

"Of course, man," Purp said. "But our girls dancing in PTC shirts and skirts, that's going to catch some eyes. Definitely."

"I don't know," Javier said. "The dancing might be cheesey."

"It could," Purp said. "Maybe so. But human mannequins, anyway. People eat that up."

* * *

Flecks of brown crud snowed down onto Javier's shirt. Knees belt like he was in labor, Javier laid on his back under the food line cabinet. He chipped at the mess with an ice scraper.

"Greg's coming next week to get the divider down and move the glass blocks over to make the window screens," Purp said, squatting down by Javier.

Javier sawed at crud. A steady stream of flakes fell on his chest.

"I thought you were going to do it?" Javier said.

"No," Purp said. "Remember the permit problems?"

"I thought you said it was simple?" Javier said.

"It is simple," Purp said. "But remember I can't do it on commercial property?"

"You said it would take you two hours," Javier said, out of breath from scraping so hard.

"When I said 'I' I meant 'one,'" Purp said. "It would take one two hours to get the divider down."

"How long does he say it'll take?" Javier said. "Could it be done for February?"

"Of course," Purp said. "He said he'll be done in a week, tops."

"That's not two hours," Javier said. "When is he going to get started?"

"The end of the month," Purp said.

"The end of the month?" Javier said.

"So what?" Purp said. "We've got until February, earliest."

Javier stretched for a spray bottle of Formula 409. Purp slid it closer.

"Betty was meeting with Needleman this morning, right?" Javier said.

Purp heard a tapping noise.

"That's the plan," Purp said. "I wasn't sure she was going to go. She hasn't really been around, just to pay the bills."

"She's been busy at the salon, and doing weddings," Javier said. "And with school. She's trying to graduate in December."

"I wish she'd just take her paycheck even though we're closed," Purp said. "I don't know why she doesn't."

The tapping noise got louder. Someone was rapping on the glass door.

"You think the sign would say it all," Purp said. He stood up, knees stiff from squatting. He saw a kid through the door, a regular. He'd spoken with him before, but he couldn't remember the guy's name. Purp walked over to the front door and opened it. He took his time. He was getting sick of guys asking when they'd be open.

"Hey Purp," the guy said.

"How's it going, man?" Purp said, bumping knuckles with him.

"I came back for homecoming. What happened?"

"Oh, it's a long story," Purp said. "One of the girls didn't tell us she was seventeen."

"Major bummer. Are you going to open back up?"

"We hope to. Not sure, though. Legal stuff," Purp said.

"How soon could you open? For this weekend?"

"Oh, no," Purp said. "Definitely not. We don't even have our hearing until the end of January, so February at the earliest."

"Bummer. I was so looking forward to coming here."

"Sorry man," Purp said. "Listen, I got to get back to work here. Good seeing you."

Purp shut the door and went back behind the food line. Javier inspected the steam pans with a Mag-Lite Purp gave him one time when they went camping, his crud-flecked shirt now wet with something, maybe just 409.

"We're stupid," Purp said. He didn't squat down, he just talked loud instead. It had made his knees too sore. He leaned against the food line.

"I'm under here and you're up there," Javier said, "so maybe it's just me that's stupid."

"You heard about the smoking ban?" Purp said.

"In bars and restaurants?" Javier said. "I read about it. Doesn't matter to us, right? We've always been non-smoking."

"It goes into effect January thirtieth," Purp said. "They're all scrambling to build outdoor patios now, so people can sit out there and smoke."

The sawing, scraping sound started again from underneath. Purp could tell by the sound coming through the steam Pan that Javier was doing the way back now, between the back of the pan and the front of the cabinet.

"When you think about it," Purp said, "where's our outdoor patio?"

"We don't have one," Javier said. His legs scrambled, as if he were trying to use his heels to push himself further under the cabinet.

"Exactly," Purp said. "That's my point exactly." Purp reached into the under-the-counter cooler next to where Javier worked. He pulled himself out a bottle of Budweiser. He'd put a case in there yesterday when nobody was around. It shouldn't sit that long anyway, until they re-open. Born-on dating.

"We've got fifteen feet of space between the glass wall and the wash bays," Purp said. He unscrewed the cap from his bottle, trying to let the fizz out quietly. "More as you get closer to the office side. You know what that is?"

"What?" Javier said.

"That's our new café," Purp said. He looked out the glass wall at the open concrete space. He sipped his beer. "We extend the awning over it, put out propane heaters and misters, and we've got an all-weather patio seating area that doubles, just about, our current."

Javier scraped.

"Are you drinking beer?" Javier said.

"You could hear that?" Purp said.

"I can smell it," Javier said.

"But don't you like the patio idea?" Purp said.

"That's awesome," Javier said. "But are you looking for something to do? Because I've got a pretty big list I made if you are."

"Somebody has to have the vision," Purp said. "And somebody has to have the paint scraper."

Javier scraped like he was going to come right through the bottom of the stainless steel pan. He didn't say anything. Purp wasn't sure Javier had heard him. It was just as well, it was a stupid thing to say. Purp made a mental sketch of how the patio seating could go. How he'd have a railing to corral off the seating area from the rest of the courtyard. He'd make it out of glass blocks. No, just clear glass. Glass panels with a one-inch open gap between them and a brushed aluminum cap across the top.

"And somebody's going to have a beer bottle stuck up his ass in a minute," Javier said, "and a paint scraper."

Purp looked at the food line. Not nearly big enough, hardly big enough for the seating they already had, let alone the eight new riser tables and all the outdoor tables. It was going to have to be twice as big with two people on the line all the time. Purp would put another touch screen up so both people on the line could do the sort the way they needed to. One on block, one on fifo. They could expand into the bar area that never got used. That was just a waste of space now, since they never got their liquor license.

"If you attack me," Purp said. "Then we must fight. And given the pace of our last bout, that, amigo, is actually something we could not get done by February."

* * *

"It's not a loan," Purp said. "It's a gift. Not a gift, I mean, I'll just pay for it. It's the least I could, you know."

"We can pretty comfortably cover the dining area renovation and kitchen expansion," Betty said. She made red stars by two columns on her spreadsheet. She spun the spreadsheet around so it would be right side up to Purp and Javier, sitting across from her at the three café tables they'd pulled together to have their meeting on.

"OK then," Purp said. "So I'll take window box lighting, awning expansion, patio glass corral, patio tile, patio – everything patio. What about the self-serve soda fountain?"

"That goes for kitchen expansion," Betty said. "That's us."

“OK,” Purp said. “So I’m looking at, basically, column E and from K on.” Purp tapped the columns with his fingertip.

“Not that though,” Betty said. “That’s the totals column.”

“Yeah, OK,” Purp said. “Good.” He tried to add up the items he said he’d paid for, but he couldn’t. He got the general idea, though, and he knew he had just about enough to cover it without selling things he didn’t want to. “Ed’s Northside will get the lighting done in the window boxes the week after Thanksgiving. The awning expansion is just about done now, definitely before Thanksgiving. Soda machine they said pretty much any time we’re ready, they already have it. They just need a week lead time. Furniture they said after one January.”

“That’s late, right?” Javier said. “That’s cutting it close.”

“It’s backordered,” Purp said, “If we want the same outside as in, which I do. They have enough for the riser tables at the warehouse, but the other they have to bring in from Italy. So worse comes to worse, if they slide the outside date back, we’ll rent them from Restaurant Supply until ours come in.”

“Fair enough,” Javier said.

“And for plumbing,” Purp said, “he’s coming one December. That’ll take a couple of weeks.”

“What’s that for again?” Betty said. She spun the spreadsheet back around her direction and drew a red box around the line item for plumbing on her budget sheet.

“For the patio misters,” Purp said, “a high-pressure hose system retrofit, and natural gas to plumb in all these heaters,” he waved toward the courtyard, “in the wash bays and for the patio dining. And also to bring gas into the kitchen in case we need it. And to plumb in the fourth wash bay properly so it’s an official thing to have four.”

Betty drew an arrow from the word “plumbing” to an empty white space on her page. She wrote notes in the empty place.

“I thought you had those heaters for the girls before,” Betty said.

“I did, but on propane,” Purp said. “I was forever changing tanks. This is cheaper, too, in the long run.”

“Like you calculated it out,” Betty said, under her breath. But Purp heard it.

“What was that?” Purp said.

“Huh?” Betty said. She scribbled a few more notes on the back of her sheet.

Javier sipped a Diet Pepsi.

“That’s going to be so much better to have the self-serve fountain,” Javier said. “It’ll be so much easier on register. And faster.”

"Yeah, and with room for two on the line, you'll be cruising," Purp said. "It won't just be a squeeze-in like it was."

"It's going to be a sad day for buffalos when we re-open," Javier said.

Purp laughed.

"Now," Purp said, "about the matter of the New Year's Extravaganza."

"Yeah, I don't know, Purp," Betty said. "I don't know if that's such a good idea."

"I spoke with Detective Butcher," Purp said, "and he didn't see a problem with it. I emailed him. He said it wasn't like we're open for business, it's just a private party."

"Mr. Needleman doesn't think it's a good idea," Betty said. "He said better not to. It might give the wrong idea so close to the hearing."

"But it's not like it's illegal," Purp said.

"It's not so good for insurance, either, Mr. Needleman told me," Betty said.

"So you really asked him?" Purp said.

"Yeah," Betty said, "why do you think I'm saying what he said?"

"I just want to make sure," Purp said, "because I emailed him, too, and he said we wouldn't be doing anything wrong, so that's funny he gave you such a different impression."

"Maybe Betty is just saying the lawyer didn't think it was a good idea," Javier said, "but that it isn't technically illegal."

"Right," Betty said.

"Well," Purp said, "I think I want to get everybody together, and get the girls psyched up again. I mean, we're going to lose a lot of them. It's not going to be the easiest thing to get our staffing up to where it needs to be." He crunched up a stale nacho chip. He and Javier had been trying to eat down as much of the leftover food they could from before they got shut down. "Especially since I'm going to try to keep all four bays wet now as much as I can."

"You do what you want," Betty said.

"It'll be fun, and it'll be important," Purp said. "I want to try to get the team feeling back as much as I can. I want to make it nice for them so they don't lose confidence in what we're doing."

"I don't think they give it that much thought," Javier said.

"I think they do," Purp said. "This whole place doesn't work unless those girls think it's cool to work here. What happened with Gina might make it uncool." Purp ate another chip. "And then again, it might make it even cooler. Some of that is going to depend on the party."

"Well, that can be your department, then," Betty said. "You can be the official party planner."

"It's more serious than you think," Purp said. "And I also want them to get used the idea that the patio seating is there now."

"I think you just miss your girls," Betty said.

* * *

Selma cut a cube of pan seared ahi tuna, the middle pink, and slid some black rice onto her fork behind it. She wore her teal-colored V-neck sleeveless top that Purp remembered from way back. It looked great on her, still. Shadows cut her shoulders and upper arms. She looked like she'd been working out even more lately. Purp didn't recognize her jeans, but they looked like they'd pop if somebody pricked them with a pin.

"So did they say when you could re-open?" Selma said.

"Not yet," Purp said. "The hearing is next month, so just after that at the earliest."

"If they let you re-open," Selma said. "I can't believe they shut you down for so long for that," Selma said. "Especially since you guys didn't know how young she was." Selma sipped her iced tea. "I mean, it was pretty creepy but I would have thought they'd just make you fire her and give you a fine or something."

"It's a big deal," Purp said.

The waiter came over. He looked like a student, maybe a guy who came into PTC. Purp couldn't tell for sure. The waiter smiled and looked only at Selma. He'd been doing that all afternoon.

"Is everything OK with your lunch?" The waiter said. "Is there anything else I can get you right now?"

"No thank you," Selma said.

"I'm all set," Purp said.

"Enjoy," the waiter said. Purp thought he saw the waiter glancing down Selma's shirt.

"You know, I'm trying to take it easy lately," Purp said. "And when we re-open, I'm planning to keep it a little more professional than the first time around."

"Easy?" Selma said. "You mean like you're on vacation?"

"No," Purp said. "Not like that. I'm working hard. I have all these ideas for when we re-open. We've got the renovations going on, I'm trying to monetize the website so we can have a subscription basis for courtyard feeds, all kinds of stuff. I'm trying to get a lot of web stuff done before we open, online apparel store, social networking so website customers can interact with the girls, and each other, lots of good stuff."

"It doesn't sound like you're taking it easy," Selma said.

"I mean," Purp said, "I guess with my behavior."

"You're trying to take it easy with your behavior?" Selma said.

"Yes," Purp said. "I'm trying to, sort of act with a little more moderation."

"You mean you're not drinking?" Selma said.

"I am cutting way back, yeah," Purp said.

Selma looked down at her ahi. She cut some more of it.

"I'm sorry you guys got shut down," Selma said. She didn't look up from her fish. "I know you have a lot of work invested in that place. And you had a good idea with it, too. I've heard guys on base talking who didn't know we were," Selma poked at her salad, "who didn't know I knew you."

"Thank you," Purp said, "for saying that."

As fit as she looked, Selma seemed small to Purp. She seemed older, too, like she'd aged a lot since she went to stay with her father.

"You know," Purp said, "I was thinking, I was wondering if you had plans on New Year's Eve?"

"I don't know," Selma said. "I hadn't really penciled in my social calendar that far ahead."

"The reason I'm asking is," Purp said, "I'm trying to get everybody at PTC together on New Year's, in the café. I want to start over with it right, you know what I mean?"

"I guess," Selma said. She scrunched her eyebrows like Purp knew she did when something was about to irritate her. "How exactly does that fit in with you taking it easy?"

"I was thinking maybe this time around," Purp said, "when we re-open, maybe you'd like to be a little more involved in the place with me. And maybe you'd like to come to the party?" he said. "You could keep an eye on me?" Purp raised one eyebrow and made a silly face.

Selma laughed.

"You could make sure I don't get out of hand?" Purp said.

"I guess," Selma said. She ate a fork full of the black rice. Forbidden rice, it said on the menu.

Purp ate the last of his gorgonzola gnocchi. The salty cream sauce made him thirsty but he didn't want take a sip of his Diet Coke because he didn't want to wash the flavor of gorgonzola away.

"You've got to taste some of this rice," Selma said. She slid her plate an inch toward Purp.

Purp took a spoonful of the black rice with a clean teaspoon neither of them had used. The rice tasted like butter and nuts.

"I wish I had five stomachs," Purp said. "Or at least three, like you."

"I have three stomachs?" Selma said. She looked a little confused, maybe offended.

"Isn't that what those are?" Purp said, pointing to her breasts with his spoon.

Selma laughed and gave him a look he knew meant, "What the crap?" Then she put on a face like she thought he was crazy, but Purp knew she liked random humor like that.

"Well, whatever they are," Purp said, "they're not getting any smaller, huh?"

* * *

"Purple," Melanie and Elizabeth screamed together. They'd just come in. They were the last two Purp expected and if they came much later, they would have missed New Year's altogether.

Purp opened his arms and the two of them, Melanie and Elizabeth, crashed into his chest. They smelled like beer and cigarettes. Purp hugged them tight together, his palm touching the skin on Elizabeth's back, his hand half on, half off her short T-shirt. He kissed the top of each of their heads.

"The Purple Pimp," Melanie said, giggling and rubbing the sable lapel of Purp's smoking jacket with both hands after the hug broke up. Purp hadn't been planning to wear his party jacket and hat, but they ended up on him. He couldn't exactly picture when. He grabbed Melanie in a bear hug and crushed her into him, lifting her off of her spiked heels. She laughed. Purp laughed. With his chin on Melanie's shoulder Purp looked over at the café table where Selma sat with Betty and Javier. Horatio Pendragon sat with them and so did Tara. And so did the man Horatio had brought along with him. Betty and Selma glanced away when Purp looked at them. They all of a sudden both seemed real interested in something Horatio said.

Melanie twisted in the hug, as if to shake Purp or wrestle him. Or just to hug him up more. Purp lost his balance and went down on one knee, one arm on the table next to him for balance. Melanie held his other hand in both of hers, bent over and dangling her hands, and Purp's hand, between her knees. She laughed so loud and at such a high pitch it hurt Purp's left ear. Purp knocked over a paper cup of something on the table and he felt it wet on his ankle. Two girls behind him screamed and then laughed. Purp felt the back of his neck go red.

Sweat dripped onto Purp's face from underneath the hatband of his velvet hat. He felt like his head was turning to the left without him trying. He had to concentrate on looking forward but it still felt like he was turning to the left. He pushed himself up using the table for a handhold. Some of the girls and guys around him cheered when he got back to his feet, the packed café more crowded than it ever was when they were open. The party had started invite only, but then people brought guests, and guests brought guests. Selma told Purp a while ago that it had gotten out of hand and people were coming in since then. Purp raised his hands over his head to the cheers of the circle around him. It felt to him like he was standing still and the circle, and the café, was moving to the right around him about twice as fast as the second hand of a clock moves.

Purp put his hands down, one still sticky with whatever had just spilled on it. He looked at his sticky hand, reached around, and wiped it onto Melanie's ass, onto her jean skirt with a frayed hem. He felt the tips of his fingers brush the bare skin of the back and inside of her thigh under the skirt. The circle got less noisy around him and faded away. One of the guys, with a beer in his hand, said, "oh," dragging it out for a long sound.

Melanie looked puzzled. She stretched her neck, trying to look behind her at where Purp had just wiped his hand.

Purp felt his whole face go red. Melanie didn't look happy anymore.

"That's a thing I did," Purp said to her, loud over the music coming from the video wall, "because it was you who knocked me over." He pointed to Melanie's ass. It surprised Purp how drunk he sounded. Even to himself. He thought he'd sounded more drunk than he felt. He'd snorted something, too, though, with a guy in the bathroom. A guy who came in with a friend of Lacy's, or something. "It's OK though," he said, "it's probably not the stickiest thing to go on the back of your skirt before the end of tomorrow."

A blond girl dancing caught Purp's eye. For a second she reminded him of Gina but Gina hadn't been invited. He didn't know the girl. He didn't know half the people there. Melanie had disappeared. Evaporated into the crowd.

“They say you like Jack and Pepsi,” a guy said. The guy handed Purp a thirty-two ounce. Purp sipped it. It tasted strong, like half-Jack maybe, but in a cup that big? Purp didn’t recognize the guy.

“You know what I was thinking?” the guy said. “I was thinking you guys need a Monkey Cam. You know what that is?”

“David Letterman,” Purp said.

“That’s right,” the guy said. “He knows. You need a monkey cam running through all this shit here.”

Purp gulped his drink and nudged himself into the crowd, shuffling over toward where Selma sat. He thought the guy might be still talking, but maybe not. He found the back of an empty chair at Selma’s table. He leaned on it, looking over the table down Selma’s dress, and Betty’s, both black short dresses, similar, but different. Betty’s, velvety with a wide, open square neck and tight short sleeves. Selma’s, a stretchy knit off both shoulders and low in the front, even lower than Betty’s.

“Did I mention,” Purp said, “that you guys, both, look really, really good tonight?”

“Yes, you did, Purp,” Selma said. “A few times now. You know you’re –

“Have you given any thought to my proposal?” Purp said.

“No,” Betty said.

“No thought?” Purp said. “Or no to the proposal?”

“Neither one,” Selma said.

“Betty?” Purp said. “Betty? How about you?”

Betty looked the other way, toward the corner of the table where Javier and Horatio’s friend seemed to be discussing something important.

“Well, you should,” Purp said, “with tits like that, you both should.” Purp sipped his drink. He felt like something else must be in it. Whatever it was, it was powerful. “I for one,” he said, “personally, wouldn’t mind seeing it happen. And I’ll tell you, in my professional life I do see a lot of –

“OK, Purp,” Selma said. “That’s enough.”

“I just mean –

“Enough,” Selma said. She stood up from the table. Betty shot her a glance and then flicked her eyes back toward the conversation.

“Enough what?” Purp said. “It’s a natural thing to notice, that’s all.”

Selma walked away toward the office.

Purp walked sort of toward the office, too, but he got off on a detour where Monica laughed in vinyl pants, platform boots, and a tube top.

"This girl," Purp said. "This girl." He put his arm around Monica's bare shoulders and tugged her toward him. "I can't wait until we re-open because this girl," he said, "is a girl I'm looking forward to seeing naked again."

The guys around Purp and Monica looked down, and at each other.

"The ass on her," Purp said. "Is really something else, the way she moves it. Really. If you put a Sharpie marker in her ass, she could seriously write her name with it."

"Hey Purp?" Monica said. She ducked out from under his arm. "This is my boyfriend Rami. I'm not sure if you've ever met him."

Rami stepped forward and put out his hand for Purp to shake it.

"Rami," Purp said. "You don't look so much like a happy man. Enjoy the party. This party. Lighten up, vato." Purp rubbed the bare skin between Monica's shoulder blades and fed himself to the crowd again.

As it got closer to midnight the throng thickened around Purp with fewer and fewer people he recognized. His armpits soaked with sweat, Purp lost track of where he put his drinks, and how many there were. So much sweat ran down into his pants Purp wasn't sure whether he pissed himself or not, or if it even mattered. At some point Ryan Seacrest counted down on the video wall and champagne ran down the back of Purp's smoking jacket, inside. He was sitting on one of the new chairs on the patio. He was smoking a joint in the girls' changing room with an Asian guy and two white girls he didn't know. A redhead, one of them. He was in his office, looking up something on the computer but he forgot what.

* * *

It looked like afternoon. Sun came in between the awning and the courtyard wall from the left, like it did on a winter afternoon, or a summer evening. Purp sat up, his numb butt on the tiles of his office floor, his back against his desk, trying not to throw up. Something tasted metallic in his cotton mouth. He smelled it, too. He looked out his office window into the courtyard. Afternoon light drew long shadows away from empty red Solo cups littering the concrete. Ghosts of the party. Purp thought of water flooding the dining rooms of the Titanic. It looked cold outside. He got the urge to check the temperature plot but sitting, even, felt like too much for him. He laid back down and his stiff hair crunched under the weight of his head. Afternoon. He wondered how it had gotten so late. He didn't hear anyone else in the building. One of the refrigerators clicked on and hummed. Purp's crotch itched from his damp pants and he thought about whether it would be better to kick them off, or if maybe it would be too chilly without them. Monkey Cam. Purp fell back to sleep.

* * *

Purp got out of his truck pretty sure that the meeting was for Betty and Javier to tell him that they'd lost. Purp felt like an idiot for missing the hearing. Javier hadn't said much on the voicemail, just that he wondered if Purp could make it in today for a meeting. If Javier had good news, Purp figured, he would have just said it. It embarrassed him that Javier couldn't just assume that Purp would be in anyway. Purp tried to count up how many days he'd been in since New Year's. It wasn't a lot. He hadn't even seen Betty since the party, maybe just the once. Purp checked himself out in his reflection from one of the apparel display windows as he walked past. He smoothed back his hair, trying to get more of it into the hair tie so it didn't look so frizzy. He tugged at his shirt so it might look less wrinkly.

The cowbell on the door clanked Purp in. He remembered the first time Tara rang the courtyard bell for their first customer. Purp wished he'd had the video wall made then, so he could have footage of that archived.

The café looked great, all ready to go with the new seating inside and out. Everything looked perfect, like they could open today. Purp wanted to get it over with, the meeting, so he didn't bother with a soda first. He heard Betty and Javier talking already in Betty's office. He stood in Betty's doorway.

"Knock knock," Purp said.

"Good morning, Purp," Javier said. "You got my message?"

"Your email? No." Purp said. "And I've been checking, too. I've been at my computer pretty much all the time, working on this monkey cam idea I have for the car wash."

"My voicemail," Javier said.

"Oh, no, I didn't. My battery died. Why?" Purp said.

Javier explained everything Purp had heard already heard on the voicemail.

"I'm really sorry," Purp said after Javier was done. "I totally lost track of which day it was, I've been working so much on the website."

"Well," Betty said. "You're here now."

"That I am," Purp said. "So how'd it go? At the hearing? Not good?" Purp thought Javier seemed somber and formal, which he took to mean bad news.

"We won at the hearing," Javier said. "We can re-open anytime we want. Betty and I were thinking the first of February." Javier's tone didn't change.

"That's fantastic," Purp said. He stood up. "That is so great. Wow." He put his hands on his head. "Oh, man, you had me going. You were all acting glum like we lost. Oh, wow. Oh, Betty, I'd hug you if I didn't think it would cause some kind of incident. Wow."

"It is good news," Betty said.

"But there's something else we wanted to go over today," Javier said.

"What?" Purp said, sitting down. "Are we on probation or something? Whatever it is, it can't be worse than being shut. I'll do whatever they said."

"It's something Betty and I have been talking about for a little while now," Javier said.

Purp got this flash like Javier was about to tell him he and Betty were getting married.

"And Selma, too," Betty said. "We've been talking about it with her since New Year's."

"Selma?" Purp said.

"She's an owner, Purp, as much an owner as you, actually," Javier said.

"On paper, yeah, but operationally no." Purp said.

"Paper's what counts," Betty said.

"But anyway," Javier said, "We've been talking about this and the three of us, all of us, Betty, Selma, and me, we think it might be better for the business – and more important, for you personally, for your health, if you left the car wash."

"If I leave it?" Purp said. "Leave like, what do you mean?" Purp looked at Betty. She just looked down at her desk. She didn't have anything on it, though, no spreadsheet, no folder, nothing. She just looked down, a curtain of shiny hair blocking out her face, her neck red.

"We think it would be better if you didn't participate in running the car wash anymore," Javier said. "Or the café."

"You want me to just walk out of here?" Purp said. "Out of my business? That I created? This place comes from me. I invented it."

"Not walk away, Purp," Betty said, still looking down. "You'll still own the property, so you'll be getting rent for that. It's not like just a complete break." Betty glanced up at Purp, her eyes about to spill. She looked down and sniffed.

"Purp," Javier said, "I don't know how to say this –

"Well you should," Purp said, "otherwise that degree of yours isn't much good."

"It's just," Javier said. "Your behavior's been getting more erratic lately. The drinking, and we suspect you're using drugs. You're kind of not so much in control anymore, and I'm not going to lie to you, it's disruptive. It is making the work of running this place more difficult."

"Javier, are you serious?" Purp said. "Do you hear yourself? You're firing me? You're my friend. That's what got us to this point to begin with."

"We're not firing you, Purp," Betty said. A round wet dot slapped onto her desktop. She left it there.

"We're asking you to sell us your stake in the business," Javier said.

"Not firing," Betty said.

"'Us?'" Purp said. "Sell to 'us?'"

"To Betty," Javier said. "We'd like you to sell your share to Betty."

"But not the property," Betty said.

"Betty doesn't have enough money for that," Purp said.

"Well, she can raise it," Javier said. "And she's got investors interested. Selma is interested in selling, too, when we told her what kind of money we're talking about."

"Selma," Purp said, "what's with Selma all of a sudden?"

"She's on the papers," Betty said. "We can't do it without her signing."

"And she agreed to it?" Purp said. "She agreed to sell my business out from under me?"

"No," Betty said, "not like that. She just agreed it was a good idea for everybody, including you, and her, to cash out here and do what you're going to do. Financially, you are going to make out very, very well, especially with the rent factored in."

"But it's not –

"Between the cash buyout," Betty said, "and the rent for the building and lot, since you've paid off the lot and the construction loan, you're talking about a very comfortable living indefinitely. Way more than you were getting at the museum."

"And for sitting home doing nothing," Javier said.

Purp looked at his shoes. Timberland, below the ankle. "Adventure Style" they called them on Shoes.com. The sole on the right one had been starting to flap, lately, on the instep. The right shoe had two faint smears of paint on it, two different shades of purple, from painting the office walls. The left shoe had a crusty patch of mortar from when Javier and Purp laid the block walls. He got some miles out of those shoes. Purp looked at Javier's Doc Martens, a new pair. Maybe Betty helped him pick them out, these ones, but Javier always had worn Docs as long as Purp knew him.

"Not for nothing," Purp said. "Not at all for nothing."

"No, Purp," Betty said. "Not for nothing. It's money you deserve."

Purp looked down at the Saltillo tiles he'd picked out for the floor. Load after load in his truck, bringing them across the border. He remembered going through them so that each room – both offices, both bathrooms, the changing room, the kitchen, the café, the entryway – every area had one with a coyote paw print in it. He thought that would be cool, good luck. The entryway tile with the paw print on it was under the new table riser now. Purp felt bad when it got covered up.

"Thanks for thinking of my health," Purp said, still looking down, "and my financial independence, but no. No, I'm not going to sell my business. Not to a college girl who thinks she can run a business because she knows how to use Excel and QuickBooks. Not to you, either, man," he said looking up at Javier. "Not to you. A guy with two degrees and nothing to do, nothing to do but work in Starbucks. I raised you up into a wealthy man –

"He worked for it, too, Purp," Betty said. "Nobody is saying you didn't earn it, but he earned it, too."

"You didn't have two dimes to rub together," Purp said. "Talk about getting too big for your britches, huh? You're telling me I'm disruptive?" Purp stood up. "If I'm disturbing you, either of you, please feel free to walk out the door. If I'm disrupting your peaceful existence, then walk away. You walk away." Purp stood in Betty's doorway. "That's my name on your tits." Purp pointed to the PTC logo on Betty's tight zipper hoodie, part of the apparel line Purp had up on clear plastic large-chested mannequins in the new window displays. "That's not your own name. You start a business if you want your own name on your tits. And that's not his name, either, notice. That's not your boyfriend's name." Purp pointed to Javier. "It said 'Starbucks' on his apron until I raised him up. My name is on the sign and I'm going to be here long after you're gone," Purp said to Betty.

"It's not so much your name on the sign anymore," Betty said, "as it is a reference to the color of the paint on the walls."

"What's that supposed to mean?" Purp said.

"The sign outside is actually right," Betty said. "This is more the 'Purple Topless Carwash' than it's been 'Purple's Topless Carwash' for a while now. You're not in control. Not of yourself, and not of this business."

* * *

Purp handed a can of refried beans up to Javier. Javier stood on a step stool, lining the cans up on the top shelf of the dunnage rack in the back stock hallway. Purp wasn't sure what to expect for the re-opening and Javier had ordered a lot of food, just in case. With the new bigger food line, the extra helper, and all that new seating, they might go through an awful lot of food on opening week. And Javier was ready for it. Purp handed him up a can of sliced jalapenos.

"I don't even know," Javier said.

"You knew the other day," Purp said.

"You do seem like you need a little help, right?" Javier said.

"Help with what?" Purp said. "So I drink. You drink. It's Betty is what it is, don't you see that? I'm telling you, man, friend to friend here. She's got you seriously whipped."

"It's not like that," Javier said. He took a can from Purp with both hands and slid it back on the shelf.

"I just want to enjoy this opening," Purp said.

"OK," Javier said. "That's kind of like, what I really want, right? I want to just enjoy this place, you know? Like we did when we first opened. Or like before we opened."

"Me too," Purp said.

"But I do agree with Betty," Javier said, "not so much about the selling, maybe the selling, but I do agree that it's possible that this isn't good for you, this place."

"I don't think that's it," Purp said.

"I knew you before," Javier said. "I knew you since. I do think you were better off before. That's all I'm saying." Javier stepped off the stool and sat on it. "You know what you should put on one of your shirts?" he said.

"What's that?" Purp said.

"You should put that it's the world's best manmade car wash, and the only manmade car wash visible to the naked eye of an observer standing on the surface of the moon."

Purp laughed.

"I should do that," Purp said.

"You should," Javier said. He dug some sunflower seeds out of the pocket of his Guayabera shirt and funneled them into his mouth.

"I should do a lot of things," Purp said.

Javier crunched shells.

"Do you think it is?" Javier said. "Visible?"

"No," Purp said. "I doubt it."

"It's wider than a road," Javier said.

"It is," Purp said. "But it doesn't cast much of a shadow, I don't think." Purp kneeled down by the pallet of cans. "I guess we'll have to wait and ask one of those Chinese guys."

"The Chinese guys?" Javier said.

"Well, they'll probably be the next ones up there," Purp said. "Who can look and tell us if they see it. I'd give them a buck to say they could."

* * *

Purp gathered the girls in a huddle under the awning. He had the heaters going almost full blast and it was actually a little too toasty under there, even though the outside temperature was fifty-five.

"OK, Nicole, can you do greeter?" Purp said.

"Aww," Nicole said. She made a sad face.

"What, you don't like it?" Purp said.

"I wanted to wash," Nicole said.

"OK. Who wants greeter? Nobody new, though," Purp said.

Marissa put up her hand, palm forward, and then flipped it, backside toward Purp. She let her hand fall and shrugged her shoulders.

"Thanks, Marissa," Purp said. "We're going to be on four bays, obviously. It might be slow, though."

"Now I need sign girls. I'd like two new and one old," Purp said. "J. J. do you remember what you did the day we opened the first time around?"

"Sign girl, woo hoo!" J. J. said. She squealed and held her hands up and snapped her head from one side to the other, whipping her hair against her arms.

“We’ll rotate you guys out so all the new girls get a shot at it by the end of the day,” Purp said. “And J. J. you show them where the signs are, OK?”

“Uh huh,” J. J. said. “In the changing room still?”

Purp nodded once.

“But can we make new ones?” J. J. said.

“Yeah, sure,” Purp said. “All the stuff is still in there, I think.”

“Cool, cool,” J. J. said.

“The other two sign girls, I’d like Shaniqua and Wendy,” Purp said. Wendy, an Asian girl, kept flexing and relaxing the muscles on the front of her thigh like she was nervous. Every time she did it Purp saw the outlines of three muscular cables running down from under her little skirt. Wendy looked like she worked those thighs hard, like with a lot of squats or something. “It’ll be fun, Wendy.”

“I just wanted to get washing,” Wendy said.

“You will,” Purp said. “I won’t have you on sign too long. Don’t worry. You’re going to do awesome.” Purp pointed to the wash bay closest to the outdoor seating. “The fourth bay, like we used to use when it was super-busy, has its own hoses now. So you don’t have to share with the one on the end. Everything else is pretty much the same, OK? Except we have high-pressure hoses now.”

“I like those little guns,” Marissa said. “They’re so cute.”

“Watch out, though,” Purp said. “Don’t spray them at anybody’s face or anything, not that you would, it’s a lot of pressure.”

Susie trotted across the courtyard, a nice sight in her halter top. Purp couldn’t wait until these girls started washing. Seeing Susie got him even more excited to open.

“Sorry,” Susie said. She sang it.

“Susie!” Purp said. “Welcome. We’re just getting organized. You’re going to be washing. Be careful with the new hoses.”

“Hi,” Susie said. She waved to a couple of the girls.

“Susie I’m not sure you’ve met Crystal, Wendy, Monet, Tyler, Shaniqua, Lindsay, and Bella,” Purp said. He said all the names fast, running them together into one long word.

The girls laughed. Susie hip-checked Purp and he took a dramatic step sideways, pretending to almost fall.

“Wow,” Tyler said, a sporty-looking girl with short brown hair.

“You have a really good memory,” said Bella, her black eyeliner and hair making her look about as Goth as a person could in super-short cutoff shorts and a PTC halter top.

“He’s wicked smart,” J. J. said. “Like a freaking evil genius.”

"I was paying attention, see?" Purp said. He looked at his watch. "All right girls, lets go."

Tara clapped her hands three times. "Woo hoo," she said, loud enough for it to echo off the courtyard wall.

"Woo hoo," the girls chanted back, the ones who weren't new.

"Girls, come on," the experienced girls said all at once, cheerleader-style, Tara leading the chant.

Purp walked back inside. Javier had Brad on the line, and a new guy, Josh, a curly-headed surfer-looking guy with a UCSB boonie cap keeping his hair out of his eyes. Purp figured Josh knew what to do since Purp had seen him in the café a million times before. Another new guy, Arturo, stood behind the register, his long, skinny arms folded across his chest as if he didn't know what he should be doing.

"OK, gentlemen," Purp said, "get ready for the show. The gate is opening." Purp waved his arms toward Marissa while she rolled back the entrance gate.

"Oh yeah," Josh said. "That's what I'm talking about, right there."

Purp turned toward the glass wall just as Susie took her shirt off. It was contagious. Nicole peeled off her tank top. Then a new girl, Lindsay, got the idea. Purp was glad for the awning, her skin looked so fair.

Purp walked into his office, keeping his eyes on the courtyard. He didn't want to miss Bella taking her shirt off in the courtyard for the first time, and he certainly got an eyeful. Her round girly-looking tits didn't seem to match, somehow, with her Goth makeup and piercings, and the straight black hair she had with the white streak in it. But it worked. It was a good day. J. J. led Wendy and Shaniqua with their signs out the entrance driveway toward Guadalupe.

Javier sat at his desk looking out into the courtyard. Purp patted Javier's shoulder as he walked by.

"We're open," Purp said. He leaned against the front of his desk, keeping his eyes on the window.

"Oops," Javier said. He stood up, his chair rolling into the wall. "Not yet." Javier scooted out of the room, shuffling his keys.

Purp heard the hex key turn in the front door.

Javier popped back into the office and sat down.

"Now we're open," Javier said. "All the way."

Marissa leaned into a neon-green Civic, the first car of the day. She crossed her arms on the driver's side door and put her face into the open window. Purp imagined the view the driver got as Marissa leaned over in her tank top. That view was way better than a machine you slide a credit card into with a green light on top.

Nicole and Lindsay played with the new high-pressure wash guns. The girls seemed to like the pistol grips. Tara jogged toward the changing room. Purp wondered if something was wrong. Tara disappeared inside and then Purp heard a Reggaeton beat thumping his window. They'd forgotten the music, that was all. Tara came back out, dance-walking. She looked ready to wash. The cowbell jingled on the front door. By nine fifteen Purp had four bays washing and a good little murmur of voices coming from the café.

* * *

Purp snapped the lid off his thirty-two ounce cup and flicked it into the trash can by his desk. He tipped the cup up and ice slid onto his nose. He breathed in the last vapors of his Jack and Pepsi.

Outside, Monet and Wendy walked arm in arm out of the changing room, clean and dry in their street clothes, Monet in a clingy bright yellow mini-dress which looked nice with her dark brown skin and blond cornrow braids. The top of Wendy's head barely came up to Monet's shoulder. The two of them looked like they were laughing.

Purp already had his cash stacked and counted and it sounded like there were still customers finishing up in the café. With all the new seating and the faster line, it had been taking Javier a lot longer lately to count his till, which was a good thing. Purp zipped the cash and Betty's cash forms into green vinyl bags and gathered them two in each hand so he could bring them to the safe. He walked into the café toward Betty's office. A group of guys had some riser tables pulled together and they watched on the video wall as the girls left the changing room.

"There she is," one of the guys said.

Purp looked over at the monitors as Crystal walked from one screen into another in jeans and a black backless apron top.

"Shit she's hot," a different guy said.

Fifteen or twenty guys and a couple of girls lingered in the café, laughing and finishing up.

"Purple J. Squirter." Max. Purp hadn't noticed Max in the café, but it wasn't possible to mistake the voice for anyone else. Max had become quite a regular since they re-opened. He'd come back on re-opening day and a few times a week all month since. Max told Purp a couple of weeks before that it broke his heart when the carwash closed and he regretted not having spent more time there. Now that he was retired, he said, it was his New Year's resolution to come to the café more.

Purp looked to his left and there was shiny-headed Max looking up at him, sitting with his arm around a brown-haired girl with pink glasses. She looked cute. And probably younger than Purp, his age, at the oldest.

"Mandy," Max said to Purp, making a gun with his fingers and pointing it at Mandy's temple.

"Hi Mandy," Purp said.

Mandy smiled. Definitely a cutie.

"This, Purp," Max said to Mandy. "They got him on manager here, or something like that. Right, Purp?"

"Something like," Purp said.

"Started washing tables," Max said, "now he's the cheese."

Mandy looked up at Purp and nodded as if impressed.

"Destination: Taco C., buddy, across the street to knock back a few more after you shut," Max said, "in case you're interested in coming with."

"Thanks," Purp said. "I'm going to be here a while cleaning up, though."

"Suit yourself," Max said. "We'll be there."

Purp excused himself and brought the cash bags into Betty's office.

"We've got a nice box today," Purp said to Betty. "I had four bays wet almost all day."

Betty looked up from her computer.

"That's what I like to hear," Betty said.

Purp handed her the green bags.

"Stacked and counted," Purp said, "t's dotted, i's crossed, ready for the safe." He felt like he was doing a Max impersonation, but he didn't exactly mean to be.

"Thanks, Purp," Betty said.

"Thank you," Purp said.

Purp ducked out of Betty's office and helped Josh clean up while Javier finished his till.

"How'd you get that bruise," Purp said, looking at Josh's eye.

"Fight," Josh said. He took the last bin of beans out of the thermotainer.

"You win?" Purp said.

"I did," Josh said. "Two-hundred fifty dollars."

"How'd you do that?" Purp said. "Win two-hundred fifty dollars?"

"Mixed martial arts," Josh said.

Purp carried three bins of cheese to the back cooler.
"Here?" Purp said.
"Albuquerque."
"Huh," Purp said.
Javier locked the door behind the last of the stragglers. He came over by Josh and Purp. There wasn't much left to do for the night, just wipe up a little on the riser tables.
"Yeah," Javier said. "Josh has been showing me the moves." He mimed a slow-motion martial arts kind of attack at Josh. Josh deflected it at normal speed, not looking amused. Javier rubbed his wrist where Josh had hit him.
They finished cleaning up. Javier went into Betty's office, maybe to wait for her to finish, and Purp let himself and Josh out. Josh walked off down Powell and Purp went around to his truck in the café lot.
"PJ," Max said. He called across Guadalupe from the Taco Cabana patio. He sat at a table outside with Mandy. "Tip one with us."
"A different time, Max," Purp said. "I'm beat."
"Cocksucker," Max said.

* * *

"Thank you so much for coming out here on short notice," Purp said to Alex, the plumber.
"No problem," Alex said. "I know you guys need it." Alex leaned against the side of his truck in overflow, keeping his eyes on the wash bays.
"We have the old hoses for backup," Purp said, "but the girls like the pressure system a lot better and it does a much better job on the cars."
"It's a good unit," Alex said. "I think it's fine now."
"Thanks again. I can't believe how fast you got here," Purp said.
"I understand," Alex said. "That system is your business. No water, no car wash." Alex didn't look at Purp at all, mesmerized by the girls washing cars.
"Hey, listen," Purp said. "You're the owner, right? That's you?" Purp pointed to the name on the side of the white van.
Alex let his eyes dart toward the van for half a second.
"That's me now," Alex said. "But it was my dad's name first."
"You think you might like to get your van washed? On us?" Purp said.

“Sure,” Alex said. “Definitely.”

“I’ll tell you, I’m a little nervous about that unit going down again,” Purp said. “And I’ll make a deal with you. If you can say you’ll be over within three hours of when I call like you were today, I’d say you can wash that van here for free whenever you want.”

Alex laughed. He looked at Purp and shook his hand.

“That’s a good deal for me,” Alex said. “Because the unit’s not going to break and I’d probably be here within three hours anyway, for BTB, even if it did.”

Purp laughed.

“And I can’t always do this,” Purp said, “because the old lady inside kind of rides me for it, but I’m going to pay you in cash today, too, OK?”

“Cash and a carwash,” Alex said, “I’ll be over here parked waiting for something to break.”

The two men laughed.

“Come on,” Purp said, punching Alex in the shoulder. Alex followed him to the box.

Purp unlocked the box and reached in. He pulled out a fistful of bills and counted out two-hundred fifty dollars. He handed the money to Alex.

“Will two-fifty cover it?” Purp said.

Alex didn’t say anything for a second.

“Yeah,” Alex said. “Cash, yeah, that’ll cover it.”

“What?” Purp said. “Not enough?”

“No, it’s fine if it’s cash,” Alex said.

“I didn’t mean to pay you less,” Purp said. “I just thought you’d say it was less than that. I mean, I was trying to give you more.” Purp felt like an ass. He got the feeling Alex was planning to charge him more than two-fifty.

“It’s fine,” Alex said. “It’s about right.”

“No, seriously,” Purp said. “What were you going to charge me?”

“It’s fine,” Alex said.

“Here,” Purp said. He gave Alex another fifty dollars. “Here. I’m not short of cash, I just thought that was about what it would be.

* * *

Purp set the thirty-two ounce cup half-full of ice and fresh Pepsi down on the floor tiles near his desk. He looked over his shoulder and then slid one of his bottles of Jack out of the bottom drawer. He tried to pour it quickly but his hands felt shaky so he used both of them at once. He got the bottle stowed, the drawer shut, and he was still bent over the cup when Javier came into the office. Purp sat up fast and put the cup down on his desk. He fiddled with opening a straw.

"What the fuck was that?" Javier said.

"Huh?" Purp said. "What's that?" Purp said. Purp figured Javier had maybe seen him pouring the whiskey.

"What the fuck was that out there with the box?" Javier said.

"Oh," Purp said. He sighed, relaxing his shoulders. "Oh, I was just paying the plumber."

"Paying the plumber?" Javier said.

"Yeah," Purp said. "He came right over and got the pressure hoses up."

"You just paid him out of the box?" Javier said.

"Yeah," Purp said. "It was three-hundred bucks."

"What were you thinking?" Javier said.

"What? He needed to be paid," Purp said. "I paid him. He came over so fast." Purp got the straw into his J and P and sipped it, hard. It burned the back of his throat, fizzy and warm feeling. "I'm nervous about the pressure unit. It's a single point of failure."

"We're not having this conversation again," Javier said. "We're not. You just lost that transaction for taxes. No receipt, no check, no records, nothing."

"What's the big deal?" Purp said. "It's three-hundred dollars."

"It could be a lot less than that if you'd capture it for a deduction," Javier said. "And it just fucks up our records."

"Oh, listen to you," Purp gulped his drink. A third of it was gone. "You sound like your old lady."

"It's not Betty," Javier said, "it's me. I don't like it either. You start paying the plumber, next thing you know you're siphoning off fifty or sixty thousand dollars, or who knows how much, for TVs, then you're –

"You know the video wall was an awesome idea," Purp said. "You know this. You can't tell me –

"I can't tell you it brought anybody into the café," Javier said. "Because you just do things, you don't take the time to study them."

"I do," Purp said. "I do study things."

"You don't, Purp. Not lately, you don't," Javier said.

"Who wrote the plate camera software?" Purp said.

"That was a long time ago, Purp," Javier said.

"Just tell me," Javier said, "you blew like fifty-grand on the video wall, min. We don't know exactly, because you didn't save receipts or pay for it with the business VISA. Now tell me how are we doing making that back? What kind of metric are you using to quantify whether that was a good investment of our money?"

"Check out the big brain on the poet," Purp said. "Quantifying the metrics. You seriously need a new girlfriend. I can help you there." Half of the cup was gone. Purp felt it kicking in.

"I'm saying no," Javier said. "Stop. We're like six weeks into this now and it's not going to be like that. It's not Betty saying it, either, it's me. If we have to put a different lock on the box, we will, Purp. I'm serious. You should focus anyway on what you're good at, operational stuff. I think I just want you out of the cash handling loop altogether if you're going to stay."

"If I'm going to stay?" Purp said. "What are you, smoking something?"

"Don't look at me, man," Javier said. "What's in your cup? I'm not the one with the problem."

"I'm drinking a soda," Purp said.

"Oh, come on," Javier said. "Don't ask me if I've been smoking something when you're sitting there with a bucket of bourbon, drinking it out of a straw like we don't know."

"What?" Purp said.

"That's just insulting, OK?" Javier said. "Look, I know it, Betty knows it, the girls know it – you have a problem, OK?"

Betty poked her head into the doorway. She had sunglasses in her hair.

"Is everything OK?" Betty said. "You guys are getting kind of loud."

"I'll get loud," Purp said. "This is ridiculous." He worked the straw like a fat baby at a nipple. It was getting down to ice, his drink.

"Did you tell him?" Betty said, stepping into the office.

"Did you tell him what?" Purp said. "I'm not giving my business to your fucking Vietnamese mafia."

"We saw you on the video wall," Betty said. "We saw you taking money out of the box."

"I was paying the plumber," Purp said. His throat hurt from yelling. "For Christ's sake, I was paying, the God, damned, plumber."

"Shh," Javier said.

Betty backed up toward the door in the clunky tall clogs that gave her Clydesdale feet. She looked startled. She had on short red shorts, ultra low-rise, glossy red thumbnails hooked into her belt loops.

Purp looked out at the courtyard. From the back Crystal reminded him of Gina. Purp wondered what Gina was doing right now. Right at that second. He looked away.

Purp hurled his thirty-two ounce cup at Betty's chest. It hit her in the head. The lid snapped off. Ice flew, and landed. The flamey scent of alcohol waved back toward Purp.

Betty grabbed at her head with both hands. Javier lunged at her, hugging her sideways around the shoulders. She shrugged him off.

"I'm fine," Betty said.

Purp got up from his chair. He almost had to sit back down again but he steadied himself and walked past Javier and Betty.

"That's it," Betty said as Purp walked past her.

Purp walked out into the café. It was quiet for being so packed. Several guys looked in his direction.

"I'm done, Purp," Betty said.

Purp looked over his shoulder. Betty followed him.

"I quit," Betty said. "No notice, nothing."

"Well," Purp said. "Goodbye then. Thanks for your help." Purp walked toward the food line.

"And I swear if Javier didn't own this place," Betty said, "you would so be hearing from a lawyer."

Purp ducked behind the food line and slid Betty's case of nuoc m'am off the dunnage rack. She'd worked through three quarters of the bottles. Purp came back around the line in time to see Betty's leg disappear into her office. She slammed her door. Purp speed walked toward her office. Javier grabbed at his elbow.

"Leaver her alone," Javier said.

"I want to make sure she doesn't forget her sauce," Purp said.

Purp opened Betty's door and kicked it wide. It slammed into the wall. Betty's diploma fell off its hook. The glass and frame shattered on the tiles. Betty stood behind her desk, her face glistening wet.

"Take your smelly fish sauce with you," Purp said. He tossed the case toward her as if she might catch it.

Betty deflected the box and it landed on her chair. Three bottles slipped out and smashed. One bounced and rolled toward Purp. He kicked it. It spun into the wall but still didn't break. Javier grabbed Purp around the neck from behind and backed him out toward the door. Purp tripped but Javier held him up, one arm around Purp's neck and the other around his chest with his thumb jammed in Purp's armpit.

"Divide your burritos in four," Purp said as Javier dragged him back. "Just put sauce on a quarter and save the other three."

* * *

Purp tipped a pillow onto his head so that it made a sandwich, two pillows as bread and his head as the meat. He curled his knees tighter toward his chest, laying on his bare mattress naked, in a ball, on his side. He heard the doorbell jingle three more times even through the pillows. Before that it had been his house phone, which he got up and unplugged. His cell phone hadn't rung at all this morning. Purp thought he remembered it beeping low battery yesterday, or maybe the day before, then it stopped.

Now, pounding on the door. Hard bangs like the door was going to rip through the frame. Purp's head hurt already, and the banging made it worse. His mouth felt like it had something in it, thick and cheesy. He remembered a dream he was just having that his mouth kept filling up with rubbery cheese and he kept scooping it out with his fingers, but it kept growing back.

The lock on the front door clicked. The door sounded like someone opened it slowly, the creaky hinge squeaking.

"Purp?" Selma said. "I'm coming in. Are you home?"

Purp reached toward a sheet on the floor. He flicked it over himself. He put the top pillow back onto his head.

"Purp?" Selma said. "Are you here? I see your truck."

The front door creaked shut. Purp heard the deadbolt snap into place.

"Purp I have my dad with me, OK?" Selma said. She whispered something, Purp figured to her dad.

Purp heard their shuffling feet on the tiles in the hall, the padding of shoes on the bedroom carpet. He tugged the sheet to make sure his ass was covered up.

"Oh my God, Purp," Selma said. "It's OK, Papa. He's OK. Go ahead."

Purp heard Selma's dad walk back down the hall.

"Purp, are you OK?" Selma said. "Hello?" She tapped his toe. "Is there anybody in there?"

Purp flipped the pillow off his head. It fell to the floor.

"I'm trying to take a sleep," Purp said. It felt like his tongue was sticking to the roof of his mouth.

“It smells really bad in here,” Selma said. “Really bad. Like flammable bad. Did you spill something? Or is that smell coming out of you?”

“I didn’t expect anybody to visit,” Purp said.

Selma straightened the sheet over Purp. She sat down on the edge of the bed near Purp’s face.

“This isn’t right,” Selma said. “It’s really smelly in here. Like crazy person smelly.”

“I didn’t have a chance to take a shower yet,” Purp said.

“Busy?” Selma said.

“I was up late,” Purp said. “Working. Monkey Cam transaction processing.” He tried opening his eyes but the light made his headache worse. He tugged some sheet up so it covered his face.

“OK,” Selma said.

“It’s for web customers,” Purp said. “They pay. They get a live feed,” he said. Just the little bit of talking made his jaw hurt, and his neck, “from a camera inside a car. They see what they’d see if they were really there. At the car wash.”

“OK, Purp,” Selma said. She patted the back of his hand. “Shh,” she said.

Selma stood up and opened a window. She sat back down by Purp.

* * *

Purp had to take a cab to the car wash. Selma left him a note saying she took his truck keys because she didn’t think it was safe for him to drive. She left him a load of groceries and it said on his note to call her when he needed more. She’d taken his Jack Daniels, too. He wanted to ask the cab driver to stop at Barrel House on the way so he could get more, but Selma also had his wallet. Purp didn’t mention that to the cab driver. He figured he’d get some money at PTC. He still had his box key, anyway, and his stash of Jack in his desk drawer.

“Javier,” Purp said.

Javier turned around. He’d been working on changing the carbon dioxide tank when Purp came up behind him.

“Wow, hey, Purp,” Javier said. “Are you OK?”

“I am,” Purp said. “But I need a couple of bucks to pay for my cab down here. It’s a long story.”

"Here you go," Javier said. He pulled a twenty off a wad of cash he had in his pocket, no wallet, no money clip, just a stack of bills folded over.

"Thanks," Purp said.

Purp jogged, as well as he could, out to the cab. He held out the twenty in a hand so shaky it worried him. He waited for his change and came back in.

"Hey," Purp said to Javier, who was still bent over the canisters.

"Hey," Javier said. He set the empty tank by the back door, near another one.

"Is that CO2 done?" Purp said. "I need a soda."

"Where have you been, man?" Javier said.

"Hang on a sec," Purp said. "I'm really, really thirsty." Purp went around to self-serve and drew himself a half-full Pepsi. He went to his office but the bottles were gone. Shit.

"Bar's closed, buddy," Javier said from behind Purp as Purp rolled his bottom drawer shut.

Purp sat back in his chair. They had four bays washing outside. Wendy had her hands on the hood of a 350Z and her knees apart. Black wet braids dripped over her shoulders, one braid on either side of her head. She moved her hips in a slow, wide oval, standing on her tiptoes, her flexed calf muscles chiseling their outline under her tan skin. She really caught on to things.

"Oh, no," Purp said, "I'm cool." He put the lid on the Pepsi but he had a hard time with the straw, getting it open and steadying his hand enough to get the straw into its hole. "What did you drink it all?" He forced a chuckle but it came out more like a raspy cackling noise. "That's cool, though."

Javier leaned against his desk.

"What the fuck, Purp?" Javier said. "You yell and throw shit around and scare poor Betty and then you disappear for four days?"

Purp got the straw into the hole.

"Do you work here still?" Javier said. "Or what? I had to beg Betty to come back here and help me. You left me all alone here."

"She's back?" Purp said.

"She's not here now," Javier said. "And you're lucky she's not. She's only helping me because you're not around. She doesn't need this shit. She's taking her CPA exam next month."

"I didn't hurt her, did I?" Purp said. He watched Wendy dancing now, bent at the waist, facing the office with her hands on her thighs, her ass toward the Nissan, looking back at the driver over her shoulder.

"No," Javier said. "You didn't. But that was the end of it, Purp. That was it. You're not drinking here anymore, you're not yelling, that was just the end. You screwed us over with all that shit. All of us."

"I was provoked," Purp said. "I was just paying the plumber." Purp finished the Pepsi.

"It was just an accident that you didn't hurt her," Javier said. "That was really irresponsible. And then to disappear like that and leave me short, with you and Betty gone."

"Everybody keeps saying I'm useless," Purp said, "so what does it matter if I'm gone?"

"I don't know your schedule with the girls," Javier said. "I don't know how you run all that. And I didn't know if you drove off a bridge somewhere, or what."

Purp turned toward Javier. Spinning in his office chair made him tremble. He felt like he was going to puke. His skin prickled with heat and he knew his ears and cheeks were bright red. Sweat rolled in his armpits.

"You called Selma," Purp said.

"I did," Javier said. "To see if she knew where you were."

"You're really stupid if you think she's your big ally," Purp said. "I know you've been talking to her about getting me to sell."

"I told you I was," Javier said. "That's no big super-sleuth."

"She's not a friend of this place," Purp said. "I know how they found out about Gina." Purp felt his breathing get fast.

"You're not making sense, Purp," Javier said. "Are you OK? Should I call somebody or something?"

"Next time," Purp said, "you're talking to her, planning against me," he had to pause to catch his breath. He started to shake so bad he had to hold onto the desk. "Ask her what Gina's real name is, and how she knows."

"Purp?" Javier said. "Are you OK?"

* * *

Purp sat in his recliner and ate a bowl of Nabisco shredded wheat. Nonfat milk. He liked whole but skim was all that was in the house. A middle-school aged girl on the Today show talked about a terrible dog bite she got and what it was like to go through seven surgeries afterward so her face could be reconstructed. Purp felt a little woozy being up so early and he wondered why Selma and Javier couldn't have just come over in the afternoon, instead. They probably wanted to check on him. He'd only been out of the hospital two days. He refused to be sent to a treatment program, but he did stay in the hospital four days for his detox. He'd pissed himself in the office when he blacked out talking to Javier. That was the part that irritated him the most.

The doorbell jingled and the lock clicked. The creaky hinge creaked.

"Purp?" Selma said. "We're here."

Purp stood up and walked into the entryway. Selma took off her blue hat as she stepped onto the tiles in her uniform skirt.

"Hi, Purp," Selma said.

Javier walked in behind her.

"How are you feeling?" Selma said.

"I'm fine," Purp said.

"Hi Purp," Javier said.

"Nothing to drink yet," Purp said.

Mr. Needleman walked in behind Javier.

"Did you go to the meeting yesterday like they told you to in the hospital?" Selma said.

"I did," Purp said. "Hello," Purp said to Mr. Needleman. They shook hands.

"Good morning," Mr. Needleman said.

"Did that guy pick you up for it," Selma said, "the one they told you to call?"

"Yeah," Purp said. "He was all right. Kind of flaky but he's OK. He's my sponsor." Purp looked at Mr. Needleman. "So, I did not expect you this morning. Is everything OK? We checked and photocopied all the licenses, everybody's. New girls, old girls – well, none of them are old. But old enough."

Nobody laughed.

"Can we sit down?" Selma said. She walked around Purp and stepped down into the living room before he could answer.

Purp, Javier, and Needleman followed her and sat.

"Can I get you guys something to eat or drink, or something?" Purp said. "I'd offer you a Jack and Coke," Purp said to Mr. Needleman, "but Selma won't leave me a bottle of Coke. Or Whiskey." Mr. Needleman smiled but Purp saw that it was forced. "And I have no car keys to get my own." Mr. Needleman held onto his fake smile. "And also, no money to get any even if I did." Mr. Needleman kept smiling, but started looking uncomfortable. "And I don't even have an ID to get money out of the bank. If I wanted to." Mr. Needleman stopped smiling. "But I can send myself a check from my brokerage account." Selma looked up at him. "But I'd have a hard time cashing it. With no license." Mr. Needleman nodded, as if trying to appear sympathetic to a four-year-old child. "But I do have Arizona Iced Tea, diet, with lemon. If you want that."

"No, thank you," Mr. Needleman said.

"So anyway," Purp said, "the moral of that story is, write down your credit card numbers and expiration dates and security codes in a very safe place, which I did not ever do, so if your estranged wife takes away your car and all your money while you're in the hospital getting detoxed because you pissed your own pants in front of your best friend, you'll at least be able to buy things over the Internet."

Javier laughed, but Selma and Needleman didn't.

"So anyway," Purp said, "all that aside, what's up, guys? Is everything OK at the shop?"

"It's fine," Selma said. "Everything's OK. But this isn't the time for you to be worrying about that," she said. "We just want you to get better, OK?"

"I wasn't expecting Mr. Needleman this morning," Purp said.

"I know," Selma said.

Javier looked at the side of his Doc Marten.

"We asked Mr. Needleman to come here to help explain some things, in case we couldn't so well," Selma said.

"I'm not sure what there would be to explain," Purp said.

"Well," Selma said. "There are some things. And they're not so pretty. I'm sorry."

"OK," Purp said.

"Javier and I," Selma said, "we have decided that it's best for the business, and also for you, if you don't come to the car wash anymore. Maybe not permanently. Maybe that will change, depending on your progress with your outpatient treatment. Can we turn that off?" Selma looked at the plasma screen. Matt Lauer bounced to Willard in D. C. showing the cherry blossoms.

Purp turned off the T.V.

"I'm not sure," Purp said, "that's for you to decide, is it?" Purp turned to Mr. Needleman.

"As a matter of law," Mr. Needleman said, "it is. This is a limited liability corporation held by two partners. For these purposes, for questions of an incapacitated partner, it is similar in the eyes of the law to a dual proprietorship."

"That makes it more clear," Purp said.

“The corporation is jointly held,” Mr. Needleman said, “and your half of it in turn is also held jointly since your business is incorporated in a common property state. So between Selma and Javier, they hold a seventy-five percent stake in the business. If you contest this, it would take a while, and you might win, but given your recent violent and erratic behavior on the premises we were able to obtain a restraining order against you to prevent you from entering the –

“You got a restraining order against me?”

* * *

Purp’s feet burned, sore and hot from the pavement. He was sure there would be blood if he took his shoes off. The clock on the bank a mile ago said six in the evening and still ninety degrees. A hot April. He’d been walking since eleven, since about an hour after Selma left, and Javier and Needleman.

Purp pressed the button, black plastic faded and cracked from the sun. He had to push it in hard for it to make contact. He remembered this. He heard the buzzing noise it made coming from upstairs. Purp figured she wasn’t home, but he was prepared to just sit and wait for as long as it took.

Footsteps thumped down the stairs. He could tell they were hers.

Gina opened the door. She had on a black dress, stretchy knit with a high waist and a wide square neck. It didn’t look like she had a bra on. The fly-away skirt looked airy and cool, even though it was black. She stood in pink flip-flops, her hair damp. A bruise on her chest, just below the collar bone. A bite.

“Oh my God, Purp, hi,” Gina said. She hugged him. Her breasts felt tight against his ribs.

“How’s it going?” Purp said. “You doing all right?”

“I am,” Gina said, breaking off the hug. “I am. I’m in school this semester, at Apache.”

“That’s really great,” Purp said. “You look fantastic.”

“Thank you,” Gina said. “Wow, what a surprise.”

“I know, sorry,” Purp said.

“No, I mean, it’s great seeing you,” Gina said. She fiddled with a flake of paint peeling off the doorframe.

“I could seriously use a glass of water,” Purp said, stepping into the doorway.

Gina put her hand on Purp's chest and didn't step back.

"Hey, Purp," Gina said, "it's kind of like, a bad time right now?"

"You busy?" Purp said.

"I kind of am," Gina said. "I mean, I have somebody. Upstairs. And it would be sort of weird." She bit her bottom lip and scrunched up her face. She blushed and that made her scar stand out white, more visible than usual.

"Oh," Purp said. "Oh, OK."

"I'm sorry," Gina said. She patted Purp's chest. "I want to catch up, and everything, it's just a bad time right this second, OK?"

"Oh, yeah," Purp said, "totally. Anyway, I was just coming by."

"OK, well, good," Gina said. "It's really good seeing you. And happy birthday, by the way."

"Thanks," Purp said. "I actually forgot."

"Aww," Gina said. She made a sad face.

"Last year was a long time ago," Purp said.

"I know," Gina said. "Crazy."

"Hey," Purp said, stepping back onto the stoop. "Do you think you could do me a huge, huge favor? Do you think you could lend me some money?"

* * *

Purp rattled the front doors. Locked. He didn't feel like he could take another step. The halogens still blazed white light, though, glittering off the glass block privacy screens. The shirts looked nice. Purp did like the clear mannequins but he thought it would be better once they got real girls in the windows. Purp rapped on the glass door with his knuckles. Josh sat at one of the café tables behind a soda cup and Brad at the self-serve fountain. They looked like they were done cleaning, getting ready to leave. It didn't seem like anybody heard him knocking. The video wall was on showing MTV. Purp thought maybe they couldn't hear him over the music. He tapped the mouth of his bottle on the glass. It made a louder noise than he thought it would.

Javier came around the food line toward the front doors. Brad followed with Josh behind. Purp waved through the doors at Javier. Javier nodded and put up a finger, as if saying, "just a second." Javier shut the video wall down and walked over to the door. He turned the hex key and Purp stepped in, but Javier backed him out.

"Hey," Purp said.

"Hey, Purp," Javier said. Josh and Brad greeted him, too.

Javier held the door open for Brad and Josh to come out. He followed them and then locked the door behind him. Brad and Josh said their goodnights and walked down Powell toward the dorms.

"What's going on, Purp?" Javier said.

"I've got to sit down," Purp said. "I walked all the way over here."

"Shit," Javier said.

"I know," Purp said. "I mean, I wasn't walking the whole time. I stopped here and there, but I walked it."

"Jesus," Javier said, looking at the bottle. "Why?"

"I was just," Purp said, "I don't know. I don't know."

"You know you're not supposed to be here, right?" Javier said.

"Just let me in for a Pepsi," Purp said. "Or some water."

"You want a little Pepsi with your Jack Daniels?" Javier said. "No, man. You're just not supposed to be in there."

"You won't let me in for a drink of water?" Purp said.

"Purp, it's not like that," Javier said. "It's just we have to draw the line."

"There's nobody here," Purp said. "Betty's not here, is she?"

"No," Javier said. "But she has been helping me."

"Well who are you worried about?" Purp said. "Selma's not here." Purp spread his arms, fingers splayed on his left hand, bottle in his right, half full.

"It's not Selma or Betty. It's me," Javier said. "Can't you get that straight? I'm on your side, but no. You're not coming over here at closing time, drunk, two days after you just got out of rehab."

"I wasn't in rehab," Purp said. "I was in detox. I'm in rehab now."

"What's the difference, Purp?" Javier said. "You're a real mess, you know that?"

"I might be a mess," Purp said. "It's just what you said was imprecise. I wasn't in rehab."

"Whatever you were in," Javier said, "you're not coming in here. We have a fucking restraining order on you. We just told you that today. You're done, Purp. You're done here. At least for a long time, you're done."

"Who are you?" Purp said. "To tell me I'm done."

"I own this business," Javier said. "More than I thought I'd have to."

"You own it because I gave it to you," Purp said.

"Just stop with it," Javier said. "Come on, I'll get you a soda or something over at Taco Cabana." Javier put his arm around Purp's shoulder.

Purp flung Javier's arm off his shoulder.

"Oh, the big man, huh?" Purp said. "You're going to do me a favor and buy me soda? Call me a cab?"

"That's kind of what I was thinking," Javier said.

"Oh, Generous Spirit," Purp said, "your charity touches me." Purp pointed the mouth of the bottle at Javier and took three steps backward toward the curb.

"You know you're not even supposed to be within a hundred –

"Well call the cops then," Purp said. "Use your phone and call the cops." He said.

"It's not like that, man," Javier said. "Look, it's me you're talking to. We were friends."

"No," Purp said, "call the cops. Call the cops. There's a crazy disgruntled employee violating his restraining order." His voice echoed off the condos across Powell.

"Purp, shh," Javier said. "Calm down. People are going to hear you, right?"

"Call the cops," Purp said, taking a swipe at Javier with his bottle. "Call the cops."

Javier shoved Purp hard in the chest with both hands. Purp just about lost his balance, taking four or five awkward steps backward, off the curb and into Powell.

"What are you to push me away from my own business?" Purp said. "What are you?" Purp pointed the bottle again. "You're an over-educated fast-food worker." A pickup drove by, moving from the right lane into the left around Purp. The driver blew his horn.

"Purp, get out of the road," Javier said. He stepped into the street and reached for Purp.

Purp backed up, swinging with his bottle, still half full. A car came at him from his right. He only saw the lights and heard the horn. The car swerved into the left turn lane around Purp and Javier.

"Get out of the road," Javier said.

"Call the cops," Purp said. "A hundred fifty feet, huh?"

Javier grabbed Purp around his left wrist and pulled him hard toward the curb. An SUV sped around them. Javier tugged Purp into the bike lane. Purp knocked Javier in the side of the head with the bottle as Javier stepped up onto the curb.

“Ow,” Javier said. “Fuck.” He stumbled onto the sidewalk, holding the side of his face. “Fuck the cops, I’m calling Selma.”

Purp hurled the bottle at Javier’s head. It missed him by a couple of feet and crashed into the brightly lit window behind him. Purp watched the glitter of high-intensity halogen lights on shattered glass and whiskey.

Javier charged toward Purp and put his shoulder into Purp’s chest knocking them both onto the pavement, half in the bike lane, half in the lane of traffic. A motor scooter whined by, tooting its European-sounding horn in short, sharp blasts that got lower in pitch as the driver sped away. Javier belted Purp in the jaw with his elbow. A solid strike. Purp’s head snapped back and bounced off the asphalt. He smelled a scent like burning plastic. Javier sat on Purp’s chest and cocked his elbow back for another blow but he was thrown sideways off of Purp, just picked off of Purp’s chest clean. Purp didn’t feel a thing. Purp rolled over to look where Javier went. A man stood in the street with his back to Purp, hands held out to his sides, stomping hard on Javier’s head and chest. Javier writhed and lashed but it didn’t even look like an effort for the man to keep big Javier down with just one foot.

“You Mexican motherfucker,” the man said, “ain’t enough they give you a job in this titty joint and what do you have to do, rob the manager when he come in here to lock up for the night?” It was Max. “You sorry wetback cocksucker.” Max stomped Javier’s head. Javier bled from his mouth and nose. He tried to cover his head with his hands but Max kicked them away.

“Max,” Purp said, getting to his feet. “Stop.” The window. The smashed window spilled black smoke over the sidewalk. Flames licked the galvanized steel awning.

“I got your back, P.J.,” Max said. He kicked Javier in the ribs. “Lucky I was over there drinking after you guys shut. I heard you saying ‘police’ and I heard glass smashing,” he kicked Javier in the ass, “I wasn’t waiting around for no written invitation.”

Purp slammed into Max from behind. Their feet, Max’s and Purp’s, got caught up in Javier and they landed on the concrete, Purp on top of Max.

“Oh, fuck,” Max said. “Fuck me Amadeus.” He let out a howl that made Purp’s left ear rattle.

“Shit,” Javier said. “Rescue.” He scrambled to his feet and it reminded Purp of a turtle trying to get off its shell.

The clear mannequins flared up and melted grotesquely, obscenely. A new stench billowed out, whatever the mannequins were made of, on fire.

"Get off of me, motherfucker," Max said.

Purp rolled over onto the sidewalk. "Not technically," Purp said.

Javier already had the front doors open. He got to his hands and knees and disappeared inside. There wasn't any smoke coming out the front door but a thick black trunk of it rolled out the broken window and darkened the underside of the awning. All the window lights went out at once. Maybe Javier had thrown the breaker. Purp stood. Max grunted as if trying to take a dump.

"I think you broke my hip," Max said. "I can't stand."

Purp heard the dragon-screech of a fire extinguisher. White powder mixed with black smoke. It looked like the fire might be too far along for Javier to get it out. Purp stepped back, forgetting where Max was until he stepped on Max's hand. Purp shifted his weight to the other foot but his ankle twisted and he fell off the sidewalk.

"Purp?" Javier said.

Javier bent over Purp from the left side, his hands on his knees. Gouts of blood caked Javier's soot-stained face, his singed curly hair an ashen halo. Purp felt like he was in a bed, but he saw black sky and the condos across Powell. And a fire truck. And an ambulance.

"Good morning, Starshine," a man's voice said. Somebody patted Purp's shoulder.

"Is it gone?" Purp said. He reached up and put his hand on Javier's, on Javier's knee.

"Is what gone?" Javier said.

"The car wash," Purp said.

"Negative," Javier said. "It just impacted on the surface."

Javier stood up and stepped back. Two paramedics raised Purp's gurney up to waist height.

"I'll call Selma," Javier said.

"A penny for the old guy?" Purp said.

Javier laughed.

"No," Javier said. "But he's hurting."

Made in the USA
Las Vegas, NV
07 February 2024

85225962R00142